D1077946

To my three dear chaps,
and Nicola

Chapter One

The church bell, cracked and faint, struck seven as Anna opened her eyes. She closed them again, and waited for the second bell to chime, three minutes later. Then she got out of bed and pushed open the heavy wooden shutters of her window. High up in the air, swallows hawked lazily across the pale blue dome of the sky. A cool breeze, smelling of thyme and wood-smoke, flowed over her bare shoulders and she stretched her arms over her head and inhaled deeply, filling her lungs with the aromatic air.

From her high window, she looked down over the roofs of the village, across the vineyards and cherry orchards towards the grey-green rolling country of the *garrigue*, with the pale lavender, jagged outline of the Cévennes in the distance.

Down below, the metal gate clanged. Anna looked down and saw Honorine coming into the courtyard, bringing with her the bread for breakfast.

'*Ciao*, Honorine! Sorry, good morning!' she called.

Honorine looked up, and waved at Anna. '*Ciao, mignonne!*' she called back, and cackled with laughter at her own humour. Honorine loved to practise her English, picked up during her years in England. It seemed natural for them all to speak English, and the children much preferred it, to Anna's secret annoyance. She really had very little sympathy with England, either its language or its people. Except, of course, Jeffrey.

Honorine disappeared into the kitchen with the bread. Anna could hear the water being drawn through the pipes. Honorine was preparing to make the coffee. Anna drew back from the window, and padded across the cool, tiled floor to the small stone wash-basin, which was neatly fitted, like a *piscina*, into a niche in the thick stone wall. Over the basin curved a tarnished brass, swan-necked tap, and Anna turned it on, so that a thin stream of cool water poured into the bowl. She sluiced water over her face, neck and arms, and, taking her toothbrush from its glass, and salt from a tin, she vigorously cleaned her teeth. She peered at her face in the spotty mirror over the basin. Dark eyes, with very blue whites, dominated her tanned face, the wet lashes stuck together in spikes. Her straight dark hair hung in limp curtains on either side of her thin face and long neck. Anna sighed, and pulled the plug from the basin.

A large, fruitwood *armoire* with ornately carved doors stood against the lime-washed wall. Inside, the cupboard was half filled with Domenica's winter clothes, furs and boots. The other half had been cleared by Honorine for Anna, and she took out a white linen sleeveless shirt, almost transparent with washing and ironing, and a long, faded pink jumble-sale skirt, with little bits of mirror stitched into the embroidered hem. She pulled back the sheet to air the bed, pulled the shutters together and closed the heavy metal latch. Slipping her feet into espadrilles, she went down the wide stone stairs. Passing Domenica's door, she opened it silently and peered in. The old high mahogany bed was draped in mosquito nets, which hung from a steel ring suspended from a beam. The white-sheeted mound of Domenica's body, with only her wild, grey curly hair visible on the heap of pillows, was very still. Anna closed the door carefully, and continued on down to the kitchen.

The vaulted room, once a cellar for wine storage, cool even in the hottest part of the day, had tall double doors in a wide stone arch opening on to the courtyard.

In summer, these were kept shut during the day to keep out the heat and the flies, but now, in the early morning, they stood slightly open, letting a shaft of light into the dark room. Honorine was pouring boiling water into the *cafetière*, while Olivia, Anna's younger child, was cutting the bread into thick diagonal slices and putting them into a basket.

'Breakfast outside, Mum?'

'Lovely,' said Anna.

Under a vine covered trellis stood a battered round iron table, painted dark green. Around it stood slatted folding chairs, painted the same dark green. Honorine put down the tray, and they sat down.

'It is unfair,' said Olivia, with her mouth full. 'Why did Josh have to go to Estagnol with his friends? It's boring here all by myself; everyone has gone to the sea. Why couldn't we have gone too?'

'Would you really like to be staying in one of those roasting little concrete flats at Grau du Roi?'

'Yes, I would,' said Olivia. 'I could have gone with Virginie. I could have shared her bed, she said so.'

Anna sighed. They had had this conversation several times already. 'Don't you think it would have been rather lonely for me here, all alone?' she said.

'But,' said Olivia sullenly, 'you've got Domenica.'

'Lucky me,' said Anna, smiling.

'And you've got Honorine,' added Olivia.

'I know I have darling, but I need you too.'

'Is Saturday,' said Honorine, interrupting. 'We go to Uzès for the market, isn't it? You'll like that, no?'

'Well,' said Anna, 'if we're going, Domenica had better get up, or it'll be too hot and crowded. Anyway, we must make a list. What do we need?'

Honorine went into the kitchen to fetch her pad, and Olivia decided to give up her sulk. Her tennis racquet and an old ball were lying on the ground by the gate, and she picked them up. 'I'll just go out into the square for a bit, OK?'

'Fine, but don't disappear, and watch out for cars.'

9

Olivia clanged the metal gate behind her, edged past Domenica's battered old Volvo estate parked outside, and took a look round the little square. Domenica's house, which had once been the presbytery, stood on one side of the square and faced the church, with its squat, square bell-tower. She wandered over to the fountain which occupied the centre of the square. The upper basin was so thickly covered in dripping moss of an incredibly brilliant green, that it was impossible to see the carved stone shell hidden beneath. From the moss, rivulets of sparkling water dripped steadily into the bigger, round stone basin beneath. Olivia leaned over the rim and dipped her hands in the cool water. A little notice said *EAU NON POTABLE*, but she drank a little anyway. Once, the fountain had been the entire water supply for the whole village, but nowadays everyone had piped water, so the fountain was now just a cool place to sit, under the huge old plane trees whose branches shaded the greater part of the square. Brutally pollarded every winter, by midsummer they had grown a new, thick green canopy. A few old ladies had already brought out their chairs, and were warming their bony old legs in the warm, dappled sunshine, outside their doors.

On the other side of the square the village houses, all three storeys high, were jammed tightly together, with the café and *boulangerie* on one side, and the *bureau de poste* on the other. Wide stone arches at each corner of the square led into and out of the village, through the encircling vineyards, to the main road three kilometres away. They also led to narrow lanes that ran right round the backs of all the houses, and down to a little river with a rusty iron bridge. This was a favourite place of the village children, and of Josh and Olivia. It was too shallow for serious swimming, but it was fun to splash around and build dams, and sometimes fish under the willow trees that grew on one bank. Olivia was forbidden to go there on her own, so she bounced her ball across the square and began to practise her forehand, with rhythmic metallic thumps against the presbytery gate.

Anna went upstairs to wake her mother. As she passed the door to the *salon*, which also served as a showroom for the antiques, and an office for Domenica, the fax machine began to clatter. She went and stood by the machine as it brought forth its long trail of shiny, thin paper. Pressing the receiver button, she tore off the message. It was from her brother Giò, in Paris.

'I will descend tomorrow, Sunday, with the van, so hope you have a lot of stuff for Place des Vosges. Will bring a new friend, does an arts programme on *Antenne 2*, very sympa. Doesn't mind van. There's plenty of room in the *remise*, I think? See you tomorrow about 6. Love, Giò.'

Anna's spirits rose, and she broke into delighted laughter. She had not seen her twin brother since Christmas. Like her, he was tall and thin, with dark eyes, but his hair was like Domenica's, wild and curly. He had also inherited his mother's temperament: kind, self-opinionated and often over-reactive. It was typical of him to assume that he could come and bring a friend when the house was full of August visitors, but she knew that Domenica and Honorine would be overjoyed at the news, and she ran swiftly upstairs to her mother's room to tell her.

She burst through the door, waving the fax. 'Giò's coming,' she said. 'He's bringing a friend.'

Domenica sat up, and pushed back her hair. 'Good, when?'

'Tomorrow evening.'

Anna pulled out the mosquito net and, knotting the end, threw it over the bed-head. She sat on the edge of the bed. 'Have we got enough sheets?'

'Don't fuss, darling. Honorine will manage.'

Honorine appeared at the door with a tray of tea.

'Honorine, Giò comes tomorrow.'

'Is good,' said Honorine.

'With a friend,' said Anna.

11

'OK,' said Honorine. 'Is work to do, sheets to wash. You will 'ave to do shopping.'

'Right,' said Domenica. 'We'll go to the market, Anna?'

'Fine,' agreed Anna. 'Have you made a list, Honorine?'

They went downstairs, leaving Domenica to dress. She stretched out her legs, leaning against the pillows, with the particular secret smile that only the promise of Giò's arrival could provoke. Of course, she loved Anna and her grandchildren, and was fond of Honorine, couldn't do without her really. But Giò was special, and adored. Domenica took good care to conceal this fact from Giò; she knew that loving someone totally made you vulnerable. She also knew that Giò, so much like herself in many ways, would not hesitate to take advantage of her weakness if he felt like it. She laughed.

She flung back the sheet and swung her bare brown legs, rather veined and bruised on the right thigh, but still in reasonable shape, to the floor. She did a few knee bends. Thank God for the hot weather and the disappearance of arthritis. Then she took a shower, and put on beige linen trousers, and a loose silk knitted top in a deep indigo blue. She ran her fingers through her wild grey hair, and stuck coral-coloured plastic combs behind her ears. She sprayed herself lavishly with Hungary Water, picked up the business-like leather satchel she carried everywhere, and went down to the courtyard.

Anna was standing by the open gate, calling to Olivia, and Honorine stood waiting with the list. 'You don't want coffee?'

'No, I'll get one in Uzès, maybe.'

'I make the bed in the *remise*, no? For the guest, and Giò in 'is own room?'

'Yes, fine, Honorine. You decide, OK?'

'And lunch, what time?'

'Don't bother, we'll get something in town.' She got into the driving seat, and Honorine shut the gate. Anna put the shopping bags into the back, locked in Olivia, and got in beside Domenica. Domenica inched her way through the Place de l'Église, and drove through the arch which led out of the village to the Uzès road.

The vineyards, which reached right to the edge of the narrow country road on both sides, were already heavy with bunches of dark, purple-bloomed grapes beneath their thick covering of leaves. The leaves were still fresh and green, and it would be two more months before the grapes were ready for the *vendange*. Anna wished that she could be here in September and October, when the weather was less fiercely hot, and the little tractors with their flashing orange warning lights drove busily with their loads of ripe grapes to the co-operative, and the beautiful clear warm days seemed to last forever. But it would be at least three more years before she could leave Olivia on her own. So, for the moment, the school holidays dictated the times of their visits. She glanced sideways at Domenica, whose strong brown hands grasped the steering wheel firmly as she drove fast and well along the narrow road. Would I really like to be here with her alone? she thought. Without the children as a buffer? She'd only start telling me how to run my life; how I've messed everything up; that I'm spineless and too easily pushed around. In fact, she's the one who does most of the pushing. Jeffrey doesn't push me around, exactly. He just walked out, without any warning. He said there wasn't another woman, though I suppose it was pretty naïve of me to believe that. He just needed space, to live alone, so he kept saying, and come to lunch on Sundays to see Josh and Olly. Anna stared out of the open window.

The shaming thing is, she thought, that I *am* spineless. I still love him. My whole stupid week in London is looking forward to Sunday, and making a really nice lunch for him. Idiotically going on hoping that he might change his mind and come back.

In the agonizing first weeks after Jeffrey's departure,

Anna often felt as if the grief she felt was mourning for his death, rather than his absence from her bed and her life. And sometimes she rather wished that he *had* died, in an accident or something, so that she could grieve for him openly and honestly, and then try to rebuild her life. As things were, and had been for ten years now, she was caught in a trap of hopeless longing for something she knew could never be rebuilt, but still hoped for.

She had sent him a card, asking him to go out to check that the canary had seed and fresh water. She despised herself for resorting to such pathetic stratagems to keep the lines of communication between them open, but seemed quite incapable of preventing herself from doing so.

Domenica slowed down as the road joined the main road to Uzès. In the distance, across the shimmering *garrigue*, the little medieval town rose, pink and translucent, its ancient towers wavering in the heat haze. The road was lined on either side with tall plane trees, banded in lime-wash, which gave a welcome shade as they drove with all the windows open to catch a breeze.

Domenica parked in the crowded car-park opposite the Rest Home for Protestant Ladies, and they walked the few hundred metres to the Avenue de la Libération. In the sandy square, a troupe of Peruvian musicians was belting out its music, with nose flutes and drums, deafeningly amplified, and Anna's depression lifted in spite of herself. They stopped for a few moments to listen, and Olivia, taking a few francs from Domenica, put them in the hat which lay on the ground.

The Boulevard Gambetta was lined on either side of the road, and under the trees, with stalls selling espadrilles, cheap cotton dresses and T-shirts in garish pinks and purples, ice-cream, sweets in lurid colours, and bikinis. Other stalls sold olive-oil soap from Marseille, and olive-wood spoons and bowls. They passed

14

under a deep stone archway into the Place aux Herbes. Here the Saturday market was in full swing. In spite of the crowds, a curious calm prevailed. In the centre of the square a large fountain sent its cooling jets high up under the canopy of leaves of the plane trees, translucent in the morning light. Many of the stalls, which fanned out from the central fountain in well-ordered lines, had big white canvas trattoria umbrellas to provide extra shade. The lanes between the stalls were wide, so that the shoppers were able to move easily along them, cooled by the moisture-laden air.

In the inner circle were the sellers of silver jewellery, dried herbs, lavender and honey. Different types of olives, black and glossy with oil, or pale green, or tiny pink-brown ones in brine, were arranged for tasting in round, earthenware bowls. The oil itself was sold in everything from elaborate glass bottles to huge tin cans. The next ring of stalls offered a wide variety of fruit and vegetables. The cherries and apricots had long finished their season, but peaches, nectarines and raspberries filled the air with their scent. Piles of splendidly deformed and brilliantly red tomatoes, with extravagant bunches of basil in buckets beside them, assaulted the eye and nose simultaneously. Alongside were piled peppers, red, yellow and green, and purple heaps of aubergines. Plaits of violet garlic hung from the wooden frames of the umbrellas, with glossy dark green branches of bay. Beautiful yellow waxy potatoes were displayed in wooden barrels, banded with chestnut, and beside them baskets of the local salad, a mixture of rocket, lamb's lettuce, radicchio and *frisée*. This was Domenica's favourite salad, and she bought half a kilo, wrapped in newspaper, and stuffed into a large plastic bag. She bought tomatoes, a free bunch of basil thrown in, aubergines and peppers, and round white onions.

'We'll get potatoes in the village,' said Domenica. 'They're too heavy to carry back to the car.'

Anna bought peaches, nectarines and lemons,

and they moved on to the fish stalls. Here, the table-and-umbrella stalls had given way to small vans, whose sides opened up to reveal the goods for sale, fish, meat or cheese. They looked at the fish, brought that morning by refrigerator lorry from Marseille: bass, *rascasse*, whiting, monkfish, red mullet and gurnard. There were soft-shelled crabs and mussels from Sète, piled on seaweed, on big slabs of ice.

'Let's get some red mullet,' said Anna, 'and I'll make a basil sauce to go with it tonight.'

'Can't we have meat, or chicken?' Olivia pulled a face at the thought of fish.

'You can have a Marmite sandwich, if you like.' Domenica gave Olivia a little tap on the head.

'I'd like an ice now,' said Olivia, looking at her mother with hostile blue eyes, and turning down the corners of her mouth. 'It's hot.'

'Um, yes, in a minute, darling,' said Anna.

'Now, then,' said Domenica, 'tomorrow?'

'The fatted calf?' Anna smiled at her mother.

'What?' said Domenica. 'I think garlic chicken, don't you?'

They moved on to the poultry van, where they bought two large chickens.

'Just cheese, then,' said Domenica, as they reached the tiny mobile cheese van. The cheese lady was famous in Uzès, and drove her van down from the Cévennes every week, stuffed with goats' cheeses, large and small, in different stages of ripeness. There were soft, moist fresh ones on vine leaves, and tiny shrivelled discs of fully matured ones, pungent and delicious. They bought both kinds, and some *fromage frais* in a muslin bag. Anna looked at her watch.

'Nearly half-past twelve,' she said. 'Home?'

'No, a drink,' said Domenica firmly, and headed for a café in the wide, vaulted arcade which surrounded the Place aux Herbes. Anna and Olivia, carrying the heavy bags, followed her. A group of young men got up and left a table as they approached, and Domenica with practised efficiency and remarkable speed, put her handbag firmly on the table and sat down. Anna followed her, trying to avoid the angry glances of a couple who had been waiting for a free table. A waiter approached.

'A *pastis* for me, lots of ice,' said Domenica. 'What do you want, darlings?'

'White wine and Badois, please,' said Anna.

'Coke,' mumbled Olivia.

'What?'

'Coke, please,' said Olivia.

Domenica gave the order, and asked for the menu.

Honorine pulled the sheets out of the washing machine and put them into the round wicker basket. Her back ached, and she was hot and tired from toiling up and down the stone stairs. She picked up the heavy load of sheets and carried them through the back court, to the rear walled garden. The line was tied to a hook in the wall, and Honorine took the other end and tied it to a branch of the ancient fig tree, which dominated the garden.

'I'm getting too old for this,' she said to herself as she pegged out the sheets. But she knew that she would stay with Domenica until one or other of them died. After that, she thought, who knows? She sat down on the stone bench for a moment, in the cool shade of the fig, and thought of the day, so long ago, when she and Domenica had met for the first time. Domenica had driven into the square at Souliac with a dark-haired man, one warm spring evening. They had got out of their open car and wandered round the Place de l'Église, looking around, laughing and chatting to each other loudly, taking photographs. Honorine had been leaning out of her upstairs window, observing the strangers rather disapprovingly.

Domenica had caught sight of her, and called up,

'*Est-ce qu'il y a, par hazard, une maison à louer ici?*'

'*Si.*' Honorine had pointed across the square to the presbytery, '*Là-bas.*'

Domenica had turned and looked across at the crumbling house. On the faded, dark green metal gate hung a piece of board with the dim message, '*Maison à vendre, ou à louer.*'

Domenica had turned back to Honorine. '*Merci, madame,*' she had said and, taking the man's arm, had crossed the street to look at the house. Honorine smiled at the memory. From that moment she had known that somehow this tall girl, with her black curly hair and grey-green eyes, would come to be the focus of her life, and she had gone downstairs, taking the presbytery keys from the hook where they hung, waiting for just such an eventuality, and went to unlock the gate.

The crawling evening traffic reached the Hogarth Roundabout. Jeffrey edged over to the left-hand lane, and turned into Church Street. He parked his car, and rolled down the window. He sat for a moment, enjoying the cool smell of the rain-washed street, and looking with pleasure at the winding jumble of eighteenth-century houses, overhung with the dripping branches of an old horse chestnut tree, the same tree that had caught his eye on their first visit to the street, and led them to the Lifeboat. He looked across the street at the little house, half hidden behind the heavy foliage of the chestnut. The closed windows of the upper floor looked blank and grimy, and the white-painted weatherboarding was yellow and peeling. He supposed he should get it repainted.

The ship's figurehead, fixed to the wall between the two upstairs windows was, on the other hand, brightly painted: pink face with red lips, black eyes and hair, and sky-blue dress with a flowing white scarf around the shoulders. Anna must have had a go at it herself, he thought. Certainly, she had always loved it, and like

Jeffrey himself, had been charmed at the idea of living in such an appealing little house. In fact, it wasn't a house at all, but had originally been a boat house, with an upper floor for storage. The big double doors were still there and led to a damp, dark cellar-like space where Anna kept her elderly Renault, and mixed gesso, and boiled rabbitskin glue on a primus stove. To the left of the double doors was a narrow door which opened on to a flight of steep stairs leading to the habitable part of the house.

Jeffrey got out of the car and walked a few yards down to the slip-way. The rain had stopped, and the gardens on the river bank added the strong scents of honeysuckle and tobacco to the seductive, faintly putrescent smell of the river at low tide. Gulls puddled with their feet along the water-line, screaming and quarrelling over every edible scrap turned up. Boats lay at their moorings in midstream, or lolled awkwardly on the mud, waiting for the return of the water. Three big houseboats were lashed together on a concrete mooring. It looks like a gypsy camp, he thought. Lines of grubby-looking washing were strung up, in spite of the weather, and gas cylinders and rusty junk were scattered about. If these were travellers, parked on a lay-by, he said to himself, there would be a huge outcry, and the local council would try to move them on. But because this is a middle-class set-up, and they know their rights on the waterfront, it's OK, even atmospheric.

Jeffrey walked back up the street to the Lifeboat, opened the door with his latchkey, and clumped up the steep, dark, bare-boarded staircase. She ought to get a light put in, he thought, someone will fall down these stairs one day and break their bloody neck.

At the top of the stairs, a door led into the big, main room. Lit by a tall Venetian window which overlooked the churchyard, Anna's long worktable stood with all her tools laid out in neat rows, and a white cotton cloth draped over the work in progress. The

19

once-white walls, which time and smoke had turned a soft parchment colour, were partly papered with old marine maps, bought at a flea-market *bouquiniste* in Paris. On one wall hung a large carved and gilded mirror, with speckled bluish glass, which reflected the worktable and the window beyond in a wavering, watery image. Around the mirror was a collection of gilded insurance plaques, quite randomly hung, so that they looked as if someone had hurled a handful of bright golden coins at the wall, and they had stuck. A group of Anna's soft, washed-out watercolours hung in gilded frames. There were several portraits, rather tentative he thought them, of Domenica and the children, and Anna's twin brother, Giò, but the pictures were mainly miniature paintings of olive trees, Roman-tiled roofs, and amphorae filled with stiff oleanders. By the kitchen door hung a vertical row of eighteenth-century prints, views of Milan, mounted on brown wrapping paper, with heavy black ebony frames. The floor of the room, like the rest of the flat, was covered in sand-coloured sea grass which still, after twelve years, gave off a pleasant smell of hay. From the floor rose the black iron spiral staircase to the gallery. A steel campaign bed, with a mattress covered in natural linen served as a sofa, and near it stood a battered brown leather armchair.

In spite of himself, Jeffrey was impressed by the calm beauty of the room. 'It's really rather nice,' he said aloud.

The sound of his voice drew an immediate response from the canary, which began to hop about its cage and bang its bell excitedly. Jeffrey remembered why he had come, and went over to the cage to check the seed and water bowls. The water seemed a bit cloudy, so he extracted the glass jar from its holder, spilling the water as he did so, and went into the kitchen. He turned on the cold tap and held the jar under it for a few moments, looking vaguely around the little galley at the once-familiar, blue flowered mugs and plates, and black iron cooking pots, all arranged on open shelves, ready for use. He smiled as he thought of himself and Anna preparing dinner together, and the smell of garlic and courgettes frying suddenly seemed to fill the air. He remembered her small childish breasts under a sweaty black singlet, and the long bony fingers pushing the damp hair off her forehead.

That had been during the early days of their marriage, when they were too broke to go to France, and the children had been too small to travel. For once, England had been hot in August, so they had sweltered in London, and had taken chairs out onto the narrow strip of concrete in front of the garage doors. They had sat under the chestnut tree in the comparative cool of the evening, drinking cheap red wine, and watching the blue smoke from their cigarettes curl up into the dark branches above, and been happy.

Jeffrey carried the jar of water back into the big room, and carefully replaced it in the cage. He shut the door, and snapped the latch firmly. 'Dozy little brute,' he said, and the canary responded with a shrill cadenza of notes, hopping enthusiastically from perch to perch. He ran his fingernail sharply across the bars of the cage, and crossed the room to Anna's worktable.

On the left side of the table were rows of lethal-looking carving tools and antique burnishers. In a jar stood several brushes, gilders' mops and tips, and beside the jar were books of gold leaf in varying shades of gold. The gilding cushion, made of layers of felt and goatskin, stood ready, protected by its shield of vellum to prevent draughts from blowing the fragile leaf about, while it was being cut to size. On the right side of the table stood a filing tray and answerphone. Jeffrey lifted the corner of the white cotton cloth to see what was underneath, and then pulled if off altogether to reveal a large, corpulent cherub, glistening with bright new gold leaf. His wings had been rubbed down a little, so that in places the reddish tint of the bole underneath was just visible, giving a delicately worn look, and throwing the carving of the feathered wings into sharper relief. The cherub's belly and thighs gleamed with their rich covering of gold. Jeffrey thought that it looked splendidly opulent, and that it seemed rather a pity to rub the expensive gold off again, just to make it look old. He sighed and not for the first time, wished that he had been able to do something like this with his life, rather than spend his time listening to other people's matrimonial disputes in his dreary office at Marsh, Bradfield and Buckmaster.

The light on Anna's answerphone was on, so he pressed the button and listened to her messages. One was from her doctor's surgery, saying that the test results had arrived, and would she telephone to make an appointment to see the doctor. The second was from the dealer for whom Anna worked. 'Anna, this is Axel. How are the *putti* going? Please call me, I have a good Japanese client interested. He isn't here long; can I bring him to see you? We need to talk. I have a wonderful triptych for restoring as soon as the *putti* are finished. Please call me, 'bye.'

Jeffrey stopped the tape, and reset it. He looked round the room, and saw the other cherub, lying in a dark corner. He was dirty, faded and cracked, and no work had been done on him at all.

'My God,' he said, 'the stupid cow has gone off on holiday without finishing the work, or telling anyone where she is. It's absolutely typical. No sense of responsibility at all, much less any idea of making a proper effort to support herself, or the kids.'

He put the cloth carefully back over the cherub, and looked at his watch: a quarter to seven; he could do with a drink. He went into the kitchen and looked in the fridge, and found a half-full bottle of white wine. Releasing the air from the vacuum stopper, he pulled it out. He sniffed the bottle, pulled a face, and emptied it down the sink. A piece of collapsing Roquefort stood on a plate beside a tomato and two lemons. In the salad drawer was an unopened pack of ready-washed salad. Jeffrey closed the door irritably. If she was going away for a month, why the hell couldn't she empty the fridge and turn it off? He needed a pee, so he climbed the spiral staircase that led to the bedrooms and bathroom. In the bathroom all was immaculate. The Edwardian basin and loo were patterned with delicate sepia leaves, and the mahogany loo seat was wide and solid. Anna had repapered the walls and ceiling with a design of wild clematis, faded reddish-brown on a sand-coloured ground. It made the little room seem warm and cosy, and threw the bright, white bath and crisp white cotton curtains into sharp focus. Beside the loo was a big stack of lavatory rolls, white again. Why so many? he wondered. In Anna's room, once his and Anna's, in the deep slopes of the roof, most of the floor space was occupied by the double bed. It was covered by a white stitched quilt which reached to the floor all round, and was piled high with a stack of cushions in faded and worn ancient textiles, in shades of ochre, pinks and tawny reds. A deep rooflight in the slope of the ceiling let in a shaft of watery sunlight, and a heavy green branch of the chestnut tree, stirred by a breeze, sent shudders of raindrops onto the glass.

On one wall, shelves held tightly-packed books, mostly concerned with Italian art and architecture, and some contemporary fiction, French and English. On another wall hung a portrait of Domenica, a watercolour done when Anna was a student, framed in a beautiful but damaged gilded frame. It had hung there for seven years or more, waiting to be restored. She'll never do it, Jeffrey thought, but in any case it looks rather good as it is. A spider plant hung from a hook in the ceiling, its clay pot in a wire basket, pale blue with verdigris. Jeffrey stuck a finger in the pot and felt the dry soil. A small brass watering can stood on a table. It had some water in it, and he carefully gave the plant a drink, holding his hand underneath in case it dripped through. It did not.

Nearly seven o'clock, thought Jeffrey. I don't want to fight my way back to Chelsea through the traffic yet. I'll walk down to the Black Lion and have a drink there. He locked the front door and clattered down the stairs, slamming the street door after him. He walked away down the street to the river without looking back.

Chapter Two

Giò drove the battered old van slowly through the quiet Sunday morning streets of the Marais towards the péripherique and the A6. Beside him, Patrick was hunched in his seat, still half asleep, and silent. They planned to drive to Beaune and stop for an early lunch and a rest before driving on to Lyon, and going through the tunnel in mid-afternoon. By then the heat of the day would be less intense, and the tail-backs of tourist cars should have cleared. Giò hoped that they would get a clear run through to Rémoulins, where they would leave the *autoroute* and head for Uzès, reaching Souliac in time for dinner. In his car, Giò could easily do the whole journey in seven hours, but the ancient transit van could only manage eighty kilometres an hour, less when loaded; so in summer it was a long, hot journey. He thought it pretty sporting of Patrick to come with him, and hoped that Souliac, Domenica and the presbytery would seem worth the effort of getting there.

They had met a couple of weeks before, when Patrick and his crew had been working in the Place des Vosges. Giò had closed the shop at noon and gone to lunch in his usual café, and had found it packed with the crew. At a table on the pavement, a grey-haired man sat alone, reading *Le Monde* and drinking a glass of Perrier.

Giò paused by the table, his hand on the vacant chair. 'Is this seat free?' he said. 'Do you mind if I sit here?'

The man lowered the paper, and glanced at Giò. 'Of course not.'

Giò sat down and signalled to a waiter. The man put down his paper as his lunch arrived. The waiter gave Giò the menu. He ordered a glass of wine and a carafe of water, and the waiter went away.

'Do you work around here?' asked the man.

'Yes,' said Giò, 'and I live here too, over the shop.'

'You are lucky, it's a marvellous part of Paris.' The man held out his hand, 'Patrick Halard.'

'Giò Hamilton,' said Giò, shaking hands.

'Joe as in Joseph?'

'No, Giò as in Giorgio.'

'But you are English?'

'My father is English, but my mother is half French, half Italian. She does the collecting side of our business.' The waiter reappeared with Giò's drink, and he ordered *crostini* and a salad.

'And what is your business?' said Patrick.

'Antiques, posh junk, lamps, interesting fabrics, mirrors, anything that people might want to put in their houses.'

'How interesting.'

Giò drank some water, and then took a sip of his wine. 'Patrick Halard,' he said slowly. 'Don't I know that name?'

'You might,' said Patrick. 'I do a late-night arts programme on the TV.'

'Of course, that's it,' said Giò. 'That must be terrific fun.'

'Actually, a lot of the time it's quite frustrating and boring. You spend more time hanging about, and repeating things endlessly, than actually making films. But yes, it has its good things too.' He looked at Giò. 'At the moment,' he went on, 'we're making a documentary about the Marais, and we're looking for locations to illustrate contemporary uses of the buildings. I wonder if I could have a look at your shop?'

'But of course,' said Giò. 'It's just a few doors down the arcade; it's called *Le Patrimoine*.'

They finished their lunch in a friendly silence.

Patrick folded his paper, and stood up. 'We usually finish filming around six. Would that be a good time to come to the shop?'

'Fine, any time,' said Giò. 'Just be sure you don't miss it, it's very small.'

'I won't,' said Patrick. 'About six, then.' He walked away through the parked cars, and disappeared under the trees.

Giò ordered coffee, and sat for a few minutes with his face lifted towards the sunshine that slanted through the arches of the arcade. What a nice chap, he thought, and in his mind's eye he saw Patrick walking away under the trees, his broad square back in a crumpled linen jacket, silvery grey short hair, and tanned neck. He remembered his eyes, pale blue and heavily wrinkled. Is this the start of something new? he said to himself. He laughed and stood up, looking at his watch: nearly two, time to open up. He walked along the arcade to his shop. He unlocked the heavy plate-glass door and went in.

The three rooms, which ran one into another through tall, connecting double doorways, were cool with air-conditioning, and dimly lit by many lamps, all shaded by dark green or black metal shades, rimmed with chipped and faded gilding. The walls were covered with brown wrapping paper, and on them hung many mirrors, a few enormous, most quite small, and many elaborately carved and gilded. Tallow candles in silvery metal sconces with brightly polished reflectors shone like stars in the gloom, their steady flames reflected repeatedly by the mirrors. A few were real, and were lit when the shop was open, but most were electrified, with very small bulbs like flickering flames. Giò would have preferred them all to be real, but the fire risk, and the insurance premiums, prevented it.

In the first room a large round table, covered in a damask cloth to the floor, was laid with a pink-and-gold Sèvres dinner service. Heavy old silver, and thick eighteenth-century wine glasses flanked the plates. In the centre of the table stood an enormous silver *épergne* hung with miniature silver baskets. Giò privately though it hideous, but he knew it would sell pretty quickly, and had filled the baskets with bogus purple grapes, and trailed a garland of plastic vine leaves around the whole edifice. A pair of Victorian branched silver candelabra stood on either side of the *épergne*, and Giò lit their candles. A set of English mahogany dining chairs, upholstered in indigo-and-ochre Provençale cotton surrounded the table, which stood on a square of orchid-pink carpet, with a beige trellised pattern edged in black.

Through the connecting open doors could be seen a small, dim book-room, with playing cards left scattered on a green baize table. Over the card table hung a large double lamp, like a billiard table light, with a deep, black metal antique shade. Small gilded chairs were pushed back from the table, as though the players had just left. A pot-bellied Provençale *armoire* stood against one wall, its doors open to reveal a collection of white porcelain, displayed on shelves in its sage-green painted interior. Shelves of old leather-bound books covered the remaining walls from floor to ceiling.

The bedroom, glimpsed through yet another pair of open, ivory-painted panelled doors, and glowing in the rosy light of a single lamp, revealed a big double bed with a tall putty-coloured headboard carved like a Chippendale mantelpiece. The fine white cotton sheets were thrown back, and fat white square pillows were heaped in an inviting pile on the bolster. A heavy piece of tapestry, in shades of brown and pink, and lined in rose-pink silk, was suspended on a black wooden pole over the bed-head like a canopy, the sides looped back against the wall, and caught by carved, gilded hooks. On either side of the bed were small rosewood tables on which stood lamps, open books, and Victorian *carafes* and tumblers. On the bed was flung an Indian crewel-work dressing-gown, and a pair of old green leather slippers lay on the floor.

Giò sat down at his little desk in a dark corner of the dining-room and began sorting the correspondence piled in a metal tray. Bills from upholsterers, plumbers, electricians, bank statements, and letters from clients awaited the return of Laure from her long August vacation. It was the quietest month of the year, but it was surprising how much he missed her. For one thing, he could not leave the shop, or even go upstairs to the apartment, without locking the front door. He always had the feeling that if he left the shop locked for five minutes, an incredibly rich client would come along the arcade, peer in through the windows and long to buy everything in sight. Then, thinking the shop closed for August, would go away again and a great sale would be missed. He had considered hanging a little sign saying 'Back in five minutes', but thought this a bit down-market. Many times he had sat at the desk, longing to have a pee, or put the kettle on, and had remained rooted to the seat, watching people drifting past, and occasionally coming in and wandering round in a nervous way before, usually, sidling out again with an apologetic '*Merci.*'

Giò and Laure had developed a very effective sales technique. Laure sat at the desk, apparently working, and gave a friendly smile to anyone who came into the shop, and let them browse around. Then Giò would appear through his secret door in the book-room wall, and engage the customer in conversation, telling him, or more often her, the history, sometimes real, sometimes imaginary, of each piece, until something, even if it was only a glass paperweight, had been sold. This routine Giò enjoyed, and sometimes these customers became one of the regular clients who formed the backbone of the business. These were the people for whom Domenica scoured the hill villages of Provence and the Languedoc, seeking out particular ancient pieces of furniture, faïence and textiles. Without Laure, Giò felt curiously inhibited, and far less effective as a salesman. He supposed that it would probably be sensible to close down altogether in August, but there were usually a lot of German and American tourists who came to Paris during the month, and somehow it seemed stupid not to catch that business if he could. Americans in particular were insatiable in their quests for Provençale chests, quilts and faïence, and Giò had a lot of these things stacked in his apartment upstairs, awaiting their moment.

Through the plate glass window, with *Le Patrimoine* written backwards on it in big gold Trajan letters, Giò watched the lazy summer people strolling past, some in the arcade, some under the trees across the sunlit street. Further down the arcade, a small group of jazz musicians played in a soft, contemplative way that seemed suited to the day, and the sound stirred Giò to the extent of opening the heavy glass door in order to hear better.

A middle-aged couple, obviously American to judge by their white buckskin lace-up shoes, the woman's crisp pink-and-white-striped shirtwaister and white sun hat, and the man's seersucker jacket and navy baseball cap, stopped and peered in at the window.

'My goodness, Sidney, is this a private house?'

'Not at all,' said Giò, stepping forward, 'it's an antique shop. Do come in.' He held out his arm in a gesture of welcome, indicating the door, and the couple entered, looking slightly stunned.

'Do feel free to look around, and ask any questions you may have,' he said gently, deciding not to bombard them with the usual flow of information. They wandered through the rooms, touching and exclaiming quietly to each other, ignoring Giò, until they reached the bedroom.

'Oh, Sidney, have you ever seen anything so delicious?' the woman cried, clasping her capacious bag to her bosom, and gazing in rapture at the bed.

'It's very nice, dear,' the man agreed.

'Oh, Sidney, do you think . . .?' her voiced trailed off, doubtfully.

'Well, dear,' said the man. 'Wouldn't it be difficult to ship? It's rather big?'

Giò stepped quietly forward. 'Actually, shipping these things is a lot easier than you might think. You don't need to buy the entire bed. Any six-foot double bed would adapt perfectly. What makes the bed is the eighteenth-century carved panel that forms the bed-head, and the canopy with its pole and tie-backs. This wonderful old tapestry,' he went on, warming to the task, 'came from the house of Mme de Sévigné, who lived nearby for over twenty years. It has been meticulously restored. Feel how soft and supple it is, and look at the exquisitely faded colours.' The couple, mesmerized, came obediently forward and felt the fabric. The woman looked at her husband longingly.

'OK, sweetheart, if you really want it?' said the man.

'I do,' said the woman, and it sounded like a vow.

They sat down on chairs conveniently placed beside the desk, while Giò took down their particulars and accepted payment by American Express Gold card. He took the telephone number of their hotel. 'Just in case I need to contact you about anything at all,' he said, and promised to dispatch the crate as soon as shipment could be arranged. After they had shaken hands, the woman pink with excitement and pleasure, and left the shop, Giò closed the door carefully and telephoned American Express for verification of the amount of the transaction. All was well there, and he replaced the receiver.

'Thank you, darling Mme de Sévigné,' he said, smiling, 'again.'

Upstairs in the apartment were stacked six or seven more bed-heads, not quite identical, but very similar, and a big pile of tapestries, some restored and already lined with silk, some awaiting restoration. Giò would not make a new arrangement exactly like this one for a few weeks; perhaps pink-and-white Toile de Jouey would be nice next time? He looked at his watch: ten to five. Suddenly he felt tired and very thirsty. He locked the shop door and, going through his secret door in the little book room, he climbed the narrow, twisting stair to the apartment, to make some tea.

Waiting for the kettle to boil, Giò lay down on his big red sofa, which was covered in a torn and faded old *indienne* fabric from Nîmes, and piled with old cashmeres and cushions, and looked around him at the chaos of his apartment. The turkey carpet which lay in front of the sofa was barely visible beneath the magazines and papers scattered over it, and all around piles of books, with empty picture frames stacked against them competed for space with tables and chairs, *armoires* and clocks, a huge pair of church candlesticks, and deep piles of carpets and fabrics.

The kitchen was really only a cupboard. It had no proper oven, just a two-burner hob, run on a gas bottle, a tiny sink with a gas water-heater over it, and a small fridge. Giò rarely ate at home, and if he did, he made an omelette or instant soup. His small bedroom was like a cell: just a narrow, hard white bed, no ornaments or mirrors or books. On the otherwise bare wall facing the foot of the bed, Giò had hung a small Russian icon of the Virgin and Child, not for any religious reasons, but because he thought it beautiful.

The bathroom was the one really immaculate room in the apartment, in spite of its ancient fittings. The nineteenth-century cast-iron roll-top bath was overhung by a huge shining copper geyser like an immense samovar, from which came both hot and cold water, not always in an entirely reliable manner. Very occasionally, the mechanism went berserk and water gushed everywhere but into the bath below. Witness to one of these disasters was a large watermark on the ceiling in the shop below, one of the excellent reasons for the dimness of the lighting. The bath and geyser had been fixtures when Giò took over the lease of the apartment and shop, and to rip them out would have been expensive and a pity, but the lavatory, bidet and basin were new and sparkling white. The walls were white-tiled, with one wall covered in mirror tiles; thick glass shelves housed Giò's shaving things and heavy, glass-stoppered bottles of bath essences and colognes. A neat stack of thick blue bath towels stood on a folding butler's tray, flanked by a square glass jar full of Floris soaps. A sliding, mirror-covered door concealed Giò's wardrobe, and made the little room seem much larger than its actual size.

The kettle boiled, and Giò got up, and putting an Earl Grey teabag into a mug, poured boiling water onto it. He looked in the fridge for a lemon, cut a slice and dropped it into the mug. He put the mug down on the long table behind the sofa. It's rather airless in here, he thought crossly, and went to open the tall shuttered windows which looked into the trees surrounding the square. This did not seem to make much difference so he crossed the room and opened wide the big panelled door which gave onto the communal stairway. At once a cool breeze blew through the apartment, and he sat down on the sofa to drink his tea. He leaned back on the cushions and closed his eyes, enjoying the warmth of the mug on his hands, and the cool breeze on his forehead. He opened his eyes just as a sleek black cat walked through the open door and paused just inside, gazing at Giò with cool green eyes.

Giò stared back. 'Hello, cat. Where did you come from?'

The cat turned and stalked out again, as silently as it had come. Giò put down his mug and followed the cat. He went out onto the landing and, looking down over the stairwell, he saw the cat slipping swiftly down the shallow stone steps to the marble hall below. At the bottom of the stairway it paused and looked up. Giò smiled. I wouldn't mind a cat, he thought. He finished his tea, had a wash and checked the ice-tray in the fridge. Then he went down to the shop to wait for Patrick.

*   *   *

In the central part of the square, Patrick walked slowly towards the retreating camera, the late afternoon sun slanting across the tops of the trees and straight into his eyes, and read from the autocue for the fifth time, 'The Place des Vosges and the houses which rise above the arcades were built in the reign of Henri IV. Previously, the site had been occupied by the Palais de Tournelles and its tournament field, where Henri II was accidentally killed while jousting with the captain of his Scottish Guard. Later, the place was deserted by the Court, who avoided it and its tragic memories, and the square deteriorated into a sinister wasteland, and became a notorious area for murders and duels. The square became fashionable once more during the reign of Louis XIV, as is well recorded by Mme de Sévigné. During the nineteenth century the Place des Vosges was visited by many celebrities from all over the world who came to see Victor Hugo. His house at number six is now a most interesting and beautiful museum, where many relics of the great writer can be seen.' Patrick turned and looked through the trees towards the corner of the square and the Musée Victor Hugo.

'Cut,' called Olivier. 'I think that about wraps it up, Patrick.' The director looked round the crew. 'Everybody happy with that?' There was a murmur of assent. 'Right. Tomorrow we do the Musée Carnavalet. It's a five o'clock start, I'm afraid, which gives us five hours till they open at ten. We could come back on Monday if necessary, but they're not keen, it's their only closing day. OK for you, Patrick? You've got that bit of the script?'

'Yes, fine,' said Patrick.

The crew started to pack up and load the cameras and lights into the vans, and the make-up girl gave Patrick a wet-wipe to clean his face. He packed his file containing his script and the schedules into

34

his briefcase, said good night to Olivier, and walked across the square to his car, parked under the trees. He put his briefcase in the boot of the car, and then locked it again. He looked at his watch: six fifteen. He walked down the arcade, looking for Giò's shop. Then he saw the gold lettering, *Le Patrimoine*, on the window. Peering in at the dim and intimate interior through the heavy plate-glass door, Patrick got an unmistakable sensation of voyeurism. Suddenly, he noticed Giò sitting writing at the little desk, and pushing open the door, entered the shop.

'There you are,' said Giò, getting up. 'Come in. How did it go? Are you tired? Would you like a drink?' He realized that he was chattering nervously, and smiled at Patrick.

'No thanks,' said Patrick, 'not just yet.' He looked around. 'What a charming place you have here. It's not like a shop at all, more like a private house, or a film set.'

Giò flushed with pleasure. 'Exactly, that's the point. I like people to feel comfortable here, but also stimulated by my ideas. Enough to want to buy them.'

'And they do?'

'Luckily, yes.'

Patrick walked slowly round the shop, gently touching things, picking up glasses and looking at their bases.

'I love old glass,' he said. 'It's so beautiful, but also robust and satisfying to hold.'

'It's getting harder and harder to find, unfortunately,' said Giò 'But Domenica seems to have a special nose for finding new sources, she has a kind of mafia in the hills, collecting for her.'

'Domenica is your mother, no?'

'That's right,' said Giò. 'I also have a sister who works in London; she does quite a bit of gilding and restoration for me, but I have a team of craftsmen all over Paris, working on carpets and tapestries, mending porcelain, repairing mirrors. You name it, I know someone to do it.' He laughed, and Patrick laughed, too.

'Where do you keep all your stock?' he asked. 'Do you have a warehouse?'

'Not so far,' said Giò. 'My apartment is upstairs, and I store stuff up there. Would you like to see?'

'I would, very much,' said Patrick.

Giò locked the shop door, and took Patrick up the little secret stair to the apartment.

'My God,' said Patrick, 'it's Aladdin's cave!'

'Or the flea-market, depending how you look at it,' said Giò. Patrick prowled around the room, studying everything with great concentration. Giò went into the kitchen and got out ice, and tipped some into a small silver bucket. He took two tumblers from a cupboard and put them on a tray with the ice, and a bottle of cold mineral water. He took the tray through.

'What would you like? Scotch? Vodka?'

'Do you have any wine?' said Patrick.

'Certainly. It's the stuff we buy at home, quite ordinary, but cheap and OK. I bring it up with me every time.' Giò went to the fridge and took out a bottle of white wine. He poured two glasses, and handed one to Patrick. 'I hope it's not too cold. It's difficult in hot weather here, with no cellar.'

Patrick took the glass, and crossed to the open window, looking out through the dappled green leaves of the trees. 'It's astonishing here,' he said. 'You could be in the country.'

'I know,' said Giò, and came and stood beside Patrick. He raised his glass. '*Salut*,' he said.

'*Salut*.' Patrick took a deep swallow of his wine. He turned to Giò. 'As I mentioned earlier, the piece I am working on at present is about the history and people of the Marais, and especially the Place des Vosges from its early history to the present day. It occurred to me that your shop, and your apartment, would be an appropriate example of the use of the buildings in the late twentieth century. How would you feel

36

about such a proposal?' He looked at Giò, who said nothing. 'Of course,' he went on. 'you would have a proper contract, and be properly paid. And,' he added, 'it would be good publicity, no?' He smiled at Giò, who emptied his glass and tried hard not to show his excitement, and remain cool.

Giò walked back to the kitchen on suddenly stiff legs and got the bottle of wine. He came back to the window, and refilled their glasses. 'I think I'd like that very much,' he said.

'Good,' said Patrick. 'Now, what about dinner? I'm starving.'

They went out of the apartment, and down the grand communal stair to the courtyard, then under the archway, and back into the Place again.

'I'm sure you know the best place for a really good dinner round here?'

'I certainly do,' said Giò.

After dinner they sat out on the pavement, and drank an Armagnac with their coffee, and Giò produced his squashed packet of Gitanes. 'Do you mind?' he said politely.

'Not at all, I'd love one myself,' said Patrick. 'I don't smoke much these days, too politically incorrect, but every now and then . . .' He took one from Giò's proffered packet.

They talked quietly of this and that. Patrick spoke of his great interest in seventeenth-century French history and architecture, and how much he enjoyed doing the preliminary research for his programmes. 'For example, tomorrow we are filming at the Musée Carnavalet which, as I am sure you already know, was the home of Mme de Sévigné for twenty years.'

'I do know, and never cease telling my clients about her, a most useful lady to me,' said Giò, and Patrick laughed.

'I'm glad,' he said. 'Some time soon I want to go

south to Grignan and see the *château* where her daughter lived. I'd really like to do a full-length feature on them all, if I could get the powers that be to fund it. De Grignan was the Acting Governor of Provence at the time. It took seventeen days to do the hair-raising trip by coach and barge from Paris, sometimes more. Provence must have been a hellish and hostile place then.'

'Grignan, that's about forty kilometres from Orange, I think, so it's not very far from Uzès,' said Giò. 'You must come and stay at Souliac and we could make a trip to Grignan easily.'

Patrick was touched by Giò's friendliness. 'What a nice idea, I'd love to, some time.' He stood up, and put money on the table for the Armagnac and the coffee.

'Early start tomorrow,' he said. 'I must get to bed. Thank you for your company, Giò. I will telephone you to arrange about the filming in *Le Patrimoine*, it should take two days at most. I'll send you a letter of agreement and the usual contract, OK?'

'Yes, that would be great,' said Giò, standing up. 'There's just one thing,' he added, 'I'm afraid I would not be happy if a "stylist" came in and tried to re-arrange the shop. In fact, I could not allow it.'

'Don't worry,' said Patrick gravely. 'With you, Giò, that would be strictly unnecessary.' They shook hands, and Patrick walked down the street to his car. Giò watched him go, then walked back through the arcade and in through the courtyard entrance. He climbed the stairs and, as he reached his landing, he saw the sleek black cat waiting outside his door. He opened the door, and the cat slipped through before him. The phone was ringing, and he crossed the room to answer it. If that's Ma, he thought, I shan't tell her about Patrick, and being on the telly; she'd be up here in a flash, taking over. I'll wait till it's all finished and tell her then. He went to answer the phone, which gave a click, and rang off as he did so. He replaced the receiver.

'I don't think I'll ring her back tonight, cat,' he said. The cat wound itself around his legs, purring. 'Come on,' said Giò, disentangling himself and walking towards the kitchen, 'let's see if we can find you some milk.'

Just before mid-day, Giò left the *autoroute* at Beaune and headed for the St Loup road. He drove along the hot, quiet, dusty road for a few kilometres until he saw the signs to Hauterive. They drove up the drive to the ancient water mill, now an hotel, and parked the van under the tall willows that bordered the river bank. They got stiffly out of the van, and Giò could see the small blue pool through the trees. As it was a Sunday in August, Giò had telephoned to reserve a table for lunch. They checked in and went at once for a swim. The water was cold and deeply soothing after the grilling heat of the old van. Giò floated on his back with closed eyes, and felt all his tiredness falling away. He thought of the cool court-yard at Souliac, of Domenica and Anna, and Honorine preparing a special dinner for tonight.

They lunched early, and then slept under the trees for an hour.

Patrick woke first. 'Time to press on? My turn to drive, I think?'

'Are you sure you can bear to?' said Giò. 'It's a real pig to drive.'

'Well, I'll give it a try, and see how we get on,' said Patrick.

They drove through the tunnel at Lyon just before three o'clock. 'Thank God for that,' said Giò. 'We should get a clear run, now.' They reached the bi-furcation at Orange at six, without any delays, and took the A9 to Rémoulins, and then the long, straight, tree-lined road to Uzès, passing the Pont du Gard, distantly glimmering in the evening sunshine. A cool breeze came through the ventilators as Patrick drove the last few kilometres towards Uzès, bypassed the town, and finally turned into the narrow road through the vineyards. He steered the van carefully under the archway, and drove at last into the square at Souliac.

'Park over there behind the old Volvo,' said Giò. Patrick parked the van and turned off the engine. They sat for a moment, and Patrick looked all round the square, at the tree-shaded fountain, at the church and the shabby, graceful houses with their crumbling eighteenth-century doorways. Most people were indoors now, eating supper, and the little square was tranquil and rosy in the last rays of the evening sun.

'What a magical place,' he said.

'Indeed,' said Giò, pleased.

At that moment, the green iron gate opened, and Olivia erupted through it. She looked cross. 'I thought it was you, Giò,' she said. 'You're late; I'm jolly hungry.'

Chapter Three

Under the vine Domenica and Anna sat waiting. A large white china jug, chinking with ice, stood on the table. Domenica had already had a couple of drinks. Through the big doors to the kitchen stole a garlicky aroma of spit-roasting chickens, which Honorine was doing her best to prevent overcooking. An old black lantern hung from the trellis, and the occasional moth hurled itself against the glass and fell exhausted onto the table beneath. Anna had lit a fat yellow *citronelle* candle to discourage mosquitoes, and it shed its soft, wavering light over the blistered green tabletop.

The gate gave its familiar protest as Olivia pushed it open, followed by Giò and Patrick carrying their bags. Domenica got up, slightly unsteadily, and enfolded Giò in her strong, brown arms. He hugged her tightly, and kissed her on both cheeks. She smelt clean and lemony, and somehow comforting, and looked wonderful in an apricot silk robe which fell in soft folds to the ground. Waiting politely to be introduced, Patrick smiled at Anna, who sat quite calmly at the table waiting for the fuss to subside. She smiled back at him and picking up the jug, she filled a glass.

'Do sit down and have a drink, you must be exhausted,' she said. 'I'm Anna,' she added. 'I expect you've already guessed that.'

'Patrick.' He held out his hand. 'Yes, the likeness is remarkable. Viola and Sebastian, no?'

Anna laughed, and shook hands. Olivia looked from one to the other, frowning, mystified. 'What are you talking about? Who's that?'

'Patrick,' said Anna, 'this is my daughter, Olivia. Olivia, this is Patrick. Will you see how Honorine is getting on, please darling, and ask her to come and have a drink before dinner?' Olivia disappeared through the doors to the kitchen.

'Wonderful smell,' said Patrick, sitting down next to Anna and taking the glass she offered him.

'Wonderful cook,' said Anna, 'and friend. My mother's so lucky, she's had Honorine for forty years now – more in fact.'

Giò disengaged himself from Domenica, and introduced Patrick to her.

'Don't get up,' she said, as he half rose to his feet. 'Relax, you must both be whacked.'

'Knackered,' agreed Giò. 'It's a hell of a grind in that van. We'll have to think about a newer one soon, Ma.' They discussed the question of a new van for a few minutes, while Domenica looked covertly at Patrick, who was leaning towards Anna, to hear what she was saying in her soft voice. He laughed, and Anna laughed too, rather shyly.

Domenica looked at her watch. 'Dinner in fifteen minutes,' she said. 'Giò, take Patrick to his room, I'm sure he'd like a wash before we eat.'

Giò drained his glass, stood up and, picking up the bags, led the way through the kitchen to the back courtyard. Honorine, red-faced and flustered, wiped her hands on her apron, kissed Giò, asked about the journey, shook hands with Patrick and turned anxiously back to her stove. Patrick followed Giò through the back kitchen door, into the little kitchen court, and through the archway into the courtyard garden beyond. A long pearwood table was laid for dinner under an ancient fig tree, and Giò led the way past it to the *remise* at the back. A peeling, faded blue door led into the garage, which gave on to the little lane running behind the houses. A rickety wooden stair with no handrail led up to the room Honorine had made ready for Patrick. A wash-stand, with a basin and jug of water, stood waiting, and beside it stood a small table with a sponge, soap and a pile of towels. The plain hospital bed, with a white cotton quilt, was already turned down.

'There's rather a grotty loo at the bottom of the stairs,' said Giò. 'I hope you won't be too uncomfortable,' he added, turning to go.

'I'm sure I won't,' said Patrick, smiling.

Patrick put his bag down on the blue-painted bench at the foot of the bed, and took out a fresh blue-and-white-striped linen shirt, and black linen trousers. A row of wooden shaker pegs were screwed to the back of the door, and he hung his jacket on one of them. He longed to stretch out on the bed for a few moments, but knew he would probably fall asleep instantly if he did so. Since Lyon, he had been rather regretting driving down with Giò; it would have been much less exhausting to have caught the TGV to Avignon, and hired a car. But then, he thought, Giò would have had to drive all the way by himself, so I suppose that was a good enough reason to go with him. He stripped off his damp shirt, jeans and pants, and poured water into the big basin, which had a faded pink pattern of Chinese birds and paeonies. He picked up the large sponge and soaked it in the tepid water. He leaned over the basin, and sloshed water over his head and neck, and then, squeezing out some of the water to avoid too much going on the floor, he poured a few drops of bath gel onto the sponge, and slowly washed himself all over. The cool breeze from the open window fanned his wet skin, and filled him with a sense of well-being, almost happiness. He rinsed the lather out of the sponge, and wiped it over himself again. Then, reluctantly, for he heard voices in the garden below, he took the towel and patted himself dry. He wrapped the towel around his waist, and went over to the window, dragging a comb through his cropped grey hair as he did so. He stood by the open window, looking down through the dark, finger-shaped leaves of the wide umbrella of the fig tree, and saw Anna

43

lighting candles on the long table, and shielding the flame with tall glass photophores. Olivia brought two flat oval baskets containing figs on vine leaves, and goats' cheeses, and put them on the side table. Then she returned to the kitchen, and came back with two more baskets filled with fat slices of bread.

'I put two *carafes* of water in the fridge,' said Anna, and Olivia obediently went off to fetch them. Anna walked quietly round, straightening knives and forks and glasses.

Patrick put on his trousers and shirt, and wiped the dust off his brown leather sneakers with the cloth he kept in his bag. He slipped his bare feet into them, and hung his wet towels, and dirty clothes on the pegs on the door. Then he went down the perilous wooden stairs. I hope I won't be too pissed later to negotiate these, he thought wryly, trying to fix in his mind the position of the light switch as he turned it off.

'There you are,' said Anna, as he came through the door into the garden, and joined her at the table. 'I do hope you won't be too uncomfortable in that rather primitive room. My mother keeps meaning to put a bathroom in, and decorate the room properly, but you know how it is, these things never seem to get done, do they? It's usually where my son Josh stays, and he likes it like that, it means he doesn't have to keep it tidy, or even clean.'

'And where is Josh, now?'

'At Estagnol, staying with friends, windsurfing for a couple of weeks.'

'So he is older than Olivia?'

'Yes,' said Anna, with a smile. 'He's seventeen.'

'Ah,' said Patrick, and smiled back at her.

Anna moved to the stone slab which stood against the wall of the house, where glasses and bottles of wine stood waiting. She turned to Patrick. 'A drink while we wait for the others?'

'Thanks, a glass of wine would be lovely.'

Anna poured the wine, and some for herself and

came back to him, handing him a glass. He looked around the garden with its crumbling high walls festooned with climbing roses, wisteria and honeysuckle. Lichen-blotched urns, filled with pittisporum, and clipped balls of box stood in groups round the walls, and a small statue of the Virgin stood in her niche, lit from below by a lamp hidden in a clump of hostas. The old stone slabs which covered most of the ground were interspersed with areas of fine gravel, and still released the warmth of the sun. The ancient fig spread its branches over the table, giving protection from both the fierce heat of the day and the dew by night.

'You people certainly seem to have a huge talent for houses,' said Patrick.

'Well, maybe Domenica and Giò do, but I'm much more ordinary.'

Patrick was just going to say that he doubted that, when Giò and Domenica, his arm round her shoulders, came through the archway, followed by Olivia carrying a big white platter of sliced tomatoes, glistening with oil and black olives, and speckled with torn basil leaves and chopped anchovies. Honorine followed with two bowls of *croûtons*.

'Sit anywhere,' Domenica said, seating herself firmly at the head of the table. 'No, you sit here next to me, Patrick, as it's your first visit, and you sit on my other side, Giò, there's so much to talk about, no?'

Olivia sat on the bench next to Giò, and leaned against him. He gave her a hug. 'How are you, sausage?'

'All the better for seeing you, my dear,' she replied, smirking.

Anna sat at the other end of the table, and Honorine, protesting that it was easier for her to get up and down if *she* sat at the end, was obliged to sit next to Patrick, who held out the chair for her.

'Thank you,' said Honorine, sitting down. Two bright pink spots appeared in her cheeks, and she unfolded her napkin with a little flourish.

'Poncy twit,' thought Olivia, peering across the table with her small, close-together blue eyes. Domenica and Giò exchanged brief glances, and Giò lifted the platter of tomatoes and handed it to his mother. Anna got up and fetched the bottles of white wine, and put them on the table, then she took the dish from Giò and handed it first to Honorine and then to Patrick.

'Let me hold it for you,' he said, getting up and taking the plate from her. When Anna had helped herself he put the dish down in front of Giò, who helped Olivia and himself, then poured the wine and passed round the *croûtons*. They ate in silence for a moment, enjoying the fruity, ripe tomatoes in their pungent dressing.

Domenica turned to Patrick. 'Tell me about yourself, Patrick. Giò tells me you work in the telly?'

'True,' said Patrick. 'And you are in the antique business, with Giò? And, of course, indirectly, Anna, too?'

'Well, yes,' said Domenica, a little taken aback. 'You seem to know a lot about us already.'

Giò put down his fork. 'Ma,' he said, 'I haven't told you yet, but *Le Patrimoine* is going to be in one of Patrick's programmes. It's about the Place des Vosges. He filmed last week in the shop. I'm in it, too. What do you think of that?'

Domenica picked up her glass, and looked at Giò. 'You didn't ask me whether I wanted the shop to be filmed, darling, did you?' She took a deep drink, and there was a small silence.

'No,' said Giò, steadily and, leaning over, kissed his mother. 'I didn't ask you, because I wanted it to be a nice surprise, and I knew you'd be delighted at such a terrific piece of free publicity.'

Domenica hesitated, and then burst into her loud, braying laugh. 'Yes, of course I'm delighted, darling, how clever you are.' She turned to Patrick. 'Should I know your name? Are you famous, a star?'

'Not really. My programme is a late-night arts show, with quite limited appeal. Most sensible people are on

46

their way to bed by eleven, which is the time it goes out.'

'Oh, well,' said Domenica, 'I'll have to watch out for it, but actually I hardly watch telly at all, it's so awful.'

Giò looked anxiously at Patrick, but he was mopping up the oily dressing from his plate with a piece of bread.

Anna said quietly, 'I watch it whenever I'm here. It's on Sunday nights, isn't it? It's an excellent programme, I love it.'

'So do I,' said Giò, smiling with relief at Anna.

'I'm sure I would, too,' said Olivia pertly, 'if I were allowed to stay up to a civilized hour.'

'Cheeky brat,' said Giò, ruffling her hair.

'Don't *do* that, Giò!' Olivia shouted, blue eyes blazing, and hitting him hard with her clenched fist. Laughing, he caught her fingers, and held them tightly in his. Ominous tears welled in her eyes, and her lower lip trembled. Oh dear, thought Anna, it's far too late for her, she should have been in bed hours ago. She stood up, and so did Honorine, and they stacked the dishes, and carried them to the kitchen.

'I'll help,' said Olivia in a small voice and, picking up the empty bread baskets, she ran after her mother.

'Poor child,' said Patrick, 'we arrived so late. I expect she's tired out and over-excited at seeing you, Giò.'

'Yes,' said Giò, getting up, 'I'll see if I can help.'

Domenica leaned back in her chair, and looked levelly at Patrick. 'Personally, I don't believe in pandering to children,' she said. 'I treat them as adults, and I expect them to behave as adults. If they behave childishly, I ignore them, and if they behave disruptively, I believe they should be packed off to bed.'

'It's a widely-held point of view,' said Patrick.

'But not by you?' said Domenica.

'Not particularly,' said Patrick, and smiled at her, his blue eyes dark behind his spectacles, in the flickering candlelight.

'Do you have children yourself?' Domenica asked.

'Sadly, no,' said Patrick.

'Ah,' said Domenica, and smiled at him, her strong white teeth emphasized by the dark maroon lipstick she wore.

Patrick had no wish to offend her, so he got up, offering to fetch the red wine from the stone slab. He came back with the bottles, put them on the table, and poured a glass for Domenica.

In the kitchen Giò carefully wiped the tears from Olivia's eyes with the corner of a dishcloth, and apologized to her. 'It was stupid of me. I know you hate having your hair messed up, I do myself,' he said. She hugged him round the waist and mumbled something indistinct into his shirt front.

Honorine shook the chickens off the spit and onto the big yellow platter rimmed with brown, piled the roasted garlic cloves around the chickens, and poured over the fragrant juices from the drip tray. Then she heated some brandy in a ladle, set it alight and poured it, flaming, over the birds. When the flames died down, Anna scattered a handful of chopped tarragon over the dish, and stood back for Honorine to carry it triumphantly to the table. Anna followed with the plates, and Olivia with the bread. Giò came behind with a bowl of green salad, already dressed. Honorine set down the dish in front of Giò, and gave him her special, sharp little knife to carve the birds.

'Goodness, Honorine,' he said, taking the knife, its blade worn thin with use, 'I remember this knife when I was younger than Olly.'

'I 'ave 'ad it longer than that,' said Honorine proudly. 'Much longer.'

Giò carved the chickens swiftly and skilfully, ladling sauce and roasted garlic lavishly onto each plate. Presently, the scented warmth of the night, the wine and the delicious food began to weave their spell. The curiously bad-tempered and tense atmosphere with which the meal had started melted away, and

Patrick began to relax and enjoy himself, joining in the laughter at the jokes between Giò and Domenica and Olivia. Anna and Honorine did not contribute much to the conversation, both apparently happy to eat and drink, and be amused by the others. Once or twice Patrick caught Anna's eye, and smiled at her, and she returned his smile, but he did not think it prudent to try to talk to her when the others were in full flow. He knew well the rules of the game. When you have performers there has to be an audience, however boring the performance, not that this one was boring at all. If the performers were also fairly drunk, it was not usually wise to distract attention from them by including others in the conversation. Domenica and Giò screamed with laughter at their own jokes, and Olivia looked from one to the other, with bright eyes and flushed cheeks, entranced. Giò stood up to refill glasses, and Olivia, her mouth full, shouted, 'What is pink and hairy, and goes up and down?'

'Oh, Olivia,' said Anna anxiously.

'OK, I give up,' said Giò. 'What is pink and hairy, and goes up and down?'

'A very ripe gooseberry in a lift,' yelled Olivia. 'Get it?'

They all laughed, Anna with relief, and Honorine stood up to clear the plates. 'Olivia, *mignonne*, will you 'elp me, please?'

'Let me help,' said Patrick, getting up.

'No, no,' said Anna, 'there's not much to clear anyway.' Honorine and Olivia went off to the kitchen, and Anna said, 'I'll see if I can persuade her to go to bed now, she's awfully tired.' She got up and followed them, taking some figs on a plate.

Olivia saw the figs as her mother entered the kitchen, and gave in without a struggle. 'OK, I am a bit tired, I'll go to bed.' She took the figs, kissed her mother and Honorine, and called out of the door, 'Good night, I'm going to bed, I'm pooped.' She departed slowly up the stairs, dripping fig juice as she went.

'Now, Honorine,' said Anna, 'you go and sit down, and relax, finish your dinner in peace, I'll make the coffee.'

'No, no,' said Honorine, 'Domenica won't like it.'

'The hell with Domenica,' said Anna, giving her a gentle push. 'Go!' Honorine gave Anna a surprised look, and went.

Anna pushed the heavy old kettle onto the hotplate, and put coffee into the *cafetière*. The cups were already set out on a tray, waiting. She slumped wearily against the table, and watched the kettle as it came to the boil. She made the coffee, picked up the tray, and carried it out to the garden. Honorine was sitting in Olivia's place, next to Giò, so Anna put the tray down at the end of the table, and sat down next to Patrick, who refilled her glass and passed her the cheese.

There was a rustle in the branches, over their heads, and the leathery leaves of the fig tree clacked together as something heavy moved in the darkness.

'What on earth is that?' asked Giò. 'A cat?'

'No,' said Anna, 'it's the owl. He's lovely, he's a barn owl. Sometimes he comes into the room at night, if you leave the shutters open.'

'How exciting,' said Patrick. 'I love owls. I wish he'd come into my room.'

'Probably shit all over the place, if he did,' said Giò. 'Cats, now, they're another matter. I didn't tell you, Ma, I've got a cat; it just appeared from nowhere, and walked in.'

Domenica, bored by the animal talk, lit a small cigar, inhaling deeply. Anna poured her coffee, and passed it to her. 'What sort of cat is it, Giò?' she said, across the table. 'What's its name?'

'Thin, black, green eyes. Hasn't got a name yet, just cat, until I think of something.'

'Odious things, cats,' said Domenica.

'Or even otiose?' said Patrick, with a little smile.

'That too,' said Domenica, laughing and offered Patrick a cigar.

Inside the house, the telephone began to ring. 'Damn,' said Giò. 'Who the hell is that, at this time of night?' The phone stopped ringing. 'Oh, good,' said Domenica, 'I must have switched on the machine.

They drank their coffee, and watched the cigar smoke rising in still columns into the dark tree. 'The old owl doesn't seem to mind,' said Anna, smiling at Patrick. The shutters of an upstairs window were flung open and Olivia, ghostly in her nightdress leaned out. The owl clattered his wings and flew away.

'It's Dad,' said Olivia. 'He wants to talk to you, Mum.' Anna got to her feet, startled, and went indoors. As she ran two at a time up the stone staircase to the *salon*, she suddenly stopped. 'Why am I running?' she asked herself. 'What am I afraid of?' She walked quite slowly to the telephone, and picked it up.

'Yes?' she said coolly, and was amazed at herself.

'Anna,' said Jeffrey, 'what are you playing at, not finishing that gilding job before you went on holiday? There's a long angry message for you on your answering machine, from that chap Axel, saying he's got an interested Jap client but he needs the stuff now, not next month.' Anna held the receiver away from her ear. She could hear the hectoring voice going on and on, and waited for it to finish. She put the receiver back to her ear. 'Anna?'

'Yes?'

'What have you got to say for yourself?'

'If it's any business of yours, Jeff.' Anna's heart began to thump.

'Of course it's my bloody business. Every time you cock up a commission, or lose a dealer, it costs me at the end of the day. You could earn a proper living if you bloody well wanted to, you could . . .' Anna put the telephone carefully down on the table, and went quietly out of the room, and down the stairs to the garden. She sat down next to Patrick again, and poured herself another glass of wine.

'Well?' said Domenica.

'Well, nothing,' said Anna.

'Good,' said Giò, and flung his arms round Honorine.

High up in the house came the haunting sound of a flute. The liquid notes floated out of Olivia's window, and hung in the night air.

'Is Olivia, she his awake again,' said Honorine.

'Doesn't matter,' said Giò.

'No,' said Anna, 'it doesn't matter at all.'

Much later, Anna lay in her bed, covered only by a thin sheet, and gazed at the intense dark blue, star-pricked rectangle of her open window. She could smell the faint odour of the anti-mosquito burner which enabled her to have the window open, and felt the cool night air caress her bare skin. She thought about Jeffrey. Why was he such a shit to her? And why was she still hung up on him? She could not think of a single really good reason, other than the fact that he was the father of her children. The way he went on about money was ridiculous really. He paid the mortgage on the house, and the heating and lighting bills, and insurance. But he only paid fifty pounds a week towards the children's maintenance. Did he have the faintest idea of how much it cost to clothe an adolescent, and how much they ate? She thought of Josh coming in from school, dropping his heavy bag of books on the floor, and heading for the bread crock. He could easily eat half a loaf, thickly spread with butter, and Marmite or cheese, and then eat a huge dinner two hours later. Olivia wasn't quite as voracious as Josh, but she would down a pint of milk at a time, and eat half a packet of biscuits. They were both at good schools in Hammersmith, and of course Jeffrey paid the fees. But Anna had to find money for the uniforms and expensive school trips, which seemed to occur with alarming frequency, and of course she had to find the cash for bus fares and school lunches. It all seemed to add up to a frighteningly large sum every week.

Anna's earnings as a restorer and gilder were not very large, and far from regular. She could never say, 'This year I will earn so much,' and budget with that in mind, because the work came in in dribs and drabs. Sometimes one job followed another quickly, sometimes she waited for a couple of months before a commission was confirmed. And always, literally always, a big job would materialize just before it was time to go to France, and she would not achieve the promised delivery date. Jeff had a point about her lack of professionalism, but if she kept her nose to the grindstone at all times and failed to give the children, and herself, their annual long break from England, what then? They were, after all, only partly English, and it was important to her that they should feel, at the very least, Europeans. Anna hated the idea of their becoming clones of Jeffrey, or of her own father, now living with his second wife in Sussex, and rarely seen by her.

But she made enough to give her children the things they needed, and always managed to find the money for them all to go to Souliac every summer, and Christmas. Domenica was generous and kind, and would not allow Anna to contribute much to the housekeeping while they were staying with her. She also gave the children money from time to time. 'One needs cash in the pocket, no?' The children readily agreed.

Anna knew that Josh would soon begin to go his own way; he had already started. He would get himself a holiday job, and be more independent. Next year he would be at university, and soon Olivia, too, would go her own way. What then? she thought. Will I have invested so many years of energy and love in them, and then be dumped? She knew that, once the children were gone, she would see nothing of Jeffrey. When the children were no longer at home, he would probably divorce her, sell the house, dividing the proceeds between them, and force her to leave the Lifeboat. The thought filled her with a huge dread. The Lifeboat was her home, and she loved it with a deep and abiding passion, it was her refuge and her comfort. She did not particularly like the English people, or the English weather, but the little house was her own place, and when she closed the front door behind her and entered her work-room, she felt like a hermit-crab retreating into its shell, safe and protected.

Patrick had negotiated the stairs to his room with comparative composure, and now lay with closed eyes on the bed. He, too, had an anti-mosquito burner plugged in, so was able to lie naked and relaxed, and enjoy the scented night air. Stretching back in his mind, the day seemed interminable. They had left Paris in the pearly mists of daybreak, and rattled down through Burgundy and the Lyonnais to Provence, getting hotter and hotter as the day wore on, and finally arriving at this little piece of the Mediterranean dream. Like most dreams, it was a fragile state, easily bruised by the people who inhabited it, and easily turned into a nightmare. Domenica, he thought, was an amazing woman, domineering and strong-willed, but a good person to have on your side in a war. He could imagine her carrying messages on a motor-bike, or blowing up bridges. He could see where Giò got his energy and talent from; but Anna? What of Anna? She seemed totally unlike her mother in every way. What about the father? he wondered. Perhaps she is like him. Giò had not mentioned his father, except to say that he lived in England.

Down below in the garden, the owl had come silently back to his roost in the fig tree, and began to hoot, tentatively. Patrick opened his eyes and listened, and then crept across the room to the open window and looked down. At first he could see nothing. Then the owl hooted again, and he saw him, perched on a high branch, his huge eyes dark pools against the white feathers of his face. Another owl hooted from the trees in the square, and Patrick's owl replied. He watched for a few minutes, then got back into his bed, suddenly chilled, pulled the sheet over himself, and fell instantly asleep. He slept heavily, and then began to dream.

He dreamt of Marie-France, his young wife of so long ago, killed in a car crash a month before the birth of their child. They had tried to save the baby, but he was dead when they delivered him by Caesarian section. He saw Marie-France's waxen face, disfigured by injury, when they took him to identify her in the hospital mortuary. He had thought that he would go out of his mind with grief and rage at the time, but after nearly thirty years he had learned to live again, in a detached sort of way, and did not allow himself to think about her too much. In his dream he held her warm, naked body close to his, her arms were clasped tightly round his neck and her kiss was deep and demanding. At the moment of orgasm he awoke, pierced by loss. He turned over, his face in the pillow, and wept.

Chapter Four

Domenica woke with a slight headache, but also the feeling that something nice had happened. Of course, she thought, Giò is here. She planned to go with him to a village near Sommières, where a dealer friend of hers had an old barn full of highly desirable pieces of furniture, and to Lodève, where she had another contact, who bought and sold faïence. Monday was a good day to go. Many places would be closed, so there would be time for quiet bargaining and a pleasant lunch with M Alphonse and his nice arthritic wife. Poor old soul, thought Domenica, who was more or less the same age as Mme Alphonse, but found that hard to take seriously.

The door opened, and Olivia peeped in, 'Are you awake?' she asked softly.

'I am, my darling.' Domenica sat up. 'Have you brought me some tea?'

'Yes,' said Olivia, advancing towards the bed. The cup rattled in its saucer, and some of the tea slopped over. 'Hang on, I'll get a tissue.' She ran to Domenica's bathroom and grabbed a handful of tissues, and mopped up the spilt tea. Domenica drank the tea thirstily. When she had first been married to Robert, she had laughed at the idea of tea before breakfast, in the afternoon, sometimes even at bedtime, but she had become addicted to it herself in the end, and now couldn't imagine life without it. Anna always brought Twining's Earl Grey down with her, no other kind suited their water so well. Giò came in, wrapped in a long towel, fresh from his shower, and sat on the bed while they planned the day.

'What about the others?' said Giò. 'Shall we all go?'

'No,' said Domenica. 'If we took the Volvo, there wouldn't be room for the things we buy, and it wouldn't be very comfortable in the back of the van for them, would it?'

'OK, then. We take the van, and if they want to go somewhere, they can have the Volvo, right?'

'Seems the best way,' Domenica happily agreed.

'Can I come with you?' Olivia asked, her arm round Giò's neck.

'No, darling, this is business. You'll stay with Anna and Patrick.' Giò stood up. 'I must send a fax to Laure at the shop, to tell her where I am. She should be back from her holiday today, I forgot to leave her a note. We'll leave about ten?'

'Fine,' said Domenica.

Giò and Olivia went down the beautiful stone staircase together to the *salon*, stone-smelling, shuttered and cool in the early morning.

'I love this place,' said Olivia, 'but it makes me feel sad sometimes, too.'

'I know just what you mean, Olly,' said Giò, squeezing her hand. 'The flip side of extreme beauty or of extreme happiness is often a feeling of regret or sadness. It's something to do with the passing of time, I think.'

Olivia looked up at him. 'You'll always be around, won't you, Giò?' she asked.

'As long as you need me,' said Giò, 'with any luck.'

'What about Dad?' said Olivia.

'I can't answer for him, sweetheart,' said Giò. He wrote a note to Laure on Domenica's paper, and crossed the room to the fax machine.

Olivia watched him closely, as he inserted the paper into the slot, dialled the numbers, and waited while the note fed itself through the machine. The machine clicked and whirred and disgorged the receipt slip. Giò tore it off.

'Is that it?' asked Olivia.

'That's it,' said Giò.

'Has it got there already?'

'Certainly has.'

'And that's all you do?'

'Yup.'

'How clever,' said Olivia, impressed.

'It is, rather,' said Giò.

Patrick found Anna and Honorine sitting in the front courtyard, drinking coffee. He sat down, and Anna poured coffee for him. 'I hope you slept well?' she said. 'You had such a long, hot drive, and we all stayed up so late.'

'Not at all,' said Patrick, 'I feel fine. It was a very pleasant evening, and a superb dinner,' he added, smiling at Honorine. He turned to Anna. 'Your owl came back. Did you hear him?'

'Yes, I did. He comes nearly every night. Domenica hates it, actually. She thinks owls are harbingers of death.'

Patrick laughed. 'Do you believe that?'

'No, I don't. I love to hear them,' said Anna.

'In spite of the fact that they are probably in the process of hunting poor little mice and voles?' said Patrick, teasingly.

'Is because of that,' said Honorine stoutly, banging her fist on the table, 'I am 'ating the 'orrible little brutes,' and they all laughed.

Giò and Olivia came out of the house, and Giò told them the plan for the day. Anna turned to Patrick. 'What would you really like to do, Patrick. Giò told me you wanted to go to Grignan to see the *château*?'

'I do,' said Patrick, 'but it's probably closed on a Monday. And in any case, frankly, the thought of driving back up that hot road again so soon doesn't really appeal much.'

'Well,' said Anna, 'we could go to Uzès, or Arles, or Nîmes. Or just stay here and have a quiet day?'

Patrick thought for a moment. 'Is it far to the Camargue?' he asked. 'I've never been, as a matter of fact. I'd love to see the white horses and the little black bulls.'

'It's not far at all, it's about an hour's drive,' said Anna. 'We could take a picnic and take the whole day.'

'Oh, great.' Olivia clapped her hands. 'Can we go to l'Espiguette, and swim in the sea?'

'Why not?' said Anna. 'Honorine, why don't you come too? It's time you had a day out.'

'No, no,' said Honorine, 'I 'ave much to do 'ere. In any way, I prefer the cool and quiet 'ere. I make the picnic for you, no?' She got to her feet.

'Really,' said Patrick, 'there's no need. We'll find a bistro somewhere, I'm sure.'

Giò, with a twinge of regret that he was going to spend the day in the van with his mother, interspersed with bargaining with dealers, and humping heavy furniture said, 'I wish I were coming with you, but duty calls,' and he went indoors to find Domenica.

'Are we ready, then?' said Patrick.

'I'll just get my swimming things,' said Olivia. 'What about you, Mum, will you swim?'

'Why not? Bring mine too, darling. Patrick, did you bring anything to swim in?'

'I did, I'll get them.' He disappeared through the kitchen to the *remise*, and got his trunks and a towel, and his wallet.

When he returned he found Anna at the car, stowing baskets and hats, and Olivia into the back. She held out the keys. 'Would you like to drive?' she said.

'Would you like me to?'

'Yes, I would. And I'll map-read for you.'

They drove out of Souliac, through the vineyards, and took the road to Nîmes.

*   *   *

In London, Jeffrey leaned back in his black leather swivel chair, his fingertips touching on a level with his chin, and stared at the woman in front of him as she enumerated the sexual extravagances of the husband from whom she wished to be divorced. The catalogue of offences seemed pretty indicative of a straightforward outcome from her point of view, so he did not feel it necessary to listen particularly carefully. In any case, the tape-recorder was switched on, and he could always replay the tape later. He began to go over his telephone call to Anna of the previous evening. He did not feel that he had managed it particularly well. Usually when he deemed it necessary to tell her to pull her socks up, her response was contrite and appeasing. Last night she had been rather offhand, even rude, and when he had finished speaking he had had the feeling that there was no-one at the other end of the line, though he had heard the sound of a flute playing, far away. Perhaps he had got a crossed line? Somehow, he thought not.

He shifted in his chair, frowning. Mrs Arbuthnot stopped talking, and looked at him with flushed face, her eyes bright with unshed tears. Menopausal old cow, he thought, and smiled at her. 'Well, Mrs Arbuthnot,' he said gently, leaning forward over the desk, 'that all seems very satisfactory. I don't envisage the petition being contested in any way by your husband, since one imagines that he would not wish to have your evidence heard in open court. I think I can safely say that we can obtain a very satisfactory settlement for you. Particularly as it appears that you have suffered considerable embarrassment and humiliation over the years.'

'Is that all?' said Mrs Arbuthnot, rising.

'Yes,' said Jeffrey, standing up, 'for the moment. We'll be in touch when the documents are ready for signature, and of course, I'll contact your husband's legal advisers. I'm sure everything will proceed very smoothly.' He crossed to the door, and held it open for her. 'Goodbye,' he said, taking her hand solicitously. 'Try not to distress yourself.'

Mrs Arbuthnot, descending the staircase of Jeffrey's chambers, clutched the fat brass handrail to steady herself. Her spectacles were splashed and misted with the tears that now fell in hot rivulets down her rouged cheeks. She took a handful of tissues from her bag and dabbed at her wrecked face, trying to pull herself together. She wiped her spectacles, and put them on again. Then she crossed the hall, turning away from the doorman, and went down the steps and into the leafy square. She sat down on a bench to compose herself. It was very strange, but she felt that it was she who had been found wanting, and not William. Her hatred of him, and her desire for revenge, was strong, but at the end of the day she knew that it would be she who would be the loneliest and saddest. He would continue his life in exactly the same way as he had done for the thirty-five years of their marriage; the only difference for him would be a comparatively reduced income, and a change of address. Mrs Arbuthnot drew a long, shuddering breath, like a child. She opened her bag, took out a small silver flask, and glancing round the square to make sure that she was unobserved, took a reviving swig.

At Estagnol, Josh, with knees bent, pulled hard on the bar of his surfboard to encourage it to even greater speed as he scudded across the crescent-shaped bay, rippled like green silk in the sunlight. Looking through the transparent window in his sail, he could see the white sandy beach, fringed by tall, sprawling Corsican pines, and enclosed at either end by jagged, rocky arms. In the middle of the bay, shaded by the pines, he could see the red dot that was Mrs King's hat, as she sat guarding all their things, and no doubt reading Proust, as usual. Close to her, he thought he could see Emma lying in the sun, getting a serious tan. After a week she was so brown that it was almost impossible to identify her from a distance. Josh himself was rather burnt and peeling on the shoulders, and his skin was crisp and dry and salty, but he felt great, and in any case he knew that Emma would insist on covering him with her sun-cream, HPF 15 whatever that meant, when he got back to the beach. He always objected, but in fact he absolutely loved the feeling when she gently rubbed his shoulders and back, and lectured him about skin cancer, and wearing a hat. Hugh, her brother, was at school with Josh, and he, too, was trying for Oxbridge. He was dark and serious, like his mother. He was also a very good windsurfer, though he seemed not to notice the glances of admiration from girls on the beach when he came ashore.

Josh thought that he had never been so happy in his life. It was wonderful to be in this heavenly place, in perfect weather, and to feel so extraordinarily strong and well. It was even more wonderful to sit in the pine-scented shade on the beach, eating peaches and drinking chilled rosé, and trying not to stare at Emma's glorious brown toplessness. Like her brother, she seemed quite unaware of her beauty, and treated Josh in exactly the same way as she treated her brother, with a gently scolding kindness.

Honorine put clean sheets on Domenica's bed, and changed the top two pillow-cases. One of them was smudged with black, obviously she was too tired to clean her face last night, thought Honorine crossly. It was difficult to get rid of mascara, you had to scrub with soap and an old toothbrush, and even then it took ages. She picked up the bundle of laundry, took the dirty clothes from Domenica's laundry basket, and carried them down to the machine. She took the pillow-case, a mug of water, some soap and the old toothbrush, and sat down at the kitchen table. As she scrubbed, she thought of the many unpleasant personal habits indulged in from time to time by Domenica. Cigarette butts in coffee cups, leaving the lavatory needing cleaning, toothpaste stuck on the basin, for example. She's impossible, thought Honorine for the thousandth time, and shook her head. Why do I put up with her? she asked herself. Honorine still slept in her own little house, and her pension was just about enough to live on, especially if she let out her parents' old bedroom in the summer. But Domenica needed her, and she, Honorine, needed Domenica, it was as simple as that. She had been an only child, and her parents had both died during the war. Then her fiancé had been killed, shot by the Germans. That had been her situation when the young Domenica, and her English husband Robert had arrived in Souliac that spring evening, so long ago now. It must be over forty years, she thought, remembering herself then, bony and sallow, prematurely aged from looking after her ailing parents and working in the vineyard, defeated and disappointed before she was thirty, and finally destroyed by the loss of her Jacques. Her neighbour worked the vineyard now, and she received half the small income from the crop, but the vines were old and not very productive, so the income grew less and less. Domenica kept urging her to get the vines grubbed up and claim the compensation from the EC, then replant with asparagus, but she was reluctant to change something so fundamental to her heritage. A stubborn pride in her parents and their way of life, which would have been also hers and Jacques's in their turn, prevented her from taking such an action. After I'm gone, she thought, they can do what they like.

Domenica and Robert had been a long time looking over the presbytery, and when they came back with the keys, they were full of excitement and plans.

'Is there anywhere to stay in the village?' asked Robert.

'The café has rooms to let,' said Honorine, 'but they don't do meals. I have a room here in my house, and I could cook a meal for you, if you like.'

'You're the answer to prayer,' said Domenica. 'Thank you, that would be marvellous.'

Honorine brought two bottles of wine from her cellar, and they all sat down at her kitchen table. The handsome young couple discussed their plans and drank the rough red local wine, while Honorine cooked a dish of rabbit, spiked with rosemary and garlic, simmered with onions and carrots, and yellow new potatoes. They told Honorine of their plan to buy the presbytery and spend their summers there.

'How does one go about it?' asked Robert. 'Is there an agent I can talk to?'

'No,' said Honorine. 'The presbytery is the property of the *commune* here, you must address yourself to the mayor.'

'Really?' said Robert. 'And where can I find him?'

'It's M Boyer. He lives right here, in the Place de l'Église.'

'Good. It all sounds very simple. I'll be able to speak to him tomorrow, perhaps?'

'I'm sure,' said Honorine, putting plates on the table.

'Why is the presbytery for sale? Is there no priest in Souliac now?' asked Domenica.

'Nowadays the priest takes care of five churches in the area. He lives in Roussac, so the other *communes* are selling off the empty presbyteries. But they are so big and in such poor condition, no-one really wants to take them on.'

Robert and Domenica looked at each other. 'Except, perhaps, us,' he said.

'Except you,' agreed Honorine.

At Gallargues, Patrick left the *autoroute*, and took the Aigues-Mortes road. At Aigues-Mortes they skirted the high stone curtain wall of the ramparts, and followed the signs to Grau-du-Roi.

'When we get near,' said Anna, 'you must try not to look. It's so awful, huge concrete blocks of flats and snack bars everywhere, and bogus little hitching posts with these poor, bedraggled fly-bitten ponies, and their *gardiens* plying for hire like taxis.'

'Good heavens, why have we come?'

'Because,' said Anna, 'just past the Port-Camargue turning, there's a tiny track that takes you to a huge empty beach. You have to leave the car and walk quite a way to the actual sea, but it's wonderful, windy and exhilarating when you get there.'

'But isn't it packed with tourists?' Patrick asked, noting the billboards selling Coca-cola and hamburgers, and advertising bullfights and fun-fairs.

'Not really,' said Anna. 'They seem to stay in their camp sites, and go where the action is, thank heaven. L'Espiguette must be one of the very few wild places still left on this coast. It's a real tragedy.'

Groups of inexperienced riders plodded in single file along the verges of the narrow road, their bare legs looking red and sore against the leather girths, the ponies docile and bored, with drooping heads.

'Look over there, to the left,' said Olivia excitedly. 'The water is pink; is it flamingoes?'

'It might be,' said Anna. 'But I think those are salt pans, and the water goes pink anyway.'

They turned off the road onto an even smaller track, marked Phare de l'Espiguette, and bumped through the tall reeds which crackled and whispered in the breeze. Suddenly they could smell the sea, and, clearing the reeds, came out onto a huge, flat expanse of dazzling white sand, with a wide band of dark blue sea in the distance and a high dome of heat-hazed blue sky above.

Half a dozen cars were parked nearby, and Patrick drove up to them and parked alongside. On the distant water's edge were scattered the tiny figures of the cars' occupants. To the right, they could just see the lighthouse, but the modern developments that disfigured the further shoreline were hidden in the heat haze.

'I'm astonished,' said Patrick. 'I can't believe that this is the Mediterranean coast in August.'

'Long may it last,' said Anna, 'but I don't suppose it will, do you?'

Olivia had already changed into her bathing suit, and began to run ahead towards the sea.

'Be careful,' Anna called after her. 'The sea is deep and rough, don't forget.'

They got out the basket, with towels and hats, locked the car and followed Olivia as she ran barefooted over the soft, fine sand. In five minutes they reached the sea, and sat down close to the coastguard's hut, high on its stilts, the wires of the flagpole clacking in the stiff breeze. The water looked quite rough, with little white horses out to sea, but the red flag was not flying, and Olivia flung herself into the water and began to leap about joyfully.

'It's a shame that Josh isn't here. It's so dull for her without him.' Anna stretched out her brown legs and wiggled her bare toes in the warm sand.

'This is more like an Atlantic beach; it's a bit spartan, isn't it?' said Patrick. 'I don't really know whether I'm brave enough to join Olivia.'

'Would you rather be in Cannes, or St Tropez?' said Anna. 'Under a beach umbrella, with a beer close by?'

'No, Anna, I would not.' He stood up, took off his trousers and pants, put on his swimming trunks, peeled off his shirt, folding them into a neat pile, put his spectacles on top and waded into the water.

'It's really quite warm!' he called. 'Come in.' He held his nose and ducked under the water. Anna watched, expecting him to pop up again but he did not, and she scanned the water round about slightly anxiously.

Then, just as she was about to call out, he shot out of the water some distance away.

'OK,' said Anna, pulling off her knickers and wriggling into her swimsuit. She put her clothes in the basket and put it on top of Patrick's things to stop the wind from blowing them about. She pulled the straps up over her shoulders and dived straight into the water.

'Show off!' called Patrick, and Anna laughed and hit the surface of the water hard with her hand, sending a shower of water over him. He swam towards her and put his hands on her shoulders, and she, laughing, put her hands on his and they sank gently beneath the surface. Under the water, Anna opened her eyes and saw Patrick's face close to hers, his blue eyes wide and questioning. She smiled and closed her eyes again, and felt the soft touch of his lips against hers, and his arm round her shoulders. Then Olivia dived between their legs, and they all three broke the surface together, spluttering and laughing, and flicking the water out of their hair. They staggered up the beach and flopped down on the sand.

'Do you do that often?' said Anna primly. Patrick began to laugh, and Anna joined in, and then got hiccups, and had to be thumped on the back.

Olivia looked from one to the other, frowning. 'I'll never understand old people,' she said to herself.

'It's nearly twelve,' said Patrick, looking at his watch. 'I don't know about you two, but I'm beginning to think about lunch.'

'Well,' said Anna, 'what shall we do? We don't really want to go to one of these tourist places. There's a nice little bistro at Le Paradou, the other side of Arles. It's a lovely drive through the Camargue proper, about an hour. Can you wait to eat as long as that? The roads will be fairly clear, everyone will be having lunch.'

'Is that what you would like, Anna?'

'Yes,' said Anna, 'I really would. Then we could go through the Alpilles and Les Baux to St Rémy, and then home by Beaucaire and Pont du Gard.'

'Sounds marvellous,' said Patrick, picking up the baskets. 'Let's go.'

Olivia stood stubbornly where she was, and said she wanted to swim again. 'Look,' said Anna, pointing to the coastguard's hut, 'they're putting up the red flag, so we can't swim anyway. We got here just in time, the sea is getting very rough now.'

'OK,' said Olivia sulkily, 'I suppose so.'

They trudged back through the soft sand to the car, and were dried by the wind before they got there. They took off their damp swimming things and dressed, shaking the sand out of their shoes.

'My hair is all sticky and horrible,' said Olivia, trying to untangle her wet, frizzy fair hair with her fingers.

'Never mind,' said Anna. 'Get in the car, darling, there's a brush in my bag. You can sort it out as we drive.'

'Do you want to drive, Anna, or would you rather I carried on?' said Patrick.

'You drive to Le Paradou,' said Anna, 'then you can have a drink at lunch, and I'll drive this afternoon, OK?'

'OK,' said Patrick, getting back in the driver's seat and starting the engine. They went back to Aigues-Mortes and then took the Arles road. They drove along the old road, fringed with tall green rushy grasses and punctuated with glimpses of marshy water, from which rose white clouds of egrets, and flocks of blue and yellow rollers and bee-eaters, which hurled themselves into the vast blue sky, swept clean by the wind blowing off the sea. The herds of small, dazzlingly white horses, with their darker foals, stood near the road, twitching their ears and flicking their tails against the flies. From time to time, they passed a *gardien's* hut, set back from the road, neat and spruce with whitewashed walls, wooden shutters, and dark brown, reed-thatched roofs. Further back from the road, some of them lying down in the long grass, or under scrubby trees in the heat of the day, they saw the little black bulls, with their long sharp horns.

'Have you been to the bullfight here?' asked Patrick, slowing down to look.

'Not for a long time,' said Anna. 'When I was a child we used to go a lot with Domenica and my father. The *course* isn't like the Spanish *corrida*, the bull doesn't get killed. Every little village has its arena here, it's fun. Unfortunately, they do the *corrida* in Nîmes now, Arles too. I think it's rather horrible.'

'Me too,' said Patrick.

Approaching Arles, Anna said, 'It might be best to get onto the dual carriageway in a moment to bypass the town, and go straight on to St Martin-de-Crau, and then up to Le Paradou. In August, there are often huge queues of tourists, even on Mondays, trying to get into the centre to see St Trophime, and the arena and the Alyscamps. Poor things, the winter or spring is the best time for sightseeing.'

'It's extraordinary,' said Patrick. 'Here you are, half English and you seem to know much more about the country than I do.'

'Oh, well,' said Anna, 'I've spent half my life here, and Domenica lives here. Also, I love it here. Who knows? Maybe one day I might live here all year round.'

Not without me you won't, thought Olivia sourly, and I'm staying in London.

They crossed the Rhône and drove along the dual carriageway, leaving the town on their left and sped towards St Martin. They took the road to Maussane-les-Alpilles and Le Paradou, and presently found themselves in a shimmering, luminous landscape of olive trees and cypresses, with huge jagged pale grey rocks thrusting up through the fertile red earth. As they drove in dark shade along a road lined on either side with immense cypresses, the cool, scented air flowed in through the open windows like a benison. At Maussane, they turned left and drove the few remaining kilometres to Le Paradou.

'There it is,' said Anna, pointing, and Patrick parked the car near a pretty white building with blue shutters and big terracotta pots of geraniums.

'Lunch,' he said.

'Can I have anything I like?' said Olivia.

'Anything,' said Patrick, and smiled at Anna.

Domenica and Giò had had a tiring morning going through M Alphonse's stock, and making notes of the prices they intended to pay for their purchases. The cool, dusty barn which served as a furniture store stood close to his farmhouse, and when he had opened the elaborate system of bars and locks which protected the contents, M Alphonse left them to browse around by themselves. He knew better than to tell Mme Hamilton the provenance and date of each piece, or to talk up its value. Much better to leave her and her sharp son alone to make their choice. That way, she would take many pieces, and give him a fair price. So he sat down on an old kitchen chair by his front door, and read his *Midi Libre*, and waited.

Giò stood before an eighteenth-century *radassié* and pondered. The walnut frame of the three-seater *banquette* was in good condition, but the long rush seat was badly rotted and damaged and would need totally renewing. What would that cost? Three thousand francs, maybe more? He might get ten thousand for it, re-seated, but it would have been a lot more if the original seating had been in good condition. Also, it was a long piece, an awkward shape for the shop. One needed space for the proper display of these things. On the other hand, it was very desirable, rare, and he was sure it would move fast. He got out his calculator and did some sums. Then he wrote F1,250 on a small ticket, and tied it to the arm. Alphonse had probably paid five hundred at most, so he wasn't doing badly out of it. He moved to a pretty pair of mid-eighteenth-century beechwood *chaises à la bonne femme* stacked one inside the other. They were hand-painted, with pink flowers and dark green leaves on a faded olive green ground, the simple carving on the legs picked out with worn gold leaf. Perfection, he thought, just the right amount of natural ageing. Beautiful. I'll tell him they need a lot of restoring. And he put tickets marked F1,000 on each of them. He knew that he would get at least fifty thousand for the pair.

Domenica in the meantime was working her way through a pile of Provençale *boutis*, the padded quilts made by nineteenth-century brides for their *trousseaux*. She selected all the intricately stitched large white ones with pretty flowered borders, for these were the ones that sold fast in Paris, and for the highest prices. She also set aside a bundle of old linen sheets and lace-trimmed square pillow-cases; these were for herself at the presbytery. Leaning against a wall, she found a stack of nineteenth-century *panetières*, and tagged them at once; small pieces like that moved very quickly, and were getting increasingly hard to find. She joined Giò, who stood contemplating a small, rather black-looking *buffet*.

'I don't think much of that really,' she said. 'The hinges are broken.'

'Actually, Ma,' said Giò, quietly, 'it's a very rare piece. It's walnut, and its very plainness and lack of ornament makes it extremely collectable. We'll make a bomb on it.' He put his tag of F300 on it.

'Clever old you,' said Domenica drily.

They went out into the sunlit yard, and M Alphonse got stiffly to his feet. 'Did you find anything?'

'Yes, a few things.'

'Good. And now, one eats, yes?' Helped by Giò, he locked up the big barn doors, and they went into the dim old house, where Mme Alphonse sat placidly at the kitchen table, her arthritic hands folded before her, waiting. On the stove, a pot of soup simmered, and a thick white bowl of bright green *pistou*, smelling strongly of garlic and basil, waited on the table, together with a large, freshly baked loaf of country bread. Four fine old blue-and-white soup plates, with scalloped edges, stood on the side of the stove. Large, heavy old silver spoons and knives were set at each place, and a *carafe* of wine stood beside another of water.

'*Pastis?*' said M Alphonse, taking a bottle from the fridge.

'Please,' said Domenica and Giò together.

At three o'clock, after a leisurely and delicious lunch, Anna, Patrick and Olivia got back into the car, and Anna drove towards Maussane, and then took the road to St Rémy. Ahead of them, the jagged profile of the Alpilles thrust its unmistakable speckled white teeth into the hazy afternoon sky, and seemed to shimmer in the heat. They drove slowly past vineyards and olive groves divided by immense windbreaks of close-packed cypresses, their colour almost black against the silvery green olives, and the sharper green of the vines.

'Do you want to go up to Les Baux and see the ruins? It's an amazing view from there. Trouble is, again, the tourists just now,' said Anna.

'Any better ideas?' said Patrick.

'Well,' she said, 'there's the little cloister at St Paul-de-Mausole, where Van Gogh lived for a while, in a tiny cell. It's really lovely, the cloister runs right round a little courtyard filled with roses and lavender.'

'Sounds charming, let's go there.'

It was a wise choice for the time of year. Very few visitors were in the cloister. They looked at Van Gogh's tiny stone cell, and then sat in the cool of the cloister and looked at the pretty sunlit garden.

'What a terrific place to work, if you happen to be having a nervous breakdown,' said Patrick.

'Yes,' said Anna. 'He did a huge amount of painting here, in between bad bouts of illness. Most people seem to associate him mostly with Arles; in fact, he was here for quite a time.'

They wandered back to the car, and drove slowly towards St Rémy. They could see the coaches, and the people queuing to visit the Roman antiquities at Glanum.

'Poor things,' said Anna, 'they look so hot and tired. What an awful memory to take home of a trip to one of the loveliest places in Europe.'

'It's the same everywhere. Look at Greece, or worse, Spain. Horrible, spoilt by man.'

'Do you know Greece well?' asked Anna.

'Pretty well. I did a programme a few years ago on classical Greek drama. We did the filming in January; it's the best time for photography. It was unbelievably beautiful, a magical experience.'

'I've never been, I'd love to go.'

'I'd like to take you there,' said Patrick, 'in the very early spring, when the shrines are empty of people but full of the ancient spirits. There are wild flowers everywhere, and the air is sparkling and new.'

'Sounds wonderful.' Anna glanced at him briefly. 'In the meantime, you'll have to put up with this little bit of paradise, won't you?'

'That's not a problem,' said Patrick, smiling.

They drove into St Rèmy and, incredibly, arrived at the Café des Arts in the Boulevard Victor Hugo just as a parked car pulled out. Anna slid the car into the free place, and switched off the engine.

'Tea?' said Patrick, putting francs in the meter.

They sat at a table on the pavement, in bamboo seats with Tuscan red cushions, and ordered tea, and an ice for Olivia, who seemed rather quiet and sleepy. The terrace was shaded with a wide, white canvas canopy, and extra coolness came from the plane trees which shaded both sides of the wide street, and from the vine which climbed vigorously over its metal framework, framing the main entrance to the café.

'You ought to take a look inside, Patrick,' said Anna. 'It's interesting, seems to be completely unchanged since Mistral's day. Lots of old photographs on the walls of the bar, and a very serious restaurant at the back. Also, the last time I was here, a very serious Alsatian dog.' She laughed.

'I'll go and look in a minute,' said Patrick, laughing too. 'I need a pee anyway, if the serious dog doesn't stop me.'

Olivia looked across the street with pursed lips. She did not much care for the tone of the conversation, and thought it silly. She ate her ice in silent disapproval.

'What a nice place this is, I always like coming here,' said Anna. 'There's that lovely little shop selling wire baskets just across the road. They're copies of antiques, but I like them anyway; and there's *L'Herbier de Provence* just down the pavement, you can almost smell it from here. After tea, we'll go and buy something nice for Honorine. She works so hard, and doesn't have many treats.'

They finished their tea and walked down to the herb shop, where Anna bought some soap and bath essence in a pretty package for Honorine. She also bought some camomile shampoo for Olivia, who took the bottle rather ungraciously.

'It's specially for fair hair,' said Anna, hopefully.

'Really?' said Olivia. 'Well, OK. Thanks.'

Patrick bought a newspaper and *Paris Match*, and they walked slowly back to the car.

'Let's look at the basket shop,' said Patrick, and they crossed the street.

'This one's nice,' said Anna, weighing it in her hand, 'just the right size for bottles and glasses.'

'We'll take it.' Patrick gave the assistant a note, and she rang the till before Anna could refuse.

'Oh, Patrick,' she said, mortified, 'I didn't mean – you shouldn't really.'

'Nonsense,' said Patrick, 'it's nothing. It's just a very small thank you for a really nice day. I never knew that being a tourist could be such fun.'

When they got back to Souliac it was almost six o'clock, and they found Giò in the square outside the presbytery unloading the van on his own.

'It's a bore,' he said crossly, for he was hot and tired and longing for a drink. 'I daren't leave the stuff in the van, so I've got to take it all up to the *salon*, and then pack the bloody things all in again when we go back to Paris.'

'Come on,' said Patrick, 'I'll help, and you will too, Olivia, won't you? We've all had a long day.'

'OK,' said Olivia, 'if I must.'

Anna put Patrick's newspapers and Honorine's present in her wire basket, took out the basket of swimming things, locked up the Volvo, and went through the iron gate to join Domenica and Honorine under the vine.

'There you are, my darling,' said Domenica. 'Drink?'

'Yes, thanks, lovely.' Anna sat down at the table. 'Honorine, this is for you, a little present.'

Honorine took the package and held it to her nose, sniffing the scent. 'Anna,' she said, 'is very kind of you, but is too snob for me, *mignonne*.'

Domenica poured cold wine for Anna. 'You look pleased with yourself,' she said. 'Is that a new wire basket?'

'Yes, it is,' said Anna. 'Isn't it nice?'

Chapter Five

Robert Hamilton sat at his kitchen table drinking hot lemon and whisky in an attempt to ward off a cold. Kate, who already had the cold, was peeling potatoes for lunch, and staring out of the window over the sink at the rain-lashed garden beyond. In spite of the appallingly cold and wet August, now drawing mercifully to a close, the tomatoes and courgettes were rampaging out of control in the greenhouse, and every surface in the kitchen harboured great bowls of produce, waiting to be eaten, or frozen, or preserved in some other more labour-intensive way. Their neighbours in the village had a surfeit of their own fruit and vegetables, so there was no possibility of lessening the burden that way. Even the vicar was hopeless as a potential recipient of his God's good things; his flower ladies had already seen to that.

Kate sighed wheezily, and rinsed the potatoes under the cold tap, added salt and mint leaves to the pan and, lifting the heavy lid of the hot plate of the bashed and ancient cream Aga, put them on to boil. She wiped her hands on the dishcloth and reached for the coffee-pot on the back of the Aga. She took a chipped brown stoneware mug from the wooden plate rack over the draining board, and filled it with the strong lukewarm coffee. She sat down at the table and, taking a roll-up cigarette from the tin in her pocket, put it in her mouth and lit it.

'Must you?' asked Robert plaintively. 'Surely, with your blocked nose, you can't even taste it?'

'Yes, I can,' said Kate belligerently, taking a deep

drag, and exhaling a thin blue cloud. The fat white cat got up in a huff and jumped down from the table.

'There,' said Robert, 'you've offended him.'

'Shouldn't be on the table anyway, moth-eaten brute.' Kate took another drag, and aimed a glance of pure malevolence at the departing cat.

Robert picked up the postcard propped against the big white jug containing his favourite red sun-burst dahlias, and turned it over in his large, work-roughened fingers. It was from Josh, his grandson, announcing his intention of coming for a weekend before the beginning of term. Robert loved his grandchildren, and Kate got on better with them than she had with his twins, Giò and Anna. With unusual perspicacity for him, Robert thought that this was probably something to do with the fact that both Giò and Anna were tall and slenderly built, like their mother, whereas Kate was below average height, and pretty broad in the beam. He hardly ever saw Giò, since Giò very rarely came to England these days, and he, Robert, never went to Paris.

When he had commuted to his job in the Historic Buildings department of the GLC, as it then was, going up to London by the early train from Pulborough, and coming down again on the five thirty in the evening, he had taken Anna out to lunch from time to time. Sometimes he had taken the afternoon off on the pretext of a site visit, and taken a taxi out to Chiswick to have tea with Anna and her children at the Lifeboat. He loved the little house, and Church Street and the Mall, and enjoyed taking the infant Josh on high tide days to see the river rise over the banks, flooding the riverside gardens and eventually the road itself, so that swans swam, hissing and proud, up the Mall. He greatly envied Jeffrey and Anna for living in the house which he had found in the first place. He would have preferred to live at the Lifeboat instead of in Sussex, necessitating daily commuting. Not that he didn't love living in Boulter's Mill, he did, particularly now that he had retired and didn't often go to

London. It was nice that his grandchildren, especially Josh, liked to come down sometimes. Anna very rarely came, he guessed largely on account of Kate's coolness towards her, but Jeffrey, oddly enough, came down quite often, even after he and Anna separated. It was strange, but Kate seemed to be very fond of Jeffrey, and was always cheerful and animated during his visits. Robert almost had the feeling sometimes that Kate regarded Jeffrey as the son she had never had, and would so much have liked.

Robert got up from the table and rinsed his glass carefully under the tap, then left it to drain on the rack. He ran his fingers through his thinning grey hair, and rammed on his old khaki hat. He picked up his basket and his secateurs. 'I'll just go and see if there's anything needing picking,' he said. 'Lunch at one?'

'I suppose so.' Kate cast her eyes despairingly at the beamed ceiling, from which already hung strings of garlic and onions, and bunches of drying herbs and everlasting flowers. Robert opened the garden door and went out into the rain, closing the door very quietly behind him.

'Oh, dear,' said Kate aloud, 'what a cow I am. He means so well, but does he really have to till his bloody acres quite so hard?' She finished her coffee and her cigarette, read Josh's card, and looked at the picture, which was of the Ile de Porquerolles by moonlight. She looked out of the window at the rain which now fell in relentless straight rods, and thought sourly, some people have all the luck, and it sure as hell isn't me. She got up from the table, stubbing out her cigarette in the ash-tray, meticulously emptied by Robert every time she used it, and went to move the potatoes to the simmering plate. She took yesterday's chicken from the fridge, stripped the remaining flesh into a pie dish, sliced a courgette and a tomato over it, poured a can of condensed chicken soup over the top, and put the dish into the hot oven of the Aga. Guiltily, she threw the carcase of the chicken into the kitchen bin, putting paper, the soup can and coffee grounds on top so that Robert would not find it. I'm bloody well not making stock, she thought. She looked at the huge bowl of courgettes, tomatoes and string beans, plums and early Worcester apples and raspberries, which glowed on the blue-and-white-tiled worktop like a photograph in *Country Living*, and groaned. She put the bowl of raspberries in the fridge where the chicken had been. 'We'll have some for lunch,' she said, and went through the little door in a deep recess behind the massive old chimneybreast, which led to her pottery.

Here all was calm. The low, lime-washed room was lit only by a small leaded window, semi-opaque with dirt and neglect, and a mountain of goosegrass and nettles clawed its way up the outside of the glass. A greenish oceanic light filtered into the little room, and lit the rows of ceramic tiles which stood on shelves along two walls. Under the window was Kate's work-bench, with her wheel close by, and against the wall opposite stood her sturdy little kiln.

She sat down on her stool and looked at the half finished set of tiles on the bench before her. All had been glazed with *Blanc Ancien*, so that the soft pink terracotta of the tile glowed through, and she was in the process of decorating them with her particular motifs of fruit, flowers or curious little warriors on horseback, all in her special forget-me-not blue glaze. When she had enough finished, they would be stacked into the kiln for their second firing. She had a big order to fulfil for the Tile Merchant in Fulham Road. Delivery was due by the middle of September, but she did not see how she could manage to complete it by that time, at the current rate of progress.

Life had changed drastically for Kate when Robert took his retirement. When he had gone to work every weekday, she had driven him to Pulborough to catch the London train every morning, and then come home, slung the breakfast things into the plastic bowl in the sink, and gone immediately to her work. She had had

79

a sandwich at one o'clock, and then worked straight through till about four thirty. Then she did her household chores, brought in logs and laid the fire, prepared the elements of dinner, driving to the supermarket if necessary, and met the evening train bringing Robert home. They had driven through the lanes to the mill, happy to be together at the end of their respective days. Robert lit the fire and poured drinks, while she prepared the dinner and set the table, lighting candles and using the good silver and china. They had sat by the fire with their stiff brandies, while Robert told Kate all about his day. Then he would fetch a suitable wine from his well-stocked cellar, and open it while Kate put the food on the table and they sat down to eat: things like smoked trout or steak, or a dover sole, simple lovely food, quickly prepared. After dinner they put more logs on the fire, poured the rest of the wine into their glasses and turned on the television. If there was a play they watched that, and then *News at Ten* or *Newsnight*, but often Robert fell asleep, lulled by the warmth of the fire, the wine and the soporific effect of the television. At eleven, Kate would wake him, fill the hot-water bottles and make camomile tea, and they would go to bed.

At weekends they had enjoyed keeping the grass cut and the worst of the weeds at bay, and collecting firewood from the long strip of woodland which bordered their land and the millpond. It had been just the right amount of healthy and enjoyable exercise to keep them fit, and left Kate plenty of time to get on with her own job.

Then Robert had retired, and the whole neat pattern of her life had been turned on its head. To start with, Robert was convinced that his pension was not enough to keep them in their customary style, and seemed to have little regard for Kate's ability to supplement their income. He therefore inflicted on them a severe cutback in the housekeeping money, and set about growing as much of their food as possible, and kept rabbits, hens, ducks and geese, which took to the millpond and proved impossible to catch when required for the pot. He was in and out of the house all day long, needing cups of coffee, or a helping hand with some task or other. At one o'clock he expected lunch, a proper lunch with a pudding, as well as tea at four thirty and dinner at eight thirty. After more than twenty years of a well-ordered life together, Kate found herself curiously lonely and extremely resentful of the new domestic role in which she found herself. The worst part was that she found it incredibly hard, constantly having to put down and pick up her work, snatching ten minutes here and half an hour there, and not being able to get up a serious head of steam. It worried her that she would lose her customers and her confidence if things went on like this. Ahead of her seemed to stretch an unending avenue of frustrating, unhappy days.

She tore off a piece of kitchen roll and blew her nose, which bled all over the paper. 'Jesus!' she said furiously, throwing the paper in the bin. Through her unblocked nose came the unmistakable smell of burning, and she rushed to the kitchen, to find the potatoes boiled dry, and the bottom of the pan burnt black.

'Bugger, shit, fuck!' she cried, and hurled the pan into the sink. 'Stupid old fool,' she said, and fetched a dish. She prised the stuck-on potatoes off the burnt pan and put them in the dish. Then she added a large lump of butter, a good grinding of pepper, and a lavish handful of chopped parsley and chives. She put them in the bottom oven to keep warm, and put plates in to warm too. Nervously, she opened the hot oven door to see what was happening to the chicken dish. Rather to her surprise, it was golden and bubbling and smelt delicious. 'Thank God for that,' she said, leaving the door slightly ajar. She laid the table, and put the raspberries into bowls, her own blue ones. She decanted *fromage frais* into a small jug. Robert had come in from the rain, and she could hear him in the

81

little book-room. The door was closed but she could hear the music. He was listening to *Tosca*.

Putting a loaf of bread on the table, Kate felt a little stab of guilt. Whenever she got into one of her baity moods, which was very often lately, he played Puccini or Verdi. Kate knew that this meant that he was thinking about Domenica, and Anna and Giò, and the happy days of his youth, now gone forever.

She went to the book-room door and opened it. 'Lunch is ready, dear,' she said, smiling. Her face felt stiff. He shot her a grateful smile and, turning off the tape, followed her to the kitchen. He glanced towards the garden door. By the steps outside stood the basket overflowing with courgettes, now really small marrows, and tomatoes and aubergines. Better not bring them in yet, he thought, and sat down at the table.

He picked up the half-full bottle of last night's wine. 'Glass of wine?'

'Why not?' Kate put the chicken dish on the table, and sat down. She filled Robert's plate and handed it to him, then served herself.

Robert lifted his fork to his mouth hungrily. 'Lovely potatoes,' he said.

'Yes, they're awfully good this year,' said Kate, permitting herself a cynical little smile.

Jeffrey parked his car and crossed the road to the Lifeboat. It was quite a pleasant evening, warmed by a low hazy sun, and the midges were out in force under the chestnut tree. He let himself in and ran upstairs, leaving the street door open to let some fresh air in. He felt angry and frustrated with Anna for ignoring his telephone call, and had come to see whether there were any more messages so that he would feel justified in reprimanding her once again for her unprofessional behaviour and failure to make a proper income.

The room smelt stuffy and airless, so he opened one of the big windows and left the door open to let a current of air through. Then he went to the answering machine and played back the tape. There was another message from Axel. 'Anna, this is Axel. Thanks for your card, I had forgotten that you always go to your mother's in August. Let me know as soon as you get back, so that we can rearrange the schedule. My Japanese client is rather impatient, but seems prepared to wait, so it's not too much of a problem. Hope your holiday is doing you good, see you soon, 'bye.' Jeffrey stopped the tape. He felt extremely irritated. These people are all the same, he thought, sloppy and lax in their attitudes. If he, Jeffrey, had been in Axel's shoes, he would have had no hesitation in sacking Anna from the commission. He pressed the button again. There was another message on the tape. 'Mrs Wickham, this is the doctor's surgery. Dr Muswell has asked me to remind you that the results of your tests are here, and that you should make an appointment to see him again as soon as possible. Thank you. Goodbye.'

What was all that about? thought Jeffrey. What tests? She's not ill. He did not feel worried by the message, or even particularly curious. Still, he thought, it gives me a good enough reason to phone her, and brace her up a bit.

Patrick drove his hired Peugeot towards Orange. A fierce mistral had been blowing for two days, making everyone feel restless and unwilling to go out, except for necessary shopping. Last night the wind had dropped, and this morning heavy grey clouds covered the sky. He decided that he had better use the bad weather to make his trip to Grignan, and get it out of the way. Giò drove him into Uzès after breakfast, and left him at the car rental office. Now, as he drove along the *autoroute* he saw that the clouds were getting blacker and lower, and in a few minutes large spots of rain began to fall on the bonnet of the car. Suddenly, it came down in torrents, like a tropical storm, and the traffic, lights flashing, slowed to a crawl. He though briefly of returning to Souliac, and then rejected the idea.

At Orange he left the *autoroute* and drove into the town, stopping opposite a newsagent. A carousel of postcards and maps stood on the pavement, protected by an umbrella. He crossed the street, and bought a map and *Le Monde*. The rain still fell steadily as he drove through Orange and took the road to Suze-la-Rousse. Through the sheets of rain he could see that the road, flanked by vineyards, would have been an attractive drive under more normal circumstances, but the day was becoming more and more depressing. After Suze-la-Rousse, he continued to Montségur and then took the road to Grignan. The rain had stopped, and he got out of the car and looked across the windswept plateau to the hills of the Drôme. Their barren-looking calcareous flanks were lit by shafts of weak sunlight, piercing the great curtains of rain-sodden clouds which formed a grim backdrop to the scene. Poor Mme de Grignan, having to live here, he thought. And poor Mme de Sévigné, coming all this way, and finding this. He drove on, and then saw the huge impressive château. He stopped the car, and opened the window. What a horrible building, he thought, it looks just like the sort of place a tax-collector *would* build.

Dismayed, he realized that he had completely lost interest in his project, the sole reason for his visit here. He sat for a few minutes staring at the château, and took a photograph of it through the window of the car. Then he looked at his map again, and decided to return to Orange by Valréas, Visan and Sérignan-du-Comtat. The road was clear and fast, being lunchtime, and he got to Sérignan just after one. He parked outside a café and went in. He ordered beer and a pizza, and sat down at a table to read his paper. He stared at the printed page, reading it but failing to take it in. What was the matter with him? Why had he suddenly gone off a project, simply on account of a spell of bad weather? It was ridiculous and illogical. After lunch, he would turn the car round, go back to Grignan and visit the château properly. After all, he hadn't come more than six hundred kilometres to scrap the whole idea on a whim, without even going into the place.

The pizza arrived. It was brittle and overcooked. Oh, dear, he thought, this is definitely not my day. He finished the beer, paid without leaving a tip, and went back to the car. He drove a few hundred metres out of the village, and parked under a dripping evergreen oak. He stared at the rain-soaked vineyards, opening the windows to get some fresh air after the stuffy café. A wave of loneliness swept over him. No-one knows, much less cares, where I am at this moment, he thought. Usually, the thought exhilarated him, and made him feel secret and free at the same time, but now a feeling of desolation rose within him, bordering on self-pity. He lit a cigarette angrily. 'What the hell is the matter with me?' he said aloud. 'I like being alone, I like my own place, my own books, my own thoughts, and not being responsible for, or answerable to, anyone.' God knows he had done it for long enough to know his own mind. He thought of his tiny book-lined apartment in Paris. Originally an attic in a shabby old town house on the Quai des Grands-Augustins, it looked across the river to the Ile de la Cité, with the Palais de Justice opposite. If one leaned out of the window and looked to the right, you could see the three arches of the Pont St-Michel, and the twin towers of Notre Dame thrusting into the sky. It was a cold and gloomy little attic in a wonderful location, and he and Marie-France had fallen in love with it the moment they saw it. After her death and the loss of their baby, he had not felt any particular wish to move. On the contrary, it was only in their home that he had felt any vestige of her remaining with him. Over the years, it had not changed much. He had finally got around to centrally heating the place, and every few years he got it repainted, and had had new shelves built as his collections of books, videos and music grew. Basically, it remained the same: one large, low room under the roof, a bedroom with a tiny bathroom, more a cupboard than a room. Behind folding louvred doors was a narrow tiled surface, with a hob, a small wall oven, a fridge and a sink. Above it, a double row of shelves housed plates, mugs, and glasses, cooking pots and storage jars. If he ate at home, which was rarely, he put the dishes into the sink and left them for Mme Caron to deal with. She came in three times a week, cleaned the apartment and took his laundry home with her. She was the perfect housekeeper. Patrick never saw her, just left the money for her every week. She bought all the cleaning stuff, and left neat little accounts for him. The only way that he could tell that she had been in the apartment was the faint smell of lavender which hung in the air on the days she came. He supposed from polish or lavatory cleaner. Patrick noticed that she always dusted the photograph of Marie-France which stood beside his bed. It had been taken in the orchard of his father's house in the spring before she was killed. She had been twenty-one years old. To Patrick now, she looked even younger than that, a child almost.

In fact Mme Caron and a couple of other cleaners before her, were the only people who had been to the apartment since Marie-France's death. Patrick's father had come from Normandy to attend her funeral, but he had not stayed with him, and had returned to St Gilles the next day, sorrowful and dignified, to look after his patients. Dr Halard had lost his own wife two years before, and knew how Patrick must be feeling, and how bleak the future would be for him, but he could not find the words to comfort his son. Patrick usually spent Christmas with his father, but they had little in common except their loneliness. Through his work Patrick had many friends, but he never invited them to his apartment, nor they him to theirs. If they met socially, it would be at the Café Flore at St-Germain, or some other convenient and amusing place. He loved his work, liked his friends and thought that on the whole he had worked out his life quite well. At least, nothing could really get to him any more. Until now, he thought. What the hell is happening to me?

He threw his cigarette out of the window, and then, guiltily, got out of the car and ground it into the damp earth. He walked a little way down the road, and back again to the car, in the grip of indecision. What should he do? Go back to Grignan, make notes, take more photographs, talk to people and get his project under way? Or get in the car, go back to Souliac, and tell Anna that he loved her?

'I love her!' he shouted to the empty road, and lifted his arms to the sky, and laughed, and then said quietly, 'I love her.'

Then he got back into the car, and tried to think clearly and sensibly. For a start, he thought, she is already married, and has adolescent children. I guess that her husband, this Jeffrey, is not living with her, but I don't really know the facts at all. Why are they not divorced? I live in Paris, she lives in London. Even if something did come of it, would I really want my life invaded by children now, even quite big ones? And what about age? Anna is only about ten or twelve years older than my own son would have been, if he had lived. He closed his eyes and saw again Anna's underwater face close to his, and felt the soft pressure of her lips when he had kissed her. He opened his eyes.

'This is ridiculous,' he said. 'Grow up. This is just a silly infatuation, I'm behaving like a schoolboy.'

He looked in the driving mirror, and drove down the road until he reached a lay-by. He turned the car and drove towards Orange, filled with a curious sensation of combined elation and dread. The sun came out again, and clouds of steam rose from the tarmac as Patrick rejoined the *autoroute* to Nîmes, and drove slowly towards Rémoulins and Uzès. He felt in no hurry to reach Souliac, and just after Rémoulins he took the turning to the Pont du Gard. He had guessed that the bad weather would have discouraged sight-seers, and he was right. The colossal Roman aqueduct stood massively against the early evening sunlight, its huge stones darkened and glistening after the rain, and reflected in the bottle-green waters of the Gardon, slowly swirling through the central pillars of the six great arches, which formed the first of the three tiers of the enormous construction.

Patrick could see someone walking across the top of the first tier: tiny, ant-like and totally insignificant. I would not care to walk over there on a windy day, he said to himself. He got out of the car and walked over to a notice, which read, 'The building of the Pont du Gard was begun in the year 18 BC on the orders of Agrippa, son-in-law of the Emperor Augustus. An important bridge over the Gardon, it was also an aque-duct, bringing water from a distant source to Nîmes. The bridge is more than fifty metres high.' Patrick took a photograph, got back in the car and drove slowly towards Uzès.

Giò and Anna came out of the *Continent* supermarket and stowed the shopping into the back of the Volvo. Giò got into the driver's seat and looked at his watch. 'Half-past six,' he said. 'How about a drink?'

'Good idea,' said Anna. 'Where shall we go? Place aux Herbes?'

'Fine.' Giò turned left to join the Uzès road. A broad pink sweep of clear sky now filled the western horizon, and beneath the heavy banks of purple cloud the evening sun slanted low over the rain-washed *garrigue* and lit the sun-bleached terracotta, Roman-tiled roofs of buildings along the road, their small windows sparkling between their faded green shutters. The air was fresh and aromatic after the rain, and their spirits rose.

'Good idea to stop for a drink,' said Giò. 'Let's hope

the old bat will be in a better temper by the time we get back.'

'Are you by any chance referring to our dear mama?' said Anna. She laughed. 'Poor old thing, she can't bear the mistral. You know that.'

'Well, why did she choose to live here then?'

'I suppose,' said Anna, 'because she hated living in England, and the ghastly weather, even more.'

'And Dad?'

'Dad, too,' said Anna sadly.

They parked in the Boulevard Gambetta and walked under the vaulted entry into the Place aux Herbes. The tables and chairs had already been set out under the arcades, spilling out from the cafés after the bad weather, and were doing a brisk trade. The plane trees, stirred by a light breeze, sent down the occasional shower of raindrops, and the central fountain shot its sparkling jets high in the air, adding to the atmosphere of enjoyment already engendered by the chattering groups enjoying their evening drinks. Giò and Anna sat down, and he ordered a whisky for himself and a rosé for Anna.

'I stepped in a puddle,' said Anna. 'My *espadrille* is soaked.' She took it off and propped it against the table leg, and dried her bare wet foot on a paper napkin. 'Ugh!' she said. 'You forget the horribleness of rain and mud when you're down here, don't you?'

'Yes,' Giò replied, 'but worse, think of what's to come in a couple of months in Paris and London. Think of boots, and heavy coats, and awful central heating bills.'

'Don't remind me, please.' A cloud crossed her face.

'Sorry.' Giò touched her hand. 'Is it as bad as that? How long is it now since he left?'

'Nearly ten years,' said Anna. 'It seems longer, somehow.' She sipped her drink.

'Why don't you divorce him?' said Giò. 'There can't be much mileage left in the sort of semi-detached arrangement you have just now.'

'You're right of course, I should. Domenica's always on at me.'

'Well, why don't you?'

'Oh, Giò, it's hard to say why not. At first it was because I still loved him. Then the children were at a vulnerable age, still are in a way. Mostly it's because I am basically lazy and feeble, I suppose.' She gave an unconvincing little laugh.

'Not really good enough reasons for hanging on, are they?' said Giò. 'You're young still, Anna, you should be getting much more out of life.'

'I've got the children,' said Anna.

'For how long?' he asked, cruelly.

Anna looked at him. 'Then there's the Lifeboat,' she said. 'I've lived there for eighteen years, I love the place. I dread having to leave it. I don't want to have to move to some horrid flat, which is all I could afford on half of what Jeffrey would get for the Lifeboat if we were divorced.'

'I see what you mean,' said Giò slowly, 'but isn't this what will happen anyway, as soon as Olivia goes to college, or whatever?'

'Don't.' Anna winced. 'Yes, of course it is what will happen. I try not to think about it. Let's talk about something else.'

'Like what?'

'Well,' said Anna, 'tell me about Patrick.'

'Tell you what?' said Giò guardedly.

'Is he a bachelor? Married? Divorced? Does he have a family?'

'As far as I know, he's a bachelor.'

'Isn't he rather old for that?' said Anna, looking Giò straight in the eye. Giò looked back at Anna, his dark eyes hostile.

'If you mean by that, is he gay,' he said coldly, 'the answer is, I don't know.'

'But,' said Anna, looking into her glass, 'you rather hope he is.'

'Yes,' said Giò.

'Sorry,' said Anna. 'Didn't mean to pry.' She looked at her watch. 'Quarter to eight, we'd better get back, Honorine needs the tomatoes for supper.'

They walked to the car, a slight feeling of constraint between them. Giò drove along the Alès road. The clouds had cleared, and the huge fiery ball of the setting sun seemed suspended in the wide red sky, which faded upwards to orange, violet and pink, finally giving way to an opalescent blue overhead.

Everything seemed to Anna to be especially bright and sharp, the leaves on the vines more acidly green, the grapes more deeply purple and bloomed, the earth more intensely ochre-coloured, the stones whiter than usual. The swallows, which swooped over the vines and hawked along the road in front of the car, seemed etched on the air, their swept-back wings an intense steel-blue, their long forked tails streaming behind them. They flew so close and low that Anna could clearly see their gleaming white underparts, and the chestnut flashes on their throats and foreheads. They seem so free and happy, she thought, though I don't suppose they really are. Probably just desperately trying to feed their babies. As they drove into the square, Anna saw the little Peugeot parked by the van, and guessed it must be Patrick's. She felt a nervous lurch in the pit of her stomach, and bit the insides of her cheeks to stop herself smiling. Giò stopped the car, and got out. They unloaded the shopping, and Anna opened the gate.

From the other side of the square, music blared from the café, and then they heard the unmistakable sound of Domenica's voice roaring belligerently above the din. Brother and sister exchanged resigned glances.

'She's probably been there all afternoon,' said Giò. 'I'd better go and sort her out.'

Anna knew what this meant. 'I'll come and get you when supper's ready,' she said, and took the shopping in to Honorine. Patrick was not in the courtyard, and Honorine said she thought he was in the café with Domenica. Anna began to say how sorry she was that her mother was sometimes such a problem, but Honorine stopped her in mid-sentence.

'Anna,' she said, 'is no-one's faults, but maybe me, because I don't get anger with her. Is because I love 'er, as I love you, *mignonne*, and Giò, and the childrens. She need me, I need 'er, OK?'

'Understood.' Anna gave Honorine a kiss on her soft, wrinkly cheek. 'Where's Olivia?' she said.

'Maybe plays the video games, no?'

'Probably,' said Anna.

Anna made a tomato salad, and dressed it with olive oil, lemon juice, a sprinkle of sugar and basil. She set the table under the fig tree, not allowing herself to think about the possible implications of her conversation with Giò. I will think about it later, when I am in bed, she thought; I must be calm and sensible. He is a kind and good man, and I am probably a sitting duck, just an unhappy and frustrated woman, just as Giò is an unhappy and frustrated man. But, she told herself firmly, I am not going to allow him, or Giò for that matter, to make a fool out of me. She smiled rather sadly, I've been making a good job of that for myself, for ten years.

She returned to the kitchen, where Honorine was tasting her *daube*. 'Smells good,' said Anna.

'Is ready,' said Honorine. 'Rice is ready, too.'

'I'll fetch them.'

Over the courtyard wall came the strains of 'The Ball of Kerriemuir,' sung word-perfectly by Domenica as she lurched across the square towards the presbytery, supported by Giò and Patrick, with Olivia bringing up the rear, doing her best to commit the words to memory.

Giò suggested to Domenica that she had had a long day, and perhaps would like to go to bed, and have her supper on a tray.

'What's the matter with you, you weedy little prick?' said Domenica loudly. 'Haven't you seen anyone a bit pissed before? I suppose you're embarrassed in front of your smart Paris chum, eh?'

Giò, with admirable forbearance, Patrick thought, stuck calmly to his point, finally promising to bring his supper, as well as hers, up on a tray. At this Domenica capitulated and staggered up the stairs with Giò behind, ready to catch her if she fell. Anna and Honorine quickly laid trays, and took them to the door of Domenica's room before she could change her mind and come down again. Giò took her tray in and came back for his own. He gave them a music-hall wink, and closed the door behind him.

Anna and the others sat under the fig tree, talking quietly and enjoying their supper. Anna realized, with some surprise, that she felt no embarrassment about Patrick's being a witness to one of Domenica's less attractive performances. He seemed totally relaxed about the whole thing, even amused. He told them about his journey to Grignan, and what a disappointment the place, and particularly the château had been to him.

'What a shame, to come for nothing,' said Honorine.

'Not at all, I've enjoyed myself enormously,' said Patrick. 'It's so long since I spent any time with a proper family, and this is such a beautiful place.'

'Except when the mistral blows,' said Olivia.

'I don't know,' said Patrick. 'Even then, because it's even more beautiful when it stops, if you know what I mean?'

'Like banging your head against a brick wall?' said Anna.

'Precisely.'

From Domenica's open window came the sound of Giò's light, high voice followed by Domenica's braying laugh.

'They sound 'appy,' said Honorine, smiling.

'Telling dirty stories, I expect,' said Olivia.

*　　*　　*

After supper, Olivia disappeared on some ploy of her own. Honorine washed the dishes, while Patrick dried them, in spite of her protests, and Anna put everything away.

'What about the trays? Shall I fetch them?' said Anna.

'Is better not,' said Honorine. 'Giò will bring them, after she sleeps.' She laughed wryly. 'Tomorrow she will 'ave 'eadache, I think. Serve 'er right, it wasn't nice, what she called poor Giò, was it?'

'No, it wasn't.' Anna smiled. 'But it was quite funny, wasn't it?' They all laughed, rather guiltily.

'Good night, then,' said Honorine, kissing Anna.

'Good night, see you in the morning,' said Anna, giving her a hug.

After the gate had clanged behind her, Anna turned to Patrick. 'What would you like to do?' she said. 'Go to the café?'

'It's such a lovely evening, what about a walk?' said Patrick. 'I feel quite crumpled after sitting in that little car all day.'

'Fine, good idea,' said Anna. 'Let's go right round the village by the outer road, it takes about twenty minutes.'

They set off. The square was deserted, and only the sound of John Lennon singing 'Imagine' came from the café. Patrick looked around him at the beautiful, crumbling old houses. 'I wonder if the inhabitants realize how lucky they are?' he said.

'Does it matter?' said Anna.

He looked at her. 'You're quite right, of course. It doesn't.'

They went under the archway, and walked along the narrow road which ran behind the houses, circling the village. Dusk was beginning to fall, the sky was an intense sapphire blue, and a few stars were beginning to appear. Bats zigzagged to and fro, and they could hear the tinkling bells and bleats of a flock of goats in the fields lower down.

'Why does anyone live in London or Paris?' said Anna.

'You may well ask,' said Patrick.

They reached the little iron bridge which spanned the stream, now reduced to a muddy trickle. Clouds of midges hummed over the water, and filled the graceful weeping branches of the unusually big willow tree which shaded the little stream beside the bridge. They leaned on the iron railing, watching the slowly moving stream below.

'Anna,' said Patrick, quietly.

'Patrick,' said Anna, straightening up and turning towards him, 'I don't mean to be inquisitive, but are you gay?' She was immediately appalled at what she had said.

Patrick burst out laughing, then turned towards Anna, and said seriously. 'No, my darling girl, I am not,' and he took her in his arms and kissed her, at first gently, and then hard and long.

Anna, her arms wrapped tightly round his waist, rested her cheek against his chest, her eyes closed, filled with joy.

'No,' she said, 'you are not,' and lifted her face to his again.

Up in the willow tree Olivia crouched, motionless in the fork of a branch, mercifully hidden in the thick leaf-cover. She was surprised and angry at what she had heard and seen, but resisted the urge to jump down and confront them. She watched as they continued up the road, their arms round each other, talking quietly as they went. Before they vanished round a bend, they stopped and kissed once more.

Olivia waited for a few minutes in case they came back, then scrambled down from the tree and made her way back home, going in through the garage gate. In the kitchen she found Giò, having a drink and reading a book.

'Hello, sausage,' he said, looking up, smiling at her. 'Where are the others?'

'Dunno,' she said glumly, and took herself to bed.

At a quarter to five the next morning Olivia, who had not slept, got up and went down to the *salon*. She looked through a filing cabinet until she found Wickham, looked in the file and took out a letter from her father to Domenica. It was on his office paper. As she had hoped, his office had a fax number. She wrote a note, addressed to Jeffrey at his office: 'Dad, please come, Domenica is pissed all the time, and Mum is having an affair with a man. Love from Olivia.'

She dialled the fax number and sent the message. She removed her note, tore off the message-received slip, and put them into an ash-tray, setting a match to them. She powdered the blackened remains between her fingers and tipped them into the fireplace.

Then she silently climbed the stairs to her room, got into bed, and fell instantly asleep.

Chapter Six

Jeffrey arrived at his office on Friday morning at seven thirty. He had a brief to prepare, and liked to work when the office was quiet, and before the telephone started ringing. Passing through the reception office, he heard the fax machine whistling and whirring and wondered what had come in during the night. He picked up the long strip of paper, and glanced through the messages. At once, his eye selected the words 'Dad' and 'Olivia'. He read the message, frowning. Thank heaven he had come in early. He could imagine the supercilious smirks of the secretaries if they had got there before him. He took a pair of scissors from the red plastic tub containing pencils and biros and carefully cut out the offending message, leaving the rest in a heap on the floor for Sharon to deal with.

He went into his office and sat down, and read the message again. He was not at all surprised that his mother-in-law was drunk, but he was very surprised at Olivia's assertion that Anna was having an affair. Silly child, he thought, it's probably pure imagination. Nevertheless, the idea, however preposterous, still made him uneasy, and he flicked through the pages of his Filofax for the number of his travel agent. He dialled the number and got an answerphone. He looked at his watch: eight o'clock. Of course, too early. He left a message asking them to get him a fly-drive to Montpellier or Marseille for that night or Saturday morning. He opened the file on his desk and began to dictate into his tape-recorder. At nine thirty he heard the staff arriving, and buzzed for Sharon to bring him coffee. At nine forty-five a call from the travel agent was put through to him. The girl said she was sorry but all the flights to Montpellier or Marseille were full. She could do him a club class from Heathrow to Marseille, departing ten o'clock Sunday morning.

'I suppose that will have to do,' said Jeffrey. 'Are you sure there's nothing sooner, even changing at Paris?'

'Sorry, sir,' said the girl. 'It's August, you see, everything's booked solid, especially at weekends.'

'Yes, of course.' Jeffrey resigned himself. 'Send the confirmation over this morning, please, and I'll pick up the ticket at the airport.'

'Certainly, sir. That's fine. I'll put it on your account, shall I?'

'Thanks, fine. Goodbye.' Jeffrey put the phone down, then picked it up again, and dialled Robert's number in Sussex. Kate answered, sounding rather low.

'Kate, hello. This is Jeffrey.'

'Jeff!' Kate brightened. 'How nice to hear your voice.'

'I wondered whether I could come for the weekend? I'm so fed up with London, and I'd like to see you both.'

'Of course, we'd love it. Will you drive or train?'

'Drive,' said Jeffrey. 'I've got to catch a plane on Sunday, earlyish, so I'll go to Heathrow from you. I'll arrive about eight, if that's OK?'

'Lovely,' said Kate, sounding positively cheerful. 'Look forward to it, see you then.' She hung up. Jeffrey smiled. Kate was not one for long telephone calls, even when she wasn't paying the bill.

In the garden, a pale sun warmed Robert's back as he picked Worcesters in the orchard. He had filled three baskets and was about to load them onto his little red trolley and take them to the apple shed. The shed had been carefully swept and sprayed, and new matting lined the shelves. The whole place smelled deliciously of late summer, and conjured up in Robert's mind visions of his distant and happy childhood in this same house. He was the third generation to live in Boulter's Mill, and he had hoped that his son would carry on after him. He thought that rather unlikely now, but maybe Josh?

He pushed the trolley load of baskets to the shed, and began to place the apples carefully on the matting, inspecting each one carefully for blemishes as he did so. When all the apples had been stored, he sat down on the old stool he kept in the shed, and looked with some complacency at his handiwork. How satisfying it was to grow so much of your own food, on your own soil, in your own good time, and go to bed at the end of each day secure in the knowledge of a good day's work well done.

He heard Kate's voice calling from the house. A cloud crossed his face, anticipating trouble of some kind. If only the two women in his life had loved the place as much as he did, and had been content to live there and help him with the work. Robert was not stupid, and he knew that Kate, like Domenica before her, felt stifled and unhappy, only looking on the place as a background to her own way of life and particular talents.

The first years of his marriage to Domenica had been turbulent, but amazingly happy. They had a small garden flat in Beaufort Street, and Domenica had a job in an antique shop in the King's Road, and shopped every day for whatever was available, which wasn't much. With typical charm and resourcefulness she soon had all the little Chelsea food shops saving special things for her, and when she became pregnant with the twins they redoubled their efforts on her behalf. They went nearly every weekend to Sussex, where Robert's widowed father still lived in perfect harmony with his three ageing servants, a cook-housekeeper and two gardeners. The post-war era had taken all prospects of younger help from them, but Annie, Sid and Walter toiled gallantly on, helped by Robert at weekends. On Sunday nights they returned to London loaded with eggs, vegetables and fruit.

The one really romantic thing that Robert had ever done was to buy the presbytery at Souliac for Domenica. He used his gratuity to pay for it, and every year they spent Easter and the long summer holidays there. Sometimes friends came down, and once or twice Robert's father had come, but mostly they were alone with the twins and Honorine. This was how they both liked it, and it was even better when Honorine came back with them to London to help with the children, enabling Domenica to return to her job. Honorine slept on a platform built over the front door of the flat. It had a half-moon window, which looked into the black gnarled branches of a mulberry tree, growing outside the front door, and which tradition purported to have been in Sir Thomas More's garden. Every night Honorine climbed nimbly up her little ladder, and settled herself in what she thought of as a real room. She loved Chelsea, and soon she, too, had built up her chain of suppliers, rewarding the best ones with little presents of fresh eggs and fruit and vegetables, brought back from Sussex. In return, she often came back home with the double pram loaded up with coffee, wine, parcels of meat or fish, and long, ultramarine-blue packets of spaghetti.

Every summer, when they were in Souliac, Domenica grew sad when it was time to go back to England. 'One day, Robert,' she would say, 'will we live here always?'

'Who knows, darling?' Robert would reply. 'Perhaps.' But he knew that when his father died nothing would prevent him from living in Boulter's Mill. He knew that it would be a struggle to maintain the place, all he would get would be the house and land, but the idea of selling appalled him. His one thought was to live and die there, and pass it on to his son, whatever the sacrifice.

The time for the move to Sussex came sooner than he had bargained for. His father died in January, 1965, quietly in his sleep, aged seventy-six. Three months later, they had sold the flat and taken the children and Honorine to live at the mill. From the start, the move proved a disaster. Domenica and Honorine both missed the glamour and fun of Chelsea. They pined for the specialist food shops, the people, the pubs and cinemas. Most of all, Domenica missed her work. She had had her job for ten years now, and had learned a great deal about the antiques business, and felt her talents were being wasted simply keeping house, and endlessly gardening in the country. The twins also had, by the nature of their upbringing, become mature for ten-year-olds and very street-wise. They thought the proper country a drag compared with Chelsea, OK for the weekend, but not during the week. All three, and Honorine, were bored, especially by the weather. In London, you didn't really notice the weather very much, except to be pleased when the sun shone. Here, the weather seemed to dominate everything. In winter it was cold, dark and wet. In summer slightly warmer, sometimes sunny, more often wet. Every weekday morning Domenica took Robert to the station to catch the London train, and took the twins to their local primary school. This, too, was a disappointment. Giò and Anna had been at a Montessori school in London, and their new school seemed to them very dull. Both children became bored and disruptive, speaking French to each other to annoy the teacher, and alienating the other children.

Every morning when Domenica drove back into the yard, she looked at the disused mill, complete with all its original machinery, which stood close to the house with the great retaining bank of the millpond towering above it at one end. The wooden sluices regulated the flow of water which had once driven the machinery, and now fell gently down into a stream that flowed along the back of the building, and through the paddock behind the main house, to join the brook further downstream. In springtime, this paddock was studded with cowslips and bee orchises. The twins had picked a beautiful bunch for Robert that first spring, but they had been given a long lecture about rare wild flowers and were strictly forbidden to pick any more. Domenica walked about the deserted mill and thought what a marvellous showroom for antiques it would make, at quite low conversion costs. She could build up a business, collecting and going to sales down here, and then supplying her dealer friends in Chelsea. Why not? she thought. At least, it would give her a good excuse to go up to London pretty often.

One night after dinner, she took Robert by the hand and led him over to the mill and told him her idea.

'Never,' he said decisively. 'Over my dead body, Domenica. This is my family home, and not a commercial enterprise. I won't, absolutely won't have the place, or its way of life, altered in any way at all.'

'I see,' said Domenica, though she did not.

Things had seemed to go on quite normally, and they all went down to Souliac as usual for the summer holidays. In mid-August Robert flew back to England, there was so much to do in the garden, he said, leaving Domenica and the children and Honorine to drive back before the start of term. But a week or two later Domenica had written to Robert and told him that she was staying on at Souliac for the time being. She was determined to carry on with her career, and if Robert would not allow her to do so at his house, then she would do it in her own. She had enrolled the children in the local school, she thought it was better for them to be bilingual anyway. Honorine was not keen to come back to Sussex, she found it too cold and lonely. London yes, the country no. So, for the moment, she would see how things went, maybe they would work out a plan that would suit them both.

At first Robert had been stunned. He had missed Domenica and his children, and the mill seemed very big, silent and empty without them. He had stared out of the Georgian windows of his elegant drawing-room, through the fine, misty rain that fell on the brilliant green grass of his immaculate lawn, and felt lonely and betrayed. After a while he became angry. What is she playing at? he had asked himself. After all, he had rescued her from a rather narrow provincial life in Aix, where her widowed Italian mother had let rooms to students at the university. Domenica's father, a Frenchman, a lecturer at the university, had been killed in the war, leaving them virtually penniless. The widow had rented the tall thin house in one of the quiet old squares behind the Cours Mirabeau, and set up a lodging house. Domenica had been twenty-one when she met Robert in 1952. He had been on his first long trip abroad after the war, driving alone through France. He was enchanted by the landscape of Provence, by the food and wine, the sunshine and the clarity of the light. He had decided to stay for a week in Aix and saw a card in the foyer of the *mairie* advertising rooms to let. Domenica had answered the door when he pulled the bell. Robert had taken one look at the tall, dark-haired girl with her incredible grey-green eyes and thought he had never seen anything so beautiful in his life. Domenica looked at the handsome, dark man, listened to his halting French, smiled and invited him in.

'Please come in,' she said in English.

'Oh,' he said, 'you speak English?'

'Yes, quite well,' she said. 'I am studying modern languages at the university here.'

After their marriage, and while the spell was still on him, Robert had undertaken to buy the presbytery at Souliac. It was easier for the house to be in her name, since she was a French citizen: so the presbytery became hers.

After the divorce it seemed sensible to let things stay as they were, and they remained on friendly terms, the children spending Easter in Sussex with him, and he going down to Souliac for part of August. Three years later, driven by loneliness and a succession of unsatisfactory daily housekeepers, Robert had married Kate, and they had jogged along fairly happily together ever since.

'There you are, Robert, I've been looking for you everywhere,' said Kate, appearing in the doorway of the apple-shed. 'Guess what, Jeff's coming for the weekend.'

'That's nice,' said Robert. 'Any chance of some coffee?'

On Sunday morning Domenica and Giò announced their intention of driving over to L'Isle-sur-la-Sorgue to the weekly flea-market.

'Shouldn't one go early for that?' said Anna.

'No,' said Domenica. 'In August it's all expensive rubbish anyway. If you get there about twelve, the crowd is thinning out and the dealers are thinking of packing up. That's when you can sometimes get the odd bargain.'

'Good thinking,' said Giò. 'What about you, Anna, do you want to come? Patrick? Olly?'

'I'd rather stay here in the cool, myself,' said Anna.

'Is there anywhere nice to swim that won't be crowded?' said Patrick.

'Yes,' said Olivia, at once. 'There's a lovely pool at Arpaillargues, but you have to have lunch to be able to swim in it.'

'Sounds OK,' said Patrick. 'How about it, Anna, would that be nice?'

'Yes,' said Anna, doubtfully. 'But it's quite expensive. Are you sure?'

'I don't think that's a problem, as long as the food's good.'

'Oh, it is. It's a huge treat to go there.'

'That settles it then. Should we telephone for a table?' They all agreed that that would be wise.

Domenica was delighted that Giò would be spending

the day alone with her, but knew that he would be sorry not to be going to Arpaillargues.

'As it's your last day, Giò, we'll have lunch at the Rascasse d'Argent, shall we?'

'Great.' Giò tried to sound pleased.

Honorine came out of the kitchen and put a fresh pot of coffee in front of Domenica. 'I go now, if nothing else to do,' she said.

'Have a good rest, Honorine,' said Anna. 'You must be exhausted.'

'What time you leave tomorrow, Giò?' said Honorine. 'You are needing me very early for breakfast?'

'No, no, we'll leave about nine. The traffic shouldn't be too bad on a Monday. We should get in by seven. That reminds me, I must phone Laure and tell her to line up a couple of chaps to help get the stuff up to the apartment.' He went into the house to telephone.

'Well,' said Honorine, 'I see you all in the morning.'

'Have a good rest.' Domenica smiled at her.

'Clean my own 'ouse is good rest?' said Honorine, taking herself off.

'In a week's time, she'll be missing you all, and complaining that there's no-one to cook for,' said Domenica. 'Giò!' she shouted, getting up from the table, 'bring my bag down when you come, we'd better get off.'

They drove away in the Volvo, and Anna and Olivia cleared away the breakfast things. Patrick telephoned Arpaillargues to reserve a table, and they locked up the house and went out into the shady square. The bell was ringing for the eleven o'clock mass, and the old ladies who sat in the sun warming their legs all week were making their way in little groups into the church. They wished Anna good morning as they passed by, and looked with curious beady eyes at Patrick, as he stowed the swimming things and Anna's bag in the boot. They drove slowly and cautiously out of the square.

Olivia sat in the back of the car and stared blankly

at the countryside, as they drove to Arpaillargues. The surprise and shock of the events of Thursday evening had rather faded in her mind, and the last two days had been fun, she had to admit. Patrick and Mum had not shut her out or ignored her. She and Giò had taken the other two on at *boules* in the square, in front of all the regulars sitting outside the café, and they had won every game. Then Patrick had asked her to be his partner, and they had beaten Giò and Mum; that had been brilliant. She smiled, and gave a little wriggle of pleasure at the memory. She was beginning rather to regret sending the fax to Dad. He had not phoned her, she could imagine him reading it, and tearing it up impatiently. He would be annoyed with her if a secretary had seen it. She hadn't thought of that at the time, stupidly. Oh, well, she thought, I can't do anything about it now, can I? She was looking forward to a swim in the beautiful big pool at Arpaillargues, and lunch in the rather grand secluded courtyard in front of the château. Usually, when they drove through Arpaillargues, they took a detour round the little road that ran between the château and the high walls of its park. The big gates of the park stood open during the season, and through them you could see the sweeping green lawns and big shady trees with tennis courts beyond. Quite near the gates was the pool, surrounded by groups of long white chairs. On the opposite side of the road, facing the park, a gated archway in the high wall surrounding the domaine led into the cool, gravelled courtyard in front of the elegant eighteenth-century façade of the château, its honey-coloured stones glowing softly in the sunshine. In the courtyard, fifteen or twenty round iron tables, with lacy ironwork chairs, were already laid for lunch.

They left the car near the park gates, and went through the archway across the road to confirm their reservation at the reception. Olivia stopped to read the menu, which was posted in a little glass-fronted display case, just inside the arch. Patrick and Anna went through the great open front door into the hall of the house, cool and elegant, with huge blue-and-white Chinese jars filled with flowers, grouped on the stone-flagged floor.

'What a beautiful place,' said Patrick. 'Civilized and peaceful.'

'It's even more magical, dining here at night,' said Anna, 'when the château is floodlit, and all the tables are lit by candlelight. There's a romantic story about the place too. Apparently, Marie d'Agoult lived here, and eloped with Liszt, or something like that.'

Patrick looked up at the sweeping stone staircase that led to the upper floors. 'One can just imagine her running down these stairs and out through the door, and into the probably muddy lane to the waiting carriage.'

'And getting her lovely dress filthy in the process,' said Anna, and they both laughed.

As they came out into the sunshine, Olivia came hopping up and began to tell them what was on the lunch menu.

'Now,' said Patrick, looking at his watch, 'lunch first, and swim after, or swim first and lunch after?'

'Swim, then lunch, then swim again?' said Olivia.

'Why not?'

Considering that it was the hottest part of the year, the water in the pool was quite cold, and after a few minutes, Anna got out and settled herself on a long chair. Patrick swam a few lengths with Olivia, then she attached herself to a small group of teenagers who were engaged in fishing wasps out of the pool, so he too got out and sat down on the grass next to Anna, briskly towelling his hair.

'The water's lovely, but incredibly cold, isn't it?' he said.

'I think it must come from a spring,' said Anna. 'It's so clean and clear, and doesn't seem to have chemicals in it.'

'No,' said Patrick, 'just wasps.' He spread his towel on the grass, and lay on his stomach, his head on his arms.

'I'll put some stuff on your shoulders.' Anna knelt beside him.

'Thanks,' he said, his voice muffled.

She squeezed the cream into the palm of her hand, and began to spread it over his back, in long sweeping strokes.

'Anna,' said Patrick, very quietly, 'no-one has done this for me for a very long time.'

'Do you want me to stop?'

'No,' said Patrick, 'please don't. It's just that I can't bear the thought of being parted from you.'

Anna did not trust herself to speak at once. She felt as if she would burst with happiness. She continued to work delicately along his spine and up his neck to the base of his skull, then across his shoulder blades and down his sides. Finally she gave him a little pat, and sat back on her feet, rubbing the surplus cream into her own thighs.

'You have a beautiful back,' she said softly.

'Really?' Patrick turned his head to look at her. 'I always think of myself as very middle-aged, grey and rather wrinkly.'

'Well,' said Anna, smiling, 'you're not. But if you were, it wouldn't matter to me.'

'Wouldn't it?' Patrick lifted himself on to his elbows, and began to tear up tufts of grass. He looked up at Anna. 'Not even if I told you that I am fifty-two?'

'Not even then,' said Anna. 'I am forty myself. What's so terribly young about that?' She bent and kissed him lightly on the mouth.

Patrick lay down again, his cheek on the sun-smelling towel, and closed his eyes. 'Anna,' he said, 'if you were free, would you marry me?'

'Yes, Patrick, I would.'

He opened his eyes, and saw that her huge dark eyes

were filled with tears. He sat up, alarmed. 'Anna, my darling, what's the matter?'

'Nothing's the matter, it's just happiness,' said Anna. 'Happiness and relief. It's been such a terribly long time for me too, though not as long as you.'

'In a way worse for you.' Patrick wiped the tears from her eyes with his fingers. 'Death is such a final thing, in the end you have to come to terms with it, or go mad, or kill yourself. But rejection is quite another horrible poker-hand, particularly when it comes from the father of your children, who still expects to come and go as he pleases. He doesn't want you, but he won't leave you alone.'

'Patrick,' said Anna, 'do you really think that it would ever be possible for us to be together?'

'Certainly, I do.'

'But the children, what about them?' said Anna, anxiously, from force of habit.

'What about them?' said Patrick. 'Anna, my dearest girl, children are tough. They grow up, they adapt. They are doing it all the time, they have to. In the meantime, the only thought that is really occupying me is that tomorrow I have to go back to Paris, and all I really want to do is to take you to bed and make love to you.'

Olivia came running up and flung herself on the grass next to Anna. 'Is it lunchtime yet?' she said. 'I'm starving.'

'Me, too,' said Anna. 'I could eat a horse.'

'I'll bet you're not as hungry as I am,' said Patrick.

Anna laughed. 'I'll bet I am,' she said.

Olivia looked from Anna to Patrick, puzzled. 'Well,' she said, 'what are we waiting for?'

Jeffrey's plane landed at Marseille at precisely one o'clock. He was not carrying anything except his briefcase, so he passed quite quickly through immigration and customs, and went straight to the Hertz office, just across the road, to pick up his hired car. By one forty-five, he was cruising along the *autoroute* towards Avignon. Reluctantly, Jeffrey conceded that you had to hand it to the French for efficiency in the matter of airports and *autoroutes*, though the long queues of Algerians at immigration contrasted rather disquietingly with the laconically dismissed visitors from the Community countries. He supposed it was the same at Heathrow with people from Asia and Africa, presumably one just didn't notice them so much.

The new Renault he had hired had a flip-top roof and he opened it, and turned on the fan full blast. He pulled off his tie, and undid the top button of his shirt. Bloody place, he thought, one forgets how horribly hot it is. Can't think what Anna sees in it.

Surprisingly soon, the big brown and white signs saying *Avignon Cité des Papes* appeared, and he left the *autoroute* at the Avignon Sud exit. He followed the signs to Nîmes, driving through the ugly modern indus-trial area to the south of Avignon until he reached the Rhône. He crossed the river, and took the Rémoulins road, glancing briefly at the Palais des Papes to the right as he drove over the bridge. He reached Rémoulins at twenty past three, and took the road to Uzès. At four o'clock, he drove into the square at Souliac, and heard the church bell chime the hour. He parked tidily behind the transit van and got out of the car. He took out his briefcase, closed the roof and windows, and locked the car. Then he walked the few metres to the presbytery and turned the octagonal handle of the green iron gate. It was locked. Irritably, he tried again, rattling it in case it was stuck. Still locked. He put his hand in his pocket and turned around, scanning the square, to see whether there had been witnesses to his discomfiture. It seemed not. He hesitated briefly, then walked to Honorine's house, and knocked on the door. He waited for a moment, then knocked again, louder this time. He heard a voice saying sleepily, '*J'arrive, j'arrive,*' then the shutters of the first floor window flew open, and Honorine's tousled grey head appeared.

'*Monsieur* Wickham!' she said. '*C'est vous!*' She did not like Jeffrey, never had even at the beginning of Anna's marriage. She thought him cold and cruel. 'What you doing 'ere?' she added, rudely.

Jeffrey looked up at her, and tried to look glad to see her. 'Hello, Honorine,' he said, smiling. 'Sorry to disturb you, but the house is locked, I can't get in.'

Good job too, thought Honorine, but then she gathered her wits and said, 'Wait a moment, I descend.' The shutters were pulled to, and Jeffrey had to wait for five minutes until Honorine, dressed and with tidy hair, opened the door. 'Come in, please,' she said, and Jeffrey followed her into her neat, dark kitchen. 'You want tea?'

'Thank you, I would love some,' said Jeffrey.

She put water on to boil, and he sat down at the table. She put a cup and saucer and a bowl of sugar on the table, and took milk from the little fridge.

'If you intending stay at the 'ouse, I am sorry, but there are no more beds, each is occupied. Anna and Olivia, Giò and his friend from Paris, and Josh will also be 'ere is possible.'

'Oh,' said Jeffrey. 'I had rather assumed there would be room.'

'If you want, you can rent my other room,' said Honorine. 'Is less dear than 'otel,' she added, insultingly, Jeffrey thought.

'Thank you, that would be very nice,' he said.

He drank his tea silently. She did not offer him a biscuit. After tea, she took the keys of the presbytery off their hook and accompanied him back to the house, rather in the manner of an elderly sheepdog, polite but suspicious. She unlocked the gate and he entered the courtyard. She made no move to open the house, but pointed to the table under the vine.

'You can sit 'ere.'

Before he could say anything, she had vanished through the gate, and was walking briskly back to her own house. Jeffrey felt he had been outmanoeuvred. Annoyed with himself for not having had the wit to put Honorine in her place, he sat down, opened his briefcase and took out *The Sunday Times*. Turning to the book pages he read a couple of reviews. He put the paper down. Why have I come? he asked himself, suddenly feeling rather foolish. Surely not as an irate husband? No, he reminded himself, I am here as a concerned father, with his young daughter's interests and moral welfare to protect; to see whether there is any basis for Olivia's alarming fax. Yes. Satisfied with his reasoning, he picked up the paper again and continued reading the reviews. They were useful as a means of familiarizing oneself with the latest publications.

An hour later he had finished the paper, and was beginning to feel extremely annoyed with his situation. He heard a car stop outside the gate, then voices and the slamming of car doors. The gate opened and Olivia, her arms full of wet towels, came into the courtyard looking brown and happy. She saw Jeffrey at once and stopped dead in her tracks.

'Dad,' she croaked, and a slow dark flush crept over her face.

'Hello, Olivia,' said Jeffrey, standing up and holding out his arms. 'Aren't you pleased to see me?'

'Yes, of course,' she mumbled, advancing towards him, dropping towels as she came. Anna and Patrick came through the gate and found Jeffrey rather awkwardly embracing his daughter.

'Good heavens, what are you doing here?' said Anna, and looked at Jeffrey with something approaching dislike. In that moment she knew that his power to undermine her and bend her to his will had completely gone, and she felt an agreeable sensation of strength and control. She turned coolly to Patrick, and introduced him to Jeffrey.

'Patrick, this is Jeffrey Wickham, Olivia's father. Jeffrey, this is Patrick Halard. He is staying with us while he does some research for a television project.'

In spite of himself, Jeffrey could not help being impressed by this piece of information, and shook hands with comparative affability.

Olivia sent up a fervent prayer that he would not mention the fax, giving it as his reason for coming, and he did not. She began to gather up the wet towels, and said to Anna, 'Mum, shall I help you get ice and things for drinks?'

Anna, startled by the unaccustomed offer of help, nevertheless got the message at once, and followed her into the kitchen. Olivia signalled her to come through to the back garden, closing the door behind them. She turned to Anna, her blue eyes troubled and close to tears.

'Mum, it's my fault,' she whispered. 'I sent him a fax because I saw you and Patrick kissing in the lane, and I was upset and jealous, and stupid. I'm really sorry, I feel awful that I've spoilt our lovely day.'

Anna threw her arms round her daughter, and hugged her. 'It doesn't matter, darling, it really doesn't,' she said. 'I quite understand how you felt, and I'm sure Patrick would too.'

'Really? You're not angry?'

'No,' said Anna. 'And thanks for putting me in the picture.'

'He's really nice.' Olivia looked through her lashes at her mother, 'even if he is rather old.'

'Who is?' said Anna, smiling.

'You know,' said Olivia, smirking.

They returned to the kitchen, got out ice, water, bottles and glasses, and carried the tray out into the courtyard, just as Domenica and Giò arrived.

'What a horrible surprise,' said Domenica, when she saw Jeffrey.

'Shut up, Ma, you rude old bat,' said Giò, who could see by Jeffrey's face that his welcome had been less than overwhelming, and he went over and gave Jeffrey a hug. 'How are you my dear brother-in-law?'

Jeffrey looked slightly mollified. 'I'm sorry I just

turned up,' he said. 'I had no idea you had the house full. But don't worry, I'm staying at Honorine's.'

'Well,' said Domenica, 'that's good. I suppose I'll have to feed you?'

'Well, if it's no trouble.'

'Of course it isn't,' said Giò. 'Not to Ma, anyway. Anna will cook, won't you, Anna?'

'And I will help her,' said Olivia, quickly.

'And so will I,' said Patrick, smiling at Anna. 'I will make a Caesar salad, it's one of my very few accomplishments in the kitchen.'

'After that wonderful lunch, I'm astonished that anyone can even think about food,' said Anna, taking a long drink of cold water.

'Oh, I can,' said Olivia seriously, 'easily.'

In the kitchen Patrick, with Olivia as his assistant, was making his Caesar salad. Olivia was gently frying little diced pieces of bread in garlic-spiked oil, and Patrick was separating egg yolks from their whites, and reserving them in their half shells.

'It should really be a cos lettuce,' he said, putting the large handfuls of mixed salad from the supermarket on each plate, 'but who cares? Anna, have we got a tin of anchovies?' Anna found the anchovies, and he snipped them with scissors over the salad, then poured the oil from the can over everything.

'God,' he said, 'I think that should have been bacon, this is going to be a disaster.'

'Smells divine,' said Olivia. 'Are you ready for my *croûtons*?'

'Absolutely,' said Patrick. 'Scatter them over the top, please, *sous chef*.'

Olivia, using a slotted spoon, scattered her *croûtons*, and Patrick arranged an egg yolk on its half shell in the centre of each plate. Then he dribbled over a bit more dressing, and a good sprinkling of basil and parsley, and a handful of grated parmesan.

'*Voilà!*' said Olivia, and clapped her hands.

They carried the plates out to the table under the fig tree, where Anna had put bread, cheese and fruit, and knives and forks and glasses. Then Olivia went to call the others to the table.

Patrick put his hand against Anna's cheek, cool in the evening dew. 'I love you, darling Anna,' he said, very softly.

'And I love you,' she replied, covering his hand with hers.

After supper, Giò looked at his watch: half past ten.

'I suppose we should get to bed early, Patrick,' he said. 'I'll have to pack the stuff into the van before we leave, so I'll get up at six.'

'Don't worry,' said Anna, 'I'll help you with it.'

'So will I,' said Olivia.

'Splendid,' said Domenica. 'That lets us oldies off the hook, Patrick,' and she gave him one of her cynical little smiles.

'Oh,' said Patrick, unruffled and amiable, 'I expect I'll manage something light.'

Jeffrey stood up, and took his leave. 'It's been quite a long day for me, and I don't want to keep Honorine waiting up for me. Thank you for supper, it was very pleasant.' He sketched a smile at Patrick.

'I'll see you out,' said Giò.

Anna lay in her bed. The church clock had just struck two, and she had not yet slept. She felt incredibly tired, but at the same time wide awake, her mind swinging between an enormous happiness and sadness at the thought of the separation so soon to happen. The clock struck the quarter, and then the half hour. She got out of bed and went to her door. She opened it quietly and listened. Then she went on silent bare feet down the stairs, through the kitchen to the back courtyard door.

She opened the door, and slipped through, looking upwards behind her to check that no lights were on. She crossed the starlit garden and went into the garage, gently closing the door. Then she softly climbed the stairs to Patrick's room, and went in.

'Hello,' he said, 'I hoped you would come.'

She crossed the room and got into the narrow bed beside him. He folded her tightly in his arms and kissed her, and felt her heart beating against his naked body, through the thin silk of her nightdress. After a moment, she pulled away from him and sat up, and pulled off her nightdress.

'I don't need this,' she said, lying down again in his arms.

Presently they slept. The church bell woke Anna at five o'clock. For a second she was startled to find herself in bed with Patrick, her arms around him and his round her, her head in the crook of his shoulder. Then she remembered, and a huge bubble of happiness filled her whole being like a warm tide. Very gently, she extricated herself from his embrace, put on her nightdress, covered him with the sheet and stole from his room.

As she ran through the garden, a slight ghostly figure in the faint dawn light, Giò, watching from his window, saw her go. He did not feel anything at the time. He knew that much later he would.

Chapter Seven

At six o'clock Giò went quietly down to the salon, and began moving some of the furniture down to the front courtyard. First, he wrapped the precious eighteenth-century painted chairs in bubble plastic, a double layer, taped them with sticky parcel tape, and carried them downstairs. The long *radassié* settee would go in first and be strapped, wedged with old blankets and cushions, to the side of the van. The chairs would then be strapped on to the seat of the *radassié* to keep them from moving, wedged in tightly with more cushions. He began to wrap the small wooden *panetières* in bubble plastic, and taped them into one solid package.

Anna appeared in the door of the *salon*, wearing jeans and a faded pink shirt. Giò looked up as she quietly entered the room. He had never seen her looking so beautiful, her enormous eyes shining in her tanned face, and her cheeks flushed. She looked as if a candle were lit inside her.

'Hi,' he said. 'Thanks for getting up. Did you sleep well?' he added rather slyly.

'I did,' said Anna, smiling. 'Shall I get you some tea, or are you ready to start carrying things down now?'

'I've taken the chairs down. It's probably best if Patrick helps me with the *radassié*, it's an awkward shape on the stairs. Yes, tea would be great.'

Anna ran down the stairs and put the kettle on, and put mugs on a tray. The door to the back garden opened and Patrick came into the kitchen. She flew across the room, and he held her close.

'My darling,' he said, 'I can't bear this. I want to wake up every morning and find you there beside me, not vanished into thin air.'

The kettle boiled and she gently unwrapped herself from his arms, and made the tea.

'One comfort,' said Patrick, trying to make himself feel cheerful, 'is that it's only an hour from Paris to London. We must make plans at once. Here is my address and phone number, and my number at work in case you need me at any time.' He tore a page out of his pocket book, and gave it to her, and then wrote down her address and phone number. 'When do you get back to London?'

'Friday afternoon,' said Anna. 'We leave on the one o'clock plane from Montpellier.'

'I'll telephone you on Friday evening, late.'

'What about the children?' said Anna. 'Won't you mind if they're listening? It's such a small place.'

'No,' said Patrick. 'The sooner they know, the better. This is forever, Anna.' He took her face in his hands and kissed her again.

Anna felt all her loneliness and pessimism falling away, in the knowledge that here was a man who would make her live again, and fill her with energy and hope, fulfilment and joy. 'What a wonderful thought, forever.' Anna leaned against him. 'I can't believe the colossal luck of finding you.'

'My God,' said Patrick, 'neither can I.' A cold fear gripped his heart. With great love comes the lifelong shadow of the possibility of loss. Please God, it won't happen this time, he thought.

They carried the tray up to the salon, where Giò was wrapping the legs of the *radassié*. 'It's good of you to get up and help,' he said, taking the mug from Patrick.

'I was awake anyway. The birds always seem to wake me here,' said Patrick, smiling at Giò and sipping his tea.

Gio looked at him sharply, wondering if this was meant to be a joke, but dismissed the thought at once.

He drank his tea, and finished wrapping the *radassié*. 'Right,' he said, 'let's get this into the van first.'

The last thing to be packed was the rare old *buffet*. Giò jammed crumpled paper into the interior space, and taped the loose-hinged doors so that they could not move. Then he wrapped the little legs, and taped them, and then made an elaborate parcel of bubble plastic, finally winding an old blanket round the whole thing. 'I sometimes wonder why I do this,' he said, sneezing at the clouds of dust that rose from the blanket.

They were gently easing the *buffet* into its corner of the van, ready for strapping, when Honorine arrived with the bread.

'Good timing,' said Giò, and ran back upstairs for the last bits and pieces, and the mirrors he and Domenica had bought in L'Isle-sur-la-Sorgue.

'Breakfast ten minutes,' said Honorine, going into the kitchen.

'I'd better go and get my bag.' Patrick went quickly through the kitchen and out into the garden to his room. He looked at the bed and, picking up the pillow, he held it to his face, inhaling the smell of Anna's hair. Then he packed his clothes and shaving things into his bag, looked carefully round the room to see whether he had forgotten anything, and went down the stairs to join the others in the kitchen.

Olivia appeared, yawning, sat down at the table, and poured herself a glass of orange juice.

'Big help you were, miss,' said Giò, drinking coffee.

'Oh,' said Olivia, in feigned surprise, 'is it all done then? Gosh, sorry.' She spread butter on her bread, and looked at Giò. 'I wish you weren't going,' she said. 'It'll be dull without you. Both of you.' She looked at Patrick with her round blue eyes. 'It was lovely at Arpaillargues yesterday, I forgot to say thank you.'

'It was entirely my pleasure,' said Patrick, and smiled at her.

Giò looked at his watch. 'Quarter to nine, I suppose we'd better get off,' he said, getting to his feet.

'Yes, especially as I have to drop off the Peugeot in Uzès,' said Patrick.

'Have you said goodbye to Ma?' said Anna.

'No,' said Domenica, appearing in the doorway, wrapped in a blue silk kimono. 'He has not, the brute. Did you both think you would just sneak off?' She frowned, then burst into her loud, coarse laugh. They all laughed, a little uncertainly, and went out into the square to see them off. Giò and Patrick put the bags into the back of the van, and then came to the gate to say goodbye. Domenica flung her arms round Giò, kissing him three times, and then held out her hands to Patrick.

He saw that her eyes were full of tears. It had the curious effect of almost bringing tears to his own eyes. He stepped forward, and hugged her. 'Don't worry,' he said, 'I'll look after him.'

'I know you will,' said Domenica, and hugged him back.

Olivia hugged Giò, and then held out her hand to Patrick, but he bent down and kissed her on the cheek. Silently he turned to Anna and took her hand. He kissed her on each cheek, and then bent and kissed the palm of her hand. Then he shook hands with Honorine, got quickly into the little Peugeot, and drove away.

As the van followed the car out of the square, the four women stood sadly at the gate, waving, each trying not to feel that the point had gone out of the day. They went back to the courtyard, and Honorine made a fresh pot of coffee. Olivia brought the bread and honey out to the old iron table, and they began to make plans for the rest of the week.

The gate opened, and Jeffrey came in. They all looked up, open-mouthed.

'My God, you gave me a fright,' said Domenica. 'I'd completely forgotten you were here!' She looked at Honorine quizzically. Honorine raised her shoulders slightly, pursed her lips and looked down her nose into her cup.

'Do you want some coffee?' said Anna, quietly.

'Yes, if there is some.' Jeffrey sat down next to Olivia. 'Otherwise, I can go to the café, I suppose,' he added sarcastically. Domenica ignored this, and poured his coffee. She felt depressed and old, as she always did when Giò left, and could not be bothered to wind Jeffrey up. Olivia silently passed him bread, looking sad and thoughtful.

Inside the house, the telephone began to ring, and Olivia ran to answer it. In a few minutes, she came back. 'It's Josh,' she said. 'He says the Kings are starting the drive back to England at lunchtime. They're going to stay the night in Uzès, and Josh wondered if he could bring Hugh and Emma to stay for the night. They've got sleeping bags,' she added.

Anna turned to Domenica. 'Is it OK?'

'Yes, why not?' said Domenica. 'If it's OK with Honorine?'

'Is fine. We will be cheer up, no?'

Olivia ran back to the house, glad that Josh and his friends were coming, and relayed the good news to him.

'Brilliant,' he said. 'See you this evening, Ol.' He hung up.

Honorine got to her feet, relieved at the need for action. 'I will go for washing sheets,' she said.

'I'll help you.' Anna got up. 'I'll go and strip the beds and bring the things down to you.' She went into the kitchen and picked up the laundry basket. Then she went through the garden to Patrick's room. She stared at the bed, fighting off the tears that threatened to overwhelm her. Then she stripped off the pillow-cases, pulled off the sheets and bundled them into the basket. She took his towels from the pegs behind the door, held them briefly to her face, and then put them into the basket. She went back to the kitchen, shoved the laundry into the washing-machine, and then ran upstairs to Giò's room. His shutters were open, and she leaned out of his window, looking at the garden below, shimmering already in the early sun. Honorine came out and pegged tea-cloths on the line. Anna looked at Patrick's window, and then again at Honorine as she went back to the kitchen. Oh dear, she thought, poor Giò, I hope he didn't see me. Somehow, she felt sure that he had, and it saddened her to think that her own happiness should cause him pain. It was odd, she never really thought of Giò as a man with a great capacity for love. He was just Giò, her much-loved twin, sweet, funny and affectionate. But also touchy, easily hurt and occasionally cruel.

She sighed, stripped Giò's bed, and went down to Honorine in the kitchen. 'I suppose we will have to shop?' she said.

'Well, we need meat or chicken for the young people,' said Honorine. 'Is no good for them, just pasta or rice, isn't it?' Anna noted that Jeffrey's needs appeared not to concern Honorine.

'Maybe Jeffrey will take us all out to dinner?' she said, smiling.

'A pig might fly,' said Honorine, stuffing Giò's sheets into the washer.

'What's the best plan?' said Anna. 'Shall we get Domenica to shop, and take Jeffrey with her while I help you sort things out here?'

'No,' said Honorine. 'She will be sad for Giò's going. I think she will maybe wish to go back to bed for a while. I stay 'ere with 'er, and take care the beds. You take Jeffrey and go to town for me. It will give you chance to talk to 'im, no?'

'I don't particularly want to talk to him.'

'But I think is maybe you should?'

'But why?' said Anna. 'What about?'

'Anna, I am not stupid, or blind.' Honorine washed cups under the tap. 'You and Patrick love each other, isn't it? Is plain to see.' She turned and put her wet hand on Anna's arm. 'Poor sad girl, you try so hard with Jeffrey, is no good, and now you 'ave chance of 'appiness. Patrick is dear, good man, we all love 'im.'

'But it isn't going to be easy,' said Anna, though she was comforted by Honorine's outspokenness. 'I'm so afraid that Jeffrey will find some horrible way of getting back at me through the children, or something.'

'You so negative, Anna, you always looking trouble,' said Honorine. 'The children are old enough to choose, don't forget.' She looked at Anna sternly. 'And so are you, *mignonne*. You do not belong Jeffrey, though one might be forgive to think that you think that, for all this years.'

Anna felt her cheeks reddening with mortification. 'You don't have a very good opinion of me, do you?' she said. 'You're like Domenica and Giò, you think I am feeble and cowardly.'

'Anna, it's to understand, we all love you. But is so bad to see someone you love 'aving her leg twisting all the time.'

'Arm,' said Anna, automatically. She hugged Honorine. 'You're right, of course. I'll take him to town, now.' She took a basket from a hook in the ceiling. 'And I won't let him bully me!'

'Is good,' said Honorine. 'Take the cow by the 'orn, is better that way.'

Anna went out to the courtyard, and found her mother with her feet up on a chair, reading *The Sunday Times*. 'Where's Jeffrey?'

'He went out with Olivia,' said Domenica, without interest.

'Oh.' Anna felt annoyed, the wind rather taken out of her sails.

'I don't think they've gone anywhere, his car keys are here.' Domenica indicated the table.

'Good,' said Anna. 'I'm going to go to town to do the shopping, and I want to talk to him.'

Domenica look up at Anna, surprised. 'You amaze me,' she said. 'You don't usually care for confrontation, Anna.'

'What makes you think it's a question of confrontation?'

'Well, isn't it?'

'As a matter of fact, yes, it is.'

'Good,' said Domenica. 'About time too.'

Anna took the Volvo keys, put her bag into the basket, kissed her mother and marched firmly to the gate, which clanged shut behind her. Domenica looked after her, her eyes thoughtful and sad. My poor Giò, she thought.

Jeffrey and Olivia were sitting on the rim of the fountain. Jeffrey was talking, and Olivia swung her legs, looking mulish.

'There you are,' said Anna, going briskly across the square. 'Olivia, I'm going to take Dad into town to do some shopping, and I want you to go in and help Honorine get ready for Josh and his friends.'

'OK, Mum,' said Olivia with alacrity, jumping down from the fountain and running back to the house before Jeffrey could interfere.

'Aren't I going to be allowed to see my daughter?' he said coldly. 'She seemed very keen for me to come, after all, or don't you know that?'

'Yes, Jeffrey, I do know. It was silly of her, and she thinks so herself now, so there's no mileage in that line of reasoning,' said Anna crisply.

He got reluctantly into the passenger's seat of the Volvo, and Anna drove out of the square, towards the Uzès road. As they made their way through the vines, Jeffrey looked about him with distaste. 'Can't see what you see in this place,' he said.

'I know you can't, Jeffrey, that's precisely your problem,' said Anna, keeping her eyes on the road ahead. Jeffrey was silent. He was not used to assertiveness from Anna, though he had so often wished that she were more like her mother. He looked furtively at her profile as she drove along, staring straight ahead. Her hair was pulled back and knotted into a rubber band, so that her neck was uncovered, and Jeffrey saw, with a small shock, the face of Giò. It was bizarre, he thought, for a man and a woman to have the same face, really quite disturbing. He shifted in his seat, and looked out at the passing landscape.

'When are you leaving?' said Anna.

Jeffrey gave an exasperated sigh. 'Tomorrow lunch-time,' he said, sullenly.

'Right,' she said, 'as long as we know.' Jeffrey said nothing, but cracked his knuckles angrily.

Anna parked the car in the Boulevard Gambetta and headed for the little Casino mini market. Jeffrey trailed after her with the basket. She bought big, waxy potatoes, tomatoes, cheese and milk, salad and peaches. Then they crossed the road to the butcher and she bought a handsome rolled loin of pork, beauti-fully tied with string and already spiked with thyme and garlic.

'Isn't that rather a large joint?' said Jeffrey. 'Surely you'll be eating it for days?'

Anna looked at him. 'Haven't you ever noticed the amount of food consumed at one meal by a hungry ado-lescent? No, you obviously haven't. This meat will be enough for eight of us tonight, and if there's anything left, Josh will certainly make himself a sandwich before he goes to bed.'

'In that case,' said Jeffrey, as Anna proffered a hun-dred franc note for her meat, 'why on earth don't you buy mince, and make *bolognese* for a tenth of the price?'

'Because,' Anna replied coolly, 'the Kings have given Josh a marvellous holiday at Estagnol, as you very well know, and I have no intention of not returning a little of their hospitality in a proper manner.'

'You might not feel quite so generous if you paid all the bills,' said Jeffrey sourly.

'I wondered when you would play that card,' said Anna, walking back to the car, and putting the shop-ping in the back. She looked at the parking meter. 'There's still a quarter of an hour,' she said. 'We'll

125

go and have a coffee.' They sat at a café table on the pavement, under the shade of the huge ancient plane trees which lined either side of the road, their branches forming an arch across the wide street, giving a welcome coolness in the heat of the day. Anna ordered coffee, and Jeffrey asked for cold beer. She leaned back in her chair, consciously relaxing. She drew a deep breath. 'Jeffrey,' she said, 'I want us to be divorced.'

He looked at her, frowning in disbelief. 'Why? You never have until now.'

'Well, now I do.'

'But I don't particularly, at this juncture,' said Jeffrey.

'No, because it suits you that I have all the hard work and responsibility of bringing up Josh and Olivia.'

'Well,' said Jeffrey defensively, 'you're their mother, that's your job.'

'Yes,' said Anna, 'and the moment both of them have left home, it will be a different matter, won't it? You'll sell the Lifeboat and pay me off with the smallest amount your vile little legal mind can justify, won't you, you rotten little shit?'

Anger and adrenalin made the blood rush through Anna's veins, and she took several steadying breaths. She was astonished at herself, she had not intended to say anything other than that she wanted a divorce.

Jeffrey was equally astonished, and was glad of the diversion of the arrival of his beer, and Anna's coffee. He collected his wits. 'I presume,' he said, 'that Domenica has put you up to this?'

'You would be wrong to presume anything of the sort. I have managed to reach the decision all by myself, it may surprise you to know.'

Jeffrey sat back, and took a long pull at his beer. 'And what, may I ask, are your plans?'

'What business is that of yours, Jeffrey?'

'It's certainly my business if it affects the lives of our children.

'Yes,' said Anna, 'that's true. But I expect the lives

126

of my children will be very much enriched by what I intend to do.'

'Oh, really?' said Jeffrey sarcastically. 'And what may that be?'

'I intend to marry Patrick Halard.'

Jeffrey looked at Anna with a mixture of contempt and triumph. 'I see,' he said quietly. 'Olivia was right when she faxed me that you were having an affair. And you think that you can calmly take my children to live with your elderly fancy man in Paris, do you? Over my dead body, Anna.'

'What a total prat you are, Jeffrey. I don't think that at all. We haven't worked out the details yet, but I see no reason why I should not keep the Lifeboat and the children's lives going in exactly the same way as at present, during term time, and Patrick and I can commute between London and Paris. The children will have the best of all possible worlds.'

'But,' said Jeffrey, 'if I sue you for divorce as a whore, and get custody of the children, my dear Anna, what then?'

'In that case, Jeffrey, as I'm sure you are very well aware, both children are well over the age when they can choose which parent they want to be with. In any case, we must stop referring to Josh as a child, he is seventeen, almost a man.'

'None the less, you risk losing them,' said Jeffrey smugly.

'If I have the misfortune to run up against one of your ghastly old judges in our divorce, who takes no account of the ten years of your absence from the family home, Jeffrey, then it will be you who runs the risk of having to be chauffeur, nurse, cook, cleaner, shopper, supervisor of homework, and most of all constant presence in the lives of Josh and Olivia for five more years.'

The very idea appalled Jeffrey. He decided to try another tactic. He looked at Anna with his too-close-together blue eyes, and produced the crooked smile that used to work so well on her. 'Anna,' he said, leaning forward and taking her hand, 'what is all this? You know that you and Josh and Olly are the three people I love best in the world, and always will. Why do you want to rock the boat now? I am not ungenerous to you with money, am I? I pay all the bills, don't I? Hm?'

Anna withdrew her hand from his. 'Jeffrey,' she said very quietly, 'I loved you for a very long time. To all intents and purposes, apart from the children, you have ruined my life. Now, thank God, everything is different. I love someone else, and he loves me, and nothing you can do can destroy that. Nothing.'

'Even if it means losing your children?' said Jeffrey.

Anna looked at him coldly, and the last pathetic remnants of her feeling for him shrivelled and died. 'Yes,' she said, 'even then.' She stood up. 'We must go, or I'll get a parking ticket.'

They drove back to Souliac in silence, each pre-occupied with their own thoughts, bitter in Jeffrey's case, and increasingly positive and confident in Anna's. She could not believe that the change in her could be so swift and absolute. The memory of her hours in Patrick's bed came strongly back to her, and she felt again the closeness of his body against hers. A warm flood of desire flowed through her, and she felt the palms of her hands sweating. She gripped the steering wheel more tightly, swerving slightly to avoid the kamikaze swallows.

'Chill out, Anna,' she said, smiling at herself.

'What?' said Jeffrey.

'Nothing,' said Anna. 'Just an expression of Josh's.'

Jeffrey looked at her profile, so thin and androgynous, beautiful and suddenly strong. Like a Piero della Francesca, he thought with a rare flight of imagination. Perversely, after all these years, she was radiating a strong sexuality, and against his will he felt desire rising in him. It's this bloody place, he thought, it's the heat and the beer. Sweat prickled his armpits and his scalp, under the thick thatch of greying blond wavy hair, and he longed for the cool, grey peacefulness of Lincoln's Inn.

Lunch was a scratch affair of bread and cheese and tomato salad in the kitchen, out of the heat. Domenica took the coffee tray out to the garden, and Jeffrey followed her, with Olivia. Honorine looked at Anna as she washed the dishes, and Anna dried them. 'You 'ave spoken to 'im?' she asked.

'I have,' said Anna. 'I amazed myself.'

'Good,' said Honorine. 'Is better, you will see.' She gave Anna a little pat. 'I go now, for little sleep. I come back six, for making dinner, OK?'

'Wonderful,' said Anna. 'You're an angel.'

Honorine stomped across the square to her house. She felt happy at the thought of a future that included the frequent presence of Anna with Patrick, and pleased with herself for helping Anna to get up the courage to treat Jeffrey in the way that Honorine had no doubt at all that he deserved.

'*Ce petit merdeux*,' she said, as she unlocked her door, and went in, slamming it behind her.

At four o'clock Jeffrey stood up and announced his intention of taking Olivia for a drive. 'Where would you like to go, Olly?' he asked. Olivia looked very much as if she didn't want to go anywhere, and looked uncertainly at Anna, who sat quietly under the fig tree, making a minute watercolour of a golden lizard.

Anna smiled at her and gave a little nod. 'Just be back by six,' she said. 'Josh will want to see you.'

Domenica said nothing, but kept her eyes closed as she lay in her shabby old rattan *chaise longue*, letting the sun soak into her bones.

They heard the front gate clang as Jeffrey and Olivia departed. Anna looked across the garden at Domenica.

'You all right, Mum?' she said quietly, in case she was asleep.

'I'm all right, darling,' said Domenica. 'Just sad.' She opened her eyes, and smiled at Anna.

'I am too,' said Anna, 'but I'm happy underneath.'

'I know you are. I'm glad for you, and for Patrick, too. He is a dear good man, like a rock. I am sorry now that I was a bit rude to him in the beginning.'

'He didn't mind,' said Anna, and laughed.

'I know,' said Domenica. 'That's his strength. It's impossible to wind him up.' She closed her eyes again, and after a few minutes Anna could see that she really was asleep. She washed her sable brush, and began applying minute dots of gamboge to the back of her lizard.

As they passed through the kitchen Olivia pulled her swimsuit off the rack over the stove, and suggested that they go to Collias, and swim in the Gardon. She offered to fetch a pair of Giò's trunks for her father, but he declined, as she had thought he would. Good, she thought, if I stay in the water most of the time, he won't be able to hassle me.

'Is it awfully crowded?' he said, as they bumped along the rough *garrigue* road and passed through Sanilhac.

'Not really, except at weekends,' said Olivia. 'The schools here have gone back, so it's not too bad. You still have to pay ten francs to park the car, though.' She looked at Jeffrey sharply.

'I expect I can find that,' he said without expression.

They parked under a shady tree on the high edge of the river bank, and went down the sandy little path to the flat grey rocks below. The river here was wide and shallow, and it was possible to wade over to the opposite bank. Jeffrey sat down on the rocks and watched a small flotilla of kayaks passing by, going downstream. The canoeists appeared to be

German, or maybe Swedish; they were a family of stunning blonds, blue-eyed and deeply tanned. Jeffrey admired the Germans, he thought them efficient and hard-working; serious, like himself.

Olivia changed into her swimsuit and sat on the edge of a rock, dangling her long brown legs in the water, watching the shoals of little fish that darted around under the overhanging slabs of rock.

'How do you like this Patrick, Olivia?' said Jeffrey without preamble.

She was taken by surprise. 'Um,' she said, 'er. He's OK.'

'You don't like him, then?'

'Yes, I do,' said Olivia, truthfully. 'He's kind, and he's funny.'

'And I am neither of these things?'

Olivia looked at her father, feeling awkward and embarrassed, as she knew he intended her to feel. 'It's not that, Dad,' she said at last, rather lamely. 'He's just different, that's all.'

'And better?' said Jeffrey, relentlessly.

'No!' Olivia almost shouted. 'Not better, just different,' and she slid off the rock, and swam away from him to the middle of the river. Jeffrey noted with some surprise what a strong swimmer his daughter had become, and how muscular and athletic her slender young brown body was, still boyish except for her small, immature breasts. Her body is like her mother's he thought, but her blue eyes and fair hair are mine. Poor child, he thought, with a flash of humility, and for a second was seized with something like despair. He waited on his rock, watching Olivia playing with a tiny, dark-haired little girl, whose mother sat on a rock nearby, reading a magazine, occasionally glancing towards her child, smiling with approval at Olivia. After twenty minutes he began to feel bored and called out that they should be thinking of going back to Souliac.

'OK,' she replied, and took the little girl back to her

mother. She swam the few metres that separated the rocks.

'The water's awfully cold,' said Jeffrey. 'I'm surprised you can stay in so long.'

'I suppose you get used to it.' Olivia hauled herself onto the rock. 'It's lovely, really.'

'What about that sign by the bridge?' said Jeffrey. 'The one that says *Danger de Mort*?'

'Oh,' said Olivia, 'that's just for oldies.'

'Like me?'

'You're not that old, really.'

'Well, then, what about Patrick? He's pretty old?' Jeffrey was unable to stop himself.

Olivia looked at him. 'I suppose he is,' she said, 'but it's not a crime to be old, is it?' She started off up the track to the car, and stood waiting for him, while he followed her rather laboriously, annoyed with himself for his lack of subtlety.

'What's the time?' said Olivia, twisting her head to see the car clock.

'Twenty past five.'

Olivia gave a little hop of excitement. 'Hurray,' she said. 'Josh will be home soon.'

They bumped through the back roads to Souliac, and arrived in the square to find the King family just getting out of their car with Josh. They were all looking amazingly healthy, with sun-bleached hair and tanned skin. Olivia jumped out of the car as soon as it stopped and ran over to Josh, who seemed to have grown about a foot, and looked incredibly grown-up. Really cool, she thought, and suddenly felt rather shy of him. She punched him on the arm, and he put his arm round her shoulders and gave her a little squeeze, propelling her towards the Kings.

'This is Olivia, my kid sister,' he said, introducing her to everyone.

Jeffrey came up and stood behind them. 'Hello, Josh,' he said.

Josh turned and saw him. 'Dad!' he exclaimed,

surprised to see his father. 'I didn't know you were here, I thought Olly was with Giò.' Then he introduced Jeffrey to the Kings, and they all went through the iron gates to the courtyard, while Olivia ran ahead into the house to call Domenica and Anna.

At seven twenty, after a hot but uneventful journey, Giò and Patrick arrived at Place des Vosges. They drove the van into the courtyard entrance to the apartments and climbed the main staircase to Giò's flat. On the coffee table was a note from Laure. 'The chaps should be waiting for you at seven thirty; hope you had a good trip, L.'

'Let's have a drink. I'm dead,' said Gio, going to his little kitchen and taking out ice from the fridge. 'What do you want, Patrick? Whisky, wine?

'Water, please,' said Patrick, and Giò handed him a small bottle of Volvic out of the fridge.

'Like that?'

'Perfect.' Patrick unscrewed the cap, and drank the water at one go.

'Another?' said Giò.

'No, that's fine. Now I need a pee.'

'You know where it is,' said Giò, and laughed.

He filled a tall glass with wine, water and ice, went to the tall French windows, and opened them wide. The cool, tree-smelling air flowed gently into the room, and Giò walked about, with his drink in his hand, stretching his legs and enjoying the breeze. Patrick reappeared, rubbing his chin.

'I need a shave,' he said.

'You look fine.'

'Ought we to go and check whether these guys have turned up?'

'Yes.' Giò looked at his watch. He drained his glass, and they went down to the van. The two men stood patiently waiting. Giò apologized, and unlocked the van.

When the last load had been carried carefully up the wide stone staircase, and arranged at the far end of the apartment, Giò gave them a drink and a large tip, and they clattered away down the stairs, well pleased with their evening's work.

'What about the van? Is it OK to leave it there for a couple of hours?' said Patrick.

'Yes, it's fine. Everyone who lives here knows it's me, the *concierge* will keep her eye on it.'

'Good. In that case, let's go and eat somewhere in the arcade, and then I can get a cab home afterwards. I think we've both done quite enough driving for one day, don't you?'

'Good idea,' said Giò. 'Do you want a wash first, or a shower?'

'Yes, a wash would be nice,' said Patrick. 'If I sit down, I'll go to sleep.'

'I'll run down, and bring up the bags.'

'And could you bring my jacket? It's hanging in the van.'

Giò ran down to the van. He felt tired and depressed. He had intended to offer to cook omelettes. Laure, as she always did when he was away on a trip, had put butter, milk, eggs and salad in the fridge, and fresh bread stood on the tiled worktop, covered with a cloth. He did not really feel that Patrick was trying to avoid being alone with him, and maybe it was for the best, anyway. He did not wish to make a fool of himself by blurting out his feelings when he had had a few drinks. In a restaurant he would have greater control, he hoped. He got out the bags and Patrick's coat, locked the van and took the keys to the *concierge*, in case it needed moving.

'I'll take it to the garage in the morning, OK?'

'Very good, Mr Hamilton, that'll be fine,' said the *concierge*, winking at Giò lasciviously. Giò gave her a hard stare, and walked away carrying the two bags and the jacket, feeling foolish.

'No such bloody luck,' he said furiously. 'Stupid old cow.'

They ate at the bistro where they had first met.

They had *crudités*, and rabbit with glazed onions, and a plain green salad, and drank a Côtes-du-Rhône. Patrick ordered coffee and bought a packet of small black cigars. He opened the pack and offered it to Giò.

'No, thanks,' Giò took his squashed packet of Gitanes from his shirt pocket. 'I'll stick to these.'

They smoked in silence for a few moments.

'Giò,' said Patrick, and Giò's heart leapt, knowing what was coming. Patrick looked straight at Giò, his blue eyes gentle. 'I expect you've already guessed?' he said.

Giò took a deep drag of his cigarette. 'You mean Anna? You and Anna?' His voice sounded croaking and strange. 'It wasn't very hard to guess,' he added, with a small, unnatural laugh.

'No,' said Patrick, 'I don't suppose it was.'

The coffee arrived with the bill. The waiter poured the coffee, and left the *cafetière* on the table. Giò drank some coffee, and inhaled another lungful of smoke. He tried to smile, to feel pleased. 'I'm glad for you both,' he said. 'Poor old Anna, she had a rotten time with Jeffrey. What about you, Patrick? Are you married, or divorced, or what?'

'I was married, briefly, nearly thirty years ago. My wife was killed in a car smash, just before the birth of our child. The baby was stillborn.'

Giò looked at Patrick, appalled. His shocked dark eyes filled with tears. 'Oh, Christ,' he said, 'how frightful for you. And you've been alone all these years?'

'Yes, quite alone.'

'And to think, I thought . . .' Giò broke off, dismayed.

'You thought I was gay? Don't worry, lots of people think that. It doesn't worry me at all.' They laughed then, the tension broken.

'Oh, well,' said Giò, 'lucky old Anna! At least I'll have you for a brother-in-law, anyway.'

They walked down the arcade to the shop, where Patrick picked up his bag, and hailed a passing taxi.

'See you very soon, Giò,' said Patrick, his hand on the

handle of the cab door. 'I'm very glad we're going to be brothers-in-law, you're a terrific family.'

'Oh,' said Giò, 'wait till you meet my father. He's so English, it's a joke.'

'Your mother will do for the moment,' said Patrick wryly.

'Yes, she is rather hard to take, isn't she?' They laughed, and Patrick got into the cab and drove away. Giò watched the cab out of sight and then walked slowly back to the shop, locking the door behind him.

The roast loin of pork had disappeared, along with a small mountain of potatoes, a dish of spinach and an enormous salad. The young people were now demolishing a platter of goats' cheeses and two baskets of bread. The basket of peaches waited on the stone table, and Olivia had picked ripe figs from the tree and arranged them among the cheeses.

Anna looked down the table at the four eager young faces, so unselfconsciously enjoying everything that life could offer them, and smiled at Domenica, who sat smoking quietly at the other end of the table. Domenica smiled back, squinting through the smoke. Anna got up and refilled Domenica's glass, and Jeffrey's, and then filled her own, putting the bottle down in front of Josh, in case he should feel it necessary to offer more to his guests. He did so, and they refused politely, asking for water. How sensible they all are, thought Anna, and my children are the same, they're not like us at all. Except perhaps Olivia. Anna could see that she was making a big effort to be cool, not at all like the over-excited child who had been the life and death of Giò's homecoming dinner.

Jeffrey sat silently, next to Domenica. He had watched with some concern the vast amounts of food being consumed, and was fast rethinking his plans to deprive Anna of her children. Reconciliation, he thought, that's the best thing. I will go and see a marriage guidance counsellor the minute I get back to London. The church clock struck ten, and he looked at his watch. He had caught the sun on the back of his neck at Collias, and had a slight headache. He felt irritated by the young people, eating and talking so confidently, as if they ate dinner under the stars at ten o'clock every night of their lives.

He turned to Domenica. 'I have a headache, I think I'll turn in.'

'Why not?' she said. Jeffrey left the table and went into the house through the kitchen, and Domenica heard the front gate clang. No-one else noticed him go.

Presently Honorine got up to make coffee, but Anna stopped her. 'No,' she said, 'sit down. You've done more than enough for one evening. I'll do it.' She disappeared into the kitchen before Honorine could object.

She sat on the edge of the kitchen table, watching the old black kettle as it slowly came to the boil. A thin wisp of steam issued from the spout at last, and the lid began to rattle. Anna poured the boiling water onto the coffee.

The telephone began to ring upstairs in the *salon*. Anna's heart leapt, and she put down the kettle and ran up the stairs two at a time. She lifted the phone.

'Anna?'

'Patrick! Is everything all right?'

'Everything's fine.'

'I thought you weren't going to ring till Friday.'

'Can't wait that long. I miss you.'

'I miss you too,' said Anna softly.

'This is an awful line, I can hardly hear you. I'll ring you tomorrow night.'

'Please take care of yourself; sleep well,' said Anna.

'You too, though I wish it were last night.'

'You must come to London soon.'

'Yes, and you must come to Paris,' said Patrick.

'I will.'

'You will? That's wonderful!'

'Talk to you tomorrow?' said Anna.

'Goodnight, my love,' said Patrick.

'Goodnight.'

She went downstairs and took the coffee out to the garden. 'That was Patrick,' she said to Domenica. 'They got back safely.'

'Good, how kind of him to ring,' said Domenica, and smiled at Anna. 'Giò never does.'

'Honorine,' said Anna, 'have your coffee and then go home. All these willing hands will soon deal with the dishes.'

'Of course,' said Emma King, and added, 'that was the best dinner I've had in my life, thank you so much.' Josh and Hugh added their thanks to Emma's, and Honorine departed in a glow of appreciation. She walked across the square to her house. A full moon rose behind the church tower, and the plane trees cast long black shadows along the ground. A few lights still glowed warmly in upstairs windows, and the owl hooted in the top of a tree. As she approached her door, rattling her keys, she saw something lurking in the shadow of the porch, and gave a little start of fear. But it was only Jeffrey, leaning against the door, waiting for her to let him in.

Chapter Eight

Honorine took a tray of tea up to Domenica's room at nine o'clock. She put the tray down on the night table and half opened the shutters, letting in cool, scented air and a shaft of early sunshine.

Domenica groaned and turned over. Then she opened her eyes unwillingly and looked at Honorine as she poured her tea, and a cup for herself. Honorine settled herself in a little walnut nursing chair that stood near the bed.

'So,' said Domenica, lifting herself on to her elbow and drinking some tea, 'what's happening?'

'Anna 'as taken the children to Uzès. They meet the parents of Emma and 'er brother at Place l'Évêché, and after they go to Place aux Herbes for shopping.'

'And Jeffrey?'

'Jeffrey is 'ere. 'E drinks 'is coffee now.'

'What sort of a mood is he in?' said Domenica.

''E is very quiet. I think 'e is not very 'appy.'

'Not really very surprising. What time is he leaving?' said Domenica.

'About ten, I think; 'e 'as 'is bag 'ere.'

'Oh? So Anna has already said goodbye?'

'I think so.' Honorine got up, and put the cups on the tray. 'I better go and see to 'im.'

Domenica got out of bed and padded through to the bathroom. How tiring they all are, she thought as she brushed her teeth, it will be a nice rest when they have gone. She brushed her hair and put on her old towelling bathrobe. Quite good enough for boring old Jeffrey, she said to herself, as she stuck out her tongue and

139

examined it in the magnifying mirror. 'Ugh,' she said and, tightening the belt of the robe, she went downstairs to the front courtyard. Jeffrey was sitting at the iron table, writing a note. She sat down, and Honorine appeared with more coffee.

Jeffrey folded the piece of paper, and slid it under *Midi Libre*. 'Good morning, ' he said. 'I am just writing a note to Josh. I did not get a chance to speak to him last night, and now he has gone off with Anna and his friends, and I shall have to leave for Marseille before they get back.'

'What a shame.' Domenica stifled the urge to laugh. 'Don't let me interrupt your train of thought.' She poured her coffee.

'It doesn't matter,' said Jeffrey, 'I'm glad of the opportunity to talk to you.'

Domenica's heart sank. 'I'm afraid the feeling is not mutual.'

'What do you mean?'

'Well, what is there to talk about?' said Domenica.

'There's bloody everything to talk about,' said Jeffrey, his voice rising. 'Your bloody daughter is threatening to divorce me and split the family apart, as you very well know, I'm sure.'

'Not before time,' said Domenica coolly, staring at Jeffrey, her grey-green eyes huge behind her owl-like spectacles. Anger and fatigue had made his blue eyes small, so that they appeared even closer together than usual. I can't think what Anna saw in him, even in the beginning, she thought.

'What the hell do you mean, not before time?' said Jeffrey angrily. 'Haven't I kept the whole family, paid all the major bills, paid the bloody mortgage, for eighteen years?'

'You did it for the sake of your children, and that in itself gives you quite a few brownie points. But from Anna's point of view, you have been absent from her bed for ten years, and yet have continued to come and go as you please. What kind of life is that for her?'

140

'Well, she seemed quite happy to put up with the arrangement. She was always whining at me to come back to her,' said Jeffrey, defensively.

'And now she doesn't want you any more, you don't like it, do you?'

Jeffrey flushed a dark unbecoming red, and ran his fingers through his hair. 'What a fucking old cow you are, Domenica,' he said.

'Sticks and stones, Jeffrey.' Domenica laughed her coarse hyena's laugh, and stood up. 'I'll leave you to finish your letter to Josh,' she said. 'You'll have to leave in a few minutes, won't you?'

She went into the kitchen, and Jeffrey could hear her voice and Honorine's, and the sound of muffled laughter. He crumpled the letter and put it in his pocket, then picked up his bag and walked to the gate. He went through it, closing it silently behind him. He stood by his hired car for a moment, and looked up at the house behind its high, secret wall. At least I'll probably never have to see this bloody place again, or that frightful woman, he said to himself, as he got into the car and drove away.

At Boulter's Mill, Kate lit a cigarette and looked at the row of tiles in front of her. They really are nice this time, she thought, the blue is perfect and they have a good rhythm. She inhaled deeply. Her cold had almost gone, and for the first time she could really taste the tobacco. She stared out of the spotted, cobwebby little window at the tiny shred of blue sky that slashed the pearly grey clouds, visible over the tops of the tall trees which made a backdrop to the sodden garden. Blue, she thought, it's definitely my favourite colour. If only there was more of it in this vile country. She longed for days of unbroken blue skies and hot sun. She looked at her hands, beginning to be swollen around the thumb joints with arthritis, and thought with dread of the onset of yet another cold, damp winter. She looked at Josh's postcard which she had propped against the window, and wondered for the fiftieth time why it was that almost everyone they knew had an annual supercharge of sunshine, warm sea and wine, and yet she and Robert, who were not exactly paupers, never did.

Since Robert's retirement they had rarely left Sussex, and then only to deliver tiles to London every few months. Of course, they dined with local friends from time to time, and the same friends dined with them, though increasingly people seemed to find cooking for several people too much to manage. Instead, they fell back on the annual drinks party, either at Christmas or Easter. Kate loathed this form of entertaining, either giving or receiving it, and was conducting a rear-guard action never to go to one again, or give one themselves. But Robert enjoyed himself at such affairs. After several drinks he became positively animated, buttonholing any reasonably pretty young woman and engaging her in flirtatious conversation. The curious thing was that the girls seemed to enjoy it too. Kate could never understand why, and thought them feeble-minded, and Robert embarrassing.

She wasn't much good at village life, and didn't even try to be. She never went to church, and didn't join the WI, wouldn't do meals-on-wheels, or go to fundraising lunches, or the village fête. Of course, Robert more than made up for her anti-social behaviour by attending every church or village function, and contributing quantities of produce to the Harvest Festival, and armfuls of flowers to the flower ladies.

Why did I ever marry him? she thought. I was perfectly happy in Chelsea, still would have been today. She had had a big, light, cold studio in Beaufort Street, where she had worked all day, and then met her friends in the Roebuck in the evening, to talk and drink. They ate in one of the cheap restaurants in the King's Road, or bought fish and chips, or a take-away curry, and repaired to someone's flat to eat, drink, talk till two in the morning, and go to bed together if they felt like it, or not. It had been a perfect way of life, totally work-oriented and free, without the boring constraints of marriage.

Robert and Domenica had occasionally come to the Roebuck for a drink. Kate remembered them very well, a beautiful dark couple, totally wrapped up in each other, happy. They would sit at a table, heads close together, whispering to each other. Then Domenica would bend her head and kiss Robert, and Robert would smile at her, and soon afterwards they would leave the pub and go home, their arms round each other.

What on earth possessed me? thought Kate. After Domenica had left Robert, and was living in France, he had sometimes come to the Roebuck alone, and Kate had felt sorry for him. They had had dinner together quite often, and a few times he had spent the night in her studio. Not that these encounters had proved particularly rewarding for either of them. Robert had been missing Domenica too much, as well as the twins. From time to time, Kate would spend the weekend at Boulter's. She liked the space and the light, and after the numbing cold of her studio, she fell idiotically in love with the elderly Aga pouring forth its comforting warmth throughout the year. To Kate, it represented all she had never had in her life, a kind of stable, reliable maternal presence. After Robert's divorce they saw each other even more frequently, and in the end it had seemed logical to marry and move to the mill. If only I had kept on the lease of the studio, thought Kate. It would have made a huge difference if I had kept part of my life independent.

She sighed and looked at her watch: nearly half past twelve; she had better go and get something for lunch. She went through to the kitchen and looked in the fridge. Cold risotto congealed in a bowl. That will have to do, she thought, taking the bowl from the fridge, and breaking up the risotto with a fork.

She sliced tomatoes, poured olive oil and a splash of vinegar over them, and sprinkled them with a little sugar. She set the table and put bread and cheese out. Then she poured herself a stiff gin, and waited for Robert to appear.

After lunch she made coffee and brought it to the table. The telephone rang, and she glanced at Robert, catching his eye as he looked up from *The Times*. He put down the paper and went to answer the phone.

'Of course,' Kate heard his voice from the book-room. 'How nice, why not stay for the weekend? You will? Lovely. See you Friday, lateish. Look forward to it. 'Bye.' He came back to the table, rubbing his hands and smiling.

'That's nice,' he said. 'That's old Jim Bolt from the department. He and Marcia are going to Chichester on Friday night. I've invited them for the weekend.'

'Robert,' said Kate, through gritted teeth, 'why is it that you always make arrangements without consulting me first?'

'Why?' he said. 'We're not doing anything, are we?'

'You may not be,' said Kate, 'but it may have escaped your notice that I am desperately trying to finish my tile order.'

'Oh, that,' said Robert, drinking his coffee. 'Surely you take a break at the weekend?'

'Normally, yes. But in order to deliver on time, I'll have to work all day, every day, until it's finished. In between the sodding domestic work,' she added resentfully.

'Oh, come,' said Robert, 'it's not all that important, is it? It isn't as if you earned much from it. Rather poorly paid, like all craft work, isn't it?'

Kate felt rage rising in her like a kettle coming to the boil. She stood up. 'That's not the fucking point, you selfish old bastard. It earns enough to give me a little bit of independence and self-respect, and I intend to finish this order and deliver it on time. And when I've been paid, I'm going to take myself on holiday, probably the Greek Islands. Anywhere hot and sunny and far away from this soul-destroying place.'

'Have you quite finished?' said Robert quietly.

'No,' said Kate. 'If your bloody friends come for the weekend, you will have to prepare their room and do the cooking, and entertain them all by yourself. I shall be working.'

'I see,' said Robert politely. He got up from the table, sending her a baffled spaniel look, and went into the book-room, closing the door.

'And you can play bloody Puccini till the cows come home!' she yelled through the door. 'See if I care.'

The door opened and Robert stood in the doorway. 'Kate,' he said, 'why are you being so unkind? What have I done?'

'If you don't know,' said Kate, 'you're even more of a fool than I've always thought,' and she stomped off to her studio, slamming the door behind her.

Robert sighed. He looked at the remains of their lunch, still cluttering the table. Pensively, he fetched a tray and began to clear away.

Jeffrey stood at his office window, staring down into the square below. The rain had stopped, but the trees drooped with the weight of water, and dripped into the large, oily puddles on the paving slabs beneath them. The air was moist and mild, and he could see that clouds of midges had already formed, although it was only four o'clock.

After a search through the Yellow Pages, under the section marked Counselling, he had finally decided to make an appointment with an organisation describing themselves as 'Crisis in the Family', in Richmond. He chose Richmond because, as far as he was aware, neither he nor Anna knew anyone there. The business-like woman to whom he had spoken offered him an appointment in two weeks' time. When he expressed surprise at the delay, she was sympathetic but firm, and he had had to accept the date proposed. He noted the appointment in his diary, writing CF 3.30 p.m., and cancelling the rest of the afternoon.

Jeffrey felt tired. In fact, he felt exhausted and irritable. He was finding it difficult to concentrate, and Sharon, the inquisitive little bitch, had twice asked him if he felt all right.

'You look really done in, Mr Wickham,' she said. 'P'raps you should go home and have a sleep?'

'Thank you, Sharon, I'm perfectly all right,' he replied, resisting the temptation to put his head on the desk, and give way to the tears that had threatened to humiliate him since his arrival back in London, on Tuesday afternoon. Tomorrow, Friday, Anna and the children would fly home, and he would be able to start his campaign to persuade her to give up this wretched little frog, this *old* wretched little frog, so that maybe they could start again. 'I'll meet them at the airport. She'll like that; it'll save them having to get the train to Victoria, and a taxi out to Chiswick.'

He felt quite cheered up at the idea, and then thought of an even better one. He would go to Waitrose in the King's Road, do the weekend shopping for her, and take it out to the Lifeboat and put it all away in the fridge. Then he could check her answerphone in case there were any messages from the frog, see that Mrs Thing had made the beds up, and had fed the mad canary. He signed his letters and took them through to Sharon.

'I'm going home now, Sharon,' he said. 'I'll be in tomorrow morning as usual, but please cancel tomorrow afternoon's appointments. There's nothing that can't wait till next week, I've checked.'

'Goodnight then, Mr Wickham,' said Sharon, 'I hope you feel better soon.'

'I'm fine,' said Jeffrey. He took his umbrella from the coat-stand by the door, his bowler from its hook, picked up his briefcase and departed.

Sharon and Beryl looked at each other with round, kohl-rimmed eyes and bold, pouting red lips. 'What's eating him, then?' said Beryl, folding letters and slipping them into their envelopes.

'Didn't stay long in France, did he?' said Sharon, with her knowing little smile, and began putting the mail through the franking machine.

'Don't forget his cancelling,' said Beryl.

'Plenty of time for that,' said Sharon, taking a packet of biscuits from her drawer. 'Let's have another cuppa first, shall we?'

Jeffrey walked through Lincoln's Inn Fields and down Chancery Lane to the Strand, where he stood on the edge of the pavement with his umbrella raised, trying to get a taxi. Eventually one cruised alongside him and stopped, purring, and Jeffrey got in.

'Where to, guv?' said the driver, sliding back the glass.

'King's Road, Waitrose's,' said Jeffrey.

'Right,' said the driver, shutting the glass, and doing a U-turn in the middle of the traffic.

As they drove slowly along the Mall towards Buckingham Palace, Jeffrey pushed down his window and let the cool air from the park blow into the cab's interior. There was a 'No Smoking' sign on the glass partition, but it still smelled of stale tobacco. He sank back in his seat and watched the trees go slowly by through tired, half-closed eyes. The driver turned into Buckingham Gate, and went down Buckingham Palace Road until he reached Elizabeth Street. At the top of the street he turned into King's Road, drove around Sloane Square, and stopped the cab at Chelsea Town Hall.

Jeffrey got out and paid the fare. He crossed the road and went into Waitrose's. It felt quite strange to be in a supermarket after so many years. He normally used the local small shops near his flat in St Loo Avenue; a modest food store run by an Asian family, a laundromat, and a local Oddbins. He picked up a trolley and began to walk through the long aisles, each stacked high with a bewilderingly large choice of the same product. This is awful, he thought, how the hell do I know what kind of cornflakes they eat? If at all? Then he pulled himself together, took a firmer grip on the handle of the trolley, which seemed to have a mind of its own in respect of steering, looked at the signs hanging over the aisles, and headed for one marked 'Fresh Chilled Meat'. He studied the section marked Tender Lean Lamb, and was both astonished and dismayed at how much one had to pay for three Leg Steaks, Bone Out. The whole legs of lamb seemed better value for money, so he chose a small Half Leg, Shank End. Even so, it cost more than seven pounds. He moved to the 'Fresh Poultry', and bought a corn-fed chicken. It was imported from France, he observed, that would please her. Still, at three twenty-five it was cheap compared with the lamb. Then he bought a pound of sausages, and some bacon. That should do, he thought, and moved to the fruit and vegetables. It's no good, I can't keep totting up the cost, he said to himself. I'll just get what I think will please her, and pay up.

He bought potatoes, carrots, onions and leeks. Then two packs of ready-washed salad, tomatoes and courgettes, and apples, oranges and lemons. 'What now?' he said, looking about him vaguely.

The trolley was filling up alarmingly. Then he remembered butter, cheese, eggs, yoghurt and milk. Better get tea and coffee, and bread, too, he thought. At last he headed for a check-out, and waited impatiently in a queue. When his turn came, the girl took pity on him, as he was unable to prise open the plastic bags and was so slow in packing them, that the people behind him grew restive and began to push. The bill came to £72.93, and he handed the girl his Visa card. He wheeled the trolley through the exit and onto the pavement, wondering how he was going to get the four heavy bags of shopping, plus his umbrella and briefcase, into a taxi. He pushed the trolley along the pavement, feeling like a criminal. At any moment, he expected a security man to tap him on the shoulder, and ask him where he thought he was going with the cart.

By great good fortune, a taxi stood ticking over by the kerb.

'Are you free?' Jeffrey asked the driver, anxiously.

'Where do you want to go mate?'

'St Loo Avenue.'

'OK.'

Jeffrey hurled the bags of shopping onto the seat, and got himself, his briefcase and his umbrella swiftly into the taxi, abandoning the trolley on the pavement. The taxi drove away. Jeffrey did not look back. Ten minutes later he was stowing the shopping into the boot of his own car, which was parked in the street outside his studio flat. He heaved a sigh of relief, and looked at his watch: nearly six o'clock. God, what a time it takes, he thought, I could use a drink.

'Drink!' he said. 'I forgot wine.' He got into his car and drove round the corner to his local shops. In Oddbins he bought two bottles of Pinot Grigio and two bottles of Beaujolais for Anna, and a bottle of whisky for himself. Next door, in the mini market he bought a frozen pizza for his own supper, and two bunches of freesias in silver foil cornucopias. Then, feeling light-headed at the rate at which he was spending money, he bought chocolate for the children, and *Vogue* and *Interiors* for Anna.

He asked Mr Patel for a couple of empty cardboard boxes, and took them out to his car, where he carefully repacked everything, so that the shopping would not be hurled around the boot during the journey out to Chiswick.

At twenty past seven Jeffrey parked outside the Lifeboat, and got out of his car. He opened the boot and carried the boxes of shopping to the doorstep. He put his hat and umbrella carefully into the boot, out of

149

sight, and locked the car, checking each door afterwards. Unlocking the street door with his latchkey,
he put the boxes and his briefcase on the lower steps
of the stairs. He closed the door, and then carried the
heavy boxes, one at a time, up the stairs and through
the house to the kitchen. The canary, glad of some company, banged its bell and leapt about its cage. 'Stupid
thing,' said Jeffrey, and went down for his briefcase.

As he came back into the big room and shut the door,
his arms and legs aching from the unusual exercise, he
looked longingly at the campaign bed, and thought of
his bottle of whisky. No, he thought, if I sit down
I'll never get the beastly stuff put away. He took off
his jacket, and went purposefully into the kitchen.
He opened the fridge door. It was clean, thank God,
and empty. He turned up the thermostat, and began
to put everything away. He could not decide whether to
put the meat in the freezer or not. In the end, he
thought it better to take the lamb and the chicken
out of their wrappings and put them on dishes in
the bottom part of the fridge. Washing his hands
after this unappealing task, he reflected on how
much tedium and unpleasantness was attached to
the acquisition, storage, preparation and disposal of
food. Not to speak of the attendant endless cleaning
of cooking pots, plates, glasses, knives and forks and
so on. All this elaborate family cooking was all very
well once in a while, he thought, but he couldn't help
feeling that they made far too much of a big deal out
of it, practically a way of life.

He dried his hands and looked at the box of vegetables and wine, still waiting to be unpacked. He
sighed wearily. Why the hell did I buy so much? he
thought crossly, and began to stow the vegetables in
the salad compartment of the fridge. He was pretty
sure that Anna did that, to keep them fresher. He
seemed to remember that Kate, down at Boulter's, kept
great baskets of the things on the stone-flagged floor
of her kitchen. Maybe things were done differently

in the country. The bunches of freesias still lay on the worktop in their bright foil wrapping. Jeffrey found a bucket under the sink and filled it with water. He plunged the flowers in, wrappers and all. She can arrange them herself, he thought, I'm bound to make a mess of it.

At last everything was done. Jeffrey looked at his watch: nearly half past eight. God, where had the evening gone? He broke the seal of his bottle of whisky, and poured a generous tot into a glass. He opened the freezer and took out the ice tray. A strong, fishy smell came from the ice, and he had to throw it down the sink, and refill the tray from the tap. He ran the tap till it was really cold, and then put some in his whisky. Then he took the glass and went through to the big room. Sipping his drink, he crossed to the worktable. Mrs Thing had brought up Anna's mail and left it in a neat pile on the table. He riffled through the letters, and extracted a thick white envelope with a French stamp and a Paris postmark. The handwriting was small, neat, scholarly and in black ink. Jeffrey was sure it was not Giò's. He held it up to the light but could not see through the expensive paper. It was firmly sealed in one of those clever tamper-proof envelopes with little nicks on the flap. He felt pretty sure that if he tried to steam it open, something unpleasant would happen which would give him away. He could, of course, just destroy it. On balance, better not, Anna would find out. He restacked the pile of mail, and played back the tape. Nothing new there.

Jeffrey refilled his glass, and lay down on the campaign bed, taking off his shoes and socks to cool his throbbing feet. He took a deep swallow of whisky, and contemplated his feet, flexing his long, knobbly toes and blue-veined ankles sticking out of his black-striped city trousers. How white and morbid they looked, bloodless, like something in a mortuary, he thought. He thought of Anna's slender brown legs and narrow tanned feet, as she

151

padded around barefooted in the garden at Souliac. Into his mind's eye came the image of her profile, her long neck and flat-chested body in a thin pink shirt, her strong arms and thin, long-fingered hands on the steering wheel, and felt again the stirrings of desire. He stared into his whisky, and tears of self-pity filled his eyes. Angrily, he brushed them away.

'This is ridiculous,' he said aloud. 'I've been out of love with her for years. The only reason I've kept everything going here is my sense of responsibility.' The canary gave a little chirp. 'So why am I rushing around like a demented fool, trying to stop her leaving me for another man?' He drained his glass and got up to refill it. He walked to the kitchen, slightly unsteadily on his bare feet, and poured another drink. Better put the pizza in the oven, he thought. He lit the oven, and ripped the packaging off the pizza. He set the timer to go off in fifteen minutes, put the pizza in the oven and returned to the big room. It felt rather stuffy, and smelt rather strongly of whisky and, it had to be admitted, feet. He opened the tall window, and stood staring down at the overgrown churchyard below. A wave of depression engulfed him, and a deep sense of injustice.

He tried to remember why it was that he had left Anna in the first place. His brief and well-concealed affair with the senior partner's wife had not really been the entire reason for his move to St Loo Avenue. He thought that a contributory factor had been the advent of babies into the tiny house, with their screams and smells, and endlessly demanding presence. They had seemed to take up all of Anna's time, robbing her of her capacity to work, and thus make a proper contribution to their finances. A hot, angry flush crept up his neck as he remembered that she had nevertheless always managed to earn enough money to buy quite frequent airfares for herself and her children to go to Souliac. She also bought books and compact discs and tapes, and had always been an avid reader of glossy magazines. Piles of them stood in neat stacks under the worktable. Reference material, she claimed, but he thought that just an excuse. And clothes, too, had always been a source of disagreement. Anna always said that her clothes came from Oxfam, or thrift shops, but Jeffrey was not fooled by that. He was not naïve enough to believe that jackets from Emporio Armani could be bought in a thrift shop for five pounds. Equally, when they were babies, she had bought Petit Bateau clothes for the children, always saying they were presents from Domenica, and OshKosh dungarees at crazy prices, or so it seemed to Jeffrey. Admittedly, his own clothes were extremely expensive. In his profession you had to have a proper appearance. Equally, he couldn't drive around in a clapped-out old banger like Anna's. In fact, his Mercedes convertible was his most treasured possession.

The timer rang in the kitchen, and Jeffrey went to the oven and took out his pizza. He slid it onto one of Anna's blue-and-white plates, and poured himself another drink. As he replaced the cap, he noticed with some surprise that he had drunk nearly half the bottle. He looked at the whisky in his glass, it was rather strong-looking.

'Oh, shit,' he said. 'I suppose I'd better not drive back tonight.'

He found a fork, and picked up the plate and glass. Might as well be hung for a sheep as a lamb, he thought, and went back into the big room. He turned on the television to watch *News at Ten* and settled himself again on the campaign bed. As he ate the rather dull pizza, he watched, unmoved, the picture of appallingly wounded old people, women and young children in a Sarajevo hospital after a shelling incident. Whether the victims were Serbs or Croats or Moslems, Jeffrey had no idea, and could not feel any particular interest. Either way, these awful things seemed to be an ordinary part of everyday life now, whether happening to Cambodians, Ethiopians, or the poor old Kurds, and now Yugoslavia, or whatever it would eventually be called. Lord Owen's tired and disappointed face came onto the screen. Poor sod, thought Jeffrey, I know just how he feels.

He washed up his supper things. Deciding against another drink, he made himself a cup of tea instead. He took off his trousers and shirt and hung them over the back of a chair. He needed a pee, and looked at the spiral staircase which had to be negotiated to get to the bathroom. I don't think so, somehow, he said to himself. He went to the tall open window, and urinated through it into the bushes below. Then he closed the window, turned off the television, and settled himself on the campaign bed for the night. As he drank his tea, he looked with disfavour at his pale, hairy legs emerging from his boxer shorts. These had a design of ants on them, a Christmas gift from Olivia. At the thought of his younger child, so like himself in many ways, with the same hair and eyes, his eyes pricked with tears again. I don't want to lose them, he thought, and I don't want them to know that Anna wants someone else, especially that elderly frog, God rot him.

In a horrifying moment of self-knowledge, Jeffrey realized that that was the truth of the matter. He preferred to live alone, he liked his own company, and he liked to have the odd affair from time to time, but he still thought of the children and Anna as belonging to him. However illogical it might seem, he wanted things to stay exactly as they were. He did not want Anna, or the children, to allow some other man to usurp his rightful place, as her husband and their father. But that seemed to be precisely what was happening, whether he wished to or not. The tears spilled over and slid down Jeffrey's face. He was too tired, and too drunk to stop them. In a peculiar way, his uncontrolled sobbing became almost pleasurable in its intensity, and for the first time since he was twelve years old, Jeffrey Wickham cried himself to sleep.

He woke at half past seven with a splitting headache and a vile taste in his mouth. He was also very cold, and went straight to the kitchen and put on the kettle. While it boiled, he looked for aspirin, and found some on the herb rack. Where else? he thought. He took two, made tea with a teabag in a mug, and returned to the big room to drink it. He took his shirt and trousers, and went up to the bathroom. He looked in the mirror; he looked as atrocious as he felt. God, he thought, I don't think I can drive to Gatwick like this. I'd better go home and have a bath, and then meet the train at Victoria this afternoon. I'll phone the office and say I'm unwell.

He tidied away his mugs and glasses, and smoothed the cover of the campaign bed. His back ached, and he had a stiff neck. Bloody uncomfortable thing, he thought. I should have slept in Anna's bed – our bed. He took a last look round the room, and went down to his car, clicking the door to behind him.

Two hours later, Mrs Taylor arrived at the Lifeboat with two bags of shopping she had done at Anna's request, unlocked the door with her latchkey and went upstairs to make everything nice for the return home of Anna and her children.

At the presbytery, Anna and Honorine finished sorting the clothes to be left behind for the next holiday, and those to be packed for London. Both felt sad, as they always did at such times. Olivia floated in and out with odd pieces of clothing, and Josh was having breakfast with Domenica.

'We should leave at ten thirty,' said Anna. 'We have to be at Montpellier by midday.'

The plane did not leave till one, and the airport was not especially strict about checking-in times, but she had a horror of missing the plane, and always insisted on getting to the airport in good time. Domenica, on the other hand, always tried to keep them till the last possible minute, elaborately pretending that nothing unusual was happening, and trying to postpone the moment of departure. However, now that she and Anna were on such good terms, and she was so pleased with her daughter for finally breaking out of the trap that had enmeshed her for so long, she had no wish to make the parting more difficult, so when Anna called out of a window for Josh to come and get the bags, Domenica did not try to detain him.

At last they were all ready to go, and they piled into the car, Olivia carrying a small basket of figs, carefully picked that morning so that they were almost, but not quite, ripe.

'You come too, Honorine,' said Domenica. 'We'll go and have lunch somewhere, when we've got rid of them.' Honorine looked at her, anxiously. 'Don't worry,' said Domenica, smiling at her, 'I won't get pissed, I promise.'

Not till we get home, anyway, she added silently, as Honorine got her bag, locked the front gate, and climbed into the back seat next to Josh and Olivia.

The flight to Gatwick was uneventful, and they descended through the familiar cloud cover to land on time. They had the usual interminable wait for the baggage to appear, went though immigration and customs and headed for the train. Josh, with his formidable height and weight, forged his way through the crowd, pushing the luggage trolley, with Anna and Olivia following in his wake.

As the train pulled in to Victoria, Josh heaved the bags off the luggage rack and prepared to hurl them onto the platform.

'Wait here,' he said bossily, 'I'll get a trolley.' He vanished through the crowd. Isn't it nice to have a grown-up son, said Anna to herself, as she stood with Olivia beside the stack of suitcases.

'Hello, Anna,' said Jeffrey, 'I thought I'd never find you in this crush.'

'Jeffrey!' said Anna, whirling round.

'Dad,' said Olivia. 'What on earth are you doing here?'

'I've come to take you home,' said Jeffrey. 'Is that so surprising?'

Chapter Nine

Kate drove her little van down the Fulham Road, devoutly hoping that Fred had remembered to put cones on the road outside his shop, so that she could park and deliver the tiles. It had been a real slog getting the order finished, but she had managed it and now felt a small glow of satisfaction at having achieved her goal and proved herself reliable.

'Good old Fred,' she said, as she approached the shop, and saw the row of cones, and a sign saying 'No Parking Please, Delivery expected'. She drew up by the cones and gave a little toot on the horn. Fred came out and moved the cones, and Kate carefully backed into the space. She opened the back doors of the van, and she and Fred carried the two heavy boxes of tiles into the shop.

'Coffee?' said Fred. 'Only instant, I'm afraid.'

'Thanks,' said Kate, 'I prefer it, given the choice.'

They drank the coffee, and Kate produced her invoice.

'I suppose you'd like the cheque now?'

'Well,' said Kate, 'it would be very welcome. I'm completely skint at the moment.'

'OK.' Fred smiled at her, 'how much is it, then?'

'Five hundred,' she answered, and Fred wrote the cheque. 'Thanks very much.' Kate carefully folded the cheque and put it in her wallet. 'If there are any damaged ones, let me know at once. But there shouldn't be, they're very carefully packed.'

They shook hands, and Kate got back into the van and drove to King's Road, where she still kept her old bank account. She paid in the cheque, parked in Smith Street and walked to the Chelsea Potter. She bought herself a gin and tonic and a pack of cigarettes, and installed herself at a table. Absent-mindedly, she sipped the gin, and tipped handfuls of nuts down her throat from the dish on the table, crunching noisily. She looked round the pub. It had changed quite a bit since she was a regular. It seemed larger, and a bit smarter, but it still had a good atmosphere, and Kate imagined that in the evening, when things hotted up a bit, it was very likely nearly as much fun as it used to be, with much the same sort of crowd.

The street door opened, and a tall man with a grey beard and steel-rimmed, round spectacles came in. He was wearing a blue denim shirt and jeans, and a black beret and black motorcycle boots. He went to the bar and ordered a beer, and Kate realized with a little shock of surprise that it was one of her old drinking chums, Ted Macey.

She got up, and went over to the bar. 'Hello, Ted,' she said.

The man turned and looked at her. 'Hello, Kate. What'll you have?'

'Gin, thanks,' said Kate. She felt as though she had never been away.

Two hours later, after more gin and a big plate of sausages and mash, with onion gravy, Kate and Ted came out of the Potter, and strolled round to Smith Street in the warm September sunshine. When they reached Kate's old van, she was not surprised to find that it had not got a parking ticket. The poor thing was so old and tatty that wardens and policemen seemed to ignore its misdemeanours. Kate and Ted embraced warmly, and promised to meet again soon.

'You should never have left, old darling,' said Ted.

'Too damn right, I shouldn't,' said Kate. She watched him as he ambled off down the street and disappeared round a corner. She got into her van and switched on the ignition. Then she switched it off again, and leaned back in her seat, going over the events of the last week or two in her mind. Somewhat to her surprise, Robert had managed the visit of his friends for the weekend with considerable aplomb. He had gone out and done the shopping quite alone, and she had noted with interest that the quality and quantity of his purchases had exceeded her own usual standard by a long way. The cooking on Saturday and Sunday had been done with much hilarity and huge success by Marcia Bolt, with massive assistance from Robert, and her husband Jim. They had greatly enjoyed and appreciated Robert's wonderful fruit and vegetables and salads, and had rushed about with baskets picking anything ripe, like sodding Marie Antoinette playing at milk-maids, Kate had thought sourly, peering through her spotty studio window. She had appeared at mealtimes, and had smilingly endured a good deal of heavy badinage on the subject of women's liberation. As a revenge, she had smilingly left them all the washing-up. Infuriatingly, the sounds of good-tempered laughter accompanied even that gruesome chore, leaving Kate with a mixed feeling of guilt and annoyance at feeling guilty. On Sunday evening she was lurking in the bathroom over the front door when the Bolts left, and heard the goodbyes through the half-open window.

'Don't know where she's got to, I'm afraid.'

'Oh, well, say goodbye for us, and thanks so much,' said Jim.

'Poor old Robert,' said Marcia. 'Keep your pecker up, darling.'

Robert had murmured something inaudible and the Bolts had driven away with much scrunching of gravel and tooting of the horn in the lane.

Kate stared at her funny arthritic hands, with their square nails, cut short but still chipped and cracked by constant wetting and contact with clay.

'I won't go back, I won't,' she said angrily. 'Why should I put up with their boring middle-class values, and conservative, politically correct opinions? I'll give

Jeffrey a ring and see if he can put me up for a couple of nights, while I sort myself out.' She drove round to Cheyne Walk and parked the car. She found a phone box, and telephoned Jeffrey's office. He was engaged, said Sharon, could she take a message? Kate left her message, and then drove round to St Loo Avenue to await Jeffrey's return. She parked her van just behind his lovely Mercedes. I'm having good luck with the parking holes today, she thought, grinning at the passing car she had just carved up. She switched off the engine, looked at her watch, and then settled herself for a nice little sleep, while she waited for Jeffrey to come home.

Anna sat at her worktable and contemplated her unrestored cherub. He was encased in a thick coat of damp papier mâché, in which he had lain overnight to soften the badly damaged gilt and gesso. His twin, now completely restored and gilded, and subtly distressed, rested on his padded cradle, gleaming in a weak shaft of sunlight. Anna began to peel away the papier mâché from his body and wings, revealing the crumbling, softened gilt and gesso underneath. Then she picked up the special little knife she used for this stage of the work, and gently and painstakingly began to scrape back to the original wood.

Josh and Olivia had gone back to school, so she had at last been able to get on with her work, and deal with her mail and messages. She had telephoned Axel, and he was bringing his client, Mr Yamamoto, to see the completed cherub this afternoon. Anna was quite surprised that Axel was prepared to show the pair half finished: usually the business of restoration was a closely guarded secret, dealers apparently feeling that they could charge more if they could pass a piece off as being in its original state, or at any rate, with only the patina of time on it. Maybe Mr Yamamoto was himself a dealer? She had telephoned the doctor's surgery and made an appointment to see Dr Muswell. She had also telephoned British Telecom and asked them to install an extension phone in her bedroom. Patrick telephoned every night, quite late, and it was difficult to talk privately in her tiny house, with the television on and the children around, trying to look as if they weren't listening.

Since the return to London, Anna had felt curiously cut off from Patrick, and he seemed in a sense further away than when he had left her in Souliac, and somehow unreal. Thank God for the telephone, she thought, smiling. Each night when his call came and she heard his voice, so warm and near and reassuring, she felt again the excitement and certainty of the past two weeks, and longed to be with him. She knew that it was not going to be simple, or easy. In the first place, Josh and Olivia couldn't be uprooted and taken off to Paris at a moment's notice. Josh especially was at a critical time at school, and would be taking his A-levels next summer. In any case, neither of them would necessarily feel that they should leave their background and their friends and follow her to Paris. In the second place, it was obvious that Jeffrey was going to fight her tooth and nail every step of the way. Though God knows why, after all these years, she thought. Just sour grapes, I suppose.

Scraping the old gesso out of her angel's eyes, she thought of their return to the Lifeboat in Jeffrey's car, and nearly laughed aloud as she remembered his fury when he realized that Mrs Taylor had done Anna's shopping for her, and that she had two legs of lamb. She had done her best to behave civilly towards Jeffrey, and had offered him tea, but he had declined and had helped himself to whisky from the bottle he had left behind the night before. He had stood at the window, staring moodily at the churchyard, while Josh and Olivia took the bags upstairs, and then rather self-consciously said

162

they were going for a walk. Rats, thought Anna, as they clumped down the stairs, leaving her alone with Jeffrey. She had poured herself a mug of tea and sat down at the worktable, and picked up the pile of mail. She had come to the thick white envelope with the French stamp just as Jeffrey turned round from the window. Her heart had leapt when she saw it, but she had put it carefully on the bottom of the pile, and replaced the letters on the table.

'Aren't you going to open your letters?' Jeffrey had said, coldly.

'No, I'll open them later.'

'Please yourself,' said Jeffrey, reddening.

'Jeffrey,' said Anna, 'what is all this about? Why are you here?'

'Because,' said Jeffrey, 'Josh and Olivia are my children, and you are my wife, for better or worse, remember? And I want to make things all right between us.'

'And how exactly do you propose to do that?'

'Well, for a start, I've made an appointment for us to see a counsellor, next week. It's a service called, 'Crisis in the Family'.

'You've done what?' Anna had stared at him incredulously. 'You can't be serious.'

'I'm perfectly serious. The appointment is next week, Thursday at three thirty. Please make a note of it, I'll collect you here at three o'clock.'

For a moment Anna had been speechless with shock and fury. Then she had got to her feet and opened the front door. 'Please go, Jeffrey, and don't come here again without making an appointment. If you want to see a marriage guidance counsellor, by all means do, God knows you have a lot to learn about marriage, you rotten little shit. But don't try to drag me into your silly games.'

Jeffrey had put down his glass and walked to the door. He was tempted to hit Anna as hard as he could, and wipe the expression of contempt off her face, but had felt that such an action might be counter productive at this juncture.

'I'll be in touch,' he had said quietly, and had gone downstairs to his car in what he hoped was a dignified manner. Anna had closed the door behind him, and leaned against it, her eyes shut, until she heard the Mercedes drive away. Then she crossed to the table, extracted Patrick's letter from the pile, and went upstairs to her bedroom. She took off her shoes and lay down on her bed. She switched on the bedside lamp and held the letter to her face for a moment. Then she opened it and read it, over and over again.

When the children came in, they were surprised not to find her in the kitchen or the workroom.

'Mum?' Josh called.

'I'm here,' Anna called back.

Josh appeared at her door, his face anxious. 'You all right, Mum?'

'I'm fine, just tired, darling.'

'Has Dad been foul to you?'

'Oh, just the usual,' said Anna, opening her eyes and smiling at him. She sat up briskly. 'We must get the supper on. What shall we have?'

'How about leg of lamb?' said Josh, and they had fallen about with laughter.

'Oh, Josh, what a comfort you are,' she had said weakly, wiping the tears from her eyes.

Anna finished scraping back the cherub, brushed away all the loose bits, and then cleaned the wood with methylated spirit. She removed all the rubbish carefully from the worktable, and hoovered the floor round it. Then she went downstairs to the garage to make a fresh batch of rabbitskin glue.

Josh came out of school at five o'clock, strapped his briefcase onto the carrier of his bike, and set off home. He crossed Hammersmith Bridge, pushing

164

his bike along the footpath, and then cycled slowly along the north bank towards Chiswick, dismounting and walking over the one-way sections. He loved the river, and found it a peaceful place to walk when he needed to think things out. After the long, hot weeks at Estagnol and Souliac, it seemed really weird to be back in grey old London again, and the Lifeboat seemed terribly cramped and poky after the presbytery.

Olly had told him the riveting news about Mum and Patrick, and after the first surprise he had felt rather glad for her. He just wished that he had got back in time to meet Patrick, but for the moment he had to take Olly's word for it that he was 'very OK'. Some time ago, he had begun to realize that after he and Olivia had left home, Anna and Jeffrey would probably split up completely, and had wondered what would happen then. He supposed Anna would go to Souliac; he never really got further than that in his mind. As for Jeffrey, his feelings about him were mixed, and on the whole negative. He knew that his father thought him a mummy's boy and a wimp because he helped Anna with the housework, went to the supermarket for her sometimes, and made sure that she didn't carry very heavy things up the stairs. Josh himself felt that he was only doing what a more normal, and resident, father would have done as a matter of course. He did not, however, say this to Jeffrey when he made his snide little remarks during the boring Sunday lunches that they were forced to endure nearly every weekend. None the less, Josh was a kind-hearted boy, and it pained him to see Jeffrey's gauche attempts at reconciliation.

'Too late, sunshine,' he said to the river, 'the bird has flown.'

When he reached Chiswick Steps, he wheeled his bike down to the water's edge. The tide was ebbing. Oily swirls of filthy water spread greasy slicks on the gull-puddled mudflats, and in midstream chunks of battered polystyrene bobbed along the surface towards the sea, or piled up against the moorings of the craft that lay at anchor. Josh leaned on his handlebars and inhaled the smell of the rotting Thames. He knew that whatever happened to him in his life, or wherever he went, the river smell would always mean home to him. His earliest memory was probably wading in his gumboots along the Mall with his grandfather, when the spring tide had flooded the road. The swans had swum along, proud and hissing in front of them as they sloshed along. He had held very tightly to Grandpa's hand, and had been secretly quite relieved when it was time to go to the Lifeboat and have tea with Mum and the baby Olivia. Suddenly Josh remembered the card he had sent to Grandpa and Kate from Estagnol. He thought he had promised to go down to Boulter's for the weekend. It occurred to him now that very likely Mum would be glad if he and Olly took off for a couple of nights, to give her a chance to see Patrick alone. I'll talk to her when I get home, he said to himself, and ring Grandpa tonight.

He cycled the last few metres up Church Street to the Lifeboat, and put his bike in the garage, which was smelling of warm glue mixed with the petrolly smell of the old Renault. Maybe Mum would let him take the car to Sussex? That would be great. Josh got out his latchkey to let himself into the house. The key refused to work, and he tried again, without success. He rang the bell and then stood back, looking up at the kitchen window. The blind shot up and he saw Anna's face peering down. He waved, and then heard her running down the stairs to open the door.

'Sorry, Josh,' she said, 'I had the locks changed.'

'Crikey!' said Josh.

'It's OK,' she said, 'I've got several sets of keys. Come on up, Axel's here with Mr Yamamoto.'

Josh followed her upstairs, and was friendly and polite to the visitors, who were having a glass of wine with Anna. It was the white wine that his father had provided, Josh noted with amusement.

Then he mumbled something about having a load of prep, and went up to his room.

Jeffrey walked down St Loo Avenue, and saw Kate's van parked behind his car. He had been given her message by Sharon, and found himself quite pleased that she was to stay for a night or two, though the idea of giving up his comfortable bed to her, and sleeping on the sofa, did not greatly appeal. Still, he was fond of her, and maybe she would lend a sympathetic ear to his problems. God knows, he thought, she has plenty of experience of the bloody Hamilton family. As he drew level with the van, he saw Kate slumped in the driving seat, fast asleep. He bent down and tapped on the window, waking her at once. She looked up, pink-faced, and smiled at him.

'Hope you don't mind me invading you, darling,' she said cheerfully, as she got stiffly out.

'Not at all, delighted to see you,' said Jeffrey, holding the door for her.

'My, you look smart,' she said, kissing him.

'Just the working gear,' said Jeffrey, feeling complimented, none the less.

He unlocked the street door, and they climbed the stairs to the first floor. Jeffrey opened his flat door and they went in. His hall was square, and lit by a window looking over the deep well at the back of the flats. He used it as a dining-room, and a round table covered with a green baize cloth stood in the centre of the thick oatmeal carpet, surrounded by three Chippendale chairs with tapestry-covered seats. The walls were panelled with limed oak, and were hung with a few of Anna's watercolours in gilded frames.

'Tea, or a drink?' said Jeffrey, putting his briefcase, hat and umbrella away in the cupboard concealed in the panelling.

'Um,' said Kate, 'is it too early for a drink?'

'Certainly not,' said Jeffrey. 'Whisky?'

'Great,' said Kate, 'but first, I'd better nip out and buy a toothbrush, I haven't brought anything with me at all.'

'No need,' said Jeffrey, pouring whisky. 'There's a spare one in the bathroom cabinet.'

'Thanks. I suppose I'd better phone Robert and tell him I'm not coming back for a day or two.'

'Yes, of course,' said Jeffrey. 'It's in here.'

They went into the sitting-room, the original studio, with its high floor-to-ceiling windows, and the gallery housing Jeffrey's bed and chest of drawers. The room was spacious and light, and was dominated by a long sofa covered in a thick natural linen, and piled with cushions made from faded Aubusson carpets, heavily fringed in beige silk. Tall, grey marble table lamps with big cream shades stood on either side of the sofa, on black lacquer coffee tables. Books and magazines were stacked in neat piles, and the severity of the room was softened by many green plants, a palm tree, and two weeping figs in antique terracotta pots. Under the wide windows, a bench was filled with more pots containing spindly, scented-leaf geraniums, which clawed their way up the windows to reach the light. The whole feeling of the room was reposeful and restrained.

At the foot of the stairs which led to the gallery bedroom, stood a mahogany console table with a glass top, and on it stood the telephone, directories, a diary and a silver pot containing freshly sharpened pencils.

'Help yourself,' said Jeffrey, indicating the phone. 'I'll just go and let the cat in.'

He went back to the dining-room and pushed up the window. Immediately his large, tiger-striped cat jumped down from the window sill and wound himself round Jeffrey's legs, purring noisily. He opened another secret panel which led to his microscopic galley kitchen, and the small adjacent bathroom. He opened the fridge and got out a tin of Whiskas.

Kate dialled the Boulter's number. It was engaged. She replaced the receiver and took a good swallow of her whisky, wandering round the room with the glass in her hand. How tidy Jeffrey is, she thought, everything is so cunningly thought out, plenty of storage, all hidden behind secret panels. Not like an architect's house, all room and no cupboards to speak of. It was as if they couldn't bear to part with a single centimetre of visible space. Over the Chippendale-style fireplace, which faced the sofa, and had logs in it, fired, Kate observed, by a gas pipe, hung a large watercolour of Josh and Olivia as very young children, presumably the work of their mother. Kate did not particularly like Anna, thought her spoilt and tiresome, and beneath the little girl exterior, quite like her mother. She re-dialled the number, and Robert answered at once.

'Robert?'

'Who else?' said Robert, drily.

'It's me, Kate. Just to say that I'm staying with Jeffrey for a couple of nights.' There was a pause. 'I've got a new order to discuss,' she added, feebly. She did not know why she bothered to lie to Robert.

'Very well,' said Robert. 'See you when you're ready to come home.'

'Yes,' said Kate, uncertainly, 'fine. Who was that on the phone before me?'

'Oh,' said Robert, 'it was Mary. She was asking us to go and take pot-luck with them, but I said I was waiting for you.'

'Well, you can go now, can't you?'

'Yes,' said Robert, 'I will. I'll ring them back, now. Good night, my dear.' He hung up before she could reply.

She put the phone down, slightly annoyed that he was amusing himself, but glad not to be feeling guilty. 'Jeff,' she called, 'all done. Now, I'm going to take us out to dinner. Where's a nice place that won't cost an arm and a leg?'

Jeffrey, the cat in his arms, came into the room, looking thoughtful. Where was a nice place, cosy and dark, where you could take an older relative and tell her all your troubles? 'There's a little restaurant I sometimes go to, quite quiet, good food, no music.'

'Sounds perfect,' said Kate, who would have preferred something more lively-sounding.

'I'll book a table, shall I?' said Jeffrey. 'Half eight?'

'Great.' She sat down on the sofa, suddenly feeling quite tired.

At a quarter to nine they had settled themselves into a far corner of the basement restaurant, womb-like with its dark, crimson painted walls and total lack of daylight. The tables had red leather banquettes and were lit by low, pink silk-shaded lamps, which illuminated the food and very little else. The waiter brought a bottle of house red and a plate of *crudités*. He lit the solitary candle and left them to study the menu.

'I'm going to have gambas and a steak,' said Jeffrey. 'What about you?'

'Calf's liver and onions with rosemary sounds nice.'

'Aren't you afraid of mad-cow disease?'

'No, I'm not,' said Kate. 'And I'll have the warm duck-liver salad to start with.' She looked at Jeffrey with bright eyes. 'You see, I'm inordinately fond of offal,' she said, crunching a raw carrot. She burst into a loud laugh, and Jeffrey did the nose trick into his glass of wine. The evening had got off to a very good start.

Two hours later they sat back, replete, and Jeffrey ordered coffee and brandy. They had dispatched a second bottle of wine quite easily, finishing it with the cheese.

'Good job we came by taxi,' said Jeffrey, lighting a cigar, 'you've got me pissed.'

Kate laughed, she felt fairly pissed herself. They had each listened with sympathetic attention to the other's tale of betrayal and lack of appreciation, and both felt quite a lot better for the sharing of their problems.

'The bloody Hamiltons,' said Jeffrey. 'They're all the same. They're parasites. Look at Robert, he just

170

uses you as an unpaid housekeeper and slave to that huge house and garden. And as for Anna, she wouldn't last five minutes on her own. I've been coughing up for everything all these years, and look at the thanks I get for it. She's screwed me up properly. Her children aren't much better, they have their eyes to the main chance, selfish little brutes.'

'Poor you,' said Kate. 'I don't suppose it's much fun having the dread Domenica as a mother-in-law, either.'

'Interfering old cow,' said Jeffrey. 'I hate her guts.'

They were enjoying themselves enormously. The waiter brought the coffee and brandy, and Jeffrey asked him to phone for a taxi in fifteen minutes.

At half past eleven they climbed the stairs to Jeffrey's flat, holding on to each other and giggling like children. Jeffrey found a pair of his pyjamas for Kate, and she emerged from the bathroom ten minutes later, looking like an ancient baby, with her round pink face gleaming and her short grey hair sticking spikily out from her head.

'Hope you don't mind my sheets?' said Jeffrey. 'It's too late to change them, I haven't got the energy.'

'Don't give a damn.' Kate mounted the stairs to Jeffrey's bed, clinging to the railing as she went. She fell into bed with a groan.

Jeffrey undressed and hung up his clothes in one of his secret cupboards. Then he lay down on the sofa, making a soft pile of cushions at one end, and covering himself with a plaid rug. He tossed and turned on the hard sofa, trying to make a soft dip for his hip, without success. He sighed. 'Kate,' he said, after a moment, 'are you asleep?'

'Yes,' said Kate. 'Well, nearly.'

'It's bloody uncomfortable on this sofa.'

'OK,' said Kate, 'you'd better come up.'

The sex was a revelation to them both, especially Jeffrey. He had never really understood that you could go to bed with someone for the sheer hell of it, as a totally selfish experience. Never, in his entire life had he done anything as mad and impulsive, and he felt his anger and frustration draining away, as he lay sweating and exhausted in Kate's arms afterwards. As for Kate, she hadn't had a really proper orgasm for years, except in her head. Somehow, with Robert, there was always a slight holding back on his part, she never knew why, and never asked. Certainly, she had always been careful not to be too boisterous with him; it was always strictly the missionary position with them. Jeffrey, his face bristly on her ample bosom, gave a slight snore, and she smiled. His weight on her arm was becoming uncomfortable, and she was beginning to get pins and needles in her hand. She thought about trying to extract her arm, but was unwilling to disturb him. In any case, it was such a pleasure to prolong the physical contact, after the best blow-through she'd had in years. She stroked his back with her free hand. Eat your heart out, Robert, she thought as she fell asleep, there's more to life than freezing sodding spinach.

Anna got out of her bath and wrapped herself in her big white bath towel. She sat down on the little Strawberry Hill Gothic chair in front of the basin, brushed her hair, and put moisturiser on her face and neck. She cleaned her teeth, and then unwrapped the towel, and put on her nightdress, which hung on a hook on the back of the door. Then she padded across the bedroom, and got into bed to wait for Patrick's call. Downstairs, she could just hear the television, it would be Josh, watching *Newsnight*.

It had been quite a good day. The work had gone well, and she had got the first coat of gesso onto her angel. Little Mr Yamamoto had been impressed with the work, and she had promised to have the second piece finished by the end of the month. Axel had seemed pleased with her, and this had been reassuring. He had always been patient and understanding, but Anna often feared he would finally consider her too unreliable, and go to someone else. The man from BT had installed her extension phone, and a locksmith from Chiswick had changed the lock on the street door. Anna had always wondered whether Jeffrey poked around the place in her absence, or might just walk in at any time, but she had to remind herself that up to now she had always been desperately hoping that he would do just that. When she thought about it, she was astonished at how long she had gone on clinging to a lost cause, and equally how quickly and completely she had walked away from the situation. When did it happen, she asked herself. Was it when they were having dinner under the fig tree on the first night of Giò's and Patrick's visit to Souliac? She remembered Patrick saying that he loved owls. Then Jeffrey had telephoned to bully her about not finishing the gilding job before she went on holiday, and she had put the phone down on the table and gone downstairs again, leaving him nagging away to the airwaves. She remembered sitting down next to Patrick, and pouring herself a glass of wine, and Domenica saying 'Well?' and herself replying 'Well, nothing', and really meaning it.

There was a tap on the bedroom door and Josh poked his head round.

'Can I come in, Mum?'

'Yes, of course,' said Anna.

He came into the room, and sat on the foot of the bed. 'Mum,' he said shyly, 'I hope you won't mind, but Olly and I have been thinking. Would it be a good idea if she and I went to Grandpa's one weekend soon, so that your Patrick could come and see you?'

Anna looked at her son with love as he stared, red-faced, at his feet.

'Darling Josh, it would be tremendously kind, what a wonderful idea,' she said.

He looked up, relieved that he had not been stupid or insensitive. 'Oh, good,' he said. 'Brilliant. Just let me know when you want us to go and I'll phone Grandpa.' The phone rang by Anna's bed. 'That'll be him.' Josh got to his feet. 'Good night, Mum.' He left the room, closing the door behind him. Anna lifted the telephone and lay back on her pillows. 'Hello,' she said softly.

'Hello, my darling,' said Patrick. 'How are you?'

'Apart from missing you, my love, I'm all right.'

'It's the same for me. I so wish you were here; it gets worse every day, worst still every night.'

'Patrick,' said Anna, 'I've got something really nice to tell you.' She told him about Josh's idea.

'Anna,' said Patrick, 'what amazing children you have. They must really care for you to think of such a thing.'

'Yes, I know. And Olivia thinks you're brilliant, she talks about you all the time. What do you think, darling? Are you free next weekend, or are you working?'

'I'm not working, and I could be with you on the late plane on Friday,' he said.

'I was wondering,' said Anna, 'whether perhaps this first time I could come to you? This little house is so full of bad memories and unhappiness. I would really love to come to Paris, it would be an escape for me.'

'Anna, my dearest girl,' said Patrick, 'nothing would give me greater happiness.'

'Are you really sure I wouldn't be treading on your sad memories? I would hate to do that.'

'Thirty years is a very long time, and in any case Marie-France, if she knows, will be happy for us, she was that kind of person.'

'If you're sure?'

'I'm very sure. Tell me which plane you'll arrive on, and I'll meet you at the airport. Oh, Anna, I can hardly believe you'll be with me in a few days.'

Anna's eyes filled with tears. 'Nor can I,' she said, her nose blocking.

'Anna, my love, are you crying?'

'Yes.' Anna laughed shakily, 'From happiness.' She blew her nose. 'That's better,' she said.

'Good,' said Patrick. 'You'll start me off. What have you been doing? Where are you now?'

'I'm in bed. The man came and put in a phone by my bed, so that I can talk to you more privately.'

'Good idea, what else?'

'Had the lock on the front door changed.'

'Anna! What courage! Aren't you afraid of a huge row?'

'Not really, Josh is here at night-time. I'm sick of Jeffrey going through my things and listening to my answerphone.'

'Quite right, good girl.'

She told him about Axel and Mr Yamamoto, and he told her that he had been out for a drink with Giò, who had sent her his love.

'If I see him before the weekend, I won't tell him you're coming. You can decide later whether you want to see him, or whether we'd rather be alone.'

'I wish we were alone now,' said Anna, 'here, in my bed.'

'Anna, don't wind me up,' said Patrick, laughing.

'Is it so easy?'

'Very.'

Chapter Ten

The next evening Josh telephoned Robert at Boulter's. Anna had told him that she had decided to go to Paris and stay with Patrick, so there was no need to go to Boulter's if he and Olly would rather stay in London on their own.

'What,' said Josh, 'and cook Sunday lunch for Dad? Forget it. If Grandpa can have us, we'll go.' He was, in any case, greatly looking forward to the chance of driving the car.

Robert answered the phone, and was delighted to hear Josh's voice. 'Kate's away for a few days,' he said cheerfully, 'but I'm sure we'll manage very well without her, don't you? I'd love to hear all about your holiday, and Souliac. Bring your photographs if you have any.'

'Ace,' said Josh, 'I'll do that. Mum sends her love. She's off to Paris for the weekend, so I can have the car.'

'Jolly good,' said Robert. 'Work, is it? Or going to see Giò?'

'Yeah,' said Josh, 'bit of both, probably.'

'Well, old chap; see you about eightish, Friday?'

'Great, see you then, Grandpa. 'Bye.'

''Bye,' said Robert, and hung up.

Josh put down the phone, making a mental note to tell Olivia not to mention Patrick to Grandpa until Mum said they could.

On Friday morning Anna kept the appointment to see her doctor. Or rather, she arrived just before the specified time, and waited for forty minutes before her name was called. This procedure always irritated her, and compared unfavourably with the system in France, where you were treated as a valued paying customer, with punctuality and courtesy. In England, the women in the reception area appeared to maintain the deeply held belief that the patients were a thorough-going nuisance, and must be kept from the doctors as long as possible, preferably altogether, if they had anything to do with it. The doctors themselves were not as hostile as their watchdogs, but they did not, on the whole, display the same interest in their patients' health as their counterparts in France usually did. Anna was sure that the chief reason for this state of affairs was that in France you pay at once for treatment and drugs, and claim the bulk of the charges back from the State. Equally, in France, if you did not like your doctor, you simply changed him. In England, you did not pay the doctor, and many patients received their drugs free, the implication being that the service was a charity, which Anna knew to be far from the case. She wondered, as she looked around the dreary waiting-room at the depressed, pasty-faced, patiently waiting British sick, what would happen if she brought along a piece of gessoed carved wood, and cleared a space on the table carrying dog-eared old copies of *Woman's Own*, and began cutting back the gesso with her lethally sharp little tools, while she waited.

At last her name was called, and she went through the frosted-glass swing door to the badly-lit corridor, leading to the individual doctors' doors. Her doctor's door was number three, labelled 'Dr Muswell'. She knocked, annoyed at being intimidated into doing so (presumably he was expecting her, so would not be changing his trousers?)

'Come,' said a muffled voice, and Anna entered the poky, overheated room. The doctor remained seated.

'Mrs Wickham, isn't it? Yes.' He shuffled the papers on his desk.

Anna sat down on the chair provided.

'I don't seem to have your notes.' He pressed a button, and spoke into an intercom. 'Hester, I don't seem to have Mrs Wickham's notes. Would you mind?' He regarded Anna with a faint smile, benign behind his spectacles. He was a man of about her own age, possibly a little younger. 'You're looking well, Mrs Wickham. You don't look at all in need of my services. Been to the south of France, have we?'

'As a matter of fact, I have,' said Anna, 'and as far as I know, I am very well, thank you. I am here because your secretary left several messages on my answerphone telling me to make an appointment to see you.'

'Oh,' said Dr Muswell, looking slightly nonplussed, 'I see.'

The door opened and the secretary bustled in with the notes, and put them on the desk in front of the doctor. She left without an apology, muttering about being very busy this morning.

He flicked quickly through Anna's notes, and then said, 'Ah, yes, of course, Mrs Wickham,' as if he had just remembered who she was. He read the notes more carefully, and then leaned back in his chair.

'Mrs Wickham, I have the report on your scan. It appears that there may be a possibility of your having fibroids. This would account for some of the problems you have been experiencing with your menstrual cycle.'

'I am not particularly surprised,' said Anna. 'If you consult your notes, you will see that I have been complaining of heavy periods for quite some time now.'

'Ah, well,' said Dr Muswell, 'these things often take time to manifest themselves.' He hoped that she was not going to suggest that the problem could have been diagnosed sooner. He hurried on: 'I will make an appointment for you to see the gynaecologist, as soon

178

as possible, and he will decide what action, if any, is necessary.' He wrote briefly on her notes. 'I'll send you a note when we have made the appointment for you.' He stood up and, edging past her chair, opened the door. 'Goodbye, Mrs Wickham,' he said, smiling as she passed him. 'Family all well? Good, good.'

Anna walked out of the surgery without bothering to say goodbye to the women in the reception. They did not even notice her leaving; they were having their coffee. As she walked down the mean little street to the bus-stop, it began to rain.

'God, I hate this place,' she said to no-one in particular, quickening her step. The bus overtook her and she ran, leaping onto the platform as it pulled away from the stop.

Jeffrey had departed for the office at ten to nine, after a rather giggly breakfast eaten standing in his minute kitchen, where there was barely enough room for one person, let alone two, one of them quite broad in the beam. Much to his surprise, he did not have a headache, and felt remarkably cheerful after his bizarre night of passion. He swung his umbrella as he walked briskly to the bus-stop, and rather hoped that Kate would stay on for a few nights. At this particular juncture, he felt that their association was very therapeutic. He began to plan the evening. He would buy some nice wine at lunchtime, and maybe go to Harrod's food hall on his way home and get something for dinner. Veal chops, or some wild salmon, nothing too elaborate to cook. He thought it would be better to eat in rather than go out again to a restaurant. Much less expensive, for a start, and one avoided the extravagance of taxis, too. Deep down, Jeffrey knew that he was also anxious not to run into anyone he knew, and they all tended to use the same clubs and restaurants. The idea of introducing Kate as his stepmother-in-law gave him a feeling of guilt and slight shame, as if he had committed some obscene act. He knew this to be a ridiculous idea, but none the less, the thought remained in his mind.

Kate had spent the first part of the morning in estate agents' offices in the King's and Fulham Roads, trying to find a not-too-expensive studio to rent. Then she looked at three possible places. Two of them were lovely big posh studios with north-facing light, the other a grubby little basement flat down a flight of area steps, not really a studio at all, though half the rent of the other two. She told the negotiator she would think it over and get back to them later, and then drove her little van round to the Potter. It took her quite a time to find a space, ending up in a little side street some distance from the pub. But she enjoyed the walk, lifting her face to the thin fine rain that hit the warm pavement, releasing a spicy, pungent smell as it laid the dust. She felt young and light-hearted as she headed towards her pub lunch, and thought with amusement of her night on the tiles with Jeffrey. What a weirdo, she thought. He may be a clever chap, and make tons of money and own a sexy motor-car, but I bet I could teach him a thing or two about love. Not that love had had anything to do with their activities of the previous night. He could be quite good, with a bit of practice, she said to herself as she pushed open the side door and headed for the bar. Ted was already ensconced on a stool, and she gave him a friendly thump as she joined him.

'Hello, old girl, what'll you have?' said Ted.

'It's my shout, what'll *you* have?' said Kate.

'Guinness, thanks,' said Ted. 'For strength,' he added, leering at her.

'I could do with a bit of strength meself,' said Kate, laughing. 'I think I'll stick to gin though.' She ordered the drinks, and looked at the lunch menu chalked up on a blackboard. 'Shepherd's Pie, chips and baked beans,' she read out. 'Sounds great, and only one ninety.'

'Sadly,' said Ted, 'I shall have to forego the beans. I've been farting like a trooper all morning as it is. Shouldn't have had the vindaloo last night.'

'Shame,' said Kate, downing half her gin.

'What you been up to, then?' said Ted, as they carried their plates to a table and sat down.

Kate told him about her morning's viewings of studios, and asked his advice about rents. He studied the particulars with interest.

'Rip-off merchants, the lot of them,' he said, handing the papers back, and picking up his knife and fork again.

'Do you really think so? After twenty odd years, I've no idea how much rents are now.'

'Well, the studios look all right, but they're a frightful rent. It's those bastards who buy them to turn into arty flats that are the trouble,' said Ted, cramming bread into his mouth and chomping noisily.

'I know,' said Kate, 'I slept in one last night. It belongs to my stepson-in-law,' she added primly.

'There you are then,' said Ted. 'Those are the people you're up against. As for the other one, the basement, it looks a real hole.'

'Hell,' Kate agreed. 'So it's back to the drawing board.'

'Not necessarily,' said Ted, filling his mouth with Shepherd's Pie, 'You can share with me if you like. I don't need all my space, and I could do with the money. What do you think?'

'I think thanks very much, Ted,' said Kate. 'Are you still in the same place?'

'Certainly am,' said Ted, grinning. 'It hasn't changed a bit, just like me.'

'Still no heating?'

'Still bloody cold in winter, and like a furnace in summer,' said Ted, mopping up gravy with a lump of bread. 'Mind you, if you pay half the expenses, we could probably afford to make some improvements. Might even put a bath in.'

'You're on,' said Kate. 'When can I move in?'

'Any time you like,' said Ted. 'Don't you want to have a look at it?'

'No need,' said Kate, 'I remember it perfectly.'

'I remember you perfectly,' said Ted, and they smiled at each other, very tenderly.

Kate arrived back at St Loo Avenue at seven o'clock, to find Jeffrey preparing dinner in the kitchen. She and Ted had spent the afternoon in the Tate Gallery and had then gone back to Ted's studio for a cup of tea. They had settled without fuss the terms of their sharing the studio and Kate had agreed to move in on the first of October.

Jeffrey poured her a glass of chilled wine and she sat on a chair in the dining-room, talking to him through the kitchen door.

'Well, Jeffrey,' she said, 'I've done it.'

'Done what?' he asked, wrapping the salmon in foil.

'I've arranged to share a studio in Chelsea. I'm going to move back to London. I'm pissed of with being buried in the boring country. I can't wait to get back and start living properly again.'

'Great idea,' said Jeffrey, 'but how will you afford it? Aren't rents quite prohibitive now?' He opened the oven door and put his foil-wrapped fish on the lower shelf, closing the door gently.

'You're damn right they are,' said Kate cheerfully.

'So how will you manage? Surely potting doesn't pay that well?' He poured himself some wine and topped up her glass.

'Well,' said Kate, 'I reckon Robert can cough up. He owes me for twenty-five years hard labour at his precious house.'

'But surely Robert only has his house and his pension? How could he possibly afford it?'

'If he takes that line I shall divorce him.' Kate's eyes were suddenly cold and hard. 'Then he'll be forced to sell the bloody place, and I shall get half the proceeds, which I imagine will be a not inconsiderable sum.'

'True,' said Jeffrey, 'but it seems rather a dire thing to do, doesn't it?' He walked over to the big window in the studio room and began dead-heading the geranium, his mind preoccupied with the awful prospect of his children's inheritance disappearing into alimony and the pockets of lawyers.

'Do you really think so, Jeffrey?' said Kate, very quietly. 'Isn't that exactly what you will do to Anna when the children leave home?'

'Certainly not,' said Jeffrey, reddening. 'What on earth gave you that idea?'

'Oh,' said Kate, 'Robert seems to think it's a foregone conclusion.'

'Does he indeed?' Jeffrey looked at his watch. 'The supper will be about half an hour. Would you like a bath? There's plenty of hot water.'

'Good idea,' said Kate. 'I will, thanks.' She held out her glass for a refill, and went into the bathroom, locking the door behind her.

Jeffrey laid the table carefully, and made a salad. The potatoes were simmering nicely, giving off a pleasant smell of mint. Deliberately, he tried to forget the conversation he had just had, but at the back of his mind he was quite appalled at the ferocity of women when they turn against their men. He thought about his escapade with Kate last night, and suddenly felt a deep revulsion, both with her and with himself. After all, Robert was his father-in-law, it had been a betrayal of some sort, whichever way you looked at it. He took the fish out of the oven, and left it to rest on top of the stove. He put plates in the oven to warm. The cat mewed to be let in, but Jeffrey thought better not till after dinner. He sighed, and took a sip of his drink. Better not get pissed again, he thought, I don't want a repeat performance of last night. It'll have to be the bloody sofa.

He tapped at the bathroom door. 'Ready, Kate?'

'Yes, just coming.' She came out of the bathroom, letting out clouds of scented steam. 'Jeffrey,' she said, 'I've been thinking. I've got such a lot to sort out, and think about. I think I'll push off after dinner, and drive down to Boulter's.'

'Oh,' said Jeffrey, taken aback. 'Really? Are you sure?'

'Quite sure.'

'Well, perhaps, if you think it best.'

Anna sat in front of her bathroom mirror, drying her hair. Her overnight bag was packed, and lay on her bed, waiting for the last minute additions. She had decided to take the absolute minimum of clothes so that she would not have to wait for her bag at Charles de Gaulle airport, but could go straight through passport control to Patrick.

Josh and Olivia had departed for Sussex in the old Renault, with strict instructions not to let it overheat, and a large plastic jerrican of water in the boot in case it did. They had discussed with her the matter of prep, and had decided to leave Boulter's after lunch on Sunday, in order to get home in plenty of time to get it done. They had also decided, though they had not told Anna, to drive out to Heathrow and meet her plane. Josh did not want her to have the hassle and expense of a taxi, and in any case it would be fun.

Anna switched off the drier and gave her hair a good brushing, with her head bent over her knees. Then she straightened up, flicking her hair back over her shoulders as she did so. It looked glossy, and thicker than usual, and she smiled at her reflection. She applied a small amount of brown eye shadow from a fat soft pencil, and lipgloss to her mouth. She was wearing a new, thin white T-shirt, which emphasised her tan, still unfaded and golden. She put on her best pale-blue stone-washed jeans, and her polished black loafers. Round her waist she slotted her soft black leather Italian belt with a plain silver buckle. Her fine wool Armani jacket, toast-coloured with olive green window-pane checks lay on the bed beside her overnight bag.

She looked at her watch: nearly half past six. She had ordered a taxi for seven o'clock, in plenty of time for her check-in at Heathrow, at seven fifty-five. She put the last bits and pieces in her bag and closed it. Then she walked round the bathroom and bedrooms, checking all the windows. She went back to her bedroom and checked her handbag, tickets, passport, keys, money. She slipped on her jacket, picked up her bags and went downstairs to wait for the taxi.

Robert drove down Boulter's Lane with the back of the Morris Traveller full of supermarket bags. He was rather appalled at the amount of money he had spent on meat, French bread, biscuits and cakes, coffee, tea, fresh orange juice, yoghurt and cheese, and a lot of other things he thought might give pleasure to his grandchildren. At least he had not had to buy fruit or vegetables, and when he noticed the prices of these things was amazed at how costly they had become. Perhaps, he thought, he should consider selling his surplus stuff. There was always such a lot of it, it was becoming quite a problem. Deep down, he knew very well that his efforts at self-sufficiency had become a burden to Kate, but he couldn't really think of a satisfactory answer that would suit them both. At the same time, he couldn't help thinking her ungrateful and obstinate. After all, not many women had the chance to live in such a place, in such a lovely old house, in such a perfect setting. Surely the extra effort required to maintain it all was more than worth the necessary sacrifices?

He drove into the yard and parked by the kitchen door. He carried all the bags into the kitchen and unloaded everything onto the tiled worktop. Then he put everything away in the fridge and cupboards, except the beef, which was to form the basis of dinner.

He extracted Kate's dog-eared copy of Elizabeth David's *French Provincial Cooking* from the little row of cookbooks by the Aga, and looked up *Boeuf à la Bourguignonne*. He read the recipe carefully, checking the ingredients and setting them out on the counter in an orderly manner, ready to start cooking. 'Marinate for three to six hours', said the recipe. Oh. Robert looked at his watch. Nearly midday. Well, he thought, if I marinate the beef for four hours, that should do, that will leave plenty of time for the cooking if we don't eat till half past eight or so. He cut up the beef as directed, putting it in a china dish, covered it in wine, sliced onions, herbs, olive oil and pepper, and gave it a stir. He stretched cling-film over the dish as he had seen Kate do, and left it on the work-top. He arranged the rest of the vegetables, the baby onions and button mush-rooms, more herbs and garlic, ready for the cooking later, and made half a pint of beef stock from a cube. He looked at his watch again: nearly quarter to one. Lunch, he thought, and cut a large hunk of Cheddar cheese and treated himself to a couple of fat slices of French bread. He opened a can of lager, and sat down at the table to have his lunch, and read *The Spectator*.

He had a short nap after lunch, and then listened to *The Archers* on the radio. He despised himself for doing this, he thought it terrible rubbish, but went on listening just the same. Just until that woman has got herself sorted out, he thought, then I'll stop listening. But he knew he would not. When it had finished, he washed up his glass and plate, and went out into the garden. He dug up a basket of potatoes, cut a cos lettuce and a frilly red-edged one, couldn't remem-ber the name, the label had disappeared, and picked some parsley and rocket. In the greenhouse he selected three beautiful, warm Marmande tomatoes, grown from seed sent by Domenica from France. He held them to his nose, sniffing the deliciously pungent, fresh-picked smell. It was a shame, the basil had rather gone over, but he took a few leaves of what remained.

At four o'clock he started on the cooking proper, and at four forty-five he transferred the dish from bubbling on top of the Aga to the slow oven. So far so good, he thought. He made himself a cup of tea. Really, he felt quite tired. He sat down and drank his tea. He would check the bedrooms and pick some flowers for the table. It would have to be dahlias, there wasn't much else just now, except Michaelmas daisies. The potatoes were so fresh and good that they only needed a rinse under the tap before boiling, so that just left a salad to make, and a jar of plums to be opened and arranged in a dish, for pudding.

Robert thought about bringing in some logs for a fire, it was getting quite chilly in the evenings now. He sighed, and decided not to bother. If the children want a fire, they can bring in the wood and light it, he thought wearily.

By five to six he had washed the potatoes and laid the table, putting a flat glass dish with yellow dahlias floating in it, in the centre of the table, and the heavy old silver candlesticks on either side. He opened the door of the slow oven, and was pleased when a delicious smell wafted into the kitchen. He bent down and listened, to make sure it wasn't cooking too fast. It sounded fine, and he closed the door again carefully. He put plates to warm on the side of the Aga, and a dish for the potatoes. When the clock in the hall struck six Robert thankfully poured himself a stiff medicinal brandy and turned on the television news. He stretched out in his comfortable old armchair, putting his feet up on the low table in front of it. He drank his brandy and pretended to be paying attention to the news. He put down his empty glass and thought about getting another one. Better not, he thought, I'll wait until seven. Anna Ford is lovely, he thought, same name as my Anna, she's lovely too. That shit Jeffrey, smarmy little bugger, coming down here and sucking up to Kate, he won't get a penny out of me, he thought sleepily, his eyes glazing over, and then closing.

'Hi, Grandpa. It's us, we're here,' said Josh's voice, breaking Robert's dream, and he felt a gentle hand shaking his arm. He opened his eyes, and saw the close-together blue eyes of Olivia peering anxiously into his face.

'My God, Olivia, you're here already,' he said, startled, sitting up. He sat there for a moment, coming to.

'Shall I get you a drink, Grandpa?' said Josh. 'You look pooped.'

'Well,' said Robert, stretching his stiff legs, 'I have had quite a busy day. Thanks, Josh, open some wine, dear boy, I expect you could do with a drink yourself, couldn't you? Long drive, was it?'

'It's cold in here, Grandpa. Shall I light a fire?' Olivia looked competent. How she has grown, thought Robert.

'Thank you, my darling,' he said. 'I was rather hoping that you'd take over when you got here.'

Patrick sat huddled in the corner of his taxi, on his way out to Charles de Gaulle to meet Anna. It was a beautiful evening and the scents of early autumn came through the open window, warm and leaf-smelling. He had spent the whole day and early evening cooped up in the stuffy, cramped editing room with Françoise, his editor, working on the Place des Vosges material, and was thankful to breathe clean, fresh air again. It was now ten-fifteen and he had not yet eaten, or even had a drink. Anna's plane was due just before eleven, and he felt tense with excitement at the thought that in less than an hour she would be with him. What unlooked-for-happiness she had brought him; he could still scarcely believe that it was all really happening to them both.

He had got up very early that morning, and gone out and done some shopping, so that they could go back to his apartment straight away, and have a late supper there. In the little local shops he had bought oysters, butter, eggs, prosciutto and bread, and several bottles of wine, including champagne. Rather a cliché, he thought, but after all this is a celebration, one doesn't have to be too blasé about it. Anna isn't that kind of woman, anyway.

The taxi drove up at the arrivals entrance, and Patrick got out and took out his wallet, to pay.

'Are you meeting someone, M Halard?' said the driver politely.

'Yes, I am,' said Patrick, startled. 'How do you know my name?'

'I watch your programme every Sunday. I like it very much,' said the driver, smiling. 'Would you like me to wait, and take you back into Paris?'

'Thank you, that would be very kind,' said Patrick. 'And thank you again, I'm glad you like the show.'

The taxi drove away, and Patrick walked through the doors into the arrivals building. He looked at a flight information screen, and saw that the plane from London Heathrow was on time but not yet landed. He looked at the clock: ten forty-five, five minutes to wait. He bought a paper for something to do, and pretended to read it, leaning against a pillar so that he could see both the information screen and the gate through which he expected Anna to appear. His heart was beating fast, he could feel the pulse in his neck thumping. He smiled to himself. This is ridiculous, I'm behaving like a schoolboy, he thought. He looked at the clock: ten fifty-two, and then looked at the screen just as the 'landed' sign flashed up beside Anna's flight number. Relief surged through him, and his heart began to slow down. Five minutes more, maybe ten, he thought. He opened his paper, and turned to the middle pages, and made a serious effort to read something, but it was impossible. He folded the paper and put it in his jacket pocket, to give his full attention to the arrivals gate. One or two people began to trickle through, and his heart leapt. Then he saw her, walking swiftly, carrying her little bag, looking flushed and beautiful as she threaded her way past her fellow travellers, mostly businessmen, by the look of them. Suddenly she saw him and began to run towards him. He held out his arms, and she ran into them, dropping her bag beside them as they held each other tightly for a long moment without speaking. Then she turned her face upwards towards his, and he kissed her very gently.

'My darling,' he said. 'Thank God you're here.'

'You didn't think the plane might crash?'

'I'm ashamed to say I did,' said Patrick.

'Me too,' said Anna, and they laughed.

He picked up her bag, and they headed for the exit, into the fresh air. The taxi appeared like magic, and pulled up at the kerb beside them. Patrick opened the door for Anna, and spoke to the driver. 'That was a good piece of timing, how did you manage it?'

'Ah,' said the driver, smiling, 'I have my system, sir.'

'Whatever it is, it's a good one,' said Patrick.

'Where to now, sir?'

'Pont-Neuf,' said Patrick. 'Just by Henri Quatre, please.'

'OK,' said the driver.

Patrick got in beside Anna, and the taxi pulled away from the kerb, heading back towards Paris.

'Unfortunately,' said Patrick, 'the driver turns out to be one of the secret army of my fans, which is quite a bore, because I most terribly want to kiss you.'

Anna leaned against him, relaxing for the first time all day. She felt quite light-headed and sleepy. 'Does it matter?' she said. 'About the driver, I mean? I don't suppose he's got a hidden camera in the cab, do you?'

'You don't mind?' said Patrick, turning and taking her in his arms.

'I don't mind if the whole world sees us,' said Anna, smiling. 'This is Paris, after all.'

190

Presently the taxi stopped, and the driver slid back the glass. 'The Vert-Galant, sir,' he said.

'Thanks,' said Patrick, and they got out. He paid the driver, and gave him a large tip. 'That's for being a fan, and a good chap,' he said.

The driver laughed, and took the money. He handed Patrick his card. 'Any time, you can call me,' he said. 'Be happy, both of you.'

'Goodbye, and thanks,' said Patrick and Anna, as he pulled away, with a little wave of his hand.

'Why is he called the Vert-Galant?' said Anna, as they stood looking up at the statue of Henri Quatre on his horse.

'I imagine because he loved women, sensible chap,' said Patrick. 'Come on, let's go home, I've got some stuff for supper. I hope you haven't eaten?'

'No, I haven't,' said Anna. 'I'm starving.'

They walked across the rest of the Pont-Neuf, and along the Quai des Grands-Augustins, and climbed the shabby but elegant stairway to Patrick's apartment. He opened the windows and shutters of the windows overlooking the Seine and the Ile de la Cité, and they stood for a few moments looking down at the river and the traffic far below, and the great bulk of Notre Dame, floodlit, further down the island on their right.

'This has to be the most romantic place in the world,' said Anna.

'It is, now that you're here to share it,' said Patrick. 'A drink? What would you like? White wine, red wine, champagne? Come and look in the fridge and choose.' They went into the tiny kitchen, and Patrick opened the fridge door, and Anna saw the oysters, prosciutto and cheese, and the chilled champagne.

She laughed and hugged him. 'It's lovely, just like a seduction scene in a movie.'

'Exactly,' said Patrick, laughing too, 'but who is seducing who, or is it whom?' He opened the champagne, and they went back to the sitting-room, taking the bottle with them. They sat very close together on the big sofa, drinking the cold wine, saying very little, overjoyed at being together again.

Presently Anna put down her glass on the coffee table and, turning towards Patrick, she took off his spectacles. Then she put her arms around his neck and kissed him. 'I don't know about you, my darling,' she said, 'but I don't feel hungry any more. Shall we go to bed now, and eat later?'

Patrick looked at her, his blue eyes soft with love, his mouth smiling and tender. 'What an excellent idea,' he said, and kissed her on her forehead, on her neck and on her mouth. 'The only thing is, can I have my specs back, please? I can't see you properly without them.'

'No,' said Anna, laughing and standing up. 'Much better without. You can have them back later.' She picked up the spectacles and her bag, and went into the bedroom.

Patrick picked up their glasses and the half-empty bottle and followed her, closing the door behind him.

At half past three they woke, and, putting on his spectacles, Patrick went to the kitchen. In ten minutes he came back with a tray. On it were the opened oysters, bread, butter, wedges of lemon, a plate of prosciutto and some cheese. He dumped the tray on the bed, and went back to the kitchen for the wine and glasses. When he returned, Anna was sitting, cross-legged and naked, tipping an oyster down her throat.

Patrick put down the wine, and got carefully back into the bed beside her. He stretched out his hand and stroked her breast. 'Now I'm allowed to see them,' he said. 'You have beautiful little breasts.'

'They're getting bigger lately,' said Anna, helping herself to another oyster. 'It must be because of you, dearest, darling, wonderful Patrick,' and she leaned over and gave him a salty kiss.

'God, I'm hungry,' said Patrick. 'Lay off, will you?'

'What?' said Anna. 'No repeat performance?'

'We'll see about that,' said Patrick. 'This is the in-termission.'

They ate the food hungrily, and drank most of the wine, and then Anna took the tray back to the kitchen and made some coffee. They lay in bed, drinking the coffee and talking softly, planning their life together.

'Anna,' said Patrick, 'would you like to come with me to Normandy, and meet my father?'

'When?' said Anna.

'Tomorrow,' said Patrick, 'I mean today.'

'I'd love to,' said Anna, 'very much indeed.'

They made love again, slowly and tenderly, and then slept deeply, warm and relaxed in each other's arms.

After dinner Kate offered to wash up, but Jeffrey seemed anxious to get rid of her, so she picked up her bits and pieces, said goodbye and thanks, and went down to her van. She drove round the corner into Tite Street, in case Jeffrey was looking, and parked, while she thought things out. She did not really feel like driving back to Sussex, and in any case she had had quite a few glasses of wine. I think I'll drive round to the pub and see if Ted's there, she thought. Then we'll see. She drove to Smith Street and found a parking space quite near The Chelsea Potter. In the pub, which was crowded and noisy, she found Ted sitting on his usual stool, talking to another man. She tapped him on the shoulder. He turned round and showed no surprise at all at seeing her.

'Hello, old girl,' he said, and gave her a hug, 'I was hoping you'd come back.'

On Sunday morning Jeffrey got into his car and drove out to Chiswick, to have lunch with his family as usual. It was a fine, warm September day and the leaves on the chestnut tree outside the Lifeboat were turning crisp and golden. The sun sparkled on the river, and the gulls wheeled in the clear air, screaming abuse at each other, fighting over every piece of garbage turned up at the water's edge. He sat for a moment, enjoying the sun, and regretting, not for the first time, that he no longer lived here. He walked down to the edge of Chiswick Steps and stood with the small waves breaking close to his shoes. He sniffed the melancholy river smell, and thought how extraordinarily like the country it all was. It seemed a million miles from London, except for the relentless passing of aircraft on their way to Heathrow.

He walked back up Church Street to the Lifeboat. Perhaps Josh would like to walk up to the Black Lion with him, for a drink before lunch. He took out his latchkey and inserted it in the lock. It failed to turn. Frowning, he tried again. Nothing. He pulled out the key and inspected it carefully. It looked perfectly all right. He tried once more, without success, then rang the bell. No response. He stood back and looked up at the windows. Nothing. He went to the garage doors, and peered through the slit. The car had gone.

Jeffrey walked slowly back to his car and got in. He did not feel angry yet, just numb and very lonely. Did they all three hate him so much that they couldn't even be bothered to tell him that they wouldn't be at home if he came? He looked at his watch. Nearly half twelve. There was an awful lot of Sunday still to get through. He stared at the river miserably, with unfocused eyes, and felt depression engulf him. The sun had disappeared behind a big, black cloud, and a small chill breeze ruffled the water's surface. A pleasure boat throbbed by, crowded with people, belting out an old Bony M song, the sound bouncing cheerfully over the grey waters of the river.

Jeffrey sighed and switched on the ignition. He had a brief in preparation at home, he supposed he had better go back and get on with it. He turned the car, and drove slowly back to St Loo Avenue.

Chapter Eleven

Honorine sat at her kitchen table, cutting up unripe melons into two-centimetre pieces and putting them into her large copper preserving pan, which already contained chopped tomatoes and sugar. It was hot in the dark kitchen, though a small breeze blew through the plaited string fly-screen which hung over the open door. Outside in the square the cicadas shrilled lazily in the plane trees, and she could hear the old ladies' chatter as they sat on their little hard chairs, enjoying the afternoon sun. She piled the last of the melon cubes into the pan, and carried it over to her old iron stove. She had a small gas stove, run on bottled propane, but much preferred her mother's stove, though it was hot in summer and took quite a bit of cleaning, and she had to buy in wood for it. She left the pan on the top to come slowly to the boil. In three or four hours she could begin the serious business of testing for a set.

She looked at the clock: nearly four. At six she would go over to the presbytery to start making dinner for Domenica and Giò, who was coming down on the TGV for the weekend. Honorine was glad that he was coming, she was beginning to be a bit worried about Domenica, who seemed to her to be rather quiet and depressed since Anna and the children left. She would try to speak to Giò about her worries. She had diffidently suggested to Domenica that maybe she needed a tonic, should perhaps see the doctor, but her suggestions had been totally ignored, Domenica leaving the room silently, leaving Honorine feeling rebuked.

Domenica sat in the car park, in front of Avignon station, waiting for the train bringing Giò from Paris. It was hot in the car, and she opened all the windows to try to catch a breeze, and leaned back in the seat for a moment with her eyes shut.

Poor Giò, she thought, he is disappointed about Patrick, I can tell. If only he could find the right chap; all his affairs seem to fizzle out in the end, and he won't always have me to fall back on. It's bloody lonely on your own, and I should know. She smiled rather sadly, it was pointless now to regret the past. Though I wish I had had the sense to work out for myself that it's better to have someone with you, even if you fight with them all the time. Sleeping alone in the big, empty bed, eating alone in restaurants, making all your decisions on your own, isn't what I would really recommend to anyone, except perhaps a Trappist monk. She gave a rueful laugh at her small joke. Then she opened her eyes, blinked at the sunlight, and shook her head.

'Anyway,' she said aloud, 'what am I on about? I have dear old Honorine, I can't say I'm totally alone.' None the less, she thought, she doesn't share my bed, does she? She smiled at the thought. She opened her bag, found her little silver flask, and took a good swig. Perhaps Honorine was right, she ought to see the quack and get something for depression. But she knew she would not. She took another mouthful of brandy, and screwed the cap back on just as the Paris train roared into the station. She got out of the car, and waved cheerfully when she saw Giò emerging from the crowd hurrying out of the station.

'Will you drive?' she said, after they had embraced.

'Love to,' said Giò, slinging his bag onto the back seat, and opening the passenger's door for her. He settled himself behind the wheel, adjusting the seat to suit his longer legs, and then drove out of the station towards the Nîmes road. They crossed the Rhône and headed towards Rémoulins. 'Have you planned anything?' he asked.

'No, nothing.

'Would you like to go out to dinner tonight?'

'I don't think so, darling, thanks all the same. I think Honorine is cooking something nice for us.'

Giò glanced briefly in Domenica's direction. He was surprised at her turning down an invitation to eat out. A little thing like Honorine's preparing something special had not always prevented her from accepting last-minute invitations. Oh well, he thought, I suppose she's slowing down a bit now, poor old soul. 'Whatever you like,' he said.

On Saturday morning Josh woke early and lay examining the beams of the low ceiling over his bed. Through the open casement to his right he could hear blackbirds singing in the orchard and the rattling twitter of sparrows in the mass of dusty clematis which clothed the wall beneath his window. Fresh, dew-smelling air flowed through the window and over his bed, and the sky, visible over the tops of the apple trees, was a pale pearly blue. He lay for a while, enjoying the quiet country sounds, and then got out of bed, pulling on his old jeans and a jersey. He went quietly down the ancient oak staircase with its bare, polished creaking boards and carved balusters, carrying his trainers in his hand. In the kitchen he paused for a moment to put them on, and then unbolted the garden door and let himself out.

He went down the brick path that led to the kitchen gardens, the greenhouses and hotbeds, and the fruit cages. In a high, rose-red brick wall, a faded green door was closed with a piece of baling twine in place of the original latch. It had been waiting to be repaired for the whole of Josh's conscious life, and he felt, as he pulled the string, a deep affection for the unchangingness of life at Boulter's.

Inside the walled garden the rows of vegetables and salads stretched out, with gaps where things had been harvested, and little piles of outside leaves, waiting to be gathered up and put on the compost heap. On the far wall espaliered pear trees stretched their arms along their wires, the fruit hanging ripe and golden like lanterns in the early sun. Between them, outdoor tomatoes made glowing green-and-red clumps, which spilled exuberantly over the edges of the path.

My God, thought Josh, as he wandered round feeling and smelling, there's enough to feed an army here. What do they do with it all? He picked a ripe tomato and ate it as he continued his early morning tour of the gardens. He inspected the dessert grapes ripening in the greenhouse, and the gnarled old fig tree on the outer brick wall.

Then he crossed the deep, velvety dark green lawn that stretched from end to end of the house, and was guarded by a tall old holm oak, and walked round the back of the house to the kitchen door again. He looked behind him as he turned the corner, and saw the trail of his own footsteps etched in the dewy surface of the grass.

In the kitchen, Olivia was setting the table for breakfast, while Robert fried bacon and made toast and coffee.

'Can I help?' said Josh.

'Yes,' said Robert, 'watch the toast, will you? I nearly always burn it, too many things going on at once.'

'I know the feeling,' said Josh.

Old Dr Halard said goodbye to Mme Aubry, reminded her to keep on taking the tablets, wrote a new prescription which he left on the kitchen table, and went down the garden path to his car parked in the lane outside. As he fastened his seatbelt, he glanced at the car clock: nearly ten thirty. Good, he thought, plenty of time for a bit of quiet gardening before lunch. He looked in his rear mirror, let in the clutch and drove slowly down the lane to St Gilles. He had the same

198

myopic blue eyes as his son, and the same spiky hair, though his was not cropped as closely as Patrick's, and was a good deal whiter. He was very tall, and had lost weight with age, so that he looked rather wasted in his dark doctor's clothes. But his face, sunburnt and dominated by a strong Norman nose, was strangely unlined and youthful, and full of a kindly curiosity. At seventy-seven, he was a solitary but philosophical man, with few friends and no enemies. It had been his intention to retire for some years past, but every time he tried to suggest it his patients persuaded him to carry on a bit longer, 'until someone we really trust comes along'. He did not need much persuading. After all, the patients were, in fact, the entire focus of his life.

Dr Halard lived in an old farmhouse on the edge of the village. He and his wife had bought it when they came to St Gilles, a year before Patrick was born. What had attracted them to the place had been the former farmyard, surrounded by dilapidated, unused cowsheds, granaries and barns at the back of the house, and the cider-apple orchard beyond. The young Philippe and Jeanne had stood in their orchard that first spring and visualized a future with five or six children spending an idyllic childhood in those granaries and barns, with geese and hens in the orchard, and dogs and cats in the house. In fact, Patrick had turned out to be their only child, but Dr Halard thought that he had had a happy, if rather solitary, childhood. And when, in his second year at university, Patrick had brought Marie-France home to stay with them, Philippe and Jeanne once more dreamed of the place being filled with grandchildren at holiday times.

But the dream was never realized. Soon after Patrick's marriage, Jeanne, at the age of forty-four, had a cerebral haemorrhage while hanging out the laundry in the orchard. She had been found an hour later when their little maid, wondering where she had got to, went to look for her. Dr Halard remembered very well what a beautiful day it had been: the apple trees in full bloom, and late daffodils making yellow stars in the lush green grass below.

And then, unbelievably, a year later poor little Marie-France had been killed in her car, and the unborn baby too. Those had been cruel years for him, and for Patrick, but work, it seemed, was the salvation of them both, and the times they spent together, Easter and Christmas, were no longer unbearably sad. They had developed a sort of sympathetic privacy with each other, neither talking to the other about his grief. If there wasn't a hard frost at Christmas, Patrick did the heavy digging in the vegetable garden, and in the evening they played chess in front of the fire.

Dr Halard drove up the track at the side of the house and into the yard at the back. He drove his old car into the open-fronted cowshed he used as a garage, and got out, rather hoping that he would not be called out again, and could change into his gardening clothes, and be comfortable.

As he crossed the yard Marie-Claude, his housekeeper, came galloping out of the kitchen door, flapping her blue apron in a state of high excitement.

'Dr Halard!' she cried. 'Guess what? Mr Patrick is coming, he brings a friend, a lady! They will stay the night, I told him you would wish it, naturally! They will be here for lunch, about two o'clock. What a surprise, no?'

'It's a very nice surprise, Marie-Claude,' said Dr Halard calmly, though his heart was hammering behind his thick black jacket. They walked back to the kitchen together.

'There is only one thing, Doctor,' said Marie-Claude rather shyly. 'What about the bedrooms?'

Dr Halard poured himself a cup of coffee from the pot on the stove and considered this problem. 'Well,' he said, 'if it does not make too much work for you, I think perhaps we should make up the big bed in the guest room for the lady, and Patrick's bedroom for him, just as usual. More delicate, don't you think?'

'You are right,' said Marie-Claude, seriously. 'And in any case, maybe the lady is a colleague at work, nothing more?'

'I do hope not,' said Dr Halard, smiling at her.

'Mother of God, so do I,' said Marie-Claude. She looked at the kitchen clock: eleven ten. She had three hours to get everything ready. 'I have the brace of pheasants from that patient in the cellar. I will prepare them for tonight, à la crème. And there is a nice Camembert and some figs. But what about lunch? I have only a small piece of ham for you. It's not enough.'

'Shall I go over to Port-en-Bessin and get mussels? It's only about a quarter of an hour's drive, I'd be back before noon.'

'Good idea, and in the meantime I will get the rooms ready.'

'You're an angel, Marie-Claude,' said Dr Halard.

'I know it,' said Marie-Claude, complacently.

At ten past two Patrick's Peugeot went past the kitchen window, was driven straight into the cowshed and parked beside his father's car.

Marie-Claude, scrubbing mussels at the sink, watched, fascinated, as first Patrick and then a tall, slender woman with dark hair got out of the car, and emerged into the sunshine. Dr Halard came round the side of the barn from the orchard, carrying a basket, and Patrick and his companion went to meet him. Marie-Claude watched, smiling, as Patrick introduced his father to Anna, who held out her hand to him. Dr Halard took her hand and, bending, kissed it in the old-fashioned, formal manner. Then Patrick and his father embraced, and they all walked slowly across

201

the yard to the kitchen, talking and laughing as they did so. Marie-Claude flung the scrubbed mussels into the big pan, all ready to cook, wiped her hands, and doing her best not to grin in a meaningful way at Patrick, came to be introduced.

'As this is a special occasion, Marie-Claude has insisted that we eat in the dining-room,' said Dr Halard. 'Patrick, we have prepared the old guest room for Madame, perhaps you would like to show her where everything is? Your own room is, of course, ready as usual. When you are both ready, perhaps you would care for a drink before lunch? I'll be in the conservatory.'

Patrick took Anna upstairs. He opened the door of the spare room and they went in, closing the door behind them. They hugged each other, trying not to laugh.

'Oh, dear,' said Anna, 'am I going to have to sleep alone?'

'Are you crazy?' said Patrick, holding her close. 'Of course not. They're just being tactful. I'll tell him we'll sleep here together. I'll find a good moment, don't worry.'

'What will you tell him?' said Anna.

'The truth. We are in love, we plan to marry the moment you are free. In the meantime, we are lovers, OK?'

'Very OK,' said Anna, looking at the bed. 'Shall we try the bed?'

'No, my love,' said Patrick, laughing. 'We must behave properly, and go down and have a drink, and enjoy Marie-Claude's no doubt excellent lunch.'

They went downstairs together, holding hands, Anna admiring the lovingly waxed oak staircase and dark panelling hung with Victorian portraits of former Halards, and the faded and frayed rugs on the worn flagstones of the hall floor.

'It's strange,' said Anna. 'You father's house and Dad's are similar in many ways, though I haven't seen

202

much of him lately. I don't terribly like my father's second wife; I expect that's why I don't go down to Sussex very often. But Josh and Olly love it there, it's quite like this, in an English way, of course.'

'I'd like to meet your father, Anna,' said Patrick.

'Of course,' said Anna, 'we'll go down and see him when you come to London. I know he'll think you're a huge advance on Jeffrey.' She laughed. 'Just like Domenica does, she told me so.'

'I don't think that that would be terribly difficult to achieve, would it?'

'You may have a point,' she conceded, and they went into the conservatory where Dr Halard, having restrained himself from opening the champagne he had in readiness, was dispensing chilled Muscadet in tall, thick old wine glasses. He had arranged little silver dishes of nuts and green olives on the shabby rattan table which stood in the warm September sunshine, slanting through the dusty hanging baskets of ferns and jasmine.

After lunch, Dr Halard retired to his study to read the paper, which he was very soon doing with his eyes closed, and Patrick and Anna drove to Port-en-Bessin to walk along the beach in the wind and sunshine. He showed her all the caves and rock-pools of his childhood, and the ledges along the cliffs where he had stolen the eggs of various seabirds for his collection. Anna began to have a very clear picture of the odd, blue-eyed, spiky haired, solitary little boy he must have been, roaming around on his bicycle with his rods and nets and collecting boxes strapped to the carrier.

They lay in the wind-blown, bleached grass behind the dunes, their heads close together. Patrick told Anna about his mother, and about Marie-France, and found that at last it did not give him pain to talk about them. Anna told him about her childhood, so closely shared with Giò, in Chelsea, in Sussex and in Souliac with Domenica and Honorine. Then she told him of her meeting with Jeffrey, when she was a student at the Courtauld Institute, and he was reading law. Robert was still working in Historic Buildings then, and she saw quite a lot of him, and went to Sussex often to spend weekends with him. It was a chance invitation to her father's home that had quickened Jeffrey's interest in Anna, and they became engaged soon after that first visit.

'I think he thought I was an heiress,' said Anna sadly. 'But Dad has only the house, it is his passion, and his millstone now, I think.'

'And when did you go to live in your Lifeboat?'

'We were engaged for about eighteen months, and planned to marry as soon as we were both qualified. We were looking for a little house all this time, and we found this place quite by chance. Actually, it was Dad who first spotted it, and told me. And he gave us the down payment on the mortgage, too.'

'Lucky you and Jeffrey.'

'Indeed. Trouble was, it made Jeffrey all the more sure that I would come into money one day. I think he felt cheated when he found out that this was not the case. I always had the feeling that he thought I had misled him.' Anna rolled over in the grass, and stretched her arms above her head. 'So now you are in no doubt,' she said, smiling her dark, secret smile. 'You will have to take me as I am, with no dowry.'

Patrick leaned over her, and she folded her arms round his neck, pulling him close to her.

Across the Channel, at Clymping, Robert, Josh and Olivia sat on a plaid rug eating ham sandwiches gritty with blown sand, and pretending that it was not really spitting with rain. Josh and Olivia had bravely had a freezing swim, or rather a quick dip in the moody grey sea, and had run up and down the beach, climbing over the slimy wooden breakwaters, and throwing ducks and drakes to get warm again.

'Not exactly the warm south, is it?' said Robert.

'It's all right, Grandpa, it's lovely here, really,' said Olivia loyally, crunching her sandwich.

'Just bloody cold,' said Josh, and they all laughed uncontrollably, as if he had said something tremendously witty.

'Good job I brought some hot coffee.' Robert extracted the thermos from the picnic hamper.

They drove back to Boulter's Mill along the quiet leafy lanes, beginning to turn yellow now, with flurries of leaves like golden coins blown from the trees by the snatching wind. They left the car outside the kitchen door, next to Anna's Renault, and walked up the paddock to the millpond to check the levels of the old wooden sluices, and look at the ducks and moorhens whose home it was. One old pair, Quacky and Mrs Poo had been there for years, and Olly recognized them immediately.

'They're pretty amazing, really,' said Robert. 'By normal standards, they should have been dead years ago.'

'Bit old for the pot, I should think,' said Josh, to tease Olivia, who hit him a hard blow on his upper arm, with deadly accuracy.

'Ow!' said Josh. 'Olly, you're a cow.'

'You're just like your mother and Giò used to be.' Robert smiled at them tolerantly.

They went into the mill, and climbed the rickety wooden steps to the upper floor. Looking down a deep hole they could see the water gushing through, far below, on its way into the stream which flowed along the rear of the building, and on into the paddock beyond. Robert sat down on a mouldy bale of straw and looked at his grandchildren, as they stared down at the foaming white water, fascinated.

'You look very solemn, Grandpa,' said Olly, coming over and sitting down on the dusty boards beside him. 'What are you thinking about?'

'I am thinking about the time, long ago, when Anna and Giò were younger than you are now, Olly. And I

205

made the biggest mistake I've made in my life, and one I've never ceased to regret bitterly.'

Josh came over and sat down too, his arms round his knees, dark eyes troubled beneath his thick brows, and sun-bleached, wind-blown hair.

'Do you want to tell us about it, Grandpa?'

'Yes,' said Robert, 'I rather think I do.' And he told them, quietly and without leaving anything out, the story of how he had lost Domenica, and how he had missed her every day of his life since that time.

Olivia sat looking at her grandfather, her eyes round with concern and deep interest. 'But what about Kate?' she asked.

'You may well ask, my dear child.' Robert passed a hand over his face. 'I'm afraid that was the second stupidest mistake of my life. Poor Kate, she finds it every bit as boring here as your grandmother did.'

'Well,' said Josh, getting up and dusting himself down, 'I, for one, don't find it at all boring. I love it here.'

'So do I,' said Olivia.

'Well,' said Robert, 'thank God for that. Let's go and have some tea, shall we?'

Domenica and Giò sat under the fig tree after dinner, with coffee and cognac on the table, smoking Domenica's little black cigars. In the kitchen, they could hear Honorine clattering the dishes as she washed up before going home.

'Quiet, isn't it?' said Giò.

'Do you mean by that, that Honorine is noisy?' said Domenica, querulously.

'No, of course not.' Giò glanced at his mother uneasily. 'I just mean, it's rather quiet now that the others have gone.'

'Are you bored?' said Domenica. 'I suppose it is boring, just you and me.'

Giò sighed, and took a sip of brandy. 'No, Ma, I'm not

206

bored. In fact, I came down specially to see you alone, without the others always around.'

'Why?' Domenica looked at him sharply. 'Is anything wrong?'

'Not exactly. It's just that I'm rather depressed, nothing seems to go right for me lately. I thought you might cheer me up a bit; you usually do.'

'Oh,' said Domenica, mollified. 'Is it Patrick, by any chance?'

'I'm afraid it is, yes. I'm trying hard to be glad for Anna, and for him, come to that.'

'But you wouldn't try to come between them in any way?'

'No chance,' said Giò, sadly. 'They're lovers already.'

'How do you know? Did he tell you?'

'Certainly not. He's not that kind of man. I saw them.'

'What do you mean, you *saw* them? Where?'

'Here, actually. I just happened to be looking out of my window, and there was Anna, crossing the garden in her nightie, coming back from his room.'

'My God! They didn't hang about, did they?'

'I know, and they'd only known each other a week!'

'When you think,' said Domenica, 'what a totally feeble creature she was all those years, pining for the vile Jeffrey.' She laughed, and Giò, in spite of himself joined in.

'There's nothing like the speed of the worm when it really turns, is there?' he said. 'A bit like you and Dad, I suppose. Except that you didn't leap into the arms of another man, did you?'

'No,' said Domenica, 'I didn't.'

'Why not?' Giò looked at his mother. 'You must often have been awfully lonely, at the very least.'

'Because I never met another man as attractive as Robert,' said Domenica, inhaling cigar smoke. 'And there was another reason, if I'm totally honest with myself, which isn't often.'

'And what was that?' said Giò, gently.

'I always thought he would come back to me, and we would find a way to make it work for both of us. I didn't want anything to get in the way of that.'

'But what about the dreaded Kate?'

'Exactly,' said Domenica. 'The bloody cow wrecked everything, stupid, big-bummed potter.' Giò burst out laughing, and Domenica joined in, and both of them felt better than they had for quite a while.

'There you are,' said Giò, 'I said you'd cheer me up, and you have.'

'And you've made me feel better too, darling. I'm so glad you came. I have been a bit low lately.'

'Any particular reason?' said Giò lightly, carefully. Honorine had told him privately of her concern.

'Not really. A few aches and pains. I expect it's my age, and all that crap.' Domenica squinted through the smoke of her cigar.

'Well,' said Giò, 'be sensible, won't you? See the doctor if you think you should.'

'OK,' said Domenica, non commitally.

'Promise?' Honorine called good night from the kitchen door, and Giò stood up. 'Shall we go over to the caff for a nightcap?'

'I don't think so, not tonight. You go if you want to.' Domenica got to her feet. 'I think I'll turn in, I'm really quite tired.'

Giò watched her as she climbed the worn stone steps to the second floor. She reached her door, and turned and gave him a little wave of her hand. Then she went into her room and closed the door. Giò brought in the coffee tray from the garden, and locked the kitchen door. Then he went out of the front gate into the square. He walked slowly across to the fountain and sat on the rim, letting his hand trail in the cool water. Looking back at the house, big and blackly solid against the starry night sky, pierced by the solitary rectangle of rosy light that was Domenica's window, he felt a sudden sense of the swift passage of time, of loss, as if an important part of his life was over. At a deeper level, he was frighteningly aware that he had nothing at all to take its place. He sat for a long time, staring into the water, with its trembling reflection of dark leaves against a starry sky. Then he went back to the house, locked the door and went upstairs to his room. As he passed the door to the *salon*, a sudden impulse came to him and he went in and sat down at the big desk. He picked up the phone and dialled Robert's number in Sussex. Robert answered, almost at once.

'Hello, Dad, it's me, Giò. How are you?'

'Giò, what a surprise. I'm fine, how are you?'

'I'm fine. I'm in Souliac actually, with Ma for the weekend.'

'Oh. Good. Is Anna with you?'

'No, should she be?'

'No, of course not. I've got Josh and Olivia here for the weekend, and she's in Paris, I thought that . . .' Robert's voice faltered, as if he had perhaps made a blunder.

Oh, God, thought Giò, will I ever stop tripping over Anna? He took a deep breath. 'Dad,' he said, 'I thought, it's ages since I saw you. Could I come soon for the weekend?'

'My dear boy, of course. What about next weekend?'

'Terrific. I suppose it'll have to be ghastly Gatwick?'

'I can meet you there easily. Let me know day and time, won't you?'

'I'll ring you Monday evening. See you soon, Dad.'

'I look forward to it, Giò. Goodnight, my boy.'

Giò, smiling, put down the phone and went off to his bed, feeling curiously comforted.

Patrick and Anna got back to St Gilles just before six. They found Marie-Claude in the kitchen, plucking the young pheasants, and filling the room with a delicious smell as she gently simmered the giblets with garlic, herbs and cider for the sauce. Dr Halard was seeing a patient in his consulting room.

'Can I do anything to help?' said Anna to Marie-Claude. 'I feel quite useless doing nothing.'

'It's kind of you, my dear,' said Marie-Claude, 'but really, there's very little to do. And for me, it's so nice to cook for you all, not just one.' She stopped, her cheeks pink, anxious not to say too much, too soon.

'If you're sure?' said Anna.

Marie-Claude smiled at her. 'I'm sure,' she said.

'Marie-Claude,' said Patrick, 'is there plenty of hot water? Is it all right if Anna has a bath?'

'But of course it is. Of course. And there are plenty of nice warm towels in the airing cupboard. Please, my dear, help yourself.'

'Take your time,' said Patrick, as Anna went upstairs. 'It'll give me a chance to talk to Dad. You can tell, they are ready to burst with curiosity, can't you?'

'Yes,' said Anna, 'it's time to tell him,' and she ran upstairs, pretty well bursting with happiness herself.

Patrick went into the shabby, comfortable sitting-room to wait for his father's patient to depart. The kindling and logs were laid in the black iron firebasket, and he knelt down and put a match to the crumpled paper under the sticks. The dry twigs blazed up at once, and a curl of smoke went straight up the wide, soot-blackened chimney. The smell of his childhood winter nights, as the logs caught fire and began to crackle, brought a nostalgic smile to Patrick's lips. He remembered those cold, long-ago Normandy evenings, when he and his mother roasted chestnuts on a shovel, kneeling in front of the fire, waiting for his father to come home from his evening round. He remembered how his mother raised her head and looked towards the window, when they heard the engine of his father's Citroën as he drove into the yard, and they would both run to open the kitchen door, to light up the yard, and carry his bag.

When the fire was well alight, Patrick got up and crossed to the table, which was round and covered with a faded paisley shawl. On the table stood a simple brass lamp with a milk-glass shade. It had once been run on oil, but was now converted to electricity, for safety's sake, though this was regretted by both Patrick and his father. Piles of books and medical journals were stacked beside the lamp, and an ornate silver presentation tray, engraved with his grandfather's name, held bottles and glasses. Patrick poured himself a drink and sat down by the fire. Through the open window he could see the orchard, framed by a gap in the barns and byres. A pair of blackbirds were singing, hurling their beautiful liquid notes from tree to tree, the sky behind luminous, the light fading.

The door opened, and Dr Halard entered the room.

'Finished?' said Patrick, standing up.

'Yes,' said his father, 'as long as there isn't another emergency. They always seem to happen at weekends.'

'Can I pour you a drink?' said Patrick.

'You certainly can. Calvados, thanks,' said Dr Halard, sitting in the other armchair by the fire. 'Where's Anna?'

'She's having a bath.' Patrick handed his father his drink. 'It gives me a chance to talk to you alone.' He sat down and took a sip of his drink, smiling at his father over the rim of his glass.

His father looked back at him attentively, his eyes bright behind his spectacles. 'I think, and hope, that I can guess what it is you have to tell me,' he said. 'Just to see you together gives it all away.'

'Is it so obvious?' said Patrick, and laughed. 'It's a bit complicated because Anna is not yet free to marry again. She lives in London and has two teenage children. But as soon as we possibly can, we will marry, and try to arrange things so that the children will not suffer.'

'But what of their father?'

'He left the home to live alone ten years ago. Poor Anna has been hanging onto the idea that he might come back, but he has treated her very badly, visiting the children when it suits him, never making a complete break and letting her make a new beginning, playing an endless game of cat-and-mouse with her.'

'I see. Poor young woman. And now?'

'We met at her mother's house in Provence this summer. I went down with her twin brother, Giò, who lives in Paris. I did a little piece about his shop for a documentary about the Marais I'm working on, and there she was. We fell in love almost at once; we became lovers. We will marry as soon as we can.'

Dr Halard looked into his glass, and took a sip of his drink. He stood up, and Patrick rose to his feet. The older man put his hands on his son's shoulders. 'Thank you for telling me everything,' he said, his blue eyes warm and bright. 'Sometimes, the most wanted things are difficult to achieve. I'm sure you will both be very happy together, however long it takes. The marriage certificate is only a piece of paper, after all. As far as I am concerned, you are already married. It makes me very happy, my dear boy. You can have no idea.'

Patrick hugged his father. 'I think I have,' he said. 'I knew you'd understand.'

'There's only one thing,' said Dr Halard.

'What?' said Patrick, anxiously.

'Marie-Claude will never forgive me it we don't share the good news with her, and drink the champagne that is chilling in the refrigerator.'

Patrick laughed. 'I'll go and get Anna, and move my things into her room. OK, Dad?'

'But of course,' said Dr Halard. 'Where else would a married man be?'

'We'll be five minutes.' Patrick left his father and ran upstairs, whistling.

The old man looked out of the window at the darkening orchard. 'Well, my love,' he said, 'it looks as though we might have some youngsters around the old place from time to time, after all. Even stepgrandchildren are a blessing.' He crossed to the fireplace and threw the remains of his calvados into the flames, sending a flash of blue up the chimney, and a shower of sparks.

Then he went to the kitchen and took the champagne out of the fridge. He closed the door and turned to Marie-Claude, who was putting her brace of birds into the oven. 'Would you care to join us for a glass of champagne, Marie-Claude?'

Marie-Claude clapped her hand over her mouth to stop the scream of excitement which threatened to emerge. Then she washed her hands, undid her blue apron, and followed the doctor to the sitting-room.

Chapter Twelve

'Sodding golden October,' said Kate to herself as the worn tyres of her van skidded on the soggy fallen leaves in Boulter's Lane. She turned in at the gateway to the mill and drove round to the kitchen door which stood open in spite of the chill wind and rain. She switched off the engine and got out of the van, flexing her knees, stiff after the drive from London. She glanced briefly round the yard, noting the dripping, yellow-leaved climbing roses, needing dead-heading, and the wheelbarrow full of rotting manure left standing by the kitchen door.

She went into the kitchen, and found Robert heating soup in a pan on the Aga. He looked round, surprised, as she entered.

'Oh, hello, it's you,' he said. 'I didn't hear the car. Have you had lunch, or would you like some soup?'

'Thanks,' said Kate, looking at the table, set for one. 'Is there enough?'

'Plenty,' said Robert, 'I'll get another bowl.'

She sat down and waited for Robert to set another place at the table, and bring the bowls of hot soup — carrot and leek, her least favourite. He cut hunks of doughy white bread, and brought the pepper mill and a carton of grated pecorino cheese to the table, and sat down. He took a long swig of what looked like gin and tonic, but did not offer Kate a drink. She picked up her spoon and tasted her soup. It was salty, and tasted strongly of stock cube. Nevertheless, she was hungry, so she drank the soup without comment, and ate some bread. She waited for Robert to say something, but he seemed absorbed in his lunch, and his eyes kept straying to a copy of *The Oldie*, which lay open on the table.

Kate got up and poured herself a gin. The tonic was finished, so she added a small amount of tap water, and some ice. She returned to the table.

'Do you want some cheese?' said Robert. 'There may be a bit in the fridge.' If this was meant to sound pathetic, Kate ignored it.

'No, thanks, that was fine,' she said, drinking the gin.

'Have you come back?' said Robert. 'Or what?'

'No. I've come to get my stuff, and to discuss future plans with you.'

'And what exactly do you mean by future plans?' Robert looked steadily at her for the first time.

'I mean that I am going back to London to live. I've arranged to share a studio with a chum, and I want a thousand pounds a month allowance from you, or a divorce if you prefer, and I'll take half the proceeds from our property and call it quits.'

'Are you serious, Kate?'

'Never more so, Robert.

'But you know perfectly well that after tax and so forth, we don't have a thousand pounds a month.'

'Well, that's your problem, I'm afraid. I've wasted twenty odd years of my life running round after you and your precious house and garden, and now it's time to stop the whole stupid thing. You never loved me anyway, not in the way you did that bitch Domenica, so let's not fool each other any more. I want out, and if you have to sell this ridiculous place so that we can get divorced and both of us remain solvent, so be it.'

Kate lit a cigarette, and looked coolly at Robert, who sat slumped in his chair, staring down at the table. Two bright spots of colour burned in his cheeks, and his long lashes hid his downcast eyes, so that she could only guess at what he must be feeling. A small muscle twitched at the corner of his mouth, and she saw that the knuckles of his clenched fist were white. Probably wants to kill me, she thought. Robert looked up, his eyes miserable.

'Well,' he said, 'that seems fairly conclusive, doesn't it? We'll have to see what we can work out, won't we?'

'No, Robert, we won't,' said Kate. 'I have taken advice, as a matter of fact, and it's either one way or the other. I'll give you a month to choose. In the meantime, I'd like a cheque for a thousand, please. I'm going upstairs to pack my things now, so I'll collect the cheque on my way out. I'll have my kiln and all the other heavy gear collected in a few days. I'll phone you when I've made the arrangements.'

When she had gone upstairs Robert sat for a moment, stunned and blinking stupidly. Then he got up and went out into the garden. He crossed the lawn, which badly needed cutting, and went through the arch in the yew hedge, into the orchard. Slowly he passed through the rows of apple trees, heavy with fruit, until he came to the ancient Bramley at the top of the orchard. A swing, green with age and damp, frayed and smelling of rot, hung in the tree, and he sat down on it, rather gingerly. He swung himself very gently, his feet scuffing the worn patch beneath. A terrible sadness welled up in him, a deep aching feeling of the pointlessness of everything. How idiotic my life here has been, he thought, chasing round like a blue-arsed fly, weeding, cutting grass, clipping hedges, growing and picking all the stuff, and all the time, there it all is, lurking, waiting to jump on you and overwhelm you, like a great green wave. The only time there is a break is in the middle of winter, and that's not a rest, more like a kind of death. Except for all the jobs waiting to be done in the house, and the log cutting, and repairing of burst pipes. Dad always said he'd go out of here in his box, and so he did. He sighed, and a great lethargy crept over him, a reluctance to move ever again, much less get out the temperamental old mower, and attack the lawn for the umpteenth time that year.

'It was all very well for Dad,' he said, 'he always had help in his day.'

He limped slowly back to the house, his right knee stiff and painful, his back aching. Kate was stuffing suitcases into the back of the van, grim-faced and silent. He went into the house and through the kitchen to the book-room. He took the cheque book from its pigeonhole in his desk, and wrote the cheque. Then he returned to the kitchen, put the cheque on the table, and went out again to the shed where the machines were kept. He got out the mower and filled it with petrol. Then he wheeled it round the side of the house towards the lawn.

He heard the van doors being slammed, and then the engine sputtering reluctantly into life. Kate drove a short distance down the drive, then, catching sight of Robert, she stopped the van and wound down the window, calling to him across the grass.

'My solicitor will be in touch. Presumably, you'll be going to Forbes in Worthing?'

'Not necessarily,' said Robert. 'A London man might be more appropriate.'

'As you wish, of course,' said Kate. 'But why waste money? There's nothing very difficult to discuss really, is there?'

'We shall have to see,' said Robert, 'won't we?'

Kate wound up her window and drove away. As the van disappeared through the trees, Robert noticed with malicious joy that one of her rear tyres was very flat indeed.

'Serves her right, bloody old cow,' he remarked to no-one in particular, and laughed out loud at the prospect of Kate having to change the wheel on the motorway. He pulled the starting cord, and the mower sprang into energetic life. 'Thank God for that anyway,' said Robert, quite cheerfully, and followed the noisy machine over the lush green grass.

*   *   *

217

Giò's plane was a few minutes early on Friday evening, and he made his way swiftly through passport control. He had only his briefcase, which doubled as an overnight bag. He saw the tall figure of his father waiting just beyond the barrier.

'Hello, old chap, good to see you,' said Robert. 'Is that all your luggage?'

'Hello, Dad,' said Giò. 'Yes, this is all. I can't bear waiting for the stuff to arrive.'

'Couldn't agree more. Let's get out of here, shall we?'

In ten minutes they were bowling along the minor roads towards Boulter's, the mild air full of midges, and the late evening sky red with a promise of fine weather tomorrow.

'How's the weather in Paris?'

'OK,' said Giò. 'Bit like this, perhaps a bit warmer than here. But you don't notice weather so much in town, do you?'

Robert swerved to avoid a pheasant that had decided to hurl itself across the road in front of the car. 'How are you, Giò? Busy?'

'Pretty busy,' said Giò. 'What about you?'

'Frantic, as usual, and not helped by the fact that Kate has done a runner on me.'

'Holy shit! You're not serious?' said Giò, startled.

'Only too serious, my dear boy.'

'Why, for God's sake?'

'Oh, you know, fed up with life in the country, feels I treat her as an unpaid slave, can't find time to do her pottery, the usual stuff.'

'Oh, well,' said Giò, comfortably, 'she'll probably be back pretty soon. After all, how can she manage on her own?'

'Only too easily, it seems,' said Robert. 'She's arranged to share a studio in Chelsea, and is demanding a thousand pounds a month support from me, or failing that, a split-down-the-middle divorce.'

'My God, how awful! What can you do?'

'I don't quite know yet, Giò. I should like to talk it over with you; after all, it does affect you and Anna, and the children too, come to that.'

'Don't worry about us, Dad. It's you and Boulter's that's the crucial thing, as far as I'm concerned, anyway.'

Half an hour later they drove up Boulter's Lane and in at the mill gate.

'Here we are,' said Robert, getting out of the car. 'Welcome home, my boy.'

'It's good to *be* home, Dad,' said Giò, and meant it.

'I think we deserve a stiffish drink, don't you?' Robert led the way into the kitchen.

'Sounds like a great idea,' said Giò, following his father.

'Put a match to the fire, will you? It's all ready,' said Robert. 'What would you like? Whisky? Cognac? I've got some good wine for supper.'

'Cognac, thanks,' said Giò, lighting the fire.

Robert opened the oven door of the Aga, where a casserole was simmering away nicely, and a warm, garlicky scent filled the kitchen.

'Smells good,' said Giò. 'I'm getting ravenous.'

'I've made enough for several meals. I hope you won't find it too monotonous.'

'Not if it tastes as good as it smells,' said Giò, smiling at his father affectionately.

Robert put two large potatoes into the oven to bake, and closed the door. 'Let's have our drink,' he said, 'and then we can go and pick some salad, and a couple of apples.'

'Sounds lovely.' Giò lifted his glass. '*Salut*, Dad.'

'*Salut*, Giò.'

After supper they washed the dishes together, and then brought the rest of the wine to the fireside, and watched the *Nine O'clock News* on BBC1.

'I don't know why one bothers, really,' said Robert. 'They keep on broadcasting the same stuff over and over again, and really they're only interested in disasters, anyway.'

'It's the same in Paris,' said Giò. 'But at least you do get the cricket in the summer, don't you?'

'Giò! I'm amazed. Do you like cricket?' said Robert.

'Actually, I do, very much,' said Giò, smiling rather shyly at his father.

Robert turned off the TV and put another log on the fire. He settled in his chair, and lit his pipe. 'How're things in Souliac?' he said. 'Did you have a good summer?'

'Yes, it was good to see Anna and the kids. Though I didn't see Josh, he was with friends at Estagnol, lucky chap. But Olly was in good form. She'll be a handful in a year or two.'

'They were here last weekend. We had an amusing time, they seemed to enjoy themselves anyway. Though it must seem tame after Souliac. If only we had more sun, what a difference it makes.'

'I don't know,' said Giò. 'It's rather special here, Dad, and very beautiful, and the dodgy weather is part of it somehow.'

'You can get bloody sick of it after months and months of rain and wind, old chap,' said Robert. 'I don't blame Kate for buggering off, really. Or your mother, if it comes to that.'

'Dad,' said Giò, lighting a cigarette, 'that's one of the reasons I wanted to see you. It's Ma, I don't think she's well. Honorine is worried about her. She seems quiet, for her, and rather depressed.'

'Really?' said Robert, frowning. 'Any particular reason, do you think?'

'Well, I thought at first it was just being a bit lonely, with Anna gone and everything. But I think it's more than that, I think she's very tired, and feeling her age at last.'

'Maybe she needs a holiday herself, after having you lot coming and going all summer.'

'Maybe, Dad,' said Giò, 'but you know Ma. Honorine

220

does everything in the housekeeping line, and Anna helps her.'

'I wonder,' said Robert thoughtfully. 'Do you think she might like to spend a couple of weeks here, with me? Or is that a daft idea?' Giò looked at Robert, squinting through the blue haze of his cigarette smoke. His father was relighting his pipe, puffing away. He sent Giò a shy, almost anxious glance.

'No, Dad,' said Giò, gently, 'I don't think it's a daft idea, at all. I'm sure she'd love it.'

'Well, that would be marvellous,' said Robert, 'and what's more, I'll bet she'll think of a way to sort Kate out.'

'I'll bet she will,' said Giò, and they both laughed at the prospect.

'I'll phone her tomorrow. It's a bit late now, with the time difference.'

'Don't worry about that, Dad,' said Giò. 'She'll be up, she doesn't go to bed before midnight, usually.'

'Right.' Robert went to the book-room, closing the door behind him.

Twenty minutes later, he reappeared, bright-eyed and smiling.

'OK?' said Giò, half asleep in his chair.

'Very,' said Robert. 'She'll phone me in a day or two, and tell me which plane to meet.'

'Great,' said Giò. 'Well done, Dad.'

On Saturday morning, the rain falling in torrents outside his bedroom window, Robert lay in bed, worrying about how he was going to continue paying an allowance to Kate. He had a deep-rooted aversion to the idea of overdrafts and loans, and knew himself to be simple-minded when it came to money matters. After a while, he got up and went downstairs to make some tea.

To his surprise, he found Giò in the kitchen making toast and boiling water for eggs, with the coffee already

221

made and keeping hot on the back of the Aga. Robert felt a rush of affection for his son, and a sudden feeling of tiredness and inadequacy. It isn't only Domenica who's feeling her age, he thought, as he sat down at the table, already laid for two.

'How kind of you, Giò,' said Robert. 'One doesn't usually take the trouble on one's own.'

'I know,' said Giò, putting butter and toast on the table.

'Of course you do,' said Robert.

After breakfast, Robert began to tell Giò about his financial problems, and Giò listened without interrupting.

'I understand,' he said, when Robert had finished. 'In the first place, I don't think you should give Kate anything more at all, not a penny, until the whole business is settled. Secondly, I think it would be a good idea if you had a backstop fund for emergencies, and legal fees and so on. This house must be stuffed from top to bottom with things you have no particular affection for, and which I could dispose of for you. You would probably be very surprised at how much we could raise.'

'But, Giò, I hate the idea of selling the family silver, so to speak,' said Robert, looking pained.

'Dad,' said Giò, 'I'm not talking about the silver, I'm talking about the stuff that you would probably think of as junk.'

'Oh,' said Robert, 'is that what it is?'

'Dad,' said Giò, laughing, 'just as an experiment, let's go round the house, and you can choose any pieces you could bear to part with, and I'll value them for you, OK?'

'OK.' Doubtfully, Robert followed Giò up to the attics – three long connecting rooms, thick with dust and festooned with cobwebs, dimly lit by ancient, dirty rooflights. They picked their way through the paraphernalia of generations of family life. Cots, prams, dolls' houses and sledges, Lloyd Loom chairs filled with teddies and dolls, train sets and skates were scattered through the rooms, together with big old cupboards full of antique clothes, riding boots, velvet hats, whips, and heaps of beautiful old articulated shoe- and boot-trees. A magnificent rocking horse, dappled grey and white, with a flowing silvery mane and tail, stood proudly amid the clutter.

'I remember him.' Giò gave the horse's rump a push to set him rocking.

'So do I,' said Robert, and his mind flew back sixty-five years to his boyhood.

'Dad,' said Giò, briskly, 'obviously, there are certain things you want to hang on to. But just up here alone, at a quick guess, there's a good ten grand's worth of stuff. That painted cupboard alone will fetch seven hundred and fifty, at least.'

'You're not serious, Giò.'

'I am.'

'Good heavens,' said Robert, sitting down heavily in a dusty rattan chair.

Gio sat on a tapestry-covered music stool nearby and regarded his father protectively. He waited for a few minutes, to allow Robert to get used to the idea. 'It's entirely up to you, Dad,' he said. 'I don't want to pressure you in any way.'

'No, no,' said Robert. 'Of course, you're absolutely right, I must be sensible. And of course, it would be very nice not to have to worry about every last cent.'

'Precisely,' said Giò. 'Now, let's go out. It's stopped raining, so you can show me all round the place, and then we'll go to a pub for lunch. I haven't been in a proper pub for years.'

'Thank you, Giò,' said Robert, 'what a comfort you are. I feel much better about everything already.'

'Good,' said Giò, 'it's what I'm here for.'

They went down the wooden attic stairs and the main staircase and out into the garden, damp and dripping, but with a watery gleam of sunshine breaking through the clouds from time to time. Robert took Giò through the walled garden, with its rows of imperfectly weeded vegetables, past the raspberry canes and strawberry beds, the espaliered apples and pears, and into the glasshouses, where three or four bunches of grapes still hung in their bags.

'It's wonderful, Dad,' said Giò, 'but how the hell do you manage it all without help? I couldn't do it.'

'Well,' said Robert, 'I just about managed it, when Kate did the cooking and shopping and so on. But now, I suppose, it's not really feasible, is it?'

Was it ever? thought Giò to himself, sadly. 'Well,' he said, 'whatever, it's a terrific achievement, Dad. You deserve a medal.'

'I'm glad you think so, Giò. Most people think I'm completely off my trolley.'

On Sunday morning, Robert got quite into the spirit of the thing, and he chose the things that Giò would take to Paris and sell for him. They arranged that he would come the following weekend with his van to take the stuff away. They finished off Robert's beef stew for lunch, with pasta and a bottle of Burgundy from the cellar, then drove up the lane to the Downs, and flew the old Chinese fish kite that Giò had found in a box in the attic. It was gusty on the top of the hill, and the brightly coloured kite flew straight up into the blue, windswept Sussex sky. Walking backwards, father and son took it in turns paying out and pulling on the string, getting the kite higher and higher in the brilliant air, until it was like a small red-and-yellow comma in the sky.

'I haven't had so much fun in years,' said Giò, as they walked back to the car.

'Nor me,' said Robert. 'I've forgotten how to play.'

Anna drove her little Renault to Richmond to keep her appointment with the gynaecologist. His consulting rooms were in a large, red brick house set back from the road, with a gravel sweep to the front door, through an entrance marked 'IN' and an exit marked 'OUT'. As she drove in she was relieved to see that there were several parking spaces, two of them vacant. She parked her car next to a brand new, dark green Jaguar, and noticed that its parking space was labelled 'Consultants only'. She looked at her watch: five to eleven. She got out of her car and locked it. Then she walked the few metres to the front door, painted a glossy black with shiny brass letterbox, doorknob and nameplates. Rather nervously, she rang the bell. It was answered almost immediately by a young, blonde nurse in a starched cap and crackling apron over a dark blue dress. She wore a wide, dark blue webbing belt with a silver buckle, and a brooch pinned to the bib of her apron.

'Mrs Wickham?' she said, brightly. 'Do come in.'

Anna followed her to the waiting-room, which was large and filled with chintz-covered sofas and easy chairs, and coffee tables bearing glossy magazines. 'Mr Carpenter won't keep you a moment,' said the nurse, and left the room.

Anna glanced round at the other women, as she perched on the edge of an easy chair, reluctant to allow herself to become marooned in its depths. Most of them looked rather older than Anna, perhaps in their fifties. It was hard to tell, they all wore jeans, or shell suits and trainers, except one much older woman who wore a tweed skirt and a boxy, geranium-coloured jacket, and good shoes. Her hair was silvery, and Anna thought she looked nice. She smiled at her, and the woman smiled back.

The door opened, and the nurse came in. Surprisingly, Anna's name was called, and she stood up and followed the nurse, feeling as if she had jumped the queue. At a door marked 'Arthur Carpenter' the nurse knocked and entered, standing aside for Anna to pass her.

'Mrs Wickham,' she said.

Mr Carpenter was a small, slight man with smooth, slicked-back silvery hair, wearing a dark striped suit and silk tie. He sat behind an enormous leather-topped desk, with his back to a wide window overlooking a garden. He stood up as Anna entered and leaned across the desk to shake her hand.

'How do you do, Mrs Wickham, do please sit down.' His voice was very quiet, and his pale blue eyes behind National Health half-moon spectacles were kind, in a detached sort of way. Anna sat down, wondering whether it was he who was the owner of the Jaguar. Mr Carpenter consulted the file on his desk, and then took some large negatives out of a brown manilla envelope. Crossing the room, he clipped them onto a display screen, and switched on the light.

'There we are,' he said, 'Mrs Wickham's fibroids. Would you like to have a look?'

'I would, thank you.' She stood beside him while he pointed out the shadows on the film, and explained the kind of problems this condition could cause.

'Is it difficult to deal with?' said Anna.

'Not at all, all things being equal,' he replied. 'But first of all, we'd better examine you, and take a little smear, routine of course, there's no need to feel anxious at all.' He went back to his desk, and rang a bell, and the blonde nurse appeared.

'Nurse,' said Mr Carpenter, 'I'm going to examine Mrs Wickham now. Please take her to the examination room, and help her get ready.'

The examination room was tiny, with a high, hard bed covered in rubber sheeting and a white draw sheet. There was a chair to hang clothes on, and a washbasin with surgeon's taps. Anna took off her shoes, her skirt, her tights and her knickers, folding them neatly on the chair.

She got on to the bed and lay down. The nurse spread a small blue sheet over her abdomen.

'You've got a super tan,' she observed cheerfully.

'Thank you.' Anna was unable to think of anything less banal to say.

Mr Carpenter came in. He had removed his jacket and rolled up his shirt sleeves. He put on a shiny pale blue plastic apron, and thin rubber gloves. Anna stared at the ceiling, feeling sick.

'Now,' said Mr Carpenter, gently turning down the sheet to expose Anna's stomach, 'let's have a little prod round the tummy first, shall we?' Anna closed her eyes as he slowly worked his way over her entire abdomen, sometimes pressing very delicately, sometimes quite deeply and firmly. 'What a very slender lady you are, Mrs Wickham. I can feel your uterus quite distinctly through your abdominal wall.'

'Really?' said Anna.

'Is there any chance that you might be pregnant?' he said.

'What did you say?' said Anna, feeling the blood rush to her cheeks.

'I can't be absolutely sure, but I think it's possible that you might be in the very early stages of pregnancy. Is there any likelihood of that, do you think?'

Anna's mind leapt back to Souliac, and the first time she had slept with Patrick. Neither of them had been equipped with contraceptives, or had given such a thing a moment's thought.

'Yes,' she said slowly, 'it is possible. But I would have thought it unlikely, with my irregular periods, and at my age.'

'Ah, my dear young woman,' said Mr Carpenter, 'if you only knew how often I have heard that said. Nature plays curious tricks, especially on women.' He covered Anna's stomach with the sheet. 'Now, turn on your left side, and bend your knees, please,' he said, 'and we'll take a look inside, and maybe get a more accurate diagnosis.'

Her heart thumping, Anna did as she was asked. She clenched her fists, fighting off panic, but in the event hardly noticed the actual introduction of the speculum.

'All done, everything looks perfectly normal,' said Mr Carpenter, stripping off his gloves, and leaving Anna with the nurse.

Anna dressed, and went back into the consulting room, where Mr Carpenter waited, his jacket on and seated in his chair.

'Sit down, Mrs Wickham,' he said, and Anna did so. 'I'm afraid there's little doubt that you are between six and eight weeks pregnant. Does that make sense?'

'Yes,' said Anna, 'it does.'

'Any other symptoms? Sickness and so forth?'

'No, nothing like that. But my breasts are a bit bigger than usual.'

'Well, if this is an unwanted pregnancy, it would not be too difficult to recommend termination, especially at your age, and with an almost grown-up family.'

'Thank you,' said Anna coldly, 'but I don't wish to consider such a thing. Unless, of course, there was anything very wrong with the baby.'

'There are several tests we can do: Down's syndrome, spina bifida and so on. But these can only be done a little later on. Why don't you discuss it with your husband, my dear, and see me again in a month's time?'

'Yes,' said Anna, suppressing a smile, 'I'll do that.'

'In any case, there's no possibility of doing anything about removing the fibroids until the question of the pregnancy is resolved, either way. If you do go ahead with the pregnancy, we will deal with the fibroids after the birth.' He stood up and accompanied Anna to the door. 'Make an appointment for mid November, and I'll see you then.'

'Thank you,' said Anna, as he held the door for her. On an impulse, she turned towards him. 'That lovely new Jaguar, is it yours?' she said.

'It is, as a matter of fact,' he said, laughing.

'Good,' said Anna, 'you deserve it. I wouldn't do your job for anything.'

*   *   *

Back in Chiswick, Anna parked the car carefully in the garage, picked up her pot of rabbitskin glue, and locked the garage doors. She unlocked the door to the Lifeboat, and climbed the stairs to the upper room. She put the gluepot to warm on a low flame on the hob in the kitchen, and then sat down in front of her cherub, who lay in his restorer's cradle, gleaming white in his coat of new gesso. In his present state, he looked like one of those winged marble cherubs found in Victorian churchyards. Dead babies, she thought, and a goose walked over her grave.

'Don't be ridiculous,' she said, and stroked the round little belly of the cherub. 'You'll soon look beautiful.' Suddenly, the full realization of what had happened swept over her, and tears of joy filled her eyes. She longed to pick up the telephone and call Patrick, and knew he would be as thrilled as she was. 'I must be calm,' she said, 'and sensible, and not allow myself, or Patrick, to get too excited until we know that the baby is all right. I'll talk to him tonight as usual.' Then she put her head down on her arms, on the table in front of her, and closed her eyes. 'Please God, let the baby be all right,' she prayed.

She got up and went to the kitchen to get the rabbitskin glue. She stirred it, then poured some into an old jam jar. She took it back to the table, and began to add yellow ochre, mixing until she had a thin, smooth, creamy paste. Taking a soft, wide brush, she painted her cherub all over, working the colour into the deepest recesses, where the gold could not reach. Then she went back to the kitchen and made herself a sandwich. She looked at the half-full bottle of wine in the fridge door. Better not, she thought, and poured herself some orange juice instead. All that champagne with Patrick and his father, she thought, and laughed guiltily. 'Poor old baby.'

She ate her sandwich, washed her plate and glass, and got out a clean jar in which to make her red bole, mixing red powdered clay to a paste with rabbitskin glue. This done, she took the jar through to the work-table and applied the bole carefully and smoothly to her angel, who now began to look as if he were made of terracotta. When the bole was dry, she buffed the surface to a smooth finish with a stencil brush until it shone, and she could not feel any little lumps or imperfections. At last the preliminary work was finished, and she could begin the most interesting part, the actual gilding.

Anna cleared away all the pots and brushes, washing them all carefully before returning them to their usual places. Then she set out all her gilding tools, her books of gold leaf, her calf-skin pad, and her gilder's knife and tips. She picked up her angel and examined him carefully all over for any flaws, and then resettled him on his cradle. I'll start with his tummy, she thought, and carefully wetted a small area. Then she lifted a page of gold leaf from its book with her knife, and deftly blew it flat on to the calf-skin pad. She cut the page into suitable pieces with the knife, then lifted each piece with her tip, laying it on the wetted surface and gently dabbing it into position. She carried on with the work until the church clock struck four, and she had gilded the angel's torso and head, and one of his arms.

'You're going to be beautiful,' she said, lightly touching the tip of his nose, 'just like your brother.'

She covered the tools with a soft cloth, and went to the kitchen to make some tea. She brought the mug back to the big room and lay down on the campaign bed. She sipped the hot, bergamot-scented tea and let her eyes wander round her much-loved room. The gilded frames of her paintings, and the golden insurance plaques scattered over the wall, all glowed softly in the late afternoon light. She saw herself reflected darkly in the blue, wavering light of the long Venetian mirror, its silver backing blotched and spotty. It had been a present from her father at the time of her marriage to Jeffrey, and she had always loved the ghostly and mysterious images it threw back to her room. She gazed at the blurred picture of herself, relaxed against the off-white cushions of the campaign bed, ankles crossed, hands curved round the Chinese mug, with its pattern of white herons on a deep blue ground, her eyes dark pools, under straight dark brows in her narrow face, her hair straggling over her shoulders.

She smiled at herself. 'Anna,' she said, 'for once, you look beautiful, and a bit smug.' She heard Olivia's key in the door, and her heavy Doc Marten-shod feet pounding up the stairs. She turned her head lazily as Olivia erupted through the door.

'Hello Mum,' she said, 'are you all right?'

'Of course I'm all right, darling. Why wouldn't I be?'

'Oh, nothing. But you don't usually have a kip in the afternoon, do you?'

'Perhaps it's time I did,' said Anna, smiling at her daughter.

Later that night, waiting for Patrick's call, Anna lay propped on her pillows, her hands resting protectively over her stomach. Slowly, through her haze of happiness, the realization came that she had many problems to deal with, not the least being Jeffrey. She had done nothing so far about divorce proceedings, and now more than ever she knew that she would have to take some action, and not let things drift. She could not think how to set about it. How to find a suitable lawyer? Yellow Pages? She couldn't very well ask Jeffrey, who had, of course, always dealt with their business affairs. I'll ask Dad, she thought, he'll know what to do. Then there was the question of where she would live. Obviously she wanted to be with Patrick, particularly now with the possibility of the baby. But what about Josh and Olivia? She couldn't just walk away from them, nor would she want to.

The telephone rang on her night table. She lifted it and held it to her ear.

'Anna?' said Patrick, 'is that you, darling?'

'No,' said Anna softly, 'it's us.'

'What you do mean?' said Patrick, quietly.

'I mean, my love, it's me and our baby.'

'Anna, are you sure?'

Anna told him about her visit to the gynaecologist, about the tests for Down's syndrome and spina bifida that she would have to have, and then, inexplicably, she began to cry.

'Anna,' said Patrick, 'don't cry, darling. Please tell me, how do you feel about it yourself?'

Anna could tell that he was close to tears himself. She blew her nose. 'I feel terribly excited, terribly worried, and terribly happy, not necessarily in that order,' she said, with a shaky laugh.

'Thank God,' said Patrick. 'Thank God. Oh, Anna, you can have no idea what this means to me. I could not imagine anything more wonderful.'

'We mustn't get too excited till we're sure, we must keep it a secret till we know that everything is all right, don't you think?'

'Everything will be absolutely fine, I feel quite sure. How are you feeling?'

'Perfectly OK. Very well; in fact, better than usual.'

'Wonderful, good girl. Is it all right if I come on the Friday night plane? I will take a couple of extra days off, we have such a lot to talk about, decisions to make.'

'Yes, of course. Perhaps Josh and Olivia can go to Dad for the weekend. I'll ask them if they'd mind.'

'I really want to meet Josh, and see Olivia again.'

'Well, we'll go down and have lunch with Dad on Sunday, and bring them back with us on Sunday evening. How would that be?'

'Excellent. I'll look forward to it.'

'I wish you were here, I need you,' said Anna.

'If only you knew what agony it was to see you walk away from me at Charles de Gaulle, you'd know how terribly I need you too, my darling.'

'And now, more than ever.'

'Indeed,' said Patrick. 'Don't worry, we'll work everything out.'

They went on talking, happy to be as close as the telephone could make them, until Patrick realized that it was after one, after midnight for Anna. 'You must get to sleep, it's late,' he said, regretfully.

'Talk to you tomorrow?' said Anna.

'Talk to you tomorrow. Better still, be with you on Friday.'

'Goodnight, my love.'

'Goodnight, darling, please take care,' said Patrick.

She hung up, and turned off the light. She turned on her right side, and, hugging her spare pillow close to her body, fell instantly asleep.

In Paris, Patrick put down the phone and, crossing to the windows, he opened the casement, pushed back the shutters and leaned out, taking deep breaths of the cool night air. A pale moon hung in the starry sky, and he gazed at its cool perfection. Then tears filled his eyes, blurring his vision, and ran hot and unchecked down his face, splashing on the the sill below. He felt in his pocket for a handkerchief. This is ridiculous, he thought, his head throbbing, and blew his nose. Why am I crying? He closed the shutters, and then took a long, hot shower. As the warm water flowed over his body, he felt as if more than his tears were being washed away; all his sadness, loneliness and bitterness seemed to flow away, too. Then he dried himself and, taking Anna's pillow from the cupboard, where he had hidden it to prevent it being laundered, he got into bed, holding it close and inhaling her smell, till he, too, slept.

Chapter Thirteen

Jeffrey drove out to Richmond to keep his appointment with the marriage guidance counsellor. In spite of Anna's point-blank refusal to go with him, he had kept the original appointment by himself and had found the counsellor sympathetic and helpful. He had decided to go on seeing her, in the forlorn hope that she would produce some magic formula that would enable him to save his marriage.

'Sit down, Mr Wickham,' said the counsellor, indicating the sofa, covered in a blue-and-green William Morris fabric, and seating herself in a slightly higher leather chair. It was just like the chairs used by old-fashioned solicitors, Jeffrey thought, rather wishing that it was he who was seated in it, instead of the sofa, which made him feel at a slight disadvantage, no doubt the intention.

'You explained to me last time the *modus vivendi* of your marriage, Mr Wickham,' said the counsellor in her low, friendly voice. 'But you didn't say when you left the family home, or whether or not it was a mutual agreement to live separately.' She sat quietly, and waited for Jeffrey to speak.

Jeffrey sighed, and wondered why he was putting himself through this examination. 'No, it wasn't by mutual agreement. My wife did not want me to leave, in fact for years she tried every trick in the book to get me to come back. Even getting the children to phone me at the office, leaving messages with my secretary that she needed to see me, things like that.' The counsellor said nothing. 'The house in

234

Chiswick is very small, rather poky. There is only one decent-sized room, and it was difficult to get any peace, or relax, or do any work in the evenings, with childrens' paraphernalia everywhere, and my wife's work cluttering the only table. And all that had to be packed away if we sat down to a proper meal, which wasn't often. Usually, it was on one's knees in front of the television, after the kids were in bed.'

The counsellor said nothing, and waited. Jeffrey began to feel slightly threatened, as if he were digging a hole for himself, but he felt compelled to continue, he could not think why. 'I suppose I just felt my capacity to do my work properly was being jeopardised. I need peace and quiet, and an orderly lifestyle,' he said, defensively.

'And you have that now?' asked the counsellor, kindly.

'Yes, I do,' Jeffrey almost shouted. 'But don't forget that I pay all the major bills, the mortgage and so on, every damn thing. Anna only pays for the food they eat, she can't say I haven't been generous to her.'

'Has she said that?'

'No,' said Jeffrey miserably. 'She doesn't seem to consider such things important.'

The counsellor said nothing. Jeffrey shifted his position, stealing a glance at his watch as he did so. Oh God, he thought, twenty minutes still to go. The counsellor looked at him, still saying nothing. Jeffrey closed his eyes briefly.

'And now she has found this elderly Frenchman, who seems to be eager to pick up the tab, God knows why, so I am no longer of any use to her. She wishes to end our marriage.'

'And the children? What of them?' asked the counsellor quietly.

'Oh, they'll do whatever she wants,' said Jeffrey drearily. 'They adore her.'

'And does she adore them, too?'

'Of course she does. And so does her horrible old mother, with her jolly house in Provence, and her daft old father, with his jolly old mill in Sussex.'

'Are there no grandparents on your side of the family, Mr Wickham?'

'Yes, there's my mother,' said Jeffrey. 'But I never see her. She lives in Sunderland; I've rather lost touch.'

'Did your wife not wish to meet your parents?'

'The question never really arose. My father died years ago, my mother married again. I haven't seen her for years, as a matter of fact. We never got on, anyway.'

'How sad,' said the counsellor.

'Is it?' said Jeffrey, rudely. The counsellor said nothing. 'Well, anyway,' said Jeffrey, 'I expect that was my fault too. Obviously I don't fit into the received ideas about the nuclear family.'

'And yet you seem anxious to preserve your own?'

'Idiotic, isn't it?' Jeffrey stood up, effectively terminating the interview. The counsellor stood up, and went with him to the door. 'Goodbye,' said Jeffrey, 'and thank you. I'll telephone, maybe next week. My diary is rather full just now.'

'Goodbye, Mr Wickham.' The counsellor smiled as Jeffrey went down the path to the gate. She had heard it all before. She knew he would not come again.

As Jeffrey walked down the pavement to his car, a dark green Jaguar driven by a silver-haired man passed him. Time I had a new car, he said to himself. I need something to cheer myself up.

On Tuesday morning Anna telephoned Robert. She let the phone ring for several minutes in case he should be outside working, and eventually he answered, sounding out of breath.

'Dad? It's me, Anna. I hope I didn't make you run, or anything?'

'No, no. I was in the attic, as a matter of fact.'

'Goodness,' said Anna, 'whatever were you doing up there?'

'Oh,' said Robert, vaguely, 'just sorting things out a bit. How are you, darling? Any special reason for phoning in the morning?'

'Yes, Dad, two reasons. I need advice. Could you come up and have lunch with me, do you think?'

'Um. Yes, of course. But tell me what the problem is, anyway.'

'Well, the thing is, I want a divorce from Jeffrey, and I haven't the first idea how to set about it. What is even more important is how to stop him making things difficult for Josh and Olivia.'

'Good heavens, my dear girl, I'm in much the same boat, myself. Kate's done a bunk, and will almost certainly want a divorce.'

'Golly,' said Anna, 'when did all this happen?'

'It's been on the cards for quite some time. I can't say I mind, except for the financial implications, which could be serious, unfortunately. Any particular reason for your sudden change of heart? Not that I don't totally approve of your getting rid of that creep Jeffrey.'

'Yes, Dad, there's a huge and wonderful reason. He's called Patrick Halard, and I met him when he came to Ma's with Giò, and we want to marry as soon as we can. I'm bringing him to lunch with you on Sunday, if that's all right?'

'Yes, of course it is. Giò will be here, too, and possibly your mother. I'm waiting to hear from her.'

'Goodness, how are you coping? What a houseful. I was going to ask you to have Josh and Olly again, but maybe that would be too much for you?'

'Not at all, I'd be delighted. They are both so kind and competent, I love them being here. I've found lots of marvellous things in the attic to show them. I had no idea that grandchildren could be such a bonus in one's dotage.'

'Dad?'

'Yes?'

'I'm bursting to tell you, but it's a secret until we've had tests and things done.'

'What is?'

'I'm pregnant.'

'Anna, how fantastic! Are you both pleased?'

'Absolutely thrilled, but trying not to get too excited until I've had the tests for Down's syndrome and so on. On account of my advanced years.'

'Well, what terrific news. I shall look forward to meeting my future son-in-law, what's his name, Patrick?'

'That's right. So you see, I do rather urgently need to see lawyers and things. You too, by the sound of things. Could you come to lunch tomorrow?'

'Absolutely. I'll be with you at twelve thirty. In the meantime, I'll do some research on the legal side.'

'Great, that's a weight off my mind. See you tomorrow, Dad.'

At four o'clock Anna floated the last piece of gold leaf onto her cherub, and gently dabbed it into position with her tip. Then she brushed away the surplus fragments of gold, and sat back on her stool to admire his warmth and brilliance. Tomorrow she would begin to distress him, burnishing and toning down the gold to produce an aged appearance, letting the rosy tones of the red bole show faintly through the coat of gold leaf, and making him a perfect pair with his brother. Gently, she lifted his cradle, and carried him to rest on the deep window sill. Then she carefully packed away all her gilding tools in the shallow top drawers of her filing cabinet, and wiped down the long table. We'll have a proper dinner at the table tonight, she thought, and then I must talk to them about Patrick coming for the weekend, and see how they feel about it.

She took a chicken from the fridge, and stuffed its cavity with garlic and herbs and half a lemon, rubbed olive oil all over it, and a grinding of pepper, and left it to come to room temperature. She washed big potatoes, ready for baking, and fennel for braising. Then she rinsed salad, dried it in the plastic spinner and put it in a green bowl in the fridge, ready for dressing.

She heard Olivia's feet on the stairs, and her voice and Josh's talking at the same time. They came through the door.

'Hi, Mum. You've tidied up, is it finished?' said Olly.

'Nearly. Just the burnishing to do now. Have you got much prep? What time would you like supper?' said Anna, as they crowded into the kitchen. 'Do you want tea?'

'Quite a lot. Eight o'clock. Yes, please,' said Josh.

Anna filled the kettle, put mugs on the worktop, got milk from the fridge and a packet of digestive biscuits from the cupboard.

'I'll do the tea,' said Josh. 'Olly, take my bag upstairs if you're going, will you?'

Olivia and Anna went into the big room and sat down at the table, waiting for Josh to bring the tea.

'Is someone coming to supper, Mum? You've tidied everything up,' said Olivia.

'No,' said Anna, 'just us. Though Grandpa's coming to have lunch with me tomorrow.'

'That's nice,' said Josh, coming in with the tea, and putting the tray on the table. 'He hardly ever comes to London, does he? Shall we see him?'

'Not tomorrow, he'll have to get back, I expect. I was wondering, would you both feel like going down to Boulter's for the weekend? I know it's a bit soon, but Giò will be there, and maybe Domenica.'

'Oh, hell,' said Josh, 'I've got a rugger practice on Saturday morning.'

'Oh, dear,' said Anna, 'have you really?'

'What's the problem?' asked Josh, sitting down and drinking his tea.

'It's not a problem,' said Anna uncertainly, 'it's just that Patrick is coming for the weekend, and I sort of thought that you would both probably rather not be here.'

239

'Why not?' said Olivia, 'I'm longing to see him again, he's quite my most favourite man.'

'Yes, why not, Mum?' said Josh. 'I want to meet him too, you know.'

Anna felt herself blushing. 'Well, it's just that we haven't got a spare room,' she said, feeling foolish.

Josh burst out laughing. 'Mum! Are you crazy, do you think we haven't guessed? He'll sleep with you, naturally, why not?' he said.

'And you won't mind?' said Anna.

'We're all adults here, Mum,' said Olivia. 'Anyway, I think it's lovely, especially about the baby.'

'What baby?' said Anna faintly.

Olivia looked at her mother with her cool blue eyes, gentle and slightly mocking, and smiled. 'Who're you kidding, Mum? You're pregnant, aren't you?'

'How can you possibly tell?'

'Easy. You're all vague and dreamy, on cloud nine. Half the time you're not even listening to us, are you?'

'How awful, I don't mean to neglect you,' said Anna, feeling guilty.

Josh laughed. 'You don't neglect us,' he said. 'What a twit you are. You're absolutely entitled to be happy, and it's great that you are.'

Anna felt very inclined to burst into tears. Instead, she blew her nose, and told them about the tests she would have to have, and warned them about not getting too excited in case anything went wrong.

'It won't' said Olivia, 'I just know it won't, it can't. I hope it's a girl.'

'What about Dad? He's not going to like it, is he?' said Josh.

'This is it, Josh. That's why Grandpa is coming tomorrow, to advise me about lawyers and stuff, and getting the divorce under way. He's in much the same boat himself, Kate's left him and come back to London.'

'Really?' said Josh. 'Good. I always thought her gross.' He crunched a biscuit and finished his tea, looking thoughtful. 'Tell you what, Mum,' he said after a while, 'I can see that it would be nicer for you to have Patrick on your own the first time, so I'll chuck the rugger this once, and go down to Boulter's with Olly.'

'Could you really?' said Anna. 'Then I could bring Patrick to meet Grandpa on Sunday for lunch, and then we could all drive back together. Would that be OK?'

'Great,' said Josh and Olivia together.

Later that night, when Anna had gone up to have her bath, Josh and Olivia sat at either end of the table, finishing their prep. They heard the bathroom door click and the water running into the bath. The lamplight fell in a pool over Josh's work, his pen scratched in the quietness of the room.

'What do you think's going to happen?' asked Olivia quietly.

Josh looked up, a small frown of concentration on his face. 'I have simply no idea,' he said. 'Yet.'

'Will Mum go to Paris, do you think?'

'I expect so,' said Josh.

'Without us? Will we have to live with Dad?' Olivia sounded anxious.

'No, I'm sure not. They'll work something out, and they have to consult us. We are legally entitled to choose which parent we wish to be with,' said Josh.

'Do you think Mum and Patrick will want to have us in Paris?' said Olivia, in a small voice.

'Is that what you'd like?' said Josh.

'Yes, I think so,' said Olivia. 'What about you?'

'Well, it would be a bit disruptive for my A-levels next summer, wouldn't it? Maybe they'll just let me stay on here, till I go to Cambridge. If I get in.'

'Would you like that?' said Olivia. 'Wouldn't you be awfully lonely? What about cooking and stuff?'

'That wouldn't be a problem, it would be great to have the place to myself. And probably Emma could help out sometimes,' said Josh, giving Olivia a look, and warming to the idea.

'You're kidding,' said Olivia, looking prim.

'I most certainly am not,' said Josh. 'I'm not a child, Olly.'

'I think I still am, rather,' said Olivia forlornly.

Josh smiled. 'Nothing wrong with that,' he said kindly, closing his books, and switching on *News at Ten*.

'Are you pleased about the baby?' said Olivia, sitting on the floor next to Josh.

'Yes, I think so. Are you?'

'Yes. I'm only a bit worried that she won't be all right. She's rather long in the tooth for it, isn't she?'

'Well, what about Patrick?' said Josh.

'God, yes, he's frightfully old. Grey hair, even. But quite sexy. He's got a nice bum."

'Shut up, you prat, I'm trying to listen.'

'Prat yourself,' said Olivia.

'I've made an appointment for us to see this chap Cunningham at three. I've explained the circumstances to him on the phone, and he doesn't see why we can't go together and kill two birds with one stone, so to speak.'

'Dad!' said Anna. 'You don't waste time, do you?'

'Is there any reason why you can't come with me?' said Robert.

'No, none, we'll go of course. Thank you for arranging everything. Would you like a drink before lunch?' said Anna, pulling herself together, trying not to feel nervous about the forthcoming interview.

'No, better not,' said Robert. 'Got to drive, remember?'

At a quarter to three he found a parking meter in a little street near Bedford Square. There were still twenty minutes left on the clock, but Robert fed it to its maximum capacity. They walked round to Bedford Square and found the solicitor's chambers. The receptionist took their names, and sent them up in the lift to the first floor where they were met by a tall, dark secretary and shown into a waiting-room.

'You go first, Anna,' said Robert. 'Your case should be pretty straightforward. After ten years of Jeffrey's desertion, I don't anticipate the slightest difficulty for you. I'm afraid it's possible I've a lot more to lose, myself.'

Feeling slightly sick, Anna stood up when the secretary came back, and followed her to Mr Cunningham's room. He was a square, red-haired man with a ferrety, freckled face and rimless spectacles, and wore a navy pin-striped suit.

'Do sit down, Mrs Wickham,' he said, half rising from his seat. 'You father has told me a little about your situation; it sounds as though there will be no problems. Your husband has not lived with you for roughly ten years, is that correct?'

'Yes, quite correct,' said Anna.

'And now you wish to divorce him, and remarry?'

'That's right.'

'There are two children of the marriage, are there not? What are their ages?'

'Josh is seventeen, Olivia nearly fourteen.'

'And they live with you?'

'Of course.'

'I understand that your future husband is French. Does that mean that you intend to take them to live in France?'

'This is the big problem,' said Anna. 'I think Olivia would move to Paris very happily, she knows France well, her grandmother is French, I am half French myself. But Josh, my son, is another matter. He will be doing his A-levels next summer, and then hopefully will go to Cambridge, so a move for him is out of the question. The ideal thing, really, would be for me to keep possession of our little house in Chiswick, at least until Josh no longer needs a base in London, and have someone to keep house for him. The trouble is, I'm sure that my husband will insist on selling the house, out of spite.'

'It does not necessarily follow that he could do that, Mrs Wickham, if such an action would not be in the best interests of your son,' said Mr Cunningham calmly, writing notes as he spoke.

'Really?'

'Apart from suitable maintenance for the children, all you really want from the settlement is the freehold of the house in Chiswick. Am I right?'

'Could that be possible?' said Anna, doubtfully.

'I think so. I imagine Mr Wickham has other assets, does he not? The flat in St Loo Avenue, he owns the freehold?'

'I think so,' said Anna. 'I've never asked him.'

'Well,' said the solicitor, 'we can easily find out.' He continued writing his notes, then stood up, smiling at Anna in a friendly way.

'I think that's all I need to know at the moment,' he said. 'I'll do the necessary research in respect of Mr Wickham's assets, and then I'll be in touch. I think your requirements are extremely reasonable in the circumstances, and I don't anticipate that your husband could possibly fail to grasp that fact. He is, after all, a lawyer himself.'

'Do you know him?'

'Not as a friend. I know of him, of course.'

'I see.'

'We'll try to make the whole thing as swift and painless as possible for you, Mrs Wickham.'

'Thank you very much,' said Anna, shaking his proffered hand. 'Goodbye. I'll wait for my father in the waiting-room, is that all right?'

'Yes, of course. I'll order some tea for you.'

'Thank you, that would be very kind.'

The secretary ushered her out, and they met Robert in the hallway, on his way in. 'Just like a conveyor belt, isn't it?' he said. He sounded cheerful, but he felt a hollow feeling of foreboding in the pit of his stomach none the less.

*   *   *

On the way back to Chiswick, Robert was very quiet, and Anna guessed that his worst fears had proved to be only too true.

'Poor Dad,' she said at last, 'isn't there anything they can do to stop her?'

'It doesn't look like it, sweetheart,' said Robert. 'I'm afraid she'll take me to the cleaners.' He dropped Anna off at the Lifeboat.

'Won't you come in for some tea? You look awfully tired,' she said, opening the car door.

'I don't think so, darling. Thanks all the same. If I sit down, I'll never get up again.' Robert smiled at her, wearily.

'Would that matter? You could sleep in Josh's bed.'

'No, really. I must get home. Your mother may ring this evening. I wouldn't want to be out.'

'OK, if you're sure,' said Anna. 'Phone me when you get home, promise?'

'Promise,' said Robert.

Anna kissed him on the cheek. 'Thanks for everything, Dad. I feel much better and more confident now. I just wish it didn't look so awful for you.'

'Don't worry,' said Robert, 'it won't be the end of the world, you'll see.' He drove away down the little street, and Anna stood waving till he turned the corner and disappeared. She knew that, for him, the end of his world was exactly what it would be.

Honorine carried the breakfast tray up to Domenica's room. She put the tray down on the cluttered night table, and went to the window to open the shutters and let in the crisp early morning air.

Domenica stirred, and sat up slowly, groaning. 'God, what time is it?' she said.

'Eight o'clock,' said Honorine. 'You 'ave still to pack, don't forget. The taxi arrives at eleven.' She poured Domenica's coffee. 'I still 'ave few things to iron for you, I do it now, and bring them up.'

'You're an angel, Honorine.' Domenica sipped her coffee.

'You won't 'ave me to look after you in England,' said Honorine gruffly, and closed the door behind her.

Domenica lay against her pillows, and stared at the massive beams above her bed. She felt excited at the thought of seeing Robert again, but equally rather nervous. It would be strange to be at Boulter's again after all these years, but Giò would be coming on Friday, Robert had said, the children as well, and Anna and Patrick on Sunday. How will poor Giò handle that, she thought. Reluctantly, she got out of bed, and put on her old blue bathrobe. Her body ached all over, and she stood in front of the window for a few minutes, bending her knees and making circles with her shoulders, to loosen her stiff joints. She touched her toes, and stood up, feeling slightly dizzy.

'Boring old crock,' she said crossly, and went to take her shower. When she emerged from the bathroom, feeling better, Honorine had made her bed, and was laying out the neatly ironed clothes on the counterpane.

'What suitcases you want to 'ave?' she asked.

The taxi arrived just before eleven o'clock, and Honorine stood waving at the gate as it drove away, taking Domenica to the airport. She returned to the house, and went upstairs to tidy Domenica's room. Then she washed up the breakfast things. For the last few days, since Robert's invitation to Domenica to go and stay with him, she had had an increasingly uneasy feeling that somehow things were going to change. Not that Domenica had said anything to give that impression. On the contrary, she had been unusually subdued and silent. Honorine poured the remains of Domenica's pot of coffee into a mug, and sat at the kitchen table to drink it. On the table was Domenica's notepad on which she had written Robert's telephone number, with all the code numbers, and the address. Honorine sighed and, tearing off the note, folded it carefully and put it in her pocket. Then she got up and went round the house, checking all the windows and closing the shutters. She double-locked the kitchen door with the big, heavy old key, and the iron gate with the smaller one. Slowly she crossed the empty midday square to her little house. She was glad that Domenica was having a holiday, but it felt lonely and strange to have nothing to do.

'Oh, well,' she said aloud, 'I suppose I can always clean my own house, and decorate the spare room, for next year.'

Then another thought struck her. 'I'll go to the vine-yard, and see if they're ready to start the *vendange*. It will be a nice change for me, in the sun and fresh air for once. It will do me good.'

Robert and Domenica drove down the lanes to Boulter's in a flurry of dry, golden beech leaves. The afternoon was crisp and clear, noticeably cooler than Domenica remembered. She wound up her window.

'Not cold are you?' said Robert. 'Shall I put the heater on?'

'Well, perhaps on the feet, it is a bit chilly.'

'You never could stand the climate, could you?' Robert switched on the heater.

Domenica laughed. 'I suppose I was always rather determined to have everything my own way, and the English weather defeated me.'

'And me,' said Robert.

'And you what?'

'And I defeated you.'

'I suppose you did,' said Domenica sadly.

'Weren't we stupid?'

'Very.'

They drove up Boulter's Lane and in at the mill gate. The kitchen court was full of ducks, waiting for their supper. They paddled about, quacking in a demanding manner as Domenica and Robert got out of the car.

'Bloody things,' said Robert, 'shitting everywhere.'
He unlocked the kitchen door and stood aside for
Domenica to enter. It was not very warm in the
kitchen, in spite of the Aga, and Robert put a match
to the fire.

'Tea?' she said, filling the kettle.

'Yes, lovely,' said Robert. 'There's a rather awful
bought cake in the orange tin, in case you're hungry.'

'Just tea will be fine.' They sat on either side of the
fire, and drank the tea. 'Now,' said Domenica firmly,
'tell me what that cow has been up to. Tell me everything, don't leave anything out.'

Slowly and carefully, Robert told her the whole
story, culminating in his painful interview with the
lawyer. 'I feel such a fool,' he concluded, 'I've really
blown everything. Why on earth didn't I have the
sense to make the place into a trust, or whatever
people do to avoid this kind of disaster. The bloody
woman's got me over a barrel.'

'Is it such a disaster?' said Domenica.

'Of course it is. I've lost the children's inheritance,
basically, as well as my family home.'

'I don't see it like that, Robert. It's only a house, and
a piece of land that's killing you with overwork, after
all. In any case, can you really see Giò living here? Or
Anna? Her life, thank God, looks pretty straightforward
now.'

'I had an idea that Josh might be interested,' said
Robert, without much conviction.

'Well,' said Domenica, 'we'll all have to talk it over,
won't we, and see?' She got up and sat next to Robert on
the sofa, leaning against him. 'There's always Souliac,
isn't there? We could sell the presbytery, and buy
the woman out, couldn't we?'

'Domenica! You wouldn't do that, would you?'

'Yes, Robert, I would, if it would make you
happy,' said Domenica quietly, 'and bring you back
to me.'

Robert put his arms round her and hugged her close.

'I never really left you,' he said, 'you know that, don't you?'

She turned her face towards him, and he kissed her. 'No,' said Domenica, smiling. 'You never did.'

'I wonder,' said Robert, passing his hand over his eyes.

'What do you wonder?'

'Is it too early for a drink?'

'Certainly not,' said Domenica, 'it's just what we both need.'

'Whisky?' said Robert, getting up.

'Whisky, and a drop of hot kettle water, please. I'd better go and deal with those vile ducks of yours, can't you hear them banging on the door?'

'And I must bring in your luggage. Do you want a bath before supper? There's plenty of water.'

'No fear,' said Domenica, 'too jolly cold, I'll catch my death in that bathroom. I'll change into trousers and a sweater, though. It's so draughty here, I'd forgotten how uncomfortable it is without the proper clothes.' She went out into the yard with the bucket of duck food, and Robert could hear her talking to the ducks as they snatched and gobbled round her feet. He poured the drinks, threw more logs on the fire, and switched on the central heating. He took the beef stew out of the fridge and put it on the warming plate of the Aga. Then he went out to the car, and brought in Domenica's two suitcases.

'Just look at my filthy shoes,' she said, coming in with the duck bucket and stamping on the doormat.

'Your old wellies are still in the broom cupboard,' said Robert, handing Domenica her whisky.

'Are they really?' she said. 'Nasty clammy things, how I used to loathe them.'

'Welcome home,' said Robert, raising his glass.

'It's nice to be home,' said Domenica, half-way to convincing herself that she was telling the truth.

He carried her suitcases upstairs, and paused outside the spare room he had prepared for her.

'What are we stopping here for?' said Domenica, behind him.

'Um, I thought perhaps . . .' said Robert.

'Do you seriously think I'm going to sleep alone in that freezing room?'

'Where do you want to sleep?'

'Where do you think, idiot?' she said, giving him a push.

'It's awfully untidy in my room.'

'Robert,' said Domenica, 'I haven't come all this way to admire your prowess as a housekeeper.'

'Well,' he said, as she opened the bedroom door and went in, 'at least I hope you'll be able to admire my prowess as a cook, anyway.' He put down the suitcases, and stood there, suddenly rather shy, unable to believe that his dear, maddening, lost Domenica was really there, alone with him in their old bedroom. Domenica put her arms round him and hugged him close to her, and he smelt the long-remembered scent of her hair.

'What I really hope,' she said, 'is that I'll be able to admire your prowess at something quite other, later on.'

Robert felt the old desire stir in him, and his arms tightened round her. 'Not now?' he said.

'Certainly not,' she said, laughing. 'First things first. What about your lovely dinner? I'm starving, I didn't eat on the plane.'

Robert kissed the top of her head, and released her. 'OK, ma'am, whatever you say. Hurry down, please, I need your special skills with the salad. Meat and two veg I can manage. Salads still seem to elude me, somehow.'

Domenica opened her suitcases, and took out honey-coloured corduroy trousers and a long scarlet cashmere sweater. She began to strip off her clothes. Robert stood in the doorway, watching her.

'Domenica,' he said.

'What?' she said, pulling her shirt off over her head, and shaking her wild grey curly hair.

'I love you,' he said.

'I love you, too, Robert,' she said, 'I always have.'

Robert closed the door and went downstairs, whistling.

Chapter Fourteen

Giò drove the empty van off the hovercraft at Dover, and headed for passport control.

'Funny name for a Frenchman,' said the officer, flicking through Giò's passport.

'My father is English,' said Giò, pleasantly. Nosy little sod, he thought.

'Here on business?'

'No, I'm here to collect some bits and pieces from my father's house and take them to my flat in Paris,' said Giò, trying not to sound irritated.

'Valuable antiques are they, sir?' said the officer, handing back Giò's passport reluctantly.

'No, just junk from my Dad's old nursery,' said Giò. The officer seemed to lose interest, so Giò drove slowly through the barrier and up the hill, past endless road-works, to the motorway. It was a fine, sunny afternoon, and he made good time to Crawley. He took the A23 for a few miles, and then continued by minor roads to Boulter's Mill. The late afternoon sun shone in his eyes, and he slowed down as the battered old van rattled along the lanes. He drove up Boulter's Lane and in at the drive, and parked in the kitchen court, where Robert's old Morris Traveller stood in its usual place. He got out of the van and stretched his arms above his head, taking deep breaths of the moist autumn air. A cloud of midges gathered about his head, and round the corner of the old mill building a flock of ducks came running, orange feet flapping on the brick paving, their greedy quacks filling the yard.

'Piss off, you little horrors,' said Giò, taking his bag

out of the van, and running past the importunate ducks into the house, slamming the door behind him.

In the kitchen all was calm and quiet, except for the ticking of the clock on the wall. The faint smell of a garlicky meal hovered on the air, and half a bottle of wine stood on the table, corked, with two glasses, and two coffee cups. Hell, thought Giò, I hope that bloody Kate hasn't changed her mind after all and come back. He dropped his bag on the floor, and went through to the book-room. It was empty. The evening sun shone through the tall Georgian windows overlooking the lawn, and lit up the shelves of books and the pale marble chimneypiece, with its cold, empty firebasket, rarely lit these days. How peaceful it all is, thought Giò, but terribly sad somehow. I'd die of depression here, on my own. I suppose I'm pretty depressed and lonely in Paris, but at least there I can go to the gym, or the cinema, or have a drink in a café. There's always the hope of meeting someone new, something happening, like Mr Right coming along. Trouble is, my Mr Right turns out to be Mr Wrong.

He lay down on the long, saffron silk-covered sofa, taking care not to put his shoes on the fabric. He put his hands behind his head, and looked around the room at his grandparents' half-remembered and scarcely appreciated possessions, now Robert's, and presumably one day his and Anna's. Unless that greedy cow grabs the lot, he thought.

He got up and went out to the hall. He opened the drawing-room door, and peered in. The room was in semi-darkness, the shutters closed and the curtains half drawn. Giò shivered, and closed the door. He looked up the wide stairwell, with its old Turkey carpet and bogus Reynolds portraits.

'Hullo!' he called. 'Anyone home?'

A door banged upstairs, and Giò heard footsteps on the bare wooden stairs to the attic. He waited for a moment, and then Robert and Domenica appeared on the landing above. Domenica's arms were full of Victorian wax dolls, and a crimson silk fringed Spanish shawl, lavishly embroidered with white paeonies was draped across her shoulders.

'I thought I heard someone calling,' said Domenica. 'Did you?'

'No,' said Robert, and took her face in his hands and kissed her.

'Dad, Ma, stop snogging,' called Giò. 'It's me, I've arrived. You are hopeless, Dad. Anyone could come in here and clean you out, and you wouldn't even hear them.'

Robert and Domenica looked over the balustrade at Giò, looking up at them, smiling.

'Hello, darling,' said Domenica. 'You're here then.'

'Didn't expect you so soon, old chap,' said Robert.

'Evidently,' said Giò, drily, as they came down the staircase together. 'When did you get here?'

'Yesterday,' said Domenica and Robert together, and they laughed, rather self-consciously.

'Good,' said Giò, kissing his mother, 'I can see the holiday is doing you good already.'

'Who said anything about a holiday?' said Domenica. 'Your father has been bullying me to help him sort out the stuff in that filthy attic. My nose and hair are full of dust and cobwebs.' She led the way into the kitchen, and ranged the dolls along the sofa.

'Are those to go to Paris?' said Giò.

'No, they are staying with us,' said Domenica.

Robert moved the kettle onto the hot plate of the Aga, and put mugs on the table, and milk.

'Anything to eat, Dad? I'm ravenous, no lunch,' said Giò.

Robert got out bread and cheese, and a jar of chutney bought at the WI fête. 'How's that, OK?'

'Great, thanks,' said Giò, cutting himself a hunk of bread and cheese. 'How have you been getting on upstairs? Have you decided what you want me to take?'

Robert poured the tea, handed a mug to Domenica, and slid one across the table to Giò. 'Well,' he said, 'we seem to be getting somewhere, but we've been rather fighting every step of the way, because your mother seems determined to keep everything.'

God, thought Giò, drinking tea, why does she have to interfere? She's impossible. He cut himself another slice of bread and said nothing.

'The thing is,' said Robert, uncertainly, 'she has this idea that she might sell the presbytery and pay Kate off that way.'

'Well,' said Giò patiently, 'I suppose that could be one solution. But have you really thought it through?'

'How do you mean?' said Domenica. 'As far as I'm concerned, I don't care where I am, as long as I'm with Robert.'

'Very touching, Ma,' said Giò, 'but be realistic. After a few months of the cold and wet, and the sheer slog of keeping this place going, you'd be at each other's throats again, you know you would.'

'It's true, darling,' said Robert, 'he's absolutely right.' He took Domenica's hand and held it to his lips. Domenica, reluctant to let go of the idea of herself as the saviour of the family fortune, looked at Robert, her eyes filled with tears.

'I did so want to help,' she said plaintively.

'I know you did, sweetheart,' said Robert, 'but the best help you can be, is just being here.'

'In any case,' said Giò, seizing the moment, 'it's high time you two realized that you have to slow down and take things a bit easier. Enjoy life, don't keep slaving away till you drop.' He looked at them both, sitting side by side, holding hands like a pair of elderly children, defeated by age and circumstances, and felt great tenderness for them. 'Doesn't it occur to you both,' he said gently, 'that with Boulter's sold, and Kate got rid of, you could have a little place in London, and divide your time between London and Souliac, as well as a bigger income?'

Robert looked at Giò, and Giò saw a flicker of interest and hope in his eyes. 'You're right, of course,

Giò,' he said. 'We mustn't blind ourselves to the harsh facts of our senility any longer.'

'Senile yourself, you old goat,' said Domenica, snatching her hand away, and laughing.

Robert looked at his watch. 'My God,' he said, 'the train will be here in ten minutes, with Josh and Olly.'

'Where are they getting off?' said Giò.

'Pulborough,' said Robert

'I'll go and pick them up.' Giò stood up and put on his jacket.

'Would you?' said Robert. 'We ought to get cracking on the dinner. They eat like horses, the pair of them.'

'I'll take your car,' said Giò. 'Where're the keys?'

'In the car,' said Robert.

'Dad! You're completely irresponsible.'

He drove off, shaking his head, and Robert and Domenica went down to the walled garden to get the vegetables and fruit for supper.

'Actually,' said Robert, 'I think I could get to enjoy being irresponsible.'

'So could I, darling,' said Domenica, and for no reason her mind flew back to Souliac, to that very first evening, so long ago, when they had unlocked the gate of the presbytery, and wandered hand in hand all over the empty, silent house and garden.

'After all,' she said, in an apparent *non sequitur*, 'We won't be losing both our homes, will we?'

'No, darling, we won't,' said Robert, opening the gate to the walled garden, and letting Domenica pass.

She turned towards him, and put her hands on his chest. 'And I don't think you're at all senile,' she said.

Robert smiled down at her. 'Just a touch decrepit, perhaps?'

'Nothing a bit of warm sunshine won't take care of.'

'I can hardly wait.'

*   *   *

The train was on time, and Josh and Olivia sat on a bench, waiting to be picked up.

'Don't forget,' said Josh sternly, 'not a word about the baby. Domenica will be furious if she finds out that Mum has told Grandpa and us before her. So leave it to her, OK?'

'Of course,' said Olivia. 'Do you take me for a complete moron?'

'No,' said Josh, 'I don't. I just think you're a bit impulsive sometimes.'

'Prig,' said Olivia, standing up and gathering up her bags, as the Morris rattled into the station yard. 'Oh, look, it's Giò, what fun,' she added, running to the door and jumping in beside him before Josh could get there first.

'Another nice thing, my love,' said Domenica, slicing carrots in the kitchen, back at Boulter's, 'at Souliac, we'll have Honorine to do all this, won't we?'

'Blissful thought,' said Robert, uncorking a bottle of wine, and pouring a glass for Domenica. 'Did you know that drinking red wine not only keeps the arteries open, but prevents the onset of Alzheimer's Disease?'

'Who told you that?' Domenica took the glass. 'Not that I actually need any encouragement.'

'Heard it on the telly,' said Robert.

'Well, then it must be true, musn't it?'

'Anna,' said Patrick, as he parked the ancient Renault outside the Lifeboat, and pulled on the handbrake, 'I don't like you driving this car, I'm sure it's not safe. The brakes are feeble, the steering is atrocious, and there's corrosion everywhere.'

'I know. It is rather a worry, but I really do need it here. We're not close to public transport. It's a problem.'

'We shall have to sort something out for you. I've already lost one family in a car accident, I couldn't bear to lose another.'

'Of course,' said Anna, looking at him sadly. 'You're quite right, I know. But how can I afford it?'

'We can afford it,' said Patrick. 'Is there a Renault dealer near here? Would you like a newer Renault?'

'Anything. I don't mind. I've never really thought much about cars.'

'We'll go tomorrow, and get you something safe. I can't bear the thought of you driving this awful thing a moment longer.'

'Better park it in the garage now, we're not going out again, are we?' said Anna. She got out of the car and opened the garage doors, and Patrick drove the crumbling old motor in, and turned off the engine.

She unlocked the front door, and led the way upstairs. Inside, Patrick put down his bag and looked slowly round the room. He smiled, and turning towards Anna, he took her in his arms.

'It's exactly like you,' he said. 'Exquisite, calm and totally original.' He kissed her, and she wound her arms tightly round his neck, full of relief and joy at his nearness and strength, and returned his kiss.

'You should see it when it's chaotic with my work, and the children's prep and stuff, it's not particularly calm then,' she said. She took off his glasses, put them in his pocket, and put her cool fingers on his eyes. 'You look tired, my love,' she said. 'What about a drink before supper?'

'I am tired, rather,' said Patrick. 'I was up at five, we had to do a shoot, and I've been doing voice-over all afternoon. Yes, darling, I'd love a drink. More importantly, how are you? You look quite stunning, you are more beautiful every time I see you.'

'Don't you think that has something to do with you?' said Anna. 'Come on, I'll get you a drink.' She led the way to the kitchen, and Patrick followed her. 'What would you like? Whisky, brandy, wine?'

'Whisky would be fine,' said Patrick.

'There,' said Anna. 'Take that upstairs to the bedroom. You'll find the bathroom; I'm sure you'd like a wash, and I'll get the supper going. It's all prepared, there's nothing much to do.'

He went off obediently with his drink, and Anna listened to his footsteps as he climbed the spiral staircase to the upper floor. She put the casserole in the oven, and lit the gas. She put the potatoes on the hob, and checked the salad dressing. Then she took knives and forks, plates and napkins, and set the table. She put bread, cheese and fruit on the table, and lit the two tall tallow candles in the plain silver candlesticks that Domenica had given her. Then she opened the wine, and poured herself a glass, and lay down on the campaign bed to wait for Patrick. She felt very conscious of his tiredness, and for the first time a stab of fear touched her, as she thought of the difference in their ages. I must look after him, she thought, and not let him work too hard. Dear God, don't let anything happen to him, please, I couldn't bear it.

He came downstairs, and she turned her head and smiled at him. He came over and knelt beside her, and put his hand gently on her stomach. 'I still can't believe it,' he said. 'Do you have any idea of how much I love you, Anna?'

She sat up and kissed him, on his forehead and on each side of his mouth. 'Yes,' she said, 'I think I do. Let's have supper, and go to bed.'

'Is that all right?' said Patrick.

'I don't see why not,' said Anna.

'It's not dangerous for the baby?'

'I don't think so,' said Anna. 'As long as we don't try to break any records.'

'I don't think there's much danger of that,' said Patrick, getting up and holding out his hands to her. 'I'll probably fall asleep as soon as we get into bed.'

'It doesn't matter if you do,' said Anna. 'It's just being together that matters, all three of us.'

'All five of us,' said Patrick gently.

'Of course,' said Anna, 'all five of us, what a lovely thought.'

Much later, Anna, deeply asleep in Patrick's arms, heard the shrill insistent ring of the telephone. Reluctantly, she struggled into consciousness and stretching out an arm, she switched on the bedside lamp. She peered at her little clock: twenty to twelve. Who on earth would be ringing now? God, she thought, something is wrong with the children, and she snatched the phone off its cradle.

'Hello,' she said nervously, her heart thumping.

'Anna? It's me, Jeffrey.'

Relief, followed by rage, filled her. 'Jeffrey! Why on earth are you ringing at this hour?' she said, swallowing her anger and trying to sound calm.

'Why, what time is it? It's not late, have you gone to bed?'

'As a matter of fact I have, yes. What do you want?'

'I thought I'd take the kids out to dinner tomorrow. I've booked a table at the *Del Buongustaio*.'

'I'm afraid they're not here. They're spending the weekend with Dad and Ma at Boulter's.'

'Oh,' said Jeffrey. So that old bitch is here, is she? he thought. 'Nobody tells me anything,' he muttered sulkily.

He sounded rather drunk, Anna thought. 'Well, I'm sorry, but there it is,' she said.

'Why don't you come?' said Jeffrey. 'We need to talk, anyway. We might as well have a decent meal while we're at it.'

'I'm sorry, Jeffrey, I can't.'

'Why the hell not? I'm not going to eat you.'

'I can't because Patrick is here for the weekend.'

'Oh.' Jeffrey sounded taken aback. 'Well, bring him with you. He may as well come, it concerns him too, I suppose.'

'Hold on, I'll ask him,' said Anna, covering the phone with her hand. Patrick, fully awake, lay relaxed and unruffled against the pillows. Anna filled him in briefly. 'What do you think?' she said.

'Well, I can think of better ways of spending an

evening, but if it will help to convince him that it's pointless him trying to stop us, maybe we should sacrifice a few hours, and go.'

'Are you sure?' said Anna.

'Sure,' said Patrick.

'All right, Jeffrey, we'll come,' said Anna into the phone. 'Where is this place?'

'Good,' said Jeffrey. 'Eight thirty, then. It's in Putney Bridge Road.'

'Right,' said Anna, 'we'll be there. Goodnight.' She hung up, and turned off the light, and turned to Patrick, folding herself against him, enclosing him in her arms. 'Are you really sure you want to go?' she said. 'I can always phone and cancel in the morning if we change our minds.'

'No, I think it's quite a good idea. After all, he can't make a scene in a public place, can he?'

'I suppose not,' said Anna, sleepily.

'Anna?'

'Mm?'

'I don't feel tired any more, darling. In fact, I feel rather wide awake.'

Anna opened her eyes, and smiled to herself in the darkness. 'What a coincidence,' she said, 'so do I.'

After breakfast they decided to deal with the question of the car without further delay, and they drove to the Renault dealer. They chose a nearly-new Clio, and went into the office to complete the formalities. They were able to get a small amount off the price in part exchange for the old car, and Patrick arranged to telegraph the money from Paris, after which they would deliver the car to Anna in Church Street.

'In the meantime,' he said, 'we'll hire a car for you until you can have this one.' The dealer agreed to rent them another Clio, and they drove back to Church Street in it. Anna was amazed at the speed and lack of fuss of the entire operation. To her, cars, and their purchase and maintenance, had always represented an ongoing battle, with Anna on the losing side.

She parked the car outside the Lifeboat, and turned to Patrick. 'Thank you,' she said, 'you're an angel.'

'Just looking after my interests,' said Patrick, his pale blue eyes bright behind his spectacles.

'I feel guilty about you giving me such a thing before we are married.'

'Anna,' said Patrick, leaning towards her and gently pushing the long dark fringe of hair out of her eyes, 'as far as I am concerned, we are already married. You are my wife, the mother of our child and the mother of my stepchildren. That's a lot of people to take care of, and I won't allow you to take unnecessary risks with any of them. Least of all me, it's bad for my nerves.' He laughed, put his hand on her neck and kissed her. 'I know that all sounds terribly pompous, but I'm in a perpetual state of terror that something will happen to you, I can't help worrying.'

'Darling Patrick,' said Anna, 'nothing will happen, I'm sure.' In a curious way, she felt that their roles were reversed sometimes, that it was he who was the more anxious one, and she the calmer and more mature. She had never felt confident and in control with John and Olivia. She supposed that she dominated and dressed all her life for figures and Gideon, the big buffey.

'Dominica,' she said, talking of her...

'What about...'

'She's going to be hurt unless we... that Dad and the children know... so... she doesn't. I'd better talk to her tonight and tell her... Then if she's upset, Dad will have time to calm her down before we get there tomorrow. We don't want to spoil the day, do we? I should have told her, really, shouldn't I?'

'Don't worry,' said Patrick, 'I'll tell her I haven't told my father yet.'

'What makes you think that'll make any difference?'

Anna laughed, and got out of the car, locking it carefully. 'It's heaven, driving this after my poor old banger,' she said, giving the car a little pat.

'What shall we do?' said Patrick. 'Go for a walk along the river, get some fresh air?'

'Good idea,' said Anna. She looked at her watch. 'We could have lunch at a pub, it's half past twelve, nearly.'

They walked along the Mall and Hammersmith Terrace to The Dove. It was packed, and blue with smoke, but they squeezed themselves into a corner, with their drinks and a couple of formidable-looking brown sausages in rolls.

Anna sighed as she looked at her tomato juice. 'I am trying not to drink too much,' she said, 'but I really would have loved a gin and tonic.'

'Why not just have the tonic, with the ice and lemon, and a spoonful of gin for the flavour?'

'Patrick, you're a genius. Do you think my dependence on alcohol will affect the baby? I'm a bit scared of getting like Domenica.'

'You won't' said Patrick. 'If it were totally bad for the baby, your body would tell you so, you'd be sick.'

'Do you really think so?'

'Yes, I do. Now, shall I get you the gin?'

'Yes please,' said Anna.

As he pushed his way through the crowd to the bar, she thought what a strange mixture he was, half strong and powerful, half emotionally vulnerable. Maybe that's how it should be, she thought. It's wonderful to have someone to look after you and love you uncritically, as he does me, but it's good that he sometimes needs to lean on me, too.

Patrick came back with the gin, and a separate bottle of tonic, and sat down. 'Now,' he said, 'I've got something exciting to tell you.' He took a notebook from his pocket, and opened it at a pencil sketch, a floor plan. 'The attic next to mine at Grands-Augustins is about to be vacant, for renting. I wondered if you would want us to go on living there, in a bigger space, or whether you would rather move altogether to somewhere else?'

'Of course I'd want to stay there, if you would,' said Anna. 'Explain the plan to me.'

'We could have a new communicating door here, at the top of the staircase, and it would give us three extra bedrooms and a bathroom. It would be perfect for the children, we might even manage a little kitchen in there, so that Olivia and Josh could be a bit more independent if they wish.'

'Sounds wonderful, how exciting.' They sat huddled together, making plans. Anna told him about her interview with Cunningham, and his opinion that she should keep the Lifeboat as her part of the settlement.

'That would be right, for you and for the children,' said Patrick. 'It's a dear little house, absolutely redolent of you in every way. I hate to think of everything being dismantled and taken away, it's one of the really painful elements of divorce, you don't deserve it. God knows, you tried hard enough.'

'Till you walked into my life,' said Anna. 'I changed my mind pretty swiftly then, didn't I?'

'Yes, thank God,' said Patrick. 'Just don't change it again, I beg you.'

Robert and Domenica drove to Sainsbury's to shop for the Sunday lunch party, leaving Giò, Josh and Olivia to carry down all the stuff they had chosen to go to Paris, and put it in the drawing-room. After that, everything had to be cleaned and wrapped in the bubble plastic Giò had brought with him, and then packed into the van.

'Get Ma out of the way, Dad, for heaven's sake, or we'll never get it done,' said Giò, waylaying his father on his way to the garden to dig potatoes. So Robert suggested to Domenica that the leg of lamb they planned to have for Sunday lunch wasn't really big enough to feed seven hungry people. What did she think? Should they get a second one, or go and buy something else?

Domenica looked at the leg, sitting on a dish in the fridge, and agreed that it did look a bit small. 'Let's go and get another one, and I will prepare them with garlic and rosemary and anchovies, like Honorine does. Do we have anchovies?'

'No,' said Robert.

'We'll have to get some, and we should go soon, the meat should marinate for twenty-four hours.'

'Right,' said Robert, briskly, 'we'll go now. Get your coat.' He called up the stairs to Giò, 'Giò, we have to go shopping. Can you manage without us?'

'Yes, fine,' called Giò's voice from upstairs. 'Don't hurry back,' he added, under his breath.

'You're rotten, Giò,' said Josh, 'she's only trying to help.'

'I know,' said Giò, 'that's the trouble.'

As he drove down the lane, Robert thought that it might be a good time to tell Domenica about Anna's visit with him to the lawyer, and about the possibility of the baby. It had occurred to him, as well as to Anna, that Domenica would not be pleased if she thought that she was the last to hear the news.

'It's difficult,' he said, 'but I don't think I'll be betraying a confidence if I tell you. She had to tell me on account of the lawyer needing to know, me being there so to speak.' God, I'm making a balls of this, he thought.

'Robert,' said Domenica, 'what on earth are you talking about? Is it something to do with Anna? Has she been shoplifting or something?'

'Yes,' said Robert, 'it is to do with Anna. And Patrick.'

'Oh, God,' said Domenica, 'have they called it off?'

'No, darling, of course not,' said Robert. 'It's just that she's pregnant.'

Domenica was silent for a second, and then laughed her braying laugh. 'Wicked girl,' she said. 'That was a bit swift, wasn't it? But I'm glad, it's lovely. It's funny, but I feel much more inclined to be a grandmother now than I did when Josh was born.'

'The thing is, they're trying not to get too excited about it until she's had tests for various ghastly things and they are sure the baby will be OK. But it's easy to guess, she looks so amazingly different. I can't think of the right word, sort of incandescent, somehow.'

'That's not the baby, darling, that's Patrick,' said Domenica. 'Giò's in love with him too, you know,' she added laconically.

Robert braked sharply, and stopped the car. He turned to Domenica, frowning. 'Whatever do you mean? Is the fellow bisexual, or something?'

'Apparently not, though I did rather wonder, at first, when Giò brought him to Souliac.'

'Has Giò spoken about it to you?'

'Yes, he has. Poor old boy, it seems that his feelings are quite unrequited. Nonetheless, it's odd, isn't it, that Patrick was a friend of Giò's first, and then fell in love with the female mirror image?'

'Indeed,' said Robert, sounding worried.

Domenica laughed again, and patted his knee. 'Come on, we must g__ __ __ he sa__. 'T__y're qui__ old eno__g_, he lot of __e_ t_ so__ t__in__ ou__ _or __m-selv__s V__e must __t __ _rr__ng __o__t __em__

'I__o__s __ne ev__ __a__?' __aid R__be__ le__ __ng __ the clut__h__

'I__o__s__id __Do__e__a __ d__n't __i__k __e d__s.'

Ann__a__ c__ll t__ D__m__i__ th__t e__ __ning __ok __nge__ than she had intended, as Domenica insisted on a blow-by-blow account of Anna's visit to the gynaecologist, and an explanation of the tests she would have to have.

'I'll tell you all about it tomorrow,' she said. 'I must stop now, we're late already.'

Jeffrey was already seated at a table and reading a

menu when Patrick and Anna arrived at the restaurant. Anna was surprised at his choice; he looked totally out of place in such cheerful and friendly surroundings, where the busy kitchen could be seen through an arch, and the lively young waiters wove their way skilfully and swiftly around the crowded little room, carrying steaming plates to the tables. Anna pointed towards Jeffrey, unable to make herself heard above the noise, and the waiter led them to the table. Jeffrey stood up, and Anna and Patrick sat down.

'What a delightful place this is, so friendly,' said Anna.

'Not really my cup of tea, but I thought it would amuse the kids,' said Jeffrey.

The waiter put a dish of shiny black olives sprinkled with orange zest on the table, and gave Anna and Patrick menus.

'A bottle of house red,' said Jeffrey to the waiter.

'And could we have some water, too, please?' said Anna.

'Of course,' said Jeffrey, looking pained. 'What do you want, Perrier?'

'I could have a carafe of tap water if you like,' said Anna, smiling.

'No, of course not.' Jeffrey sounded irritated. 'A bottle of Perrier,' he said to the waiter. The waiter sped away, and came back almost immediately with the wine, already opened, and the water. He poured the wine and opened the water.

'I'll have to make this glass last,' said Anna, 'I'm driving.' She popped an olive in her mouth, and studied the menu, feeling hungry.

'I think I'll have the spinach and ricotta pie, and then the prawns in prosciutto,' she said.

'Sounds lovely, I'll have the same,' said Patrick.

'I'll have the *piatto pizzicarello*, and the meatballs,' said Jeffrey. The waiter scribbled the order, took the menus from them, and departed to the kitchen. Jeffrey took a long pull at his glass of wine. 'I had a letter from

267

that fellow Cunningham,' he said to Anna, pointedly ignoring Patrick.

'Really?' said Anna. 'He doesn't hang about, I must say.'

'He appears to have done his homework concerning my total assets, and seems to think you are in a position to demand half their value.'

'Is that what he says?' said Anna. 'It doesn't sound very like my conversation with him.'

'No, that was just the underlying threat. What he says is that you want the freehold of the Lifeboat, agreed maintenance for the children, and the legal costs of the divorce. Is that correct?'

'Absolutely,' said Anna.

'In the circumstances, it seems I have very little choice in the matter,' said Jeffrey, rather sulkily. The food arrived, and they began to eat. 'Are you proposing to go on living in the Lifeboat?' he continued, after a pause.

'My chief concern, and Patrick's, is for the welfare of Josh and Olivia. I want the Lifeboat to be their London home. I haven't discussed it with them yet, but obviously Josh will want to be here until he goes up to Cambridge. Olly will probably opt to move to Paris, going to school there, but of course it's for the children to decide for themselves.'

'Surely opinion ought to be considered, is that it' said Jeffrey, putting down his fork, and pushing away his plate angrily.

Patrick looked at him and smiled sympathetically. He spoke for the first time. 'Don't you think that the children will be much more likely to preserve the English side of themselves, if they have a secure London base from which to operate?' Jeffrey looked mutinous, his mouth set and grim. 'And much more inclined to keep their good relationship with you?' Patrick spoke quietly, without emphasis.

'Oh, that,' said Jeffrey. 'It never was particularly good, anyway.'

'Oh, Jeffrey,' said Anna, 'whose fault is that?'

'And what are you two proposing to live on, may I ask? Your huge joint earnings? You're a freelance TV presenter or something like that, aren't you? Does it pay well? Can you afford a ready-made family on such a hand-to-mouth existence?'

Patrick, deciding to ignore Jeffrey's rudeness and arrogance, sighed and put down his fork. 'Since you are very properly deeply concerned for Anna's security, as well as that of Josh and Olivia, this is probably the appropriate moment to tell you that I am extremely well paid. Not that it is really any business of yours, Jeffrey, but having been widowed very early in my first marriage, I have had no-one but myself to support for nearly thirty years, and have therefore accumulated a good deal of money. I hope that sets your mind at rest?' He picked up his fork, and began to eat.

'Aha!' said Jeffrey, furiously. 'Now everything is clear to me.'

Anna felt the blood drain from her face, and a feeling of dazed shock engulfed her.

'Anna knows nothing whatsoever about my affairs,' said Patrick calmly, taking her hand. 'We have never, till this moment, discussed money. You may find this difficult to believe, Jeffrey, but it's a matter of complete indifference to us both.'

'Fine words,' said Jeffrey, sarcastically, emptying the bottle into his own glass, and signalling to the waiter to bring another. 'Anna likes money all right, she sure as hell knows how to spend it.'

'Anna,' said Patrick, 'would you prefer to go home?'

Anna looked from one to the other, hesitating. The thought of a scene appalled her, and she wished they had not agreed to come.

'I'm sorry,' said Jeffrey miserably, 'don't go, please.' For a moment he felt as if he might break down. He swallowed hard, gripping the edge of the table.

'Are you sure it wouldn't be best if we went?' said

269

Anna. 'This is painful for us all. I don't want to hurt you, Jeffrey, any more than I have already.'

Suddenly, Jeffrey's anger faded, and he looked up, his close-together blue eyes empty. In that moment, he knew that he had surrendered, knew he could not hold on to Anna, that he had to let her go, and put a good face on it. He saw them both looking at him, the identical expression of concern on their faces.

'No need to take me too seriously,' he said with forced cheerfulness. 'You'll make a better husband for her than I was.' He raised his glass. 'I'm sure you'll be very happy.'

The waiter arrived with the main course, and Jeffrey picked up his knife and fork.

'Smells good,' he said. '*Bon appetit*, or whatever it is.'

'*Merci*,' said Anna. '*Toi aussi*.'

'You sound like a bloody frog already,' said Jeffrey.

Chapter Fifteen

Olivia sat on a stool in the kitchen at Boulter's Mill, slicing string beans into a colander.

'We never eat them as big as this in France,' she said critically, holding up a huge, foot-long bean, for Domenica's inspection.

'I know, darling, it's the English. They can never bear to pick them young enough, they consider it infanticide.'

'They'll be awfully tough, won't they?'

'Just take care to get all the stringy bits off and slice them very thin, and they won't be too bad. We shall have to educate Grandpa, won't we?'

Domenica opened the door of the hot oven, and slid out the two legs of lamb, browning gently on their rack. She basted them with the oil and wine marinade, replaced the roasting tin lower down in the oven, and carefully closed the door.

'The English do understand lamb, though. The meat here is far superior to ours, especially in Languedoc,' she said. She heated oil in another roasting tin, and put in the small peeled potatoes, strewing chopped garlic and rosemary sprigs over them. She put them in the oven, above the lamb. 'Just the sauce to make,' she said, pleased with her efforts so far.

'Mint sauce,' said Olivia, 'I love it.'

'Well,' said Domenica doubtfully, 'is it vital?'

'Vital,' said Olivia seriously, trying not to laugh.

'Tell you what, then,' said Domenica, who had no wish to drown her delicious pink lamb in a cold, vinegary mint concoction. 'we'll make a nice reduction with the marinade and some more wine, and then whizz some mint and sugar in the blender, and add it to the reduction. What do you think?'

'Maybe thicken it slightly with a bit of arrowroot? I like it to pour properly not just slurp in the plate,' said Olivia.

'Sounds fine, that's what we'll do,' said her grand-mother.

'Right, they're done,' said Olivia, rinsing the beans and putting them into a heavy saucepan. 'What do you think, boil for five minutes in two centimetres of salted water?'

'How domesticated you are, Olivia, so capable. I hadn't noticed your talents in that direction in Souliac.' Domenica's tone was mocking.

'Well,' said Olivia, defensively, 'Honorine always gets there first, doesn't she? I don't think she likes being helped all that much, do you?'

'No, she doesn't. She likes being indispensable,' said Domenica. 'Long may it last.'

'I'll set the table, shall I?' said Olivia.

'Yes, darling. The blue Italian plates, and the Venetian glasses would be nice, and the proper linen napkins, if Grandpa still has them.'

Domenica checked the first course, a salad of rocket and frisée with quails' eggs and a lemon mayonnaise, keeping cool in the fridge, and then went out to the garden to find Robert. He was oiling the lawn-mower.

'What about some wine for lunch?' she said. 'It's nearly half-past one; they'll be here in a minute.'

'Well,' said Robert, 'I was thinking bubbles before, and Côtes du Rhône with?'

'Are we celebrating something?'

'What do you think?'

Josh and Giò took the last package, a child's high chair wrapped in bubble plastic, and stowed it in the van, ready for Giò's departure after tea.

272

'God, my hands are filthy,' said Giò, locking the rear doors. 'I must wash before lunch.'

'Me too,' said Josh, happily inspecting his black nails. They washed in the sink, scolded by Olivia, and then walked down the lane together to waylay Anna's car.

'Don't you mind all the toys and stuff being sold, Giò?' said Josh, who did mind himself, quite a lot.

'Yes, Josh, I mind, but I'm a pragmatist, and I'd far rather that than have Dad scratching round for every last penny,' said Giò. 'In fact, I'm going to make it my business to siphon off as much of the good stuff to Souliac, and the Lifeboat if there's room, or in store in Paris, before Dad agrees to let that parasite Kate have half of it. It's utterly wrong that she should. It's bad enough her getting half the value of the house, I'm buggered if she's going to walk off with Dad's lovely old furniture and books and pictures as well.'

'But, Giò, can you do that?' said Josh. 'Is it legal?'

'Don't be naïve, Josh, of course it isn't. But I can't see the silly cow getting the stuff back once I've spirited it away, can you?' He laughed, but Josh still looked worried.

'I wouldn't want you to go to gaol, Giò,' he mumbled.

'No chance,' said Giò vigorously. 'She hasn't got an inventory, has she?'

A little red Clio came up the lane and stopped beside them.

'Mum!' cried Josh. 'You've got a new car!'

Patrick drove on up the lane and in at the gate, with Giò and Josh running after them. They parked by Giò's van, and got out of the car.

Josh came running up. 'Mum, how terrific,' he panted. 'When did you get it?'

'First things first, darling,' said Anna. 'Patrick, you haven't met Josh yet, have you?'

Patrick held out his hand, and Josh took it, shyly. 'It's very good to meet you,' he said gravely. 'May I call you Patrick?'

'Of course, please do.'

'When did you get the car? It's great,' said Josh, inspecting everything carefully.

'Well,' said Anna, 'this one's a hire, but Patrick bought us one just like it; it'll come next week.'

'I don't want to be rude about your old one, but it really wasn't safe to drive,' said Patrick, looking slightly embarrassed.

'You're damn right, it wasn't,' said Josh, 'I nearly wrote off Olly and me last weekend, the brakes were useless.'

'Oh, God, you didn't tell me,' said Anna, looking anxiously at her son.

'Not a lot of point, was there, after the event? Don't worry, it wasn't that close.'

Domenica and Robert came out of the house, and Olivia shot past them and hurled herself at Patrick, who hugged her, laughing.

'Dad,' said Anna, 'come and meet Patrick at last.'

The two men shook hands, and Robert had a strong feeling that this square, grey-haired man, with his kind, wrinkled eyes behind steel-rimmed spectacles would be the perfect man for Anna, and more than that, a support for them all.

Anna kissed her mother. 'It's wonderful to see you here with Dad again,' she said, hugging her. 'I'm so happy for you both.'

'But your news is even more exciting, isn't it?'

'Oh, Mum, I do hope so. I daren't really believe it till the tests are done.'

Patrick came over to them, and Domenica flung her arms round him, and kissed him. 'You wicked man,' she whispered, 'you've jumped the gun, haven't you? Was it in Souliac?'

'I'm afraid so,' he said. 'Do you mind?'

'No, of course not, it's marvellous.'

'Yes,' said Patrick, 'that's exactly what it is.' He put his arm round Anna's shoulders, while Olivia held on to his free arm, and they all went into the house.

Josh and Giò brought up the rear, and Giò raised his eyebrows quizzically at Josh.

'I'm the invisible man, it seems,' he said.

'You're a nutter, Giò,' said Josh. 'How could you be, in that sweater?'

After lunch, Giò announced that he thought he would go up to the Downs and walk off his lunch, before starting the drive back to Paris.

'Good idea,' said Josh, 'we'll come with you. We can fly the Chinese kite again, if that's all right, Grandpa?'

'Of course,' said Robert, half asleep on the sofa. 'It's all yours, my dear boy, help yourself.' Josh ran upstairs to get the kite.

'Patrick,' said Olivia, 'you come too. It's lovely up there – windy – you can see the sea sometimes.'

'What about you, darling?' said Patrick to Anna.

'No thanks,' said Anna, smiling, 'I'll stay here in the warm. But you go, it will do you good to be out of doors.'

'Yes, I think I will,' said Patrick. 'After that huge lunch, the fresh air will wake me up.'

They got into the Clio and drove up the narrow lane to the top of the hill, and parked the car on the short, sheep-cropped grass. The Downs stretched away around them, their rounded hills topped with dark clumps of wind-bent trees, their valley bottoms brambly and mysterious, and peppered with rabbit warrens.

'Look.' Olivia pointed, 'there's Chanctonbury Ring. They say that white witches dance there naked on Midsummer Night.'

'Not a pretty sight, I imagine,' said Giò.

'Hopefully, you can't see much, if it's dark,' said Josh.

'Ah,' said Giò, 'but they light a bonfire, and leap over the flames.' He laughed. 'The mind does rather boggle, doesn't it?'

Josh looked prim. 'Come on, Olly,' he said, 'Let's get the kite going.' He took it carefully out of the boot of the car, and gave Olivia the reel of string. He ran away with the kite, while Olivia paid out the string. 'Ready?' he shouted, the wind snatching his voice.

'OK!' yelled Olivia, and the kite shot into the air, its tail shaking as it climbed high in the sky.

Patrick and Giò walked on together towards Chanctonbury Ring, the grass crisp, sunbleached and brittle beneath their feet, the ground flecked with white chalk.

'What a marvellous place,' said Patrick. 'I'm amazed it's not full of ramblers and dog-walkers.'

'Oh, it often is,' said Giò, 'especially in the summer.'

'It's the same everywhere, I'm afraid.'

Giò changed the subject. 'You seem to get on well with the kids, Patrick,' he said.

'I hope so,' said Patrick. 'This sort of situation is bound to be a bit fraught for them. I'm just anxious that the changes will be beneficial for them, not damaging.'

'But what about your own child? Won't it rather put their noses out of joint?'

'Why on earth should it, Giò? For me, it will just mean that we have three children instead of two. Just the two would have given me great happiness, but this new one will be an unexpected bonus, all the more wonderful for that. They will all be of equal importance to us both, I know.'

'Oh, well, good,' said Giò. He was silent for a moment, waiting for Patrick to say something, but he did not. 'I didn't know you were so keen on children,' he said, glancing towards him.

'Well, now you do.'

'I hoped I might see you again, in Paris,' said Giò, quietly. 'You've been rather avoiding me, haven't you?'

'No, Giò, I haven't,' said Patrick. 'Not particularly. But don't you think it's less painful for you if we don't meet?'

'Not really.' Giò raised his sad, dark eyes, Anna's

276

eyes, to Patrick. 'It's very hard for me, and so lonely. I wanted us to be friends, Patrick, on any terms. Now I feel excluded from your life, and Anna's.'

'I don't think that either of us intends you to feel excluded, Giò. I expect it's because we are totally wrapped up in each other just now. It's natural, after all, when people are in love.'

'You are in love with Anna, and I am in love with you. Stupid, isn't it?' said Giò, trying to laugh, and failing.

'No,' said Patrick, sighing, 'it's not stupid, Giò. I like you very much, how could I not when you are the very image of Anna? But I don't love you in the way that you would wish, and never could have done.'

'Not even if you had never met her?'

'Never, under any circumstances. I have never had the slightest inclination to have a homosexual relationship. I have had, and still have, lots of gay friends, and greatly value such friendships, like any others. But I have never had a gay lover.'

'And do you count me among your gay friends?'

'Of course I do, what do you think? More than that, you're the brother I never had. The important thing is, Giò, your gayness has nothing to do with your presence, and importance, in all our lives, not just Anna's and mine. You're Giò, you belong to us, that's all there is to say.'

'I wish it were as easy as that,' said Giò, sadly.

'It has to be, I'm afraid.'

'Yes, I realize that. I'm sorry, I'll try. I don't want to spoil things for you and Anna, you have to believe that.'

'I do,' said Patrick. He looked at his watch. 'Come on, it's time we got back,' he said, turning and beginning to walk back to the car.

Josh and Olivia were hauling in the kite, and they stowed it in the boot.

'Race you down the hill, Olly,' said Josh.

'You're on!' said Olivia, and they ran over the grass

and disappeared down the brambly lane that led to the mill. Patrick and Giò got into the car, and drove slowly down the lane after them.

'Don't worry, it'll be all right,' said Giò.

'Of course it will, I never doubted it.'

'I'm sorry I made a fool of myself. I should have kept my feelings to myself.'

'My dear chap,' said Patrick, 'it's not important.'

Giò said nothing, but stared blindly through the windscreen.

After tea, they all went out to the yard to see Giò off back to Paris and, shortly afterwards, Anna said she thought they should get back to London in good time for the children to finish their prep.

Robert and Domenica stood waving as the little red car disappeared down the drive. He put his arm round her shoulders; he knew she hated seeing everyone leave.

'Come on in, it's getting cold,' he said. 'I'll make a fresh pot of tea.'

Domenica put another log on the fire, and curled herself against the squashed cushions of the old sofa, stretching out a hand towards the blaze. Robert brought the tea, and sat down close to her.

'This is a beautiful house, Robert, and I know it will be hard for you to leave it, but it will be fun to have a house in London again, won't it?'

'Yes,' said Robert, 'I really think it will, especially with the presbytery as well.' He turned towards her, seriously. 'I heard Anna telling you about keeping the Lifeboat for Josh and Olivia. It occurred to me that, when Anna goes to Paris to be with Patrick, she will need someone in London to look after Josh, housekeep and so on.'

'And you thought the housekeepers could be you and me?'

'Yes,' said Robert. 'Is that a rotten idea?'

'No,' said Domenica, 'it's a terrific idea, if the children won't think us too old and boring.'

'I thought you might rather go back to Chelsea, though God knows it's changed since our day.'

'No point in trying to go back, is there?' said Domenica. 'In any case, I don't specially want to keep running into that big-arsed trollop.'

'Are you by any chance referring to my dear wife?' said Robert, laughing.

'You only ever had one wife, Robert,' said Domenica, with dignity, 'and that's me. We were married in the Catholic church, if you recall, and as far as I am concerned, it was till death do us part. Anything else is adultery.'

'Darling Domenica,' said Robert, 'it was you who divorced me.'

'It was you who wanted it.'

'Did I? And you didn't?'

'No,' said Domenica, 'I loved you, then as now.'

Robert blinked. His head spun. He felt as wrong-footed by Domenica as he always had. He struggled to be logical, not to let her outmanoeuvre him. 'But I always loved you,' he said. 'You knew that.'

'But you took lovers. Well, Kate, anyway.'

'And you didn't?' said Robert, in disbelief.

'No.'

'Never?'

'Never,' said Domenica, triumphantly.

'Domenica, my dear love,' said Robert miserably, 'you make me feel like an absolute shit.'

Domenica flung her arms round him, and hugged him. 'Oh, Robert, you're adorable, I do love you, you're so easy to tease.' She kissed him on the cheek, as if he were a child.

He looked at her seriously. 'But it's all true, isn't it?' he said.

'Yes, it is.'

'I'm so sorry,' he said.

'It doesn't matter,' said Domenica. 'We're together now, that's all that matters.'

Robert kissed the top of her head and held her close

to him, staring into the fire. At the edge of a log, a blue flame spurted. There'll be a frost tonight, he thought. I should go and shut up the greenhouses. He felt quite tired, and emotionally exhausted by the day, much as he had enjoyed it.

'Darling?' he said, into Domenica's hair.

'Mm?' said Domenica, sleepily.

'Is it too early for a drink?'

'It's never too early for a drink,' said Domenica. 'It's the one thing we're in perfect agreement about.'

Robert got up and went to the drinks cupboard. He poured two generous whiskies. Sod the greenhouses, he thought. There's not much left now, anyway.

Patrick sat at the big table in the Lifeboat, with Josh and Olivia on either side of him. He was showing them the plans for extending the attic apartment at Quai des Grands-Augustins, and inviting their comments.

'It must have a wonderful view across the river,' said Josh.

'It does, yes,' said Patrick. 'And it's a good part of Paris for so many things. The Louvre, Palais Royal, St Germain, the Flore and Deux Magots, and lots of good student bistros.'

'Sartre and de Beauvoir,' said Josh.

'Absolutely, the place is stiff with existentialist ghosts,' said Patrick, smiling at Josh.

'Will this be my room?' said Olivia, pointing.

'If you like, why not?'

'When will it be ready?' asked Josh. 'Will it all take months?'

'I can take on the lease at the end of November. And probably Giò will know some carpenters and decorators who can whizz through the place. I should imagine January would be a reasonable date to hope to move in.'

'Would that mean that I could come too, and start at the *lycée* in January?' said Olivia, shyly.

'What does your mother think?'

'Is that what you'd like, Olly?' said Anna.

'Yes, I'd love it,' said Olivia, 'please.'

'Hell,' said Josh, 'I wish I could come too, but I suppose I'll have to finish my A-levels first. Will I stay here on my own, Mum? I wouldn't mind.'

'We'll talk about that later,' said Anna, 'nearer the time. I think you probably should have someone here, for shopping and housework, and stuff.'

'In any case,' said Patrick, 'your room will be there, and obviously you will come over often, for weekends and holidays, whenever you want.'

'I want to read architecture at university, if I can,' said Josh. 'What about the Sorbonne? Would that be possible?'

'I don't know for certain, but I imagine one could, or may be the Beaux Arts? We must find out for you. I'm talking myself out of the pleasure of having you with us, Josh, but I should think very carefully before you give up the idea of going to Cambridge. Most people, the French included, would leap at the chance.'

'But Paris is so special, I feel I'd love to live there.'

'Maybe,' said Anna, 'it might be possible to take your degree at Cambridge, and then come to Paris for your diploma?'

'Yes, I suppose,' said Josh, but he sounded unconvinced.

'Well, anyway,' said Patrick cheerfully, 'I want you both to tell me, better still, write down, how you want your rooms to be. Colours, bookshelves, storage, extra power points and anything else you can think of. It will be a good moment to start practising your architectural skills, Josh.'

'Thanks,' said Josh, brightening, 'I'll do that with pleasure. I'll help you with your scheme, Olly,' he added, kindly.

'Get lost,' said Olivia, 'I know exactly what I want, thank you.'

*   *   *

Anna and Patrick lay comfortably in bed together, reading the arts pages of *The Independent on Sunday*, bought at a petrol station on their way back from Sussex.

It was late, and the little house was quiet. Anna could just hear Josh's radio, and the occasional hoot of an owl in the churchyard came through the open rooflight. She turned her head to look at Patrick.

'We're just like an old married couple,' she said.

'What's wrong with that?'

'Nothing,' said Anna, smiling. 'It's lovely.' She put down the paper, and turned towards him. 'Tomorrow, I have to go and have the ultra-sound scan, and they'll take some blood to do the Down's syndrome tests. Will you come with me?'

'Of course I will. Are you worried about it?'

'No, not really. Just anxious that everything is all right. What if we had to consider termination?'

'It would be very sad, but it wouldn't be the end of the world. We do have two children already,' said Patrick.

'You really think that, don't you?'

'Yes, I do, and I hope that they will feel the same way.'

'What about Jeffrey?'

'What about him? If he gets his priorities in order, and starts treating them in a more normal manner, then they'll be in the fortunate position of having two fathers, won't they? Frankly, I can't see it happening, can you?'

'No,' said Anna, 'I can't.'

'Have you finished reading? Shall I turn off the light?'

'Yes, it's been a long day. You must be tired after all that driving?'

'Not as tired as you might think, my darling,' said Patrick, taking her in his arms and holding her close.

At a quarter to three Giò arrived at the courtyard entrance at Place des Vosges, and parked the van in the
usual place.

'Been to Provence, Mr Hamilton?' said the *concierge*'s husband, coming out of his little room, bleary-
eyed.

'No, to England,' said Giò quellingly, locking the
van carefully. 'I'll get the stuff taken up in the morning.
It's too late now.'

'Very good, sir,' said the old man, and crept back into
his lair.

Giò climbed the stairs to his apartment, and found
the slim black cat waiting by his door. He unlocked the
door, and the little cat slipped in ahead of him, purring
loudly. He went to the fridge, took out a carton of milk,
and poured some into a saucer for the cat. He poured
himself a glass of wine and ate a cold potato. It tasted
disgusting, cold and wet, but he couldn't be bothered
to cook anything, and the bread was rock-hard anyway. His head ached, and his eyes felt gritty after the
long night drive in the loaded van. He went into the
bathroom and turned on the geyser for a bath, then
went into the bedroom and turned down his bed. He
undressed, hung his jacket over the back of a chair,
and threw his jeans and the rest of his clothes into
the laundry basket. He turned on the taps of the bath
full blast, and poured a generous dose of Floris Rose
Geranium bath oil into the water. He refilled his glass,
and set it carefully on the thick glass shelf behind the
bath. Then he got into the bath, turned off the taps, and
lay down in the deep, scented foaming water.

'Bliss,' he said. 'Thank God for booze and baths.'

The water soothed and relaxed him, and he drank the
wine slowly, until the painful knot in his chest, which
felt like indigestion, but which he knew was caused
by misery, began to fade. Poor old Anna, he thought,
I suppose this is just how she felt when she was trying
to hang on to that bastard Jeffrey. God, when I

think how I kept banging on at her not to waste her life pining for a lost cause. And here I am, doing exactly the same thing, more fool me.

Tears filled his eyes, and spilled over. But they were quite pleasurable tears, and soon ceased to flow. He sank under the water for a moment, and then washed his hair and face. He got out of the bath, wrapped himself in his big white robe, and went through to the bedroom, towelling his hair. The little cat lay curled in a tight ball in the middle of the bed.

'OK,' said Giò. 'I get the message.' He dried his legs and feet with the towel, then slipped off his robe and climbed into bed, disturbing the cat as he did so. The cat looked at him reproachfully, then jumped back onto the bed and climbed onto Giò's chest, gently kneading with his forepaws before settling himself. Giò stroked his silky back, and the cat began to purr like a small sewing machine, gazing at him through slitted eyes.

'Which of us is it that needs a friend, cat?' said Giò. 'You, or me?' He looked at his icon, hanging darkly on the wall at the foot of his bed. The serious youthful virgin, holding her stiff, elderly-looking baby, looked back at him with compassion.

Or both of us he thought, sadly.

In the morning, he woke at eight o'clock. The cat had departed and Giò got swiftly out of bed, praying that it had not made a mess, unable to get out. It had not, but sat composedly by the front door, waiting to be let out.

'Well done, cat,' said Giò, watching it descend the staircase like a swift, black shadow.

He went back into the apartment and put on the kettle. As he drank his coffee, he stood by the French windows of his balcony, looking across the tree-fringed square. The leaves of the trees were falling fast now, as winter approached, and the faint sweet smell of putrefaction filled the air as the leaves were swept and piled into carts.

Today, thought Giò, I will do two things. First, I'll find a warehouse to store Dad's furniture. I'm running out of space here, and the sooner I get everything away from Boulter's and hidden where no-one but me knows, the better. Secondly, I must arrange to have a cat-flap put in this window. It can't be the front door, they'd never allow it, quite right too, and the cat will soon learn to find his way in and out through the balcony. I suppose I'd better get him a tray to do his jobs in.

The phone rang. It was Laure, already downstairs. 'Good morning, Giò. How are you? Shall I bring you up a croissant? I have some here.'

'Thanks, that would be kind. Laure, the van is in the courtyard, waiting to be unpacked. Could you get the blokes to come round at once, and bring the stuff up here? I must get it unloaded, and the van back to the garage, before the other tenants start complaining.'

'Yes, of course. I'll get on to it right away.'

Giò shaved and dressed, and when he came out of the bathroom, Laure had left the croissant and a note on the table. 'Chaps will be here ten o'clock, L.'

After his breakfast, Giò began looking through the Yellow Pages for warehouse agencies. After drawing a few blanks, he found a small one in the Clignancourt area, and arranged to go and see it that afternoon. He looked at his watch: half-past nine, half an hour to wait for his helpers. He made a fresh pot of coffee, and began to plan how he would set about selling the stuff he had brought from Boulter's.

'Of course,' he said aloud, 'it's obvious. I'll turn one of the rooms in the shop into a Christmas nursery. Brilliant!' He ran down the secret stair to the shop, and told Laure his idea.

She clapped her hands, and laughed. 'What a terrific

idea. It will be enormous fun, and we should get a lot of interest from Christmas shoppers.'

They decided to make the nursery in the first room of the shop, to maximise its impact on the public.

'We'll have to do it late at night,' said Giò. 'Will you be able to help me?'

'Yes, of course,' said Laure. 'When do you want to do it? Tonight?'

'Could you?'

'Yes, of course,' said Laure. 'Any time.'

The helpers arrived, and Giò went out to the courtyard to supervise the unloading of the van. The men carried everything up to the apartment, Giò paid them, and then drove the van out of the courtyard, round the little backstreets and into the Place. He found a parking space quite near the shop, locked the van and walked down the arcade to *Le Patrimoine*.

'You hold the fort here, while I go upstairs and start unwrapping the stuff, ready for tonight, OK?'

'Fine,' said Laure, and got up from her desk as an elderly man came into the shop. Giò vanished through the secret door, and went up to his apartment, to start sorting things out. The sight of his room, chaotic with bubble plastic packages, made his heart sink momentarily. I'm nothing but a bloody labourer quite a lot of the time, he thought wearily, as he tackled the nearest package, slitting the parcel tape with a scalpel, and peeling off the wrapping. I ought to have someone to do this. I need an Honorine here, really.

By one o'clock he had finished the unpacking, and began to fold the plastic, ready for reuse. Thank heaven we cleaned everything before we packed, he thought. At least it's all ready to take downstairs. He looked at the collection of furniture and toys, the dolls and teddies and train sets, the dolls' house, the cot and the pram, the blue-painted cupboard filled with little girls' lace-collared, velvet frocks, and drawers full of frilled petticoats and striped stockings, and the boxes of Christmas tree decorations. I'll get a proper tree, he said to himself, and decorate it. He took the lid off another box, filled with fragile glass balls, transparent and shimmering, like soap bubbles. We could suspend them from the ceiling by invisible threads, so that they revolve in the air. It will be magical.

In a tin trunk were bundles of fine old lace, yellow with age, and rolls of satin ribbon, faded pale blue, interleaved with tissue paper. This will be great to tart up the cot, he thought. We'll make a lace canopy so that you can't actually see the baby, just imagine it sleeping inside. He squashed the plastic wrappings into a large box, sealed it with tape, and wrote BP on it with a markerpen. Then he went down to the shop where Laure was eating a sandwich, concealed from the public by a small folding screen. She offered the box to Giò, who took one and ate it while he outlined his plan for the rest of the day.

'I'll go now to Clignancourt with the van, and check out this warehouse for Dad's stuff. I'd really like to get the rest of his valuable furniture over here as soon as I can, out of the clutches of his greedy wife. Our van isn't big enough, so I'll arrange for a French removal van to go and pack it and bring it back, probably in the middle of next week. You'll be able to cope here without me for a couple of days, won't you?'

'Yes, of course,' said Laure.

'Angel,' said Giò. 'What would I do without you?'

'I'm sure you'd manage very well, Giò,' said Laure quietly, without irony, and flicked her long, smooth honey-coloured hair over her shoulder.

'Oh, dear,' said Giò, 'I do rather take you for granted, don't I?'

'Of course not,' said Laure, her nose going pink, 'don't be ridiculous.'

'Tell you what,' said Giò, 'I'll take you out for dinner tonight, if you're free that is, and then we can come back and do the Christmas nursery afterwards. How would that be?'

'Very nice,' said Laure, 'thank you.' She gave an embarrassed little laugh.

'I'll buy a Christmas tree on my way back from Clignancourt,' said Giò, 'and I'll let you decorate it.'

'I'm sure you won't' said Laure, smiling. 'But thanks anyway.'

Giò drove back from Clignancourt through Montmartre, and stopped the van when he saw a street stall selling Christmas trees. He bought one, about four feet tall, with thick spreading branches. 'They're a good variety,' said the stall-holder, forcing a net over the tree to make it easier to carry. 'They come from Austria, they don't shed their needles. Smell nice too, don't they?'

'They do.' Giò paid the man. 'Thanks very much, it's just what I was looking for.'

He bundled the tree into the back of the van. Dusk was beginning to fall as he threaded his way through the back streets towards Place des Vosges, avoiding the busy main roads. The street lamps cast pools of yellow light on the pavements below, wet with recent rain. The prostitutes, wearing bulky, pale fur coats and high heels, were beginning to appear, carrying pretty umbrellas, some leading little dogs on leads. In one street Giò saw a group of rather blatant transvestites, huddled under a lamp, smoking. As he drove past, one of them turned towards the van, opening his coat, revealing a sequinned black *bustier*, fishnet tights and red high-heeled shoes. His scarlet lips were parted, showing big white teeth. Giò stared, then drove on, followed by catcalls and laughter.

Poor sods, he thought. How horrible. Dear God, don't ever let me get into that sort of thing. He drove on, feeling sick and depressed. At last he reached Place des Vosges, and parked near the shop. The arcades looked cheerful and festive, the elegant shops and restaurants prosperous and reassuring. Giò's spirits rose as he extracted the tree from the back of the van. This is my world, thank heaven, he thought. I really mustn't let other people's tragedies get to me.

Laure saw him as he tried to push open the heavy glass door, and she ran to help him. 'What a lovely tree,' she said. 'It's perfect.'

'Oh, shit,' said Giò. 'I've forgotten the cat-flap.'

'No, you haven't,' said Laure. 'I did it for you. A man is coming in the morning.'

'Laure,' said Giò, 'you think of everything, thank you.' He kissed her lightly on the cheek.

'I try to be useful.'

'My dear girl, you're much more than useful. You're quite indispensable.' Laure said nothing, but she looked pleased. 'I'll just go upstairs and phone my parents and tell them what I've arranged about the furniture, and then we'll go out and eat, OK?'

'Fine,' said Laure. 'I'll just put the tree in a bucket of water.' She peeled the net off the tree, and let its branches spread themselves. She fetched a bucket of water from the small scullery, a cupboard really, at the back of the shop. The sturdy little tree balanced neatly on the bucket, its sawn-off stump resting in the water. There was still enough of the child left in Laure to feel a sense of joy at the approach of Christmas, and she hugged herself as she gazed at the tree, happy in anticipation of the evening ahead.

Chapter Sixteen

Anna sat at the table, giving her cherub his final burnishing after toning him down to an aged appearance, like his brother. Patrick had watched, rivetted, and rather horrified, as she worked away, distressing the beautiful new gold leaf with emery paper and scrapers, various dirty-looking powders and what looked like dentists' tools.

'Doesn't it upset you, to destroy such perfect work?' he said.

'Not really, this is the real skill,' said Anna. 'Anyone can learn to gild, but making it look old needs a very good eye, and knowing when to stop. I used to feel quite ambivalent about it, it does seem perverse, but now I love to see the colour of the bole showing through in the places where it would get normal wear and tear. It's a question of putting back the centuries, the passage of time, the history of each piece.'

'Yes, of course, I see. It's fascinating.' He leaned across the table, took her face in his hands and kissed her. 'Do you have any idea of how much I admire you, to be able to do that?'

Anna laughed. 'It's just a job, really,' she said. 'Just a craft, most people seem to think. And you know what they mean by that.'

'You might as well say that making movies is a craft, once you've learnt the basic skills. It's how you do it that makes it an art, the end result.'

'There,' said Anna, breathing on her cherub's stomach, and giving him a final loving polish, 'I really think he's done.' She packed all her tools away in their box, and put it in her cabinet.

Patrick looked at his watch. 'What time is the dealer coming to collect them?'

'Six o'clock,' said Anna. 'He has this triptych, it's quite a rare one. He wants me to restore it, but I told him I was moving to Paris soon, so it would have to be done there.'

'Good. How exciting. We can easily get a work-table for you. Or rent a separate studio nearby, if you'd prefer.'

'I'd much rather work at home. I like to live with a piece, really get into the feeling of it, touch it all the time.'

'How can you bear to part with them when they're finished?

'Ah,' said Anna, 'that's the difficult part. How I wish I could keep these dear little chaps. Come on, let's go for a walk and get some fresh air, there's just time before Josh and Olly get home, and Axel arrives.'

They walked down to Chiswick Steps and watched the water breaking gently on the slipway. Patrick put his arm round Anna's shoulders. 'It's frustrating for you, having to wait for the results of the blood test,' he said. 'But it's a big relief that everything is all right on the scan.'

'I know,' said Anna, 'so far, so good. But I can't help worrying a bit.' She leaned against him. 'And tomorrow you have to go back. I wish I could come with you. I hate us being apart, I'm getting more and more dependent on you.'

'Darling,' said Patrick, 'I'll be back on Friday night, I'll try and get an earlier plane.'

'Yes, of course. Don't worry. I'm just a bit tired after the hospital business. I'll be OK, really.' They turned, and walked back up Church Street. 'Oh, my God!' said Anna suddenly. 'Look, it's Axel. He's here already. I'm sure he said six o'clock.'

*   *   *

It was after eight when Axel left, carrying the carefully wrapped *putti* down to his van, and leaving behind the battered but beautiful triptych.

'Anna,' said Patrick firmly, 'you look exhausted, you have blue shadows under your eyes. I want you to have a bath and go to bed, and Olly and I will get the supper. OK, Olly?'

'Yes, of course.' Olivia looked anxious. 'Are you all right, Mum?'

'She's perfectly all right, she's just tired and needs a rest. We must look after her,' said Patrick.

'Could I really?' said Anna. 'Are you sure?' She went slowly up the stairs, and turned on the taps in the bath. She went into her bedroom, turned down the bed, and took off her clothes, which were beginning to feel too small for her expanding body. She sighed, and slipped on her bathrobe.

She lay in the bath, relaxing in the warm, scented water, her eyes closed. The door opened and Patrick came in with a glass of white wine in his hand. He put the glass down on the shelf beside her, and sat down on the little Gothic chair.

'Is that for me?' she said, looking at the wine.

'Yes,' said Patrick.

'Thank you, darling,' said Anna.

'You look beautiful. Pregnancy suits you.'

'Does it?' said Anna. 'I just wish it didn't make me feel so tired, and emotional. I sometimes wish that we had had more time just being us, it was so exciting and wonderful and somehow carefree. I felt I could push a bus over.'

Patrick put his hand gently on her stomach, no longer flat, but a smooth round shape, sticking out of the water like a pink island.

'But you're not regretting this?' he said, quietly.

'No, of course not. Not really. It's hard to explain,' she said, taking a sip of her drink.

'I understand perfectly how you feel, and I'm sure we'll be able to arrange our lives later on to have times when we can be alone, just the two of us. After all, we are blessed with both your parents, and my father and Marie-Claude, and Giò, and Honorine.'

'Do you think we'll ever make love again, like we did in Paris, and eat oysters and drink champagne in bed?' said Anna, covering his hand with hers.

'How can you doubt it?'

'Am I being idiotic?'

'You're adorable,' said Patrick, 'I love you. Get out of the bath now, the supper's nearly ready.'

Presently, she lay in bed, listening to the voices of Patrick and Olivia downstairs, and the sound of Josh's radio coming faintly from his room. She felt cherished and protected, and thought how silly she was to have feelings of depression, surrounded by people who loved her. The telephone rang, and she picked it up. It was Domenica.

'Hello, darling, how are you?'

'I'm fine, I'm in bed,' said Anna.

'Good heavens, are you all right?'

'Quite all right. Patrick made me go to bed, I'm a bit tired after the hospital thing. He and Olly are making supper.'

'Quite right too. Good. How was the scan?'

'So far, everything's OK, but we have to wait for the results of the blood tests.'

'Well, fingers crossed,' said Domenica. 'I'm sure everything will be fine. As a matter of fact, I was ringing about something else.'

'Oh, what?'

'Well, we've just had a call from Giò. He's arranged for a removal van to come from Paris and take away all the good stuff from here, and store it in a warehouse. He won't say where it is. He's coming over himself to supervise everything. I must say, Giò can certainly cover the ground when he chooses. Your father is a bit stunned, but he's getting used to the idea. Quite a lot will go to Souliac, it will be nice for Robert to keep the most precious things. And we'll just have the ordinary basic stuff left here, until we sell the house and leave.'

'Sounds like a good idea,' said Anna.

'When do you think you will move to Paris?'

'Well,' said Anna, 'it's quite tricky. Obviously I'd like to go as soon as I can, but I should really stay at least until the school term ends, and we have the results of the blood tests. And then I have to find someone to look after Josh from January, a housekeeper or something.'

'What about us?' said Domenica.

'What do you mean?'

'Well, Robert and I thought that it might be fun for us to live in the Lifeboat and look after Josh, at least until he goes to Cambridge. It would set your minds at rest, and give us a chance to look for a house for ourselves in a leisurely way.'

'Mum,' said Anna, 'do you really mean it?'

'Absolutely.'

'It's a wonderful idea, an answer to prayer.'

'Well, check it out with Josh first, and we'll talk again tomorrow.'

'I'll do that,' said Anna. 'You're right, of course.'

'Good,' said Domenica. 'Talk to you tomorrow. Good night, darling.'

'Good night Mum, love to Dad.'

Anna hung up, and lay back on her pillows. What a fool I am, she thought. Suddenly, into her mind came the image of Gò's face, his wild hair, and his dark eyes. Poor Gò, she thought, I have so much and he so little, at the end of the day.

In Paris, the cold November days crept by, their damp, leaden skies alternating with crisp, frosty nights. The last of the leaves on the lime trees in the Place des Vosges came down, allowing a wintry light to filter through the arcades of the square. All the shops were preparing their Christmas displays, and the glitter and sparkle of the decorations lent the place an air of plush enchantment. Each day the volume of shoppers grew bigger. Some came merely to look, to browse and window-shop, to have a coffee at one of the cafés, and enjoy the atmosphere, but many were genuine, and rich, customers. Their taxis would draw up at the kerb, and fur-coated, suede-booted ladies would descend from them in a cloud of scent, serious handbags hooked over their arms, their eyes bright with the lust of acquisition.

At *Le Patrimoine*, the Christmas nursery was attracting a lot of attention and was a magnet to young parents. They stood in front of the window, their eyes soft with nostalgia as they took in the details of the fairy-tale scene before them. Just inside the thick glass door stood the Christmas tree, covered in delicate old silver and gold baubles, stars, moons and snowflakes, lit by tiny candles, which looked astonishingly genuine, and flickered convincingly, like real flames. Among the branches were scattered little parcels in shiny paper tied with red ribbons, and pink-and-white striped candy in the shape of minute walking sticks. Further back, and half hidden by the tree, the Victorian cot could be seen, hung with the antique English lace, the canopy festooned with more lace, tied with the pale blue satin ribbons. A large, moth-eaten teddy bear appeared to be trying to climb out of the cot, encouraged by a cross-looking Dutch doll with a painted wooden head. An articulated acrobat doll turned endless circles on his trapeze, watched by a solemn row of toy soldiers, standing at attention before their sentry box. To the right of the window stood the rocking horse, with a Paisley shawl draped over his rump, and a large beautiful blonde china-faced doll, dressed in dark blue velvet in the saddle. Giò had already received twenty or thirty offers to buy him, but thinking of Robert, he had had to say he was not for sale. One young woman was very persistent, and begged him to change his mind.

'Or at least, could you get me one by Christmas?'

Giò took her name, and said he would try, and that night he got one of his specialist woodcarvers to come and take measurements and photographs, and ordered ten, if they could be delivered by the fifteenth of December. A week later, the first two arrived, with subtle differences from the original, and Giò called the client. She was delighted, and gladly paid the ten thousand francs on the price tag, and bought a lot of other things as well.

At the back of the room, behind the cot, stood the blue-painted cupboard, its doors open to reveal a collection of Victorian children's clothes in sumptuous velvets and heavy, Welsh striped flannels, the skirts pinned up to show the freshly laundered and starched petticoats and pantaloons beneath. The wide bottom drawer was pulled open to disclose frilled white nightdresses, and striped Alice in Wonderland stockings. Small black buttoned boots stood in neat pairs on the floor.

From the ceiling, Giò had suspended the glass soap-bubble baubles, the different sizes on different lengths of invisible nylon thread. As he had hoped, they rotated gently in the currents of warm air, and as they caught the light below, moving flashes of rainbow colours were projected onto the ceiling above. The effect was mysterious, and dreamlike.

As fast as one toy, or piece of clothing, or little chair was sold, it was replaced from the hoard awaiting upstairs, so that in effect a large part of the display was changed every day. Trade was brisk, and Giò and Laure began to congratulate themselves on their level of success.

'It's a pain, having to go and organize Dad's place thing,' said Giò. 'I'm having a really good time here with you. It's fun, isn't it?'

'Yes,' said Laure, 'it really is.'

'Do you think you can cope on your own for a couple of days?'

'Yes, of course.'

'For Christ's sake don't sell the horse, will you?'

'No, Giò, I won't sell the horse, I promise.'

'I know you won't,' said Giò. 'You know the form. If anyone wants one, take their name, wait a few days, and then bring one down from the flat, OK?'

'Understood,' said Laure, patiently.

'Mum,' said Anna, 'we were wondering, shall we all go to Souliac for Christmas?'

'Lovely idea,' said Domenica. 'We were thinking the same thing. Honorine will be ecstatic, I think she feels a bit neglected.'

'Yes, I was thinking about her,' said Anna. 'The children break up on the seventeenth. Do you think you could move here by then? Then Patrick could come over on the fourteenth or fifteenth and help me pack my things, and all the gilding stuff, and a few books and pictures, and we could drive back to Paris on the same day that you take over. It will be nice for us to have a few days by ourselves, then the children could fly down to Souliac with you and Dad.'

'No problem,' said Domenica. 'We will go down in good time, and get everything ready with Honorine, so that you won't have to rush about too much.'

'I was hoping you'd say that,' said Anna. 'Then we'll drive down with Patrick's father on the twenty-third. It will be lovely.'

'I'll phone Honorine tonight, and she can get things moving. I'll book the flights tomorrow,' said Domenica. 'Giò comes the day after tomorrow, to collect the furniture. I just hope that some local busybody doesn't see a French removal van coming up the lane, and relays the interesting news to Big-arse.'

'Awful thought,' said Anna. 'I can't bear the idea of poor old Dad involved in a punch-up.'

'Don't you fret,' said Domenica. 'If she shows up here, I'll sort her out.' She sounded as though she quite relished the prospect. Anna laughed.

'I believe you,' she said. 'Goodnight, Mum, love to Dad.'

Anna sat in Mr Carpenter's chintzy waiting-room, looking up expectantly every time the door opened, and the nurse ushered someone in, or called a patient's name. She tried to relax and feel calm, but her palms felt sweaty, and she was finding it hard to breathe deeply and rhythmically. She felt as if she needed to go to the lavatory, but put this down to nervousness. At last her name was called, and she followed the nurse to Mr Carpenter's room. He sat, as usual, behind his big desk, his back to the wintry-looking garden.

'Come in, Mrs Wickham,' he said, rising as she entered the room. 'Do sit down.' She sat down, and he put on his spectacles and read the notes on his desk. 'Well,' he said, 'that all seems very satisfactory.' He smiled at her kindly. 'Don't look so worried. You appear to be in excellent health, and so is your child; well done.'

'Thank God,' said Anna. 'It's been agonizing, waiting.'

'I'm sure it has. But now, all you have to worry about is the normal hazards of childbirth, and you seem to be a remarkably young woman. You can go ahead and make the arrangements for the birth, with reasonable confidence. Which is your hospital?'

Anna laughed. 'You'll think me mad, I expect, but I'm going to live in Paris just before Christmas, so I'll have the baby there.'

'Really. How nice for you. Are you going for good?'

Anna felt that she should explain the situation, realizing that she would need to have copies of her records for the Paris hospital, in case there should be a confusion about her name after her remarriage. Mr Carpenter seemed interested and sympathetic, and promised that everything would be sent to her in good time.

'I expect you can do the necessary translations yourself?'

'Yes, of course,' said Anna. She got up to go, and he walked to the door with her. 'Thank you for everything,' she said. 'You've been very kind.' She held out her hand, and he took it.

'It's been a pleasure knowing you. I wish you and your new husband good fortune and happiness.'

Anna left the building, feeling light-headed with relief, and walked to her car. She drove slowly home, across Chiswick Bridge and down Church Street. Someone had parked in front of her garage doors, so she parked the car on the opposite side of the road, and sat for a moment, looking at the familiar sights around her that had been part of her life for so long. Soon she would be gone, and the thought filled her with joy. But I did love this place, she thought, a little bit of me will always be here. I'm glad Josh will be here, and Mum and Dad. I'd hate to think of my little house abandoned and empty.

Robert, Domenica and Giò watched the furniture van rumble away down the drive with mixed feelings: combined relief and anticlimax.

'Well,' said Robert, 'that's that.' He turned and walked away over the lawn, towards the walled garden.

'Leave him,' said Giò, as Domenica began to follow Robert. 'He'll be all right, you'll see. Come on, let's have some tea before you take me to the airport.'

'Poor old thing,' said Domenica sadly, as she filled the kettle. 'He is minding the ripping apart of his house. I do hope we're doing the right thing.'

'Ma,' said Giò, 'don't be idiotic. It's not your fault, or mine, that things have turned out so badly for him. Of course he's upset, but he still has a lot to be thankful for. You, for one thing, and the saving of his treasures for another. He knows it, really, it's just taking time to concentrate his mind.'

'I know,' said Domenica. 'I hate to see him sad, that's all.'

'Darling,' Ma, if we blew a whistle, and Kate was back here and you in Souliac on your own, he'd bloody soon change his tune, I can tell you.'

Domenica laughed, and poured boiling water into the teapot.

Robert came into the kitchen, carrying a flowerpot full of freshly dug potatoes. 'What's the joke?' he said.

'Oh,' said Giò, 'we were just fantasizing about if Kate were still here, and Ma in Souliac without you.'

'Perish the thought,' said Robert. 'What a rotten idea. Whatever put that into your mind?'

'Can't imagine,' said Domenica, and poured the strong black tea into the thick yellow breakfast cups.

'And I never want to see those bloody cups again either,' said Robert. 'She made them, and they can go in the bin as soon as you like.'

'Well done, Dad,' said Giò, smiling tenderly at his father. 'I like it when you show a bit of spirit.'

'Well, I'm not bloody dead,' said Robert.

'Precisely,' said Domenica.

After tea, Giò packed his bag, and they drove him to Gatwick to catch the plane back to Paris. Robert and Domenica drove slowly home to Boulter's through the darkening lanes. The last yellowing leaves had been stripped from the trees by the cold north wind, their branches blackly etched against the bleak December sky. Domenica huddled into her coat, and thought longingly of the sunny courtyard at Souliac.

'I must say,' said Robert, as he skidded on the rotten leaves in Boulter's Lane, 'the thought of some winter sunshine is very appealing.'

'I wonder what made you think of that?'

'I wonder?' said Robert. 'I expect you're walking around inside my head, as usual, bossy old thing.'

'Not so much of the old,' said Domenica, 'do you mind?'

Honorine sat in the sunshine in the walled garden at the presbytery, making lists, and trying to figure out where everyone was going to sleep. Domenica and Robert would of course, be in their own old room. Giò and Olivia would be in their rooms, as usual, and Josh in the *remise* over the garage. That left Anna's room, but hers was only a small double bed, so Dr Halard would have to be there. Anna and Patrick could be in her spare room, in her parents' matrimonial bed, which would be much more comfortable for Anna.

Honorine smiled to herself. It would be nice to have someone in the house for a while, it might help her to sleep better. She slept badly, in spite of her long hours of work, and usually woke at half-past two or three. Sometimes she was able to drift off to sleep again, but more often she lay wakeful, listening to the creaks and groans of the house, and the hooting of the owls in the square. In spite of her many attempts to poison them, the resident mice in the attic not only flourished but multiplied, and she could hear them scuttering about throughout the long winter nights. Sometimes, she banged on the ceiling with the broom-pole she kept under the bed for that purpose, and there would be a brief lull in their activities. Then it would start again, at first rather timidly, and then with increasing boldness, until she gave the ceiling another whack, or turned on her little radio. And even when they were quiet, she would lie tensely, listening for a squeak or a scratch. At four thirty the smell of baking bread would drift through the open window, floating across the square from the *boulangerie*, and sometimes the comforting aroma, heralding the beginning of the end of the night, would still Honorine's squirrelling thoughts, and allow her to sleep again for an hour or two.

The sleeping arrangements decided, and a preliminary

shopping list completed, Honorine closed her note-book, fastening it carefully with a strong rubber band, and returned to her own house on the other side of the Place de l'Église. She had enjoyed her week's grape-picking at the tail-end of the *vendange* in her own vineyard. After the long, hot summer and the occasional good downpour of rain in August, the grapes had been fat and juicy, and the continuing good weather had enabled the delaying of the picking until the first week in October, which meant a big crop with a high alcoholic content. Honorine loved to see the little vineyard tractors, their orange warning lights flashing, as they towed their trailer-loads of grapes to the co-operative. It was good to be out in the hot sun, under the big blue sky, swept clear of clouds by the mistral. As the sun dropped down to the west in the afternoons, to set in a blaze of red sky behind the distant mountains, the temperature fell sharply, and Honorine would hurry home to light her fire, and then go out to the *alimentation* to buy whatever she had planned for her supper, and to the *boulangerie* for her evening loaf.

Now, as usual, she sat by the fire while her supper cooked, with her flickering telly turned on for company, and drank a couple of glasses of wine. She had not expected Domenica to stay away so long. Though she was of course glad for Domenica that she and Robert appeared to be together again, as far as she could understand and Honorine had an increasingly uneasy feeling that this probably meant that Domenica would only be in Juliac for the holidays.

'Now, for the first time,' she said aloud to the empty room, 'I know what it means to be widowed. All alone, the family gone, they have no need of me now, except to get the place ready for them when they come on holiday.'

She got up and put another long, thin oak log on the fire. It crackled and blazed up cheerfully, sending its comforting warmth into the dark little kitchen. She went to the stove and lifted the lid of her old black iron pot. The little piece of bacon simmered gently on its bed of carrots and leeks, bathed in aromatic stock.

I wonder what will happen to the business? she thought. Will Giò come down to do the collecting for himself? Well, that would be nice, but maybe he'll just find a new partner. I don't know, I'll just have to wait and see, I suppose. She wiped down her pearwood table, and set herself a knife and fork, a glass and the fresh baguette. She put a yellow plate with a brown, scalloped rim, on the edge of the stove to warm, and poured herself another glass of wine. She sat down by the fire again, and gazed into the flames. Perhaps Domenica will not be able to go on paying me, or want to, if she is not here so much, she thought. Maybe I should be thinking of looking for other work. What about the new young priest? It's possible he may not have found someone to shop and clean for him yet. It's only six kilometres to Roussac, I'll cycle over tomorrow and have a word with him. It's worth a try, and it would be nice to look after a young bachelor, a bit of a change from my dear old battleaxe friend. She laughed aloud. Then, inexplicably, the laugh turned into a sob, and tears filled her eyes and fell down the worn old furrows of her face. She brushed them away angrily, and got up to put her supper on the table.

'Don't be ridiculous, Honorine,' she said loudly, 'they will all be here in a few days now. It will be just the same as before, you'll see.'

But she knew that it would not.

Patrick and Anna drove towards Dover and the hover-port. Anna's little car was loaded to capacity with her belongings, including the precious triptych, carefully wrapped to protect it from damage.

'It was a bit crazy buying a right-hand drive car, when you'll be using it mainly in France,' said Patrick. 'Never mind, we can always change it later.'

303

'I hope they're all right at the Lifeboat,' said Anna. 'I can't help feeling guilty, leaving them.'

'Don't worry, they'll be fine. Don't forget, Olivia will be coming back with us in the New Year, and you'll be with them all in a week's time.'

'You're right, it's just like me to find something to worry about. I must stop it, or you'll begin to find me a pain.'

'Never that, my love.'

The crossing was smooth for the time of year, helped by a following wind, and by three o'clock they were making good time along the uncrowded *autoroute* towards Paris. Giò had had his workmen in the new flat for the past two weeks, and already the place had all the new shelving and cupboards finished, and the painting and decorating were almost complete. All that remained was for Anna to go out with Giò, and choose beds, and rugs, and curtain materials from his stock, his Christmas present to them both. He had offered to come to Quai des Grands-Augustins at six o'clock to help unload the car and carry everything up to the apartment, and Patrick had been happy to accept his offer. He was glad of the opportunity to paper over the cracks of his relationship with Giò for Anna's sake at the very least.

He drove round the little side street to the back entrance to the building, and parked the car. He looked at the car clock: ten to six. 'Good timing,' he said, and turned to Anna. 'How are you feeling, are you awfully tired?'

'I'm fine,' said Anna. 'Just need to walk about, and stretch myself out a bit.'

They got out of the car, and as they did so Giò, who had been keeping an eye on the street from a landing window, came briskly across the road with a couple of his workmen. He kissed Anna, and cast a professional eye on the contents of the car.

'Come on, chaps,' he said, 'we'll soon have this lot upstairs.'

'Giò, darling,' said Anna, 'this one is my triptych. You will take care of it, won't you?'

'Of course,' said Giò. 'I'll take it up myself, now. You two go on up, then you can say where you want it all put, OK?'

'Wonderful,' said Patrick, picking up a suitcase. 'Come on, sweetheart, don't stand there in the wind, Giò will see to everything.' He gave Giò the car keys, and steered Anna across the street, in at the shabby rear entrance, and into the rickety little lift. As it shuddered slowly upwards, Anna could see the staircase through its tarnished gilt wire sides, with its black-and-white tiled landings at each floor, and looked anxiously at Patrick.

He smiled at her reassuringly. 'You get used to it,' he said. 'Like flying.'

The lift came to a halt, and gave a sigh. Patrick opened the wire door, then slid back the outer landing door – heavy mahogany with a glass panel – and they stepped out.

'It's weird,' said Anna, 'but I don't remember that lift at all last time.'

'That's because we used the stairs. I usually do, it's one way of getting some exercise. I just thought you might find them a bit tiring after the long drive.'

'I think I'll try and use the stairs, I need the exercise myself. Except, maybe, when one has shopping to carry up.'

Patrick unlocked the door to the apartment, and took the suitcases through to the bedroom. The sitting-room was warm; Giò had turned on the heating, the lamps were all lit, and the room was delicately scented by the big bunch of pale yellow lilies he had thrust into a square glass vase and put on the coffee table.

'How lovely,' said Anna. 'How kind of him.'

'Come and see the new place.' Patrick opened the door across the landing, and they walked from room to

305

room, inspecting all the new work, the shelves and cup-boards, the refurbished bathroom, and the new kitchen corner – just a small counter top with a sink and a hob, and shelving above. Everything was clean and freshly painted white, with bare, sanded floorboards.

'It's perfect,' said Anna. 'You are kind. Josh and Olly will love it.'

'Couldn't have done it without Giò,' said Patrick. 'I must say, he's a positive dynamo when he gets going. When you think what he's achieved in the last few weeks, shifted all that furniture from your father's place, organized this for us, and you should see the shop. It's a knockout, and he does it all himself.'

'What do you think?' said Giò, appearing in the doorway.

'Absolutely wonderful, Giò, it's lovely. Thank you,' said Anna, giving him a hug, 'and thanks for the flowers.'

'All part of the service.' Giò looked pleased. 'Where do you want the triptych?'

When everything had been carried up and unpacked, the workmen departed.

'What about a drink?' said Patrick. He opened the fridge door and saw that Giò had put in a bottle of champagne to chill. 'My God, you've thought of every-thing,' he said, taking out the bottle. He opened it, and filled three glasses.

Giò raised his glass. 'To your own, happy future together,' he said, smiling at them over the rim of his glass, his dark eyes bright.

'Thank you, Giò' said Patrick and Anna, together.

'Now,' said Patrick, 'I think we all deserve a treat; we'll go somewhere nice to eat. Where would you rather go, Anna, somewhere chic, or somewhere small and friendly?'

'I don't mind which,' said Anna, who did, but was thinking of Giò's preference. 'You choose, Giò.'

'What about *Chez Maître Paul*, in Monsieur le Prince? The food's great, and I'm ravenous.'

'Good idea,' said Patrick. 'It's not far. I'll phone now, and book a table.'

'I've got the number here, in my little book.' Giò took it out of his pocket and flicked through the pages. 'Here is it: 43.54.74.59.'

'Giò,' said Patrick, 'you're amazing. I wish you worked for me.'

'No chance,' said Giò, and laughed. 'You couldn't afford me, and I'd drive you mad.'

'You're right, of course.' Patrick picked up the telephone and made the reservation. 'Shall we walk, or get a taxi? It's about a quarter of an hour on foot.'

'Walk there, and taxi back?' said Anna. 'It will do us good to stretch our legs and get some air. But first I must phone Mum and say we've arrived safely.'

Josh answered the phone.

'Hello, darling, it's me,' said Anna. 'We're here, everything's fine. Your rooms are practically finished. How's everything that end?'

'Oh, great,' said Josh. 'The women are in the kitchen cooking supper with a good deal of drama, and Grandpa's upstairs in your room.'

'What's he doing there?'

'Well,' Josh lowered his voice, 'I heard him complaining to Domenica that the bed was too small, I think he's trying to figure out a way of making it bigger. What is he, some kind of legover legend?'

Anna giggled. 'Really!' she said. 'At his age! Are you managing to get your prep done?'

'Yeah,' said Josh. 'Actually, I'm watching the box, there's not much prep now, too near the end of term.'

'Yes, of course, I'd forgotten. Well, take care, love to everyone, see you next week.'

'Goodnight, Mum, thanks for calling.'

'Goodnight, Josh.'

'Ready?' said Patrick.

'Yes,' she said. 'I'll just wash my hands and brush my hair. We don't need to change, do we?'

'Certainly not,' said Patrick.

They walked through the little back streets, Anna taking note as they passed of all the small local food shops, and the *boulangerie*. They crossed the Boulevard St Germain to the Rue Monsieur le Prince.

'Here we are,' said Giò, pushing open the door of *Chez Maître Paul*, and leading the way into the comforting warmth of the little bistro.

'Magic,' said Anna. 'Just the kind of place I love.'

Domenica and Olivia walked from stall to stall in the Christmas market at Nîmes, buying the various elements of the thirteen desserts of Christmas. Olivia carried an ancient vine basket, and each little package was carefully placed in it, in the correct order. Raisins, dried figs, almonds, walnuts, hazelnuts, pears, apples, crystallized plums, nougat both black and white, quince paste, and crystallized melon. Honorine would be making the special sweet bread, *pompe à l'huile*, on Christmas Eve. In addition Domenica, never one to miss an extra treat or two, bought mandarin oranges and grapes, and her favourite sweets, *Calissons d'Aix*, redolent of the Christmasses of her childhood.

Robert and Josh had gone in search of a tree, and Olivia and Domenica took the opportunity to buy their presents in their absence. For Robert, Domenica bought a plaid wool shirt, and Olivia bought him a bottle of *L'Herbier de Provence* rosemary bath oil.

'Good idea,' said Domenica. 'His poor old skin could do with a bit of dosseting.'

'Spare me the details, please,' said Olivia.

'Horrid child,' said Domenica.

For Josh, Domenica bought an old, calf-bound copy of the poems of Mistral, and Olivia bought him a box of chocolate sardines, wrapped in silver paper, in a proper tin with a key.

'What do you want, Olly?' asked Domenica. 'Any thoughts?'

'Yes,' said Olivia at once, 'a *gardien*'s hat.'

'Really?'

'Please,' said Olivia.

'Well, no time like the present,' said Domenica.

In Souliac, Honorine was making her spare bedroom
ready for Anna and Patrick. She had washed and ironed
her mother's beautiful linen, bought at the time of her
marriage, although it had all looked perfectly fresh, and
smelt of lavender when she unwrapped it from its blue
tissue paper. The sheets and big square pillow-cases
were snowy white heavy cotton, smooth with age and
laundering, and edged with deep, scalloped borders;
she stroked the sheets lovingly as she smoothed them
over the big bed. Then she replaced the long, hard
bolster in its fresh cover, and put two thick blankets
on the bed, and an extra one in the cupboard. Then
she unfolded the soft, white, stitched provençale quilt
with its flowered border, and laid it carefully over
the bed. She plumped up the fat, soft square pillows,
and put them side by side at the foot of the bed. She
walked round the little room, straightening the crucifix
which hung by the window, and giving the heavy,
dark red winter curtains a little twitch. She checked
that the bulb was working in the bedside lamp, and
made a mental note to get a few flowers for Anna
on Thursday morning. Then she smiled, a small satisfied pursing of the lips, and went downstairs, closing
the door carefully behind her.

Chapter Seventeen

On Thursday evening, just after darkness had fallen, Patrick drove under the archway, and into the square at Souliac.

'Oh, look,' said Anna, 'how lovely. It's even prettier than usual.'

The *commune* had festooned the bare branches of the plane trees with strings of bright white lights. Over the fountain hung a huge star, with *Joyeux Noël* in illuminated letters beneath. Suspended between the *boulangerie* and the *alimentation* were lights in the shape of a clog, and above the door to the post office, which also housed the village school, was fixed a little fir tree, ablaze with coloured lights.

Anna got out of the car, and tipped the seat forward to release Dr Halard, imprisoned in the back.

'Are you all right?' she asked anxiously, as the elderly man eased his long bony frame out of the car.

'Quite all right, my dear,' said Dr Halard 'just a bit stiff. I'm not designed for modern cars, I'm afraid.'

'You're not alone in that.' Anna kissed him on the cheek. 'The baby and I feel a bit compressed, too.'

'How different it all looks in the winter,' said Patrick, 'without the leaves.' He looked up at the sky. 'And look at the stars, so big and close. It's beautiful.'

'It certainly is,' said Dr Halard. 'It was worth the journey. Though I think it's time you got a bigger car, my dear boy.'

'You may have a point, Dad,' said Patrick, unloading suitcases, 'we're a big family now.'

'Isn't it nice?' said Anna, opening the green iron gate, and leading the way into the courtyard.

'That, my dear, is a grave understatement,' said Dr Halard, following her through the gate. They stood for a moment in the dim courtyard, lit only by the little lamp under the trellis, looking at the tall old house, dark blue-grey against the starry sky. A wide chink of light was visible under the big double doors to the kitchen, and they could hear the sounds of voices and laughter within.

'Sounds like Mum,' said Anna. She went quietly up to the door and opened it. The surprised faces of Domenica, Honorine and Olivia turned towards her. 'Hi,' said Anna, 'we're here.'

'Goodness, you're early,' said Domenica. 'We thought you wouldn't arrive till eight at the earliest.' She got up from the table, where she had been wrapping presents, and came to shake hands with Dr Halard. 'It's good to meet you, at last, Dr Halard,' she said. 'You'd better call me Domenica, Patrick does.'

'And my name is Philippe. I hope you will call me that. Almost no-one does nowadays,' said Dr Halard, kissing Domenica's hand.

'Oh,' said Olivia, 'how sad. I'd love to call you Philippe, may I?' She came round the table and shook hands.

'Please do,' said Dr Halard. 'I hope you all will.'

Honorine wiped her hands on her apron and came to be introduced, while Olivia hugged her mother and Patrick.

'What about a drink?' said Domenica. 'You must all be cold and tired after the drive down. Come up to the *salon*, Robert and Josh are supposed to have lit the fire. I hope they haven't forgotten.' She led the way up the stone stairs. 'They seem to be permanently engrossed in a chess marathon, not a game that has any appeal to me. Too slow and too cerebral.'

'You go on up,' said Anna to Patrick. 'I just want a word with Honorine. I'll be up in a minute.' She

311

turned back into the kitchen and went over to the stove, where Honorine was already back at work, stirring the sauce she was making for supper. They exchanged kisses.

''Ow are you, *mignonne*?' said Honorine. 'Is no need to ask, you looking in good form.'

'I am in good form.'

'And 'appy, I think?'

'Very.' Anna stuck her finger in the pan, to taste the sauce. 'And you? Have you been awfully lonely without Domenica?'

'No, no,' said Honorine, 'I am busy, I 'ave been 'elping in the vine, and I 'ave got myself small jobs with the new priest at Roussac. 'E is very nice young man, very easy, 'e does not mind when I arrive, I 'ave a key to go when I want.'

'Not quite as demanding as Domenica, then?' said Anna. 'That'll be a nice change.'

Honorine turned to Anna, her black eyes bright. 'If Domenica demand me sometimes, is not serious. She is my friend since forty years, don't forget it.'

'I don't forget it,' said Anna. 'She's lucky, very, to have you. We all are. What's for dinner?'

'Veal chop, with this sauce, Anna, if there will be some left, after you tasting,' said Honorine, slapping her hand.

Anna laughed, and ran upstairs to the *salon*. Honorine shook her head, and stirred her sauce. She knew that Anna meant to be kind and sympathetic, but she also knew that she must not allow herself to need that sympathy and kindness.

The following morning, Christmas Eve, Anna and Patrick drove into Uzès to collect the oysters and sea-bass already ordered for the *Réveillon* dinner. They had to wait their turn at the special Christmas fish stall in *Continent*, while the formidable farmers' wives, brown-skinned and black-haired, deliberately counted out piles of crumpled banknotes, and then carried away their big barrels of oysters, packed in seaweed and ice, smelling of the sea. When they finally got to the front, Patrick was glad to see that Domenica had ordered two small barrels, which fitted neatly into their trolley. The fish merchant showed Anna the three large sea-bass for her approval, before wrapping them carefully in a neat parcel. Patrick took out his wallet to pay, and Anna at once protested.

'You mustn't. Domenica has given me the cash, really.'

'Why ever not?' said Patrick. 'Just think about all the hospitality I've received from your family. It's only fair, isn't it?'

They continued round the supermarket proper, crowded with shoppers, ablaze with gaudy decorations and throbbing with Michael Jackson, and bought six packs of ready-stuffed frozen snails, some caviare and some smoked salmon.

'Oh, look,' said Anna, 'English Christmas Puddings! Shall we get one as a surprise for Dad?'

'Yes, let's,' said Patrick. 'I love it myself, and mince pies. We have them in Normandy.'

'You're kidding.'

'I am not,' said Patrick, 'it's the truth.'

They bought a medium-sized pudding, and some extra *crème fraîche* to lace with brandy. They decided to let Honorine into the secret, so that she could put the pudding on to steam in good time, to enable Anna to produce it, flaming with brandy, at the end of the meal, before the thirteen desserts.

'I hope she won't be too fussed by it,' said Anna, as they queued for the check-out.

'I'm sure she won't' said Patrick.

'I can see we shall have to make some new traditions to suit anglophiles,' said Anna.

'Well, I am a Norman,' said Patrick. 'They've always had a good rapport with the Brits.'

313

'Yes,' said Anna. 'Thank heaven for it. Don't ever stop.'

Domenica left Olivia helping Honorine to make the *pompe à l'huile* dough in the kitchen, and Robert and Josh carrying the long oak logs up to the *salon*, ready for the evening, and took Dr Halard across the square to see the church, he having expressed an interest in doing so. She turned the handle of the heavy door, and they stepped inside the dark old building. As she pushed open the inner door, covered in dark red leatherette, and studded with dome-topped, brass drawing pins, Domenica saw that the church was semi-illuminated by a few electric light bulbs, and a small group of village children were rehearsing their Christmas Eve *Crèche Vivante* under the watchful eye of the new young priest.

Domenica and Dr Halard sat quietly in a back pew, and waited for the rehearsal to end. Dr Halard's eyes strayed round the building, as he took in the architectural details of the little eleventh-century church. The rehearsal finished, the priest sent the children away, reminding them to come back in good time that evening, and to wear good thick vests under their costumes. The children clattered away down the aisle, and Domenica and Dr Halard rose, and went to greet the priest.

'Good morning Father,' she said. 'I am Mme Hamilton, I live at the old presbytery. I think you already know Honorine, my housekeeper?'

'How do you do,' said the priest, bowing politely. 'Yes, Mme Honorine is very kindly helping me get installed at Roussac. It is not easy to get settled, with five parishes to look after, as you can imagine.'

'Indeed,' said Domenica. 'This is Dr Halard, who is spending Christmas with us.'

The two men shook hands, and Dr Halard began asking him about the history of the building, but the young man explained that he had not yet had time to study the records. He seemed shy and slightly ill-at-ease. Domenica had been planning to tease him about stealing her housekeeper, but now decided against it. Instead, she asked him whether he had arranged to do anything after Midnight Mass.

'I'm afraid not,' he said. 'I'll just go home and sleep, I expect.'

'In that case,' said Domenica, 'you must come over to us. I shall be very offended if you refuse.'

'How very kind,' said the priest, 'thank you. I shall look forward to it.'

'Good, that's settled then,' said Domenica. They finished their tour of the church, then the young priest switched off the lights, and went with them to the porch, where his *mobilette* was parked. He tucked up the skirts of his cassock, put on the crash-helmet kept in the plastic box behind the saddle, and wound a long, grey woollen scarf round his neck. Then he started his engine, said goodbye and rode away across the square, watched with interest by the old ladies, sitting in the sunshine in the shelter of their doorways.

'Poor young man,' said Dr Halard. 'Awfully lonely job, a priest's.'

'Very true,' said Domenica. 'I wonder how long he'll stick it?'

When they got back to the presbytery, Anna and Patrick had returned from Uzès, and the oysters had been put in the coldest place, the log-store in the back courtyard. The sea-bass had been unwrapped and admired, laid on a large flat platter, and put on the slate shelf in the larder. The frozen snails remained in their packages, in the freezer. The dough for the *pompe à l'huile* was rising nicely under a floured cloth beside the stove, and Honorine was preparing the garlic soup, the first course of the *Réveillon* dinner, to be eaten before going to church. Olivia was laying the table for lunch, which was to be pasta with a bottled tomato sauce, and salad. She also set out bread and cheese, and a bowl of apples. She felt pretty hungry herself and knew Josh would be ravenous too.

'It's going to be a long evening,' said Domenica, pouring herself a pastis, 'and I think we should all have a siesta this afternoon. I'm going to, and Honorine must, and I think you certainly should, Anna; we mustn't let you get tired.'

'I'm not arguing with you, Mum,' said Anna. 'I haven't really recovered from the drive yesterday.'

Robert, Dr Halard and Patrick all elected to have a rest, too, but Josh and Olivia demurred. They had things to do, they said.

'Tell you what,' said Josh, 'we'll go to Avignon and meet Giò off the train. It'll save you a trip, and we'd enjoy it.'

'Good idea,' said Patrick. 'You can take my car, if you like.'

'You know the rules about the speed limit, Josh, don't you?' said Anna.

'Yes, Mum, I do,' said Josh. 'I'm not a total prat.'

'Right.' Honorine hung the dishcloth over the brass rail of the stove to dry, 'I'll be off now. I'll be back at seven, to start preparing. Have a proper rest now,' she said to Domenica.

'Hang on, we'll walk over with you, Honorine, said Anna.

Olivia had had the foresight to put a couple of pairs of secateurs in the car before they set off, and on the way back from Avignon, Josh turned off the main road just after Pont du Gard, and they took the minor roads home, through the *garrigue*. After passing through Sanilhac, the road degenerated into a stony track. Josh parked the car in a rocky little clearing, and they got out and began to cut branches of evergreen oak, with tiny brown acorns, dark green myrtle and swags of grey-green sage.

'We can get ivy and stuff from the garden,' said Olivia, 'and olive branches. And there are loads of lovely big cones under the umbrella pines in the back lane.'

When the back of the car and the boot were crammed full of greenery, all three stood for a moment, watching the sun go down, a blood-red ball descending through veils of brilliant orange, then sliding behind the jagged blue outline of the Cévennes. A sudden stillness fell over the *garrigue*, broken only by the tinkle of a sheep's bell from the valley below. They watched the flock as it made its slow way up the narrow track, followed by the bent, dark shape of the elderly shepherd, and nudged on by his equally elderly dog.

'I'd hate to think of this place covered in villas, like the coast, said Giò. 'It's still pretty special, isn't it?'

'Don't even think of it,' said Josh. 'Gross.'

'Come on, it's getting cold,' said Olivia. 'Time to get back.'

They got back into the car, Olivia sitting on Giò's knee. Josh turned on the headlights and drove slowly over the stony track to the main road, and back to Souliac. They parked in the back lane and brought the greenery in through the garage and the walled garden, quietly, to avoid disturbing the sleepers. They left some of the stuff in the kitchen, and carried the rest upstairs to the *salon*. The tree was in its traditional place between the two tall windows, and already decorated, though the lights were not yet lit. Josh got wire and pliers from the tool cupboard, and Giò sat on the floor making swags and garlands, which Olivia and Josh hung over the fireplace, on either side of the windows, and round the great carved and gilded mirror that hung on the opposite wall.

'You nip out and get the pine cones, Olly, and wire a few into the garlands,' said Giò, 'and Josh and I will do the kitchen before Honorine gets back, OK?'

By six thirty they had finished their work, and swept up the debris. Giò had brought a big box of tall tallow

317

candles from the shop, and he collected all the available candlesticks and divided the candles amongst them. Then he chose the nicest places to put them, and Olivia encircled each one with a delicate trial of ivy.

'You are clever, Giò,' said Josh, 'it looks really beautiful.'

'It certainly does,' said Olivia, gazing round the *salon*. 'It makes me feel quite soppy. If you put a Christmas carol tape on, I'd burst into tears.'

Giò smiled, and put his arm round Olivia's shoulders. 'Me too,' he said.

The kitchen door banged, and they ran downstairs to see Honorine's reaction to the transformation of the kitchen.

'Mother of God,' she said, 'what a surprise! You 'ave brought the *garrigue* into the 'ouse. 'Allo, Giò, 'ow are you?'

'Hullo, darling Honorine,' said Giò, exchanging three kisses with her. 'Obviously, we haven't done the table yet. You'll tell us when you are ready?'

'Honorine,' said Olivia, 'I'm getting pretty hungry. I don't think I'll last out till after midnight. We only have the soup before we go to mass. Shall I make some snacks, nuts and olives and stu   an *tapenade* toas s, or would I be getting in your w y?'

'No, no, you carry on,' said nor ne. 'Is goo l ide a, with the aperitifs.'

'And we don't want Mum d I ad pissed befo e church, do we?' said Giò. Hor rine gave him a ha d stare, and pursed her lips. She d n t reply.

Olivia, Josh and Giò exchang loo s. Olivia t ld t e others to go up and light the re a d get the drinks ready, while she prepared the appetizers.

Honorine set about stuffing the sea-bass, which was to be the centrepiece of the dinner. She made a stuffing of breadcrumbs, sweated onion and garlic, cream and chopped sorrel, bound with egg, and filled the cavity of each perfect fish with the mixture, stitching up the opening. Then she arranged them on a bed of cooked onions, heavily spiked with herbs, poured white wine over the fish, and covered the roasting tin with foil.

'Smells terrific already,' said Olivia.

'I 'ope.' Honorine took the fish to the larder.

Anna and Patrick came through the big door, Anna looking stunning in a long, loose red velvet dress, and a thick, matching woollen shawl.

'Mum!' exclaimed Olivia. 'You look brilliant.'

'Doesn't she?' Patrick looked pleased.

'It's my Christmas present,' said Anna, smiling.

'Some present,' said Olivia.

They went up to the *salon* to join the rest of the family. Patrick, carrying the tray, paused in the kitchen doorway.

'Are you coming, Honorine?' he said.

'No, I 'ave things to do. The oysters to open, for one. I prefer to stay 'ere, and watch everything is OK.'

'Fine, but call if you need help?' said Patrick.

'Yes, OK,' said Honorine, then added, 'is wonderful to see Anna so 'appy after all this years.'

'And I am happy, too,' said Patrick.

'Yes.' Honorine smiled. 'One can see.'

As he entered the *salon* with the tray, Patrick paused for a second to look at the family, of which he was now a member. He remembered the sad, lonely Christmasses with his father in Normandy, and sent up a thank-offering for the extraordinary change that had come about, in his own life, and in his father's too. The fire blazed up the wide chimney, adding flickering light to the candlelit room, aromatic with the scent of pine, rosemary and myrtle. Robert was pouring drinks, while Josh carried them round to everyone. Domenica, wearing her cashmere sweater and a long plaid skirt, stood in front of the fire warming her hands, and observing with affection Giò, and Dr Halard. They had just met for the first time, and the old man evidently found the younger man very amusing, for he was convulsed with laughter at something he had just said. Patrick had not seen his father laughing like that for many years, and it gladdened his heart. Not for the first time, he thought how valuable was the part played by the Giòs of this world, in bringing a light-heartedness and sense of the ridiculous to daily life, the entertainers, who give so much of themselves and get so little back.

'Where are the girls?' he asked, putting the tray down on the round, lamp-lit library table.

'Gone up to glamorise Olly, I imagine,' said Robert. 'She looked a bit put-out when she saw her mother and her grandmother looking so ravishing.' He looked with great affection at Domenica. 'Drink?' he said. 'To celebrate our joint good fortune?'

'Indeed,' said Patrick, taking the glass. 'I still can't really believe it sometimes, you know, Robert.'

'Nor me,' said Robert, rather owlishly, and they both laughed.

Just before nine, Giò poured a glass of wine and made a signal to Olivia. They went down to the kitchen to prepare the table for dinner. Following her down the stairs, Giò observed with a secret smile the festive apparel of his niece. She wore a short, tight, ribbed black wool sweater, a long flowered chiffon skirt over green leggings, and baseball boots. Anna had teased her hair, curly hair into a cloudy mass round her face. She had also subtly applied some eye shadow round her eyes which had the effect of enlarging and widening them at the same time.

'You're going to be a beauty, Olly,' said Giò.

'What do you mean, *going to be*?'

They went into the kitchen.

'Olivia, my God,' said Honorine. 'What a shock! You look so grown-up. But very nice.'

'Ready for us, Honorine?' said Giò, offering her the glass of wine. 'Time you took a breather, anyway.' Honorine took the glass and sat down on a chair, while Giò and Olly cleared the table and gave it a careful wipe. Then they spread the cream linen cloth, used only on special occasions, and arranged the candles and trails of ivy and olive sprigs along the length of the table, punctuated with small filigree silver dishes containing chocolates and *Calissons d'Aix*. Olivia set the table for ten people with the best silver and glasses, and the old Moustiers plates. Near the door to the back garden Honorine had prepared the little side table with the thirteen desserts of Christmas. In the centre of a white lacy cloth she had placed the *pompe à l'huile* loaf, sweet, golden and plump, surrounded by the small dishes containing the nuts and crystallized fruits, nougat and melon, and Giò now embellished the whole arrangement with candles, small sprigs of pine, and a few golden balls left over from the tree.

'There,' he said, 'what do you think?'

'*Impeccable*,' said Honorine. 'Now, Giò, you go up and make them descend in ten minutes, and Olivia will 'elp me make the toasts for the soup.'

'Right.' Giò gathered up the remaining bits and pieces and departed upstairs.

Honorine gently reheated the soup and watched the toasts, while Olivia got the hot soup plates out of the bottom oven and put them on the table. As each toasted *croûton* was ready, she placed one in each soup plate and piled grated cheese on it. Then Honorine took her big silver ladle and filled each dish with the piping hot soup, and Olivia lit the candles, just as Domenica, followed by the rest of the family, came chattering downstairs, and sat down to the first course of their *Réveillon* dinner.

'Right,' said Domenica, when the soup had been consumed and glasses emptied, 'time to go, if we're going to get a good view of the *Crèche*.' They rose from the table and put on coats and scarves. They crossed the square to the church, already crowded with the faithful. 'I'll be over in a minute,' said Honorine. 'Keep me a place, please, Giò.'

She closed the door behind them, and cleared away the soup plates. Then she went to the larder and checked the plates of oysters, waiting with their wedges of lemon. She took the snails out of the freezer, and took off the outer packaging, leaving them in their foil trays, ready for the oven. Then, shaking her head in disbelief, she put Anna's Christmas pudding, as instructed, in a pan half-full of hot water, and left it to simmer at the back of the stove. Then she put fresh baguettes on the table, put on her coat and scarf and hurried across the square to the *Crèche Vivante* and the Midnight Mass.

The church was quite dark, lit only by the two decorated trees on either side of the altar, and the tall festive candles used only on the special feasts of the church year. Honorine slipped quietly up the aisle, and sat down next to Giò. Then she slid onto her knees for a few moments to pray. She prayed for Anna and her baby, and for her own fortitude and health. Then she eased herself back into her seat, just as the organ began to play, and the village children walked sedately to their places to begin their Nativity play. Mary, Joseph and the Baby, attended by shepherds and animals, made their little tableau, and spoke the ancient words. Six very small angels, bearing tall candles and singing a traditional carol, appeared from behind the altar, their shrill little voices slightly off-key. Then a troupe of older children in Provençale costume came up the aisle from the back of the church, bearing garlands of vine leaves and sheaves of corn, to the music of the fife and drum. Lastly, when this lively pageant had subsided, there followed a procession of the oldest shepherds drawing a little decorated cart which contained a new-born, bleating lamb. The young priest, much moved by the ancient mystery of this pastoral Nativity, blessed the lamb and the shepherds, and they made their way to the back of the church, slowly and with dignity.

Then the Mass began. As she listened to the familiar words, heard throughout her life, Honorine felt comforted. After all, she said to herself, the good Lord was just about the one thing you could feel secure

322

about, and, of course, the Holy Mother, and maybe the real secret was to trust them and not worry about anything else. Giò, too, felt a kind of comfort, but he knew that the feeling was induced by the music, the uneven rustic singing, the touching spectacle of the children and the bleating of the lamb, drawn in his little cart by the frail old men in their dark capes, leaning on their gnarled sticks.

Anna sat with Patrick and Philippe on either side of her, the bulk of their big winter coats keeping her warm. As always, she, too, had been deeply touched by the old Christmas story, by the rough charm of the village children playing their roles with seriousness and understanding. She related strongly to the Virgin and her innocent Baby, and felt herself unbelievably blessed and content. She slipped her hand into Patrick's coat pocket, and he put his hand in too and held hers tightly and warmly. She looked up at his face, and he looked down at her, and she saw that his eyes were full of tears.

Robert and Domenica sat close together, happy to be there, and happy to have their children round them, but physical frailties prevented them from appreciating the religious implications as much as they might otherwise have done. Robert was enduring silently a bad attack of cramp in his leg, and Domenica's stomach was producing very audible rumbles of hunger. They looked at each other grimly. 'Not long now,' Domenica mouthed silently. Robert looked up at the carved angels overhead and gave a slight groan.

Josh and Olivia sat at the end of the bench. Every time someone shifted his position Josh found himself in grave danger of falling off the end. As it was, he felt as if half of his bottom was hanging in space, and had to thrust his left leg out to stay in place. He dared not catch Olly's eye for fear of breaking into uncontrollable giggles.

Philippe sat comfortably, happy to be with his son and his daughter-in-law, as, in his mind, she already was, and his approaching grandchild. He thought of Jeanne and how happy she would have been, and fleetingly of Marie-France, who seemed now like a poor little ghost. He could not imagine her as a woman of fifty years, probably a grandmother herself. She would always be that slight, young girl in a Normandy orchard.

Honorine was one of the first to receive the Host, and as the large congregation lined up to approach the altar, she slipped away, without waiting for the blessing, and returned to the presbytery to put the fish and the snails in the oven, and the oysters on the table. She put the big dinner plates and the serving dish for the fish at the back of the slow oven, and checked the water in the pudding pan. It was simmering nicely. She put the fish into the hot oven, at the back, and the trays of snails at the front. Then she brought the plates of opened oysters and set them at each person's place, filling the room with the fresh, salty smell of the sea, and finally put the bottles of chilled white wine on the table. She lit the candles, just as she heard the clang of the green metal gate, and the cheerful voices of the household returning from Mass. The door burst open, and they came in with a blast of cold air.

'Christmas has arrived,' cried Olivia, rushing over and giving Honorine a powerful embrace.

'*Joyeux Noël, mignonne,*' said Honorine, feeling at last the warmth of the spirit of the Nativity.

Robert gathered up coats and took them out to the hall, and Domenica approached the table hungrily. 'We won't wait for Gio,' she said. 'He's waiting for Father Paul. He has to say goodbye to everyone, of course. They'll only be a few minutes.'

Robert filled glasses while they all found their appointed places at the table.

'Bliss,' said Olivia. 'Oysters, my absolutely favourite nosh.'

'Philippe,' said Domenica, 'will you say grace, please?

Philippe said a short grace in Latin, and they all crossed themselves, even Robert, and sat down at the table.

Giò sat on the stone bench in the porch of the little church, waiting while Fr Paul exchanged good wishes with his flock as they streamed through the door and into the square, on their way home to their Christmas feasts.

In his white, gold-embroidered vestments, Fr Paul looked even younger than his twenty-eight years, with his close-cropped brown hair and blue eyes. His shy manner, smiling but reserved, as he shook hands and said a few words to each person as he passed, seemed rather endearing to Giò, waiting patiently, and rather longing for his dinner.

Presently, the last proud mother shepherding her children departed, and Fr Paul turned to Giò. 'I won't be a moment,' he said. 'I just have to take off the uniform and lock up.' In a few minutes he reappeared, in his black cassock, and locked the door.

'I love the *Crèche Vivante*,' said Giò as they wheeled the *mobilette* across the square. 'It's a superb piece of theatre. No wonder it's survived so long.'

'I'm glad you enjoyed it,' said Fr Paul. 'All the time one is rehearsing it, in the weeks before Christmas, it's a nightmare. The children don't turn up, or they giggle and fool around, one thinks the whole thing will be a disaster. And then, by some miracle, the magic seems to get to them, and on the night it all seems real to them; it becomes a special experience.'

Giò looked at the young man, surprised at his eloquence, and passion. 'Does it matter so much to you?' he said.

'Yes,' said Fr Paul, and laughed. 'It may sound a bit uncool, but it does. It was my first time on my own, I was anxious.'

'It doesn't sound uncool at all,' said Giò, laughing

too at the younger man's choice of words. 'It sounds great, I love enthusiasm about anything. There's so little of it about these days, more's the pity.'

'I suppose you're right, but I deeply hope you're wrong,' said Fr Paul, as Giò pushed open the gate of the presbytery and led the way into the courtyard.

'Just think,' he said, as Fr Paul propped his *mobilette* against the wall, 'in earlier times you would have been living in this house with only Souliac to care for.' The young priest looked up at the tall old house, and shook his head.

'Bit big for one, and the odd assistant,' he said. 'Much better filled with a big family.'

After the oysters, the snails and the sea-bass, Robert got up to refill glasses, while everyone sat back in their seats, pink-cheeked with good food and drink, having a pause before the desserts and the Armagnac. Everyone seemed to be talking at the tops of their voices, even Honorine, relaxing at last after her labours. Giò was in full flow, telling them all about his incredible reappearing rocking horses, the copies of Robert's. Robert looked anxious.

'Don't worry, Dad,' said Giò, 'the old chap's still there, safe as houses. We'll bring him down here with the rest of the stuff later on.'

Anna caught Patrick's eye, and they collected the empty plates together, and put them in the sink. 'You'd better give me a hand with the pudding,' she said quietly, taking a warm dish out of the oven.

Patrick lifted the basin out of the pan of water, and took off the lid, turning the rich, dark, spicy-smelling pudding onto the dish. Then he heated a ladleful of brandy over the gas flame. 'Ready?' he said.

'Ready,' said Anna, and Patrick ignited the brandy and poured it, flaming, over the pudding. Anna carried it, the flames blue and leaping, and set it down in front of Robert, amid surprised laughter. 'Happy Christmas, Dad,' she said.

'Oh, darling,' said Robert, 'how dear of you.' He had been secretly missing his turkey and Brussels sprouts, bread sauce and roast potatoes. At last it felt like Christmas dinner to him.

Anna brought the plates, and the silver jug of cream laced with brandy, and Robert ceremonially cut the pudding and passed the dishes round.

'My tummy is bursting, I don't know if I can eat any more,' said Olivia, but she did anyway.

'I 'ave to admit,' said Honorine, 'is good. I 'ad my doubts before.'

'Ah,' said Philippe, 'a convert. Well done, Robert.'

When dinner was over, Domenica led the way up to the *salon*, where Giò had already put more logs on the fire and lit the Christmas tree lights, while Josh and Olivia stacked the dishes, to be dealt with in the morning, and made coffee. Josh carried the tray upstairs, and Olivia poured the coffee and took the cups round to everyone, as they sat round the blazing fire, sleepy and relaxed, lulled into serenity by the food and the calm beauty of the room, festive with its sweet-smelling greenery and the flickering radiance of candlelight.

The young priest, tired after his long, rather tension-filled day, gazed into the red heart of the fire. He had not eaten, as he had two more masses to celebrate, but had permitted himself a little wine, and some coffee. He was aware of the buzz of quiet conversation around him, but thought of his family in Soissons, imagining his mother and his two sisters enjoying their Christmas Eve at home. Though very probably, he thought, they would have been in bed hours ago. I will telephone them tomorrow, he said to himself, it will be cheap rate all day. He put his cup on the table near him and stood up. He approached the sofa, where Domenica and Robert sat close together, his arm round her shoulders.

'Please don't move,' he said, 'you look so comfortable. It's late, I must get back to Roussac. Thank you for asking me to your *Réveillon*, it was very kind of you.'

'It was a pleasure,' said Domenica. 'I do hope that you will feel able to pop in at any time.'

'I certainly will, thank you.'

'I'll come down with you,' said Giò, getting up from his chair.

'I must go 'ome, too,' said Honorine. 'Look at the time.'

'We'll come with you, Honorine,' said Patrick. 'It's high time Anna was in bed.'

They exchanged kisses and goodnights, and went down to the hall to collect their coats and scarves, before stepping out into the cold, starry night. Fr Paul wheeled his *mobilette* through the gate, and Honorine, Anna and Patrick said goodnight and hurried across the square to her house.

Giò held the *mobilette* while the young priest put on his crash helmet and scarf, and gloves. 'Don't you have a coat?' said Giò.

'No,' said Fr Paul. 'I have a cloak, but it's not awfully safe on the bike.'

'But it's really very cold,' said Giò. 'Hang on, I'll lend you an anorak.' He ran indoors before the priest could refuse, returning in a few moments with a short padded jacket. 'There you are,' he said. 'Don't worry, no-one will see you in it at this time of night, or morning, really.'

They laughed, as at a shared joke, and Fr Paul put on the jacket, said good night and rode away across the square and under the archway, to Roussac. Giò stared after him, following the red glow of the rear lamp as it wove across the square and vanished through the archway. He felt cold, and suddenly rather lonely. He put his hands in his pockets and walked round the square, looking up at Honorine's windows as he passed her house. The lights were already out. They didn't hang about, he thought wryly.

'Don't be such a prat, Giò,' he said aloud, and, turning abruptly, walked back to the presbytery. He locked up the house and went quietly up to the *salon*, where he found Philippe, sitting alone in front of the dying fire.

'Hello,' he said, stirring the logs with his foot, and sitting down. 'All alone?'

'Yes,' said Philippe, smiling. 'It's not something I mind very much. In fact I sometimes find a lot of people quite a strain. Solitude becomes rather addictive after a while.'

'Really?' said Giò. 'I wish it were true for me. I've just been having a bit of a self-pitying wallow about my solitary state, probably induced by alcohol.'

'Ah,' said Philippe, 'that's very understandable, particularly at Christmas. It's always a difficult time for people without partners.'

'This is it,' said Giò, turning his head to look at Philippe. The old man returned his gaze, touched by the sad, dark beauty of the younger man's eyes. Giò looked back at the fire. 'It must be quite a relief to become a priest,' he said. 'All that carnal temptation out of the window for ever.'

'Whatever makes you think that, my dear boy?' said Philippe.

'Don't you think that's true?' said Giò, startled.

'I think it very unlikely,' said the old man.

Chapter Eighteen

Olivia was in heaven in Paris. She had started at the *Lycée*, and found herself very comfortable there, and rather popular on account of her fluent English. Her room at Grands-Augustins was bigger than her old one in Chiswick, and she was decorating it, bit by bit, with things chosen entirely by herself. On Sundays, when *Le Patrimoine* was closed, she often went with Laure, and sometimes Giò, to the flea-markets in search of junk. Her favourite was the *Marché de Vanves*, easily reached by *métro*. Here they wandered through the stalls, finding rusty bird cages, chrome lamps, old Django Reinhardt records and second-hand clothes, at prices that Olivia could sometimes afford. They also searched for damaged gilded frames, and nice old pieces of carved wood, for Anna. Patrick had been urging her to start collecting such things for herself, to restore and keep. He felt that it was a pity that once a piece was finished, it went out of her life to be seen no more, and Anna was enchanted at having the opportunity to work at her own pace, not nagged to get something finished, and the fee collected.

'But can we afford it?' she asked. She felt that Patrick had shouldered an enormous load of expense lately.

'We can afford it,' he said. 'Please believe it.'

'Well,' she said, doubtfully, 'you'll tell me at once if we can't?'

'I'll tell you at once, Anna. Do you want to see my accounts?'

'No, of course not,' said Anna. 'It's just that I'm not

330

used to spending money without feeling guilty about it.'

'I know you're not. That's one of the things that's so refreshing about you.'

Olivia, Giò and Laure would come back to the St Michel *métro* station, bearing Olivia's loot, walk up to her room in the apartment, and set about the delightful task of trying to find appropriate places to display everything. Soon the room began to look slightly like a flea-market itself, but Olivia loved it. At night, doing her homework, she played her Django records and burned joss-sticks. Sometimes she hung out of her window, watching the world go by below: the lovers, the taxis and the constantly changing life of the river. She heard the hooting of the riverboats, and the sonorous deep clang of the bells of Notre Dame, and sighed with pleasure.

Sometimes Giò would take her and Laure for a coffee on the terrace of the Café Flore, and they would amuse themselves spotting the occasional celebrity. Giò would hold forth about the existentialists, and gave Olivia a battered old paperback copy of *Mémoires d'une jeune fille rangée*, which she read bits of from time to time. She found it rather hard-going, but was flattered none the less that Giò thought her ready for it. She sat on the café terrace, her long legs wrapped round the legs of her tilted chair, her elbows on the table, taking the occasional drag from Giò's Gitane and feeling decidedly worldly and adult. Through her haze of happiness she became aware, as the weeks went by, that Laure was in love with Giò. There wasn't a lot you could put your finger on, just small things that Olivia recognized as evidence. She observed how Laure's face lit up when Giò praised her in any way, or even came into a room, and how deflated she looked if he said anything dismissive, which was often. Silly thing, she thought, doesn't she know? She turned over in her mind the question of warning Laure, or asking Anna or Patrick whether she should, but then dismissed the idea as uncool. It's time I learned to mind my own business, she said to herself. Why destroy the poor girl's illusions?'

Josh chained his bicycle to the railings, and looked up at the windows of his father's flat. Jeffrey had telephoned the night before and invited him to lunch, and Josh had been unable to think of a good enough reason to refuse. His reluctant mood was exacerbated by the dreariness of the sullen February day. He had the feeling that it was getting dark already, although it was only just past noon. He approached the shiny black outer door and pressed the buzzer beside Jeffrey's name. The entryphone crackled.

'Yes?'

'It's me, Dad, Josh.'

The door clicked open, and he climbed the stairs to Jeffrey's flat. The door was ajar, and Josh went in.

'Hi,' he said.

'Hello,' said Jeffrey, 'come in. I'm just finishing the washing-up. My bloody woman's useless. I don't know why I don't get rid of her, she's a slut. Too much hassle to find someone else, I suppose.'

'Looks OK to me.'

'It's too late to start cooking now,' said Jeffrey. 'We'll to to a pub, shall we? I haven't shopped yet, anyway.'

'Great, why not?' They went down to the street.

'We'll take the car, it looks like rain.' Jeffrey walked towards his beautiful new Mercedes, anxious to show it off to his son. Josh got in, after expressing suitable admiration. 'I'd let you drive,' said Jeffrey, 'but it's only insured for me. That way, one can say no with a clear conscience, if someone asks to try it.'

'Good thinking,' said Josh, suppressing a smile.

'I suppose your mother took that heap of hers to Paris, did she?'

'No,' said Josh. 'She's got a nice little Clio now, she took that. I use Grandpa's when I need a car. The bike's often more convenient.'

'Oh.' Jeffrey changed the subject. 'Where shall we go? Chelsea Potter?'

They drove along King's Road, crowded with Saturday shoppers. Josh noted with distaste the sleaziness of the endless shops selling second-hand jeans and cowboy boots, interspersed with the odd posh boutique. He had never been able to understand the appeal of this part of Chelsea; to him it looked dirty and sordid. When he said this to Robert and Domenica they smiled, with far-away expressions on their faces.

'It was magic,' said Domenica. 'I don't know why, but it was. Maybe it was something to do with being after the war, and the cold war. You couldn't get much in the way of good food, or clothes, and then suddenly it all happened here, and life was fun and exciting, and so were the people.'

Even Mum and Giò remembered their childhood in Chelsea with nostalgic pleasure, so it couldn't have been totally a generation thing, thought Josh.

'Tacky place, isn't it?' said Jeffrey.

'Oh, I don't know,' said Josh. 'It has a certain raffish appeal.'

Pretentious little sod, thought Jeffrey. He left the car on a resident's parking space, and they walked down the street to the pub. Jeffrey noticed, with slight displeasure, that his son was now taller than himself, and he lengthened his stride. The pub was crowded, cheerful and warm, and smelling of beer and sausages. Josh was relieved not to be alone with Jeffrey, and began to relax. He asked for a half of bitter, and he and Jeffrey stood close to the bar, hemmed in by the crowd.

'Pointless trying to get a table!' Jeffrey shouted over the roar of voices and thump of the jukebox and the one-armed bandits.

'That's OK,' Josh shouted back, 'this is fine.'

Jeffrey felt something hard poking him in the back,

and turned round angrily. It was Kate. 'Hi,' she said. 'I thought it was you. I see you've got the divine Joshua with you.'

'Hello, Kate, what are you doing here?' said Jeffrey feebly.

'What do you think I'm doing, you moron?' said Kate. 'I'm getting legless with my chums. It's Saturday, right?'

'Um, yes, I suppose it is,' said Jeffrey.

Kate looked at Josh, quizzically. 'Come and share our table, there's room,' she said, and pushed her way through the crowd without waiting for an answer. Jeffrey followed nervously. He did not wish to antagonize her. He knew her to be perfectly capable of making a scene, and blanched at the thought of her regaling the company with the details of their extraordinary sexual adventure. Josh brought up the rear, and Kate instructed Ted to shove their coats and bags under the table to make room for the newcomers. Ted, looking blearily henpecked, did as he was told.

'This is my future ex-step-grandson Josh,' she said. 'And this is his father, the dreaded demon lawyer, Jeffrey Wickham.'

'Aha,' said Ted, brightening 'you're the chap that lives in a studio turned into a flat?'

'That's me,' said Jeffrey, smugly.

'It's bastards like you that have robbed artists of their inheritance,' said Ted loudly, delighted that Jeffrey had fallen into the trap. 'None of us can afford the rents any more.'

Jeffrey reddened, but spoke calmly. 'Market forces, I'm afraid,' he said.

'Fuck market forces,' said Ted. 'You're a bunch of shysters.'

'I think I'll see if I can get some food, Josh,' said Jeffrey, standing up. 'What would you like, sausages?'

'Oh,' said Josh, 'I don't mind, anything. I'll come with you.' He got to his feet.

'No, no. You stay here, I want to talk to you.' said Kate, putting a restraining hand on his arm. 'Sit down. Don't take any notice of old Ted here, he's pissed. Belt up, you boring old fart.' Josh sat down reluctantly. Kate, turning her back on Ted, put her elbows on the table and gave Josh her full attention. 'How are you, Josh? What are you up to these days?'

'Oh, not much. The usual. School, work, that sort of thing.'

'Still at the Lifeboat?'

'Yup.'

'Haven't escaped from Mummy then?'

Josh looked round, hoping that Jeffrey might save him from this interrogation. He was nowhere to be seen. He gathered his wits. 'As a matter of fact,' he said, 'Mum is living in Paris now.'

'What, with lover boy?'

'Yes, if you wish to put it like that,' said Josh, coldly.

Kate hooted with mocking laughter. 'So,' she said, 'little Miss Perfect has buggered off and dumped her kids, has she?'

'Certainly not,' said Josh, beginning to get angry. 'Olivia is with them, and Grandpa and Domenica are with me at the Lifeboat.'

'No need to get your knickers in a twist, old chap,' said Kate. She patted him on the cheek. Josh drew back, affronted. 'Hoity-toity,' said Kate, laughing. 'So what's happening to the dear old family home, the aptly named Boulter's?'

Josh stood up, and backed away. 'You know perfectly well what's happening to Boulter's, you ugly old cow. It's being sold so that you can have your rotten pound of flesh. I hate you, I wish you'd fall under a bus.' He turned and pushed his way frantically through the crush, and out into the street. He ran along King's Road in the direction of Sloane Square, dodging through the crowds on the pavement, fighting back tears of rage and humiliation, until he was sure he wasn't being followed. When he reached Sloane Square he took a cab to St Loo Avenue, where he unchained his bike and cycled home. He was cold and wet, having left his coat in the pub, and also hungry. His teeth were chattering by the time he reached the Lifeboat. He put his bike in the garage, and was rather relieved to find that the car was not there. Good, he thought, that will give me time to calm down before they get back. He did not want to tell Robert about his encounter with Kate, he could not see that it would serve any useful purpose, and it would certainly upset him.

He went upstairs and put the kettle on, and cut himself a thick slice of bread. He spread butter on it, and a slice of Cheddar cheese, and opened a jar of chutney. 'Bloody sodding bastards,' he said aloud, 'the whole lot of them.'

He changed out of his wet clothes, drank his tea, and felt better. Then he got out his pocket-book, and dialled the Kings' number in Richmond. Emma answered the phone.

'Emma?'

'Yes?'

'It's me, Josh. How are you?'

'I'm fine, how are you?'

'Fine. Great. Emma, I was wondering. Are you free tonight? Would you like to go to the cinema?'

'Thank you, Josh, I'd love to. What's on? Anything good?'

'Haven't a clue about here. What about Richmond?'

'I'll look in the paper. If there's nothing worth seeing we can always cook supper here. Ma and Dad are out tonight, there'll only be Hugh and me. Not "you and me".' She laughed.

'Great, thanks,' said Josh. 'I'll come over around seven, if I can borrow Grandpa's car.'

'Great, see you then, Josh,' said Emma.

*   *   *

Just after Montélimar, Giò noticed the first almond tree in flower, its delicate petals palest pink against the sooty black network of its branches, and the pearly azure of the sky. To his right the great humps of the Ardèche mountains reared, sunlit dark green velvety flanks, backed by jagged blue peaks. To his left he could see in the distance the still snow-capped *pré-alpes*. It was at this point that Giò always felt a surge of elation at being in the south again, enjoying the sensation of leaving winter behind him. He had hired a self-drive removal van to take Robert's furniture down to Souliac, as he had promised. Honorine was expecting him, and he had asked her to find someone to help him unload the stuff and carry it into the house. The sun, pouring through the windscreen, was hot and he thought that he would take off his jacket at the next *péage*.

At one o'clock he stopped his van alongside other long-distance lorries at a service station, and ate his sandwiches without getting out of the cab. He felt slightly nervous about the possibility of the van being hi-jacked, having recently read reports of such incidents in the newspapers. He thought that it was probably rather stupid of him to travel alone in the circumstances, and he finished his lunch as quickly as he could, and resumed his journey. Once past Orange he felt somewhat safer, and stopped to have a drink from his bottle of water, and a pee.

Driving through the *garrigue* towards Rémoulins, he observed with pleasure the yellow rock roses and blue rosemary in full flower, and covered in bees. After Rémoulins he drove past cherry orchards, snowy with blossom, and vineyards with their tiny new pale green leaves just unfurling on their gnarled black stumps. At last, he drove the van very carefully under the archway into the square at Souliac, and parked by the old green gate. He climbed stiffly down from the cab, stretched his arms and legs, and flexed his aching back. The sun had gone from the square, and the air was fresh, but overhead the sky was an intense blue, and the swallows, back from Africa, wheeled and shrilled overhead, the sun catching their white underparts in its dying rays.

Giò locked the cab door and went through the gate to the house. Honorine was in the kitchen, slicing vegetables on the table. She looked up, startled. 'Giò! You are 'ere! I did not 'ear you, it's my hears are no good this days.'

Giò kissed her and sat down at the table, picking up sticks of raw carrot, and crunching them hungrily.

'You just like Anna, always pick the food,' said Honorine. 'You want tea?'

'Glass of wine?'

'Of course.' She got a bottle from the larder, and poured a glass for him. 'You 'ave good journey? You are tire, I think?'

'Knackered,' said Giò. He drank the wine and ate some more carrots. Then he got to his feet. 'What time is this bloke coming, Honorine? I must get the stuff in before it's dark.'

'My God, you do it now? I tell him come tomorrow, you will be too tire tonight.'

'Shit,' said Giò. 'I can't leave it out, the stuff's far too valuable, Honorine. I'll just have to manage on my own, hell.'

'Oh, Giò, I am get it wrong. I will 'elp you, is too much for you alone.'

'Well,' said Giò, 'i would be a help. Let's try, anyway.'

They went out into the square, and Giò let down the tailgate. They got out the first package, a carefully padded and wrapped chair. Giò sighed. He would have to close the tailgate, and lock it between the carrying in of each load. Just then, the sound of a *mobilette*'s engine caught his ear, and he turned as Fr Paul rode across the square towards them, smiling.

He stopped beside the van, and took off his helmet. 'Hello, Giò,' he said, shaking hands, 'how nice to see you. You look as if you need a hand.'

'Father Paul, you're an answer to prayer,' said Giò. 'I do.'

Fr Paul took his *mobilette* into the courtyard, and took off his cassock, carefully hanging it on a hook beside the door. Then the two men carried the stuff up to the *salon*, while Honorine kept watch over the van. Just before eight o'clock the last package had been taken from the van, and Giò locked the tailgate.

'That was terrific of you, you're a lot stronger than you look,' said Giò. 'I hope you'll stay and have a drink, and some supper with us?'

'Thank you, that would be very nice,' said the priest, putting on his cassock again, and going with Giò into the kitchen, where Honorine was putting the carrots and potatoes into her stew, simmering on the stove, and smelling delicious.

'My God, I'm starving,' said Giò. 'How long will it be, Honorine?'

'Twenty minutes,' said Honorine.

'Shall we sit outside?' said Giò. 'Is it warm enough? It feels like summer to me, after Paris.'

'Why not? The air is beautiful, and there is no wind,' said Fr Paul.

Giò picked up the bottle and the glasses, and they went out into the courtyard and sat down under the trellised vine, at the shabby old green-painted table. The little lantern bloomed overhead, shining on the pale green miniature vine leaves as they unfolded from their fat pink buds on the hairy brown branches of the ancient vine.

'I love being here in the spring,' said Giò. 'It's all so fresh and new, somehow.'

'I know,' said Fr Paul, 'it's a miracle. It lifts the heart, confirms one's beliefs.'

'Does your belief need confirming?' said Giò, looking at the serious face of the younger man.

Fr Paul looked back at Giò. 'I'm afraid so,' he said. 'Often. There's no magic formula, you know.'

'Well, that's a relief,' said Giò. 'It makes you much more human and accessible.'

'Good,' said Fr Paul, and they laughed.

Giò refilled their glasses. 'Did you always have a vocation?' he asked. 'From boyhood?'

'Not at all,' said Fr Paul. 'Quite the contrary. I wanted very much to be a doctor. But my father died, leaving my mother rather poor, with me and my two sisters. The Jesuits were prepared to take me, and after that it was a fairly foregone conclusion. She wanted it, I didn't want to make life difficult for her, it made her happy.'

'But did you want it?' said Giò, frowning.'

The priest did not answer the question. 'The sad thing was, really, that later I realized that I could have read medicine without being a burden to her. But by then it was too late, I was too deep in.'

'Jesus,' said Giò, 'how awful.'

'Not at all,' said Fr Paul. 'I'm helping people, I hope. It's just another way of doing it.'

'But so lonely, so cut off from real life,' said Giò. 'How can you stand it?'

'Well, sometime that is a problem,' said Fr Paul, 'but as they say in the movies, I'm working on it.'

Honorine put her head round the door, and told them to come and eat. They went indoors and washed their hands at the sink, like children. They sat down with Honorine, and ate her good country food, and all three felt, for the moment, carefree and cheerful, and glad to be alive.

Towards the end of March Olivia's school broke up for the Easter holidays, and she and Patrick and Anna went to spend a long weekend at St Gilles. Anna was now seven months pregnant, and beginning to feel very tired. She found it difficult to sleep at night, and felt increasingly reluctant to tackle the stairs. Patrick thought, rightly, that some country air, and being in a house with only one flight of stairs to cope with, would be much more comfortable for her.

They arrived on Friday evening, glad to be away

340

from the city and driving through quiet country lanes, already green with the first flush of hawthorn. Clouds of midges floated in the mild air, and thrushes and blackbirds flashed from tree to tree, loudly challenging each other.

'It's just like England,' said Olivia.

They drove into the yard at St Gilles, and Marie-Claude came out to meet them, barely able to conceal her excitement. 'The doctor is out on his rounds,' she said, 'but everything is ready for you. It is so nice to see you all here.' She led the way into the house, Patrick and Olivia carrying the bags. Upstairs, Anna lay down on the bed, looking pale.

Patrick sat down beside her, and took her hand. 'Are you all right, darling? You look a bit tired.'

'I'm fine, I just need to stretch out. I'm getting hopeless with cars, I keep getting cramp. I'll be OK in a minute.'

'Would you rather go straight to bed, and have your supper on a tray?'

'No, no, I'm fine,' said Anna, sitting up and swinging her legs to the ground. 'Don't fuss, darling, you're like an old mother hen.'

'I feel like one,' said Patrick. 'A broody one.'

They went downstairs and found Olivia and Philippe debating whether or not to light the fire in the sitting-room.

'Do let's,' said Anna. 'It's ages since we sat by a proper fire.'

In the middle of supper, Anna suddenly put one hand to her face and the other onto her stomach. 'Oh, God,' she said quietly, 'I think it's started.'

Philippe got up and came round to her, putting his hand on her shoulder. 'Did you feel a contraction?' he asked. 'Sometimes one gets false alarms, my dear.'

'I think the waters have broken.' Anna looked up at him.

'In that case, it's not a false alarm. Patrick, telephone

the hospital for an ambulance, the number is on my desk, and tell them to warn the special care unit. Anna, come with me into the surgery, very quietly please, don't rush.'

He took her by the elbow and led her into the surgery, and told her to lie down on the examination couch. He helped her take off her tights and pants, then sent Olivia upstairs to fetch Anna's nightdress and dressing-gown, and some pillows. 'You'll be much more comfortable,' he said.

'The contractions are very strong,' said Anna. 'I think they're coming every couple of minutes.'

'Try to relax, and breathe deeply, the ambulance shouldn't be long.' Philippe took Anna's blood pressure, and listened to the baby's heart. 'All's well,' he said. 'Don't worry, everything's fine.'

Patrick came into the surgery looking worried. 'All the ambulances are out,' he said. 'It seems they're having a busy night. Do you think we should drive her in ourselves? Wouldn't it be safer?'

'Oh, dear,' said Anna, 'somehow, I don't think so. I'm afraid I'm going to start pushing.'

'I'd better have a look, my dear,' said Philippe. 'You're quite right, you are very dilated. Relax, pant, try not to push unless you have to.' He went to the kitchen. 'Marie-Claude,' he said, 'can you bring a lot of clean white towels, and a can of boiled water to the surgery? Don't forget to scald the can.'

'Mother of God, is it the baby?'

'Looks like it, yes.'

'It's too soon?'

'I'm afraid so,' said Philippe. He went back to the surgery, got out packs of sterile dressings and his operating gown and gloves, and scrubbed up. Patrick sat beside Anna, holding her hand tightly, doing his best to be reassuring and calm, and trying not to show the panic that he felt.

Marie-Claude came quietly in with the towels and the big brass can of water, and left, closing the door.

She found Olivia hovering outside. 'Come and help me in the kitchen,' she said. 'We will only be in the way here.'

They took the half-finished dishes into the kitchen, and washed up the plates. 'You had better eat your pudding anyway,' said Marie-Claude. 'It's apple tart.'

'I couldn't' said Olivia, 'I feel too frightened.'

'Try not to be,' said Marie-Claude. 'It's a natural process, after all.'

'But it's much too soon, isn't it?' said Olivia. 'It's not supposed to come till May.'

They sat on either side of the kitchen table, waiting. The clock ticked its loud, bossy tick, and the minutes passed, one by one. It seemed to Olivia that the whole place was enveloped in total silence, broken only by the ticking of the clock. No sound came from the surgery; if felt to her as if everyone had died, and she and Marie-Claude were marooned in an eerie, Marie-Celeste dream-world. The clock made its preliminary clicks and whirrs, making them both jump, and then struck ten. A blue light went flashing past the window, and Marie-Claude got up and went to the door.

'It's the ambulance,' she said, 'at last.'

She went out into the yard. Olivia got up to follow her, and then stood stock still. She thought she had heard a thin, high wail. She rushed to the surgery door, and heard the voices of Patrick and Philippe, and Anna's laugh. She sat down hard on a chair, and covering her face with her hands, burst into tears.

In a few minutes Patrick came out of the surgery and saw her. 'It's all right, sweetheart,' he said, 'they're both fine. He's very tiny, but he seems to be OK, and Anna's fine, thank God.'

'The ambulance is here,' said Olivia, blowing her nose.

'Good,' said Patrick. 'Run and tell them that the baby has arrived. Dad is looking after them. We'll give Anna a cup of tea, and then the ambulance can take them both to the special care unit, just in case the little chap needs ventilating. Tell them to bring the stretcher in ten minutes.'

Presently, Philippe, Olivia and Marie-Claude watched the rear light of the ambulance as it drove slowly down the lane, its blue light flashing, bearing Anna and Patrick and their baby to the hospital.

'Is she really all right?' said Olivia, turning her still-anxious face towards Philippe.

He put his arm round her shoulders, and propelled her towards the house. 'She is absolutely fine, and I'm sure the baby is too. I reckon he's a couple of kilos, so he shouldn't have any real problems.'

'You're a grandfather now,' said Olivia.

'So I am,' said Philippe. 'So I am.'

On Good Friday Honorine woke early and got straight out of bed. She was expecting Domenica, Robert and Josh to arrive that night, for the Easter holidays, and she had much to do. She had already done the bedrooms and the shopping. She had the dinner to prepare, but first she had decided to have a good spring clean of the *salon*. Giò had unwrapped all Robert's furniture before he went back to Paris, taking all the packing materials with him, but things were badly in need of a polish, and were littered rather haphazardly about the room.

She drank her coffee, and then crossed the square to the presbytery. It was a beautiful spring morning, warm and sunny, and as she opened the shutters in the *salon* the sun streamed in, mercilessly exposing the dust and dirt on every surface. It's just as I thought, she said to herself, shaking her head. What do the housekeepers in England do all the time? They don't clean, I think. With a grim expression, she set to work with her can of polish, and bullied the surfaces of Robert's furniture to a shine. Then she rearranged the furniture, pushing it tidily against the walls, as far as possible. Then she cleaned the tiled floor with her squeeze-mop, and put the rugs back in place, having shaken them out of the window.

'Is better now,' she said aloud. She looked up at the beautiful crystal chandelier, caught in a shaft of sunlight. Is maybe needing a clean, after the winter, she thought. She looked at her watch: nearly one o'clock. Plenty time, she thought. Going downstairs she fetched the tall aluminium ladder, and carried it up to the *salon*. She unfolded it and set it under the chandelier, clicking the safety catches firmly in place. She returned to the kitchen, and got a bowl of warm, soapy water and a sponge, and carried it carefully upstairs. She climbed the ladder, steadying herself with one hand and carrying the bowl on her hip with the other. The bowl was placed carefully on the aluminium shelf and, holding on to the top of the ladder, she reached up and unhooked one of the heavy crystal drops. She lowered it carefully into the warm suds, cleaning the cut crystal with her sponge. Then she held it up to drain, and hooked it back in place again. It swung gently, sparkling in the sunlight, sending out showers of bright prismatic colours. Honorine laughed, delighted at the effect she had created.

'Is beautiful,' she said. She took down another drop and cleaned it, and then another, until she had almost finished the job, and the water in the bowl was quite black with dirt. She debated with herself whether or not to go down and fetch fresh water, but there were only two more to do, so she decided against it.

She reached up again to unhook another drop, and the telephone rang, jangling and shrill, and made her jump with fright. The ladder rocked, and the bowl flew off the shelf, drenching Honorine with grey, soapy water as it fell. The ladder hit the floor with a sickening clatter. For a few seconds Honorine lay there, feeling nothing. Then the telephone stopped ringing, and a great roaring blackness overtook her.

* * *

Domenica, Robert and Josh got out of the taxi, delighted to be back in Souliac for Easter. Robert paid the driver, and they went through the green gate, and into the kitchen, through the open door. In the kitchen, all was quiet, with no sign of preparations for dinner. Domenica looked in the larder. A bucket of cold water containing mussels stood on the floor, waiting, together with loaves of bread, butter and cheese, and a jug of milk.

She frowned and looked at her watch. 'I wonder if she has the time wrong, and has gone home for something,' she said. 'Josh, run over and see, will you, darling?' Josh departed, and Robert poured himself and Domenica a drink.

He looked at his hands. 'Why does one always get so filthy, travelling?' he said. 'I'll take the cases up, and have a wash.' He took a good swallow of his drink, picked up the cases and went up the stairs, whistling cheerfully as he went.

Domenica, sitting at the table with her drink, suddenly became aware that Robert had stopped whistling, and had said, 'Oh, my God.' She got to her feet, a sharp clutch of fear in her guts, knowing at once that something terrible had happened, and ran to the foot of the stairs. 'Robert, what is it?' she said, her heart pounding.

'Darling, it's Honorine,' he said. 'You'd better come up.'

'Is she dead?'

'I think so, I'm afraid so,' said Robert.

After the inquest, which was delayed until after the holiday, Honorine was buried with her parents in the family grave, in the cemetery on the outskirts of the village. It was a peaceful place, behind a high white wall, guarded by impressive clumps of old cypresses. It was a beautiful April day, sparkling and brilliant, and the entire village turned

346

out to accompany Honorine on her last journey.

Giò stood with Domenica and Robert, tears pouring down his face, full of guilt and remorse that she had been cleaning the furniture he had brought down, when she met her death.

'My dear boy,' said Robert later, 'don't be ridiculous. She was obviously cleaning the chandelier, nothing to do with the furniture. It was just a ghastly accident.'

'I still feel somehow it was my fault,' said Giò. 'If I hadn't got her fussed by filling the *salon*, she wouldn't even have been in there.'

'Rubbish,' said Domenica stoutly, 'if it was anyone's fault, I'm afraid it was her own, poor old thing. I've told her countless times never to go up the ladder without someone to hold it, but you know how stubborn she could be.'

'Your mother is right, Giò,' said Fr Paul, who was having a cup of tea with them after the funeral. 'And it is quite true, she was a stubborn lady. You must not try to blame yourself.' He looked at them all with affection. 'Perhaps her time had come,' he said. 'Her particular journey was over, her task complete here on earth.' He stood up to go, and Giò walked out with him to the church.

'That's a terrific comfort,' said Robert when they had gone, 'considering I'm the same bloody age as Honorine.

Domenica and Josh laughed. 'I reckon you'll bury us all, Grandpa,' said Josh.

'God, I hope not,' said Robert.

'Make up your mind,' said Domenica.

'Do you really believe all that stuff about Honorine's task being done here on earth?' said Giò, as he and Fr Paul walked across the square, peaceful and empty in the evening light. Fr Paul looked at him.

'I try to believe it, Giò,' he replied. 'It's easy enough if it's an elderly person like Honorine, but it's quite another matter if it's a child or little baby.'

'Do you really think so?' said Giò. 'How strange. If

Anna's baby had been stillborn, or died, I'd have been sad, of course, but more for Anna and Patrick. But Honorine was an integral part of my life. We all took her for granted, but we loved her. I'll miss her terribly, we all will.'

'I know,' said the priest. 'I remember the shock and the grief when my father died. He was not yet forty. It's not easy, or fair, is it?' He turned to Giò, as they reached the porch of the church. 'When do you return to Paris?'

'Tomorrow,' said Giò, 'after lunch.'

'I wonder,' said Fr Paul, 'could you give me a lift? I have a few days leave due, and I want to visit my mother in Soissons.'

'Of course, my dear chap, I'd be glad of your company,' said Giò. 'About half-past two, here?'

'Wonderful, thank you.' They shook hands, and the young priest went into the church. Giò walked back to the presbytery, strangely happy.

He found Robert, preparing supper. 'Want any help, Dad?'

'No thanks, old chap,' said Robert cheerfully. 'Just pour us a drink, will you?'

The drive to Paris was uneventful, the traffic fairly light, and the weather sunny and warm. The two men felt comfortable in each other's company, and the enforced intimacy of the car seemed to encourage in both of them a greater degree of candour than might otherwise have been the case. They found themselves able to tell each other many things that they would normally have been reluctant to discuss, and each felt that he had at last found a friend.

As they approached Place des Vosges, Giò said, 'I could drop you at the station, but why don't you come to my apartment for an omelette first? It's long past supper time, you must be hungry.'

'Thank you,' said Fr Paul, 'how kind of you.'

Giò parked in the courtyard, and they went up the grand formal staircase to the apartment, preceded by the sleek black cat.

'What a splendid place you live in.'

'Don't be too impressed. I only have one room really, over the shop,' said Giò, unlocking the door, and standing aside politely for Fr Paul to enter the room. Giò and the cat followed him in. The room was softly lit by candles on the small table, which was laid for dinner, for two. Out of the kitchen came Laure, carrying a bowl of salad.

'There you are, Giò' she said, 'at last. I thought you'd never . . .' her voice trailed away, as she took in the presence of Fr Paul, who stood, tall and silent, beside Giò. She gathered her wits, blushing furiously, and put down the salad on the table. 'I made dinner, it's on the hob,' she stammered. 'I'll be off now, see you tomorrow, Giò.' Without waiting for a response, she disappeared through the secret door, and they could hear her footsteps as she ran down the little staircase to the shop. Then they heard the slam of the big glass door as it shut behind her.

Appalled, Fr Paul turned to Giò, his face white. 'I'm so sorry,' he said. 'I had no idea.'

Before Giò could reply, he had slipped through the door and down the staircase, and away. The cat wound itself round Giò's legs, purring, and he went to the fridge and poured it some milk. He emptied the dinner down the garbage disposal, and cleared the table. Then he poured himself a stiff whisky, and lay down on his bed, without bothering to take off his shoes. He stared at his icon, and drank his drink, but the cathartic tears would not come.

'Fuck her, fuck her, the obscene bloody cow,' he said.

The sleek black cat jumped up on the bed, and lay down beside him, purring.

POSTLUDE

In June, Anna's divorce was made absolute, and she and Patrick were married at the *mairie* in Souliac. The entire family were there for the occasion, it being half-term, so Josh and Olivia could both be present. On the following Sunday, after mass, Fr Paul baptized the baby Thomas, and Giò and Olivia were the godparents. There was a splendid celebration at the presbytery afterwards, with the first big family lunch of the year, under the fig tree in the walled garden. Philippe had got in a locum for two weeks, and had brought Marie-Claude down with him. She and Anna had become very close in the weeks after the birth of Thomas, when Anna had remained at St Gilles, while Patrick and Olivia had commuted to Paris. She was enchanted to be an important part of the extended family, and unofficial nanny to Thomas. Robert had by this time become extremely possessive of the kitchen, both in London and in Souliac, and Marie-Claude was happy to go along with this, as was Domenica, and both helped him unobtrusively, exchanging indulgent smiles.

'The next thing,' said Domenica, 'he'll want to buy a bit of land and grow his own vegetables.'

'Splendid idea,' said Robert. 'After Josh goes to Cambridge, we could live here most of the time. Why not?'

After Anna and Marie-Claude had taken Thomas upstairs for his bath and feed, and Fr Paul had left, Patrick and Josh volunteered to deal with the dishes, and Philippe and Giò decided to walk round the village.

350

'It was so sad about Honorine,' said Philippe as they passed her house, 'she would so have enjoyed today.'

'I know,' said Giò, 'I think about her all the time. She left her house to Olly, you know.'

'Did she not have relatives of her own?'

'None. Isn't it sad?'

'Yes,' said Philippe. 'But then, life so often is sad.'

They walked on round the backs of the houses in the warm evening sunshine, until they reached the little iron bridge over the stream, at this time of the year still swift-moving and full. The big willow tree was still fresh and green, its narrow leaves shimmering in the clear soft evening light, as the branches drooped towards the river.

Philippe and Giò paused, and leaned on the iron railing of the bridge, watching the swift-flowing stream as it passed beneath them, and the swallows as they swooped and dipped over the water.

'How are things with you, Giò?' said the older man.

'Awful, actually,' said Giò. 'A chum of mine, a great friend of long ago has died of AIDS.'

'How sad,' said Philippe. 'Is there any chance of this affecting you?'

'Luckily, no,' said Giò. 'I had the tests as soon as I heard about it, of course. Thank God, they were negative. But it's given me a fright, just the same.' He looked at Philippe. 'You're the only person I've told about it. Please don't tell anyone else, I don't want them worried.'

'My dear boy,' said Philippe, 'of course I won't.'

They walked on together. Olivia, crouched in her old hiding place in the highest fork of the tree was stunned, rigid with shock and fear. Somehow, she had never allowed herself to think that such a disaster could threaten Giò. She knew, of course, about HIV and AIDS, and obviously recognized their relevance to someone like him, though she had never been aware of his actually having particular relationships. His contracting AIDS had seemed to her to have about the same degree of risk as getting cancer, or being knocked down by a bus. Now, suddenly, the world seemed like a very fragile and unsafe place.

Years later, working on her etchings in her little house in Souliac, Olivia came to recognize that moment as the one in which she left her childhood behind forever.

THE END